REACHING NEW HEIGHTS

Our bodies glistened and shone when lightning struck twice in rapid succession. Water ran down my face, stinging my eyes, invading my nose, and dripping down onto the few square inches of my body that weren't already drenched. Cor lowered me down to the wooden planks of the dock. I didn't care about the discomfort or the wet or the chill of the wind against my water-slick skin—I thought only about my need to have him close.

Though the fury of the rain and wind was chaotic, above the commotion I thought I could hear the sound of birds, and an angry, animal wail. Lightning struck again, nearby this time, accompanied by a clap of thunder from what sounded like immediately overhead. During the flash I saw Cor looking up to the sky. "You want to be with them, don't you?" I said, my ears still ringing from the thunderclap.

"More than almost anything. I love being in flight. You would, too." His hands had paused. I sensed him put them on either side of me as he balanced himself. His head dropped to nuzzle against mine. "But not more than this," he murmured into my ear. "Not more than now."

J. D. WARREN

Bedlam, Bath & Beyond

LOVE SPELL NEW YORK CITY

*This book is dedicated to
my biggest fan and autograph-collector,
Charles Lewis, in the hope that his time in California
is sunny and carefree. Many thanks as well to
Craig Symons, for helping to keep me aloft
in turbulent skies.*

LOVE SPELL®

January 2008

Published by

Dorchester Publishing Co., Inc.
200 Madison Avenue
New York, NY 10016

ISBN 10: 0-505-52698-0
ISBN 13: 978-0-505-52698-4

Printed in the United States of America.

10 9 8 7 6 5 4 3 2 1

Visit us on the web at www.dorchesterpub.com.

Bedlam, Bath & Beyond

Chapter One

"You know none of this is real, don't you?" murmured the uniformed fellow at our front door, his voice so urgent that I blinked at him, startled. "I don't know who you are or where you came from, but this is not your life."

The words left me feeling like an unsuspecting gnat meeting the windshield of a speeding vehicle. All I could do was gape at him.

"You've got to wake up," he added, handling me my half-percent milk. His whispering became more intense. "You've got to remember who you are," he concluded, before walking away with a nod and a tip of his cap.

Trust me. Four out of five doctors would not recommend it as a way to start off your week.

When the time comes for a nice nervous breakdown, show me the woman who doesn't want a say in its staging, and I'll show you the little girl who never kept a secret mental scrapbook of her future wedding day. The inner control freak tends to come out when everything's going Looney Tunes. I think I speak for all of us out there when I say we'd like some input in our outfits, the flattering lighting, and our proximity to something soft to fall and thrash upon. It's only natural.

By the next morning, though, I'd convinced myself that my previous encounter with the milkman had been an aberration. I'd misheard. He'd mistaken me for someone else. Or maybe the National Dairy Council was running a little late on April Fool's jokes. Because my life, I told myself after a brisk walk back from the little market at the street's end, couldn't be any more ordinary. I was a pretty young mother with blond hair who lived in one of the most exclusive gated communities around. Everyone knew that nothing out of the ordinary happened to my type. Especially in this neighborhood.

Hunched over her hydrangeas, my next-door neighbor looked like a garden gnome, right down to the hairs decorating her chin. Actually, in her current position, she resembled one of those tasteless painted wooden cutouts that people plant in their front yards, all leg and dress and plump, bent-over bottom.

"Well, good morning!" Mrs. McCuddy straightened up on the other side of our white picket fence. "Samantha Jones, don't you look pretty today?" The woman was employing a tone I'd grown to despise—a sickly sweet combination of saccharine and insincerity that over the past twenty-four hours I'd noticed everyone using.

Garden gnomes? I couldn't even remember the last time I'd seen one—certainly no one in this suburban enclave would dare decorate with anything so tacky. Clutching my grocery bag for comfort or protection, or maybe both, I called out brightly, "Good morning!"

My neighbor had crossed her arms over the floral print of her housecoat. Awe wrinkled her round and whiskered face. Oh, right. I got it. She'd been lying in wait for me, and was pretending to have only now noticed the new black car sitting in my driveway, gleaming in the early morning sun. "There's no keeping up with the Joneses, is there?" she asked with wonderment, and then cried out, "Henry! Henry! Come look at what that young Mr. Jones has done now!"

Instantly I wanted to shush her. It wasn't merely that Mrs. McCuddy had the loudest voice on Riviera Lane—she did, and proved it every morning and night by screeching like a banshee up and down the street for her cat, Muffins—it was that I knew exactly what was going to follow. "Oh, Mrs. M., *please* don't bother your husband. . . ."

Too late. The door of number 324 thudded as the male McCuddy, bearded and stroking his potbelly, stepped out onto the porch, thumbs hooked behind the suspenders that kept his pants riding three inches too high. "Well, would you look at that! Ain't she a beauty!"

Here it came. Low whistle from Mr. McCuddy to indicate his admiration of our new car? Check. Shake of the head to indicate disbelief? Double-check. Apparently, while I'd been sleeping one night, all the neighbors had met as a committee to set a daily quota of ways to remind me how lucky I, Samantha Jones, had been to have married that amazing Marshall, champion husband and world's best breadwinner. I knew all their techniques by now.

"It's Marshall's car, of course. I rarely drive," I said, teeth gritted.

Neither of them noticed. "That Mr. Jones. Such a provider! He gives you a beautiful house, all the clothes you could ever wear, two beautiful boys, a lovely diamond ring!" Instinctively, I covered my left hand to hide the sizeable rock it sported. "Isn't she just the luckiest girl alive?" asked Mrs. M. of her husband, who had left the porch's shade to stand by the fence, where he could gaze into our driveway more closely. "I was just saying yesterday to Annabelle Martin that our Mrs. Jones has more luck than anyone!"

I was beginning to believe the milkman, again. Something was dreadfully off here. The quickest way to convince someone she's a recovering mental patient is to pull out the white gloves and gently handle her at every opportunity. Trust me. I'd been handled enough to know.

"An Escalade!" He let out a low whistle, then looked at me speculatively. "I know my cars, and that is one pricey vehicle. Don't you go banging it up now and drive up the insurance rates."

To my horror, lighthearted laughter flew from my lips. "Oh, Mr. McCuddy!" Though I recognized the sound of my own voice, I had the alien sensation that someone else was doing the talking. Several times since my odd encounter of the day before, I'd felt it.

Yet I was in control, right? I could say whatever I wanted. I could drop this armful of heavy groceries right there on that perfect lawn and watch the Wonder Bread bounce beneath that enormous tank of a car while the canned peas rolled clean out into the street. I could shuck the cashmere cardigan smothering my skin if I wanted, and let the little pearl button that was the only thing holding it onto my shoulders pop off and disappear. I could—and should—even tell Mrs. McCuddy exactly what I thought of that mangy tomcat of hers, and how if she didn't keep him from spraying my back door three times a day, the only Muffins she'd be taking home would be from the bakery down the street.

Then, though my mouth opened to say all these things just to prove I could, something kicked in. Call it the suburban survival instinct, if you must—whenever I attempted to break from the mold of dutiful wife, devoted mother, or good neighbor, my brain clamped down on the insurrection. I found myself saying in an annoying, girlish voice, "Oh, you men. It's all about the insurance with you!" It seemed to satisfy them.

Mrs. McCuddy was still talking when our milkman's truck pulled up to the curb, yellow as a buttercup and sporting the cartoon face of a smiling cow on its side. I regarded it as enthusiastically as I might a roaming root-canal specialist. ". . . just like I was saying to Annabelle Martin. Our young Mrs. Jones always has the prettiest roasts from the butcher, the nicest flowers in her garden, and a husband who moves heaven and earth to keep her happy as a clam!" Out of a sudden perverse impulse, I clutched my grocery bag so my neighbors wouldn't see the paper-wrapped chop within. It really had been the prettiest cut in the butcher's case—and for some unknown reason, I'd actually cared. When had I become a Stepford Wife?

"That's me," I said, uneasily. "Happy as a clam." A clam who couldn't get out of the shell trapping her. I let out a whimper, but it was drowned by the sound of the delivery-eryman pulling open his truck's back door. I rallied and smiled brightly. "Could you excuse me for a minute?" I asked the old couple. They both smiled with benevolence as I turned expertly in my heels and tripped lightly to the curb, still juggling the increasingly heavy grocery bag in my arms. "Oh, Mr. Milkman?" I called out, trying to sound cheerful. Here's where I would prove that yesterday had been a fluke.

In his crisp uniform, the blue of denim dungarees, the milkman turned with a smile. The edge of his fore-finger grazed the brim of his cap. His impossibly blue eyes sparkled as he greeted me. "Morning, Mrs. Jones!"

Something was off about him. I couldn't quite place it. He seemed too tall, too lean. With long, dark hair tucked behind his ears and anchored by his cap, he seemed almost too *real* for this prefab neighborhood. "A half-pound of butter today, if you don't mind, three quarts of milk, and a pint of sour cream if you can spare it." The words came off my tongue as if I'd actually planned them.

"Oh, I don't see any problem with that, ma'am!"

Nothing out of the ordinary. See? I'd imagined his warning the day before. I could have been still sleepy. Or needed my ears cleaned. Well, whatever the aberration had been, it wasn't happening again. I let out a deep sigh of relief and began to relax.

"Anything else, ma'am?" he asked, closing the back door. Before I could speak, he laid his free hand on my wrist. His skin was still frosty from the refrigerated dairy products he'd been handling moments before, yet I felt an almost electric shock at the contact. "Do you remember?" he asked in a whisper, just as he had before. His glance flickered to where the McCuddys stood almost directly behind me before he let his hand drop. Where his fingers had lain, my skin felt raw and frigid still. "This is not your life. You have to keep telling yourself that." Those sky blue eyes bore into mine, otherworldly in their intensity. "Time is running out."

To my ears, my voice sounded high and shrill when I turned away from the man and said, "Just put everything on the stoop, if you don't mind!" Every breath cut ragged and raw in my chest; the groceries had left a damp, cold patch on my blouse.

"Mrs. Jones is not your name," he said in the same low voice. "This is important. You have to remember who you are."

I was more frightened than ever, now. "I really appreciate it! Marshall is always saying I should just get my milk and butter from the market, but somehow it seems just so much fresher, delivered!" I gushed to my neighbors, trying to ignore the milkman's uncomfortable presence as he walked behind me to my front door and deposited the dairy products with a clatter of the metal basket. "I'm sure it's healthier!"

Though they both smiled in my direction, shoulder to shoulder on their own side of the fence, the McCuddys' black eyes glittered as they scrutinized me. They were watching my every move; I was certain of it now.

Everyone here was.

Even before my milkman had begun adding dire warnings to the daily dairy, I'd known something was wrong with my every waking moment. Mornings, I'd rise from shapeless dreams and half-memories of some other place—louder, faster, powered by speed and noise and rancor. Nights, I'd lay awake for a time next to Marshall, listening to his breathing slow as he receded into slumber, marveling at the quietness of it all. There were no sounds of distant roads, or of neighbors watching their televisions late into the night, or even of dogs barking or crickets chirping or any of the nighttime noises one expects after dark.

In between, I'd wander through my house and wonder where it had all come from. The linens and silverware were all mine, but I hadn't the slightest memory of picking them out. When I looked at myself in the mirror, I saw myself wearing cheerful, feminine clothes, yet where had they come from? When had I decided to style my blond hair into a chin-length flip? Or to buy the lipsticks and perfumes covering my white enamel vanity, for that matter? I couldn't remember the last time I'd set a sensibly-heeled foot in a department store or a hair salon.

Hell, I couldn't bring to mind the last time I'd ventured past the market at the end of Riviera Lane. Was I in a gated community, or a pastel, manicured prison? Was it a very very early midlife crisis? Ennui? Rehab followed by shock treatment? Was I being medicated? Pills could make me feel out of it.

"I don't think there're pills," I murmured aloud, staring at a dining room chandelier that undeniably hung in the center of my dining room, though I didn't remember ever noticing its crystals before.

Two pigtails appeared above my living room sofa. They framed a puzzled, slightly chubby face. "No, they're M&Ms!" Nikki was my babysitter. That much I could remember. She struggled to her knees and leaned over the sofa's back, clutching a pink iPod with one hand and a bowl of candy with the other. "Want some? Seriously, Mrs. J., you have the best candy in the neighborhood. Mrs. Simmons down the street? With the new refrigerator that tells you when food's past the expiration date? You wouldn't believe the *horrifying* stuff she keeps for me to snack on. Like, tangerines." Nikki convulsed in a mock shudder. "And graham crackers. What about pills, though?"

"Oh. Nothing." Smoothing the slacks that felt too stylish for my own taste, I made my way back into the living room, where the twins sat on the floor occupied with a box of Crayolas and their coloring books. "Really. Nothing," I said, trying to cover both the gaffe and the doubt in my own mind. Of the two, the doubt didn't quite go away.

"I guess M&Ms kind of look like pills." In the world of competitive talkers, Nikki was a marathon runner—never tiring herself with a sprint when she could win with a steady pace. "Do you know the interesting thing about M&Ms? They taste better when they've been in the refrigerator for a few hours. My brother says that film's like that." She plucked out the iPod's earbuds and dangled further over the back of the sofa like some breed of boneless cat. "Snickers, too. Do you think all candy bars taste better in the refrigerator?"

"You know, I think they actually might." I was happy to be drawn out of my abstraction by any conversation that didn't have to do with how grateful I was supposed to be. "Mars bars do."

"And Butterfingers."

"Regular Hershey bars."

"But not Paydays," Nikki concluded. She ran a finger over her lips, thoughtful. "Maybe chocolate in general tastes better when it's cold. I wish they'd let me do a science fair project on *that*."

As if on cue, the twins simultaneously set down their crayons and stared at me. They acted in tandem more than I cared to realize. It always made me uneasy. Nikki noticed them, too, but her reaction was the polar opposite of mine. "Isn't that adorable?"

Lately I'd come to think that my sons Timothy and Patrick seemed less like two-year-olds who'd allegedly sprung from my loins and more like miniature adults who'd been planted in my home to keep an eye on me. Fine, shoot me—I was a terrible mother. I was the kind of monster maternal figure that Dr. Spock warned about, distant and absent and doomed to warp my tykes' psyches so that they grew up to be identical male Lizzie Bordens, using the toy tomahawks their grandmother had given them to scalp me clean.

With the sudden gymnastic energy that only teenagers seem to have, Nikki fell on her back and thrust her lithe little legs into the air, before propelling herself up again. "Twins in general are the cutest things ever. Did having them hurt?"

I blinked, not expecting the question. Not that I could ever really predict on what particular perch my babysitter's mind might alight. "What?"

"Did it hurt? Is that rude? My friend Jennifer says soon

they'll grow babies in vats. Big vats of vitamin water. I like that. Obviously a superior solution to, you know. *Pregnancy.*"

The way she whispered the word, as if it were dirty, made me laugh a little. "Well, pregnancy's no trip to the spa," I assured her, trying to sound serious without scaring her half to death. Having a girl-to-girl conversation was making me feel a little more grounded than usual. Normal, even. Like I actually belonged.

"Did they give you, like a whatchamacallit? Epidermal? Did it hurt?"

"Epidural. It's . . ." I paused for a moment. I honestly didn't remember squat about giving birth nearly three years ago—nothing. Not the trip to the hospital, not how long I'd been in labor, not even how I felt about bringing two armfuls of sweet-smelling babies home. I didn't even remember having carried them for nine months—though since we didn't have any vitamin vats on the patio, surely I had to have done it. So stinging was my shock at the memory lapse that it felt almost exactly like slamming into a plate-glass window I hadn't known was there. Giving birth was supposed to be a momentous life experience, and I didn't even have the slightest recollection of it. "Oh my God," I finished, in a whisper.

Although I must have looked as pale as a ghost, Nikki kept chattering on, popping candies in her mouth between sentences. "When I get married to Clinton Wright— he's on the football team and is soooo handsome and we're going to be steadies even though he doesn't know it yet—actually, he doesn't know I'm alive, but he will after my mother finally starts letting me wear *real* lipstick instead of the cheap pink stuff—we're going to have three children. Jamie, Jessica, and Jack. My wedding gown is going to be pleats, not ruffles, and we'll go to Bermuda for our honeymoon. Where did you go for your honeymoon, Mrs. J.?"

That answer I could supply immediately, I realized with relief. "Niagara Falls." I'd been holding my breath; the words came out with an audible panting.

"That is so romantic!" Nikki twiddled her toes with excitement. She glanced over at the boys for a moment to make certain, then sighed. "Was it beautiful? Did you go near the falls in yellow raincoats and kiss?"

"It was . . ." *Slam.* There I was again, teetering on the edge of another gaping black space in my past. I knew for a fact I'd been to Niagara Falls for my honeymoon. On the built-in bookshelves in our den, next to the box where Marshall kept his pipe and tobacco, sat a snow globe of the Maid of the Mist perched on a rock, with the name of the waterfall written in silver letters over a small Canadian flag. There hadn't been a day I'd not seen it. Yet did I remember the trip itself? Not at all. Nor did I know how long we'd stayed there, nor where. I didn't even have the slightest memory of the falls' spray on my face, or how it felt to be a young newlywed who'd only days before affixed a *Mrs.* in front of her name. "It was nice, I guess," I said, trying not to betray my rising panic. From the sofa's edge, I rose to my feet and clutched a handful of upholstery between my fingers.

From where she had slid onto the braided living room rug, Nikki didn't seem to notice any change in my behavior. "Of course, I don't think Clinton Wright will be able to afford a ring like Mr. J. bought you right away, or a house like this, but I don't care if we have to live in a one-room shack, because we'll be in love and everything will be just peachy, like on television," she said. I was having a difficult time remaining upright; my legs felt weak and shaky, as if I needed some sugar in my blood. "Well, old-time television. Not like, *24* or anything. When Mr. J. proposed to you, did he kneel down? I bet he did. He looks like the kind who would kneel. Was your cake two tiers or three? What kind of flowers did you carry? Mom says carnations are good enough for anyone and not to have champagne tastes when Dad has a Bud Light budget. Isn't that crude? But I want orchids in my bouquet."

"Nikki," I said, choking out a warning. Either the room or I was spinning. Given my mental state lately, I was betting Marshall hadn't secretly installed a Tilt-a-Whirl beneath the linoleum of our stately colonial.

"Where did you meet Mr. J.? Was it in high school? I met Clinton Wright in the cafeteria. I see him in the cafeteria, anyway. Usually with Cindy Blaine. *Her* mother lets her wear lipstick from the M.A.C counter. Dark red." I knew my babysitter didn't mean any harm with her yammering, but to my frazzled nerves every syllable felt like some kind of high-speed Chinese water torture. "Gosh, I bet you were pretty in high school, Mrs. J.," she continued, retrieving some of the fat crayons the twins had discarded and wearing them experimentally on her upper lip, like green and purple wax mustaches. "Were you on the cheerleading squad? Did all the boys want you to wear their letter jacket? Oh wait, you're not *that* old. Hey!" The crayons bounced across the rug when she dropped them to leap to her feet and bound to my side. "Mrs. J., are you all right?"

I wasn't. Not by a long shot. I think we've all had quiet moments in our lives, maybe when we're looking up at the night sky or when we're sitting by ourselves and everything's still, when we've thought about how vast and unending the universe is, until we feel empty and insignificant inside. Or else we think about infinity—a number that's as big as we can imagine, and then one, and then one more, and then one more after that, never ending—and it makes us panicky and uncertain about how we fit into it all.

Though my anxiety felt just the same, the source was the total opposite. With every question she asked, Nikki chipped away at the already-shaky foundation I stood on. It felt like infinity in reverse; every answer I couldn't provide subtracted from my sum. Take away much more and I wouldn't have anything left. "Sit down!" she implored, taking me by the arm and leading me to the sofa again. "Oh my gosh, should I call a doctor or something? Should I call Mr. J.'s office?"

While I sat down, I waved a hand at her to get her to shut her mouth. Maybe I was crazy, but I didn't want anyone to know about it. Although tears stung the corners of my eyes, I tried to slow my breathing and will them away. "No, no," I said in what I hoped was a reassuring voice. "I'm fine. Really. Just a little . . . emotional . . . today, for some reason." To say the least!

By the way Nikki bit her lip, I could tell I hadn't allayed all her worries. She didn't make a move to call anyone, though. Instead, she sat there on the sofa next to me, squeezing my fingers between her warm little hands, and staring at me with wide, blue eyes. It was the best thing that anyone could have done for me right then.

After what seemed a long, long time, we both relaxed a little. Keeping quiet was easy for the boys. Neither of them had ever uttered so much as a peep, much less a complete word. Sitting for two or three minutes without saying anything must have been absolute torture for my babysitter, though. She tried to stand it with as much self-restraint as she could summon, hopped up on half a bag of chocolate candies. At last, searching for some safe topic that wouldn't send me into another crazy woman's fit of hyperventilation, she smiled and pointed to the twins. "See?" she said, sliding down to the floor like a boneless cat. "Aren't your kids, like, the most adorable things ever?"

When she lifted up their identical coloring books to show me what the pair had been working on, any small sense of comfort I'd regained over the past minute vanished absolutely. The colored-in illustrations were exactly the same. Color for color, down to the brown mounds of dirt, green grass, and hot yellow disc of a sun, as identical as the two boys themselves. And yet I didn't find any of that as chilling as the fact that not a single stroke of their crayons had landed outside the lines.

Timothy and Patrick stared at me, judging my reaction with flat, dark eyes that were as unmoving as the placid expressions on their faces. Something deep inside warned me not to betray the horror they made me feel. "Adorable?" I echoed, not meaning it. Not at all.

"They are totally the cutest things," Nikki marveled, reaching out and ruffling the hair of the nearer one—I didn't know which. If she told me how lucky I was, I decided right then and there, I would scream. Just absolutely scream, loud and clear and without remorse, until they took me away in a straitjacket and set me down in the padded cell for which I was clearly headed. Yet the babysitter didn't say a single word about how appreciative I should be. Instead, she regarded me uneasily. "Maybe you should lie down for a while, Mrs. J.," she suggested at last, giving the coloring books back to the boys. In a slow, almost practiced movement, they reached out with their chubby hands and dragged their palms across the pulpy pages, simultaneously turning them to the next picture.

"You know," I said slowly, trying to keep a smile on my face, "I think that's a fine idea."

As I tottered in the direction of the staircase, my

hands digging their nails into the fabric of my perfectly pleated pants, I suddenly remembered why I kept a babysitter around so much: I'd been lying down an awful lot, lately.

Chapter Two

My husband was a complex collection of smells. When he leaned down at my vanity to peck me on the cheek on his way back from the bathroom where he'd changed, I caught a whiff of his after-dinner coffee, the faint, lingering tang of the aftershave he'd slapped onto his cheeks that morning, the sickly sweet scent of his after-dinner pipe tobacco, and an acrid aroma of something I could only identify as mothballs—probably from the summer suits we'd taken out of storage not too many days before. "Dinner at Mother's tomorrow," he reminded me after he'd straightened up and shuffled across the bedroom in his slippers, hands thrust deep into the pockets of his fuzzy plaid robe. "Don't forget."

"Oh, honey," I said, automatically dismayed. I should have remembered, though. Just as surely as the week started with Meatloaf Mondays and Saturday was the day we fired up the brick barbecue on the patio so that Marshall could grill hamburgers and wieners, Wednesday night we always spent at the largest house at the end of the turnabout in Riviera Lane, which belonged to my mother-in-law. "Can't we do something else? Just for a change?" Hastily, I returned to the hundred strokes I gave my hair every night. I honestly didn't know why I stuck to a routine I didn't enjoy or understand, but one hundred strokes the routine demanded, and a hundred strokes my hair got.

"A change?" Marshall had picked up the putter he kept in the bedroom's corner and tapped out a few experimental strokes. "But Mother expects us, darling. She enjoys having us over."

"I know, but . . ."

"Why, we wouldn't have this house if it wasn't for her," he said, leaning over in his pajamas and robe. "You don't know how hard it is to get into this community."

No, but I knew how hard it was to escape. "True."

"Sssh." Once I'd silenced my protests, he gently tapped a golf ball he'd set down. It rolled across the wooden floor, with a faint clink, into a drinking glass lying sideways near the dresser. "Hole in one!" he crowed, before adopting his serious voice again. "But seriously, sweetheart. You know Mother. We're expected." With the club's head, he retrieved another ball lurking before the dresser, adjusting it for another putt.

What would be the point of complaining? I didn't want to seem ungrateful when I had everything I ever needed, thanks to the prize catch Mrs. McCuddy would have called the world's best provider. "All right, then," I said, trying to sound if not cheery, at least not contentious. *Clink*. Another perfect putt for the perfect man.

Instead of going for a third, he crossed the room and stood behind me. His hands rested on my shoulders. "Sam. What's wrong?" I looked at him in the vanity mirror, wondering if he knew how impossibly handsome he was. It was true—his eyes were almost a supernatural shade of pale blue, and I'd never seen anyone with a more chiseled chin or strong, rugged brow. Even in that ridiculous fuzzy plaid robe, he managed to look broad-shouldered and masculine. He was exactly the kind of guy I'd marry, if this really was my life. "What's wrong?" he repeated, insistently.

"It's silly," I said, wishing I honestly believed what I said. With Marshall there, though, and the two of us alone and the house quiet, I felt myself wanting to open up. I stopped fiddling with my brush. My left hand reached up and rested atop where my husband's fingers gently massaged my shoulders. In the light of the twin vanity lamps, the diamonds of my wedding ring sparkled. For a moment, I felt that maybe I really might be the lucky girl everyone had been telling me I was. "I don't know. Maybe I should be taking vitamins," I said, stammering slightly. Saying my worst fears aloud wasn't a trivial act; I dreaded what he might say if he took me seriously. That's why I tried to sound as lighthearted as possible when I admitted, "I've been having some memory problems lately."

"Memory problems?" he repeated, his eyes meeting mine in the mirror.

"Little things." I swallowed, not daring to move. "Forgetfulness."

"Sweetheart," he said, more kindly than I could have expected. "You're exhausted. You have the house to look after, you have to keep an eye on the twins, and I don't know how much work you do to keep yourself the prettiest girl on Riviera Lane." He gave me a squeeze. "Don't worry about it."

For an instant, I wanted to run with that explanation, but I couldn't. What did I *do* in this house except stock the pantry from the little grocery down the road, cook the occasional meal, skulk in the corners in fear of the two children a sixteen-year-old managed to watch over while talking to every classmate in her high school on her cell phone, and gnaw my nails in worry? I swiveled in my seat and looked directly at Marshall, trying to blink back tears. "I can't remember our honeymoon," I told him. "I know we went to Niagara Falls, but I can't remember anything else. I should be able to, right?"

"Sssshh." His strong hands moved to my head, stroking my hair as he hushed me. "You remember Niagara Falls! We stayed there for three days in that funny old hotel that looked like a Swiss chalet." His fingers were at my temples now, rubbing them gently, as he might if I'd had a headache. "The owner brought us those homemade sugar doughnuts every morning. We went on the boat cruise twice, and took long walks, and spent a lot of time in our room." He grinned at the recollection. "You remember now, don't you?"

And you know, it was the strangest thing. I did remember it. With every reminder Marshall gave, I felt memories returning. It was as if he'd poured a wash of watercolors over a blank sheet of clean, white paper, magically transforming the dullness into bright hues and marvelous details. Now I could almost smell those doughnuts, fresh from the fryer and thickly crusted with sugar. I recalled the prickling sensation of mist on my face and the sudden, unexpected rainbows we'd seen on sunny afternoons. I remembered the lacy nighties I'd bought especially for the trip and blushed. "You're right," I said, feeling a hundred times better. "I do."

"See?"

"What about the twins?" I asked, hoping for more miracles. "When they were born? I was trying to think of it this afternoon and couldn't . . ."

"We were at a bridge game with the Gardeners." The slow, steady pressure of my husband's fingertips at my temples intensified. It was so soothing that I closed my eyes and allowed myself to drift on the gentle waves of his deep voice. "We'd been to dinner at that Italian restaurant downtown, and you were joking that you thought you'd had indigestion." I could bring up every detail of that dinner, now—from the red-checked table-cloth to the garlicky spaghetti to the sesame-crusted breadsticks. "I'd bid three-no-trump, and you had just countered with four diamonds, for what reason I don't know, considering it turned out you only had the ace and a four in your hand. Then you rose up from your seat and said . . ."

"*Honey, I don't think it's indigestion,*" I murmured, before he could. "I remember."

"You were in labor for six hours, and at the end of it, the nurse brought out the boys to me and I couldn't stop smiling." Of course he had, I realized. It was the perfect end to a perfect story. I opened my eyes and saw him smiling at me with tenderness. "All better?"

"Much!" I admitted, straightening up and for the first time in days, feeling almost perky.

"You always ask too many questions, darling," he said, smoothly and surely. His hands dropped from the sides of my head, and he gave me a last reassuring pat before heading back across the room to his putting. "Relax. Everything's fine. You're fine and I'm fine and the boys are fine and we'll have a fine dinner at Mother's tomorrow."

"Everything's fine," I echoed, standing and pushing in the chair. It felt so easy to believe him. Every niggling doubt I'd had over the past who-knew-how-long took flight; the fluttering of their little wings felt like a cool, refreshing breeze. "It really is." I wasn't a recovering shock-therapy patient who needed a return trip to the loony bin. I didn't need a trip to the psychiatrist, or even a tranquilizer. All I'd needed was Marshall's gentle reminders, and a little relaxation, and I felt as good as new. "Oh my gosh, you're right, honey!"

"Of course I am." Mouth puckered in concentration, he tapped another of the balls littering the shiny wood floor. "Now, why don't you trot yourself to bed, tuck your pretty little self in, and work on a good night's sleep?" He nodded approvingly when I placed the tortoiseshell brush back into its case, rose to my feet, and shuffled over to him in my bedroom slippers so I could give him a devoted peck on the cheek. The man was my hero. "Where are you going?" he asked, straightening up to look at me when, after my kiss, I sailed past him out into the hallway.

"To check on the twins," I called back, remembering at the last minute not to let the caroling of my voice ring too loudly. The poor little tykes were supposed to be asleep. In my moment of clarity, I'd realized what a bad mother I'd been lately, pussyfooting around my two-year-olds like they were junior versions of *The Bad Seed.*

They were my darlings, I told myself as I entered their shared bedroom with its bright red twin beds and the cheerful *Toy Story* wallpaper. Little darlings that I'd neglected during my week of self-absorption, poor things. How could anyone in their right mind build up some paranoid fantasy about two innocent lambs who'd never squalled or whined or given me so much as a moment's trouble? Two identical clown night-lights bathed my ankles in a soothing and subdued glow that left the room's upper reaches dark enough for sleep. Smiling, I leaned over Timothy's big-boy bed, brushing back a handful of dark brown hair—so very like his father's—from his forehead.

He wasn't asleep. For a moment, I thought I'd stirred him by sneaking into the room unexpectedly, but no. He'd been awake all along. Although Timothy lay perfectly still beneath his blue blanket with his head on the pillow, he stared at me with unblinking eyes and an expressionless face. My child looked so much like a lifeless wax doll that my heart momentarily seized in my chest and I stood upright, frightened that something might have happened to him. But no, I realized. Motionless as he was, his eyes still followed mine, joined from the other bed by an equally still and watchful Patrick. The other twin lay in exactly the same supine position, also awake.

Jolted by their uncanny correspondence to each other, for a moment I considered fleeing. "Oh, you sillies," I finally whispered, made bold by the good mood I'd been in only seconds before. "Can't you sleep?" I knew they wouldn't answer me. They never did. "Do you want Mommy to sit with you for a while?"

"Something wrong?" Marshall, toothbrush in his hand and a little bit of Pepsodent foam coloring the corner of his mouth, stopped in the doorway.

From my perch on a toddler-sized stool, I shook my head to let him know everything was fine. Then, before he could pad back to the bedroom, I called out, "Marshall?" He backtracked and cocked his head. "The twins . . ." I said, keeping my voice low. The sensation was palpable that they were still looking at me from either side, but I tried to ignore it. "I just wish they were a little bit more normal."

"You mean talking?" Marshall laughed. "Darling, you'll rue the day you ever worried about it. Mother says I was the same way. Mute for months, then suddenly talking entire sentences. And now you can't shut me up." He let out another sharp bark of amusement and walked away again. "You will rue the day!" he called again, through a mouthful of toothbrush.

Maybe I would, at that, I thought to myself.

What did they need, these two round-faced strangers of mine? "Do you want a story?" I asked them, when I couldn't take the staring any longer. "Do you want to hear about Mike Mulligan and Mary Anne the steam shovel? Ferdinand the Bull?" I turned myself around on the stool and thumbed through the half-shelf of picture books. All of them seemed dog-eared and familiar, as if I'd read them aloud a hundred times apiece. "Here's one," I said, my index finger brushing against a spine that seemed newer than the others. "Have we done this one? I don't recognize it."

I was talking to myself, of course. Neither of the twins made so much as a peep as I pulled out the thin volume and flipped on the lamp between their beds. On the glossy cover, a flock of dark, almost formless birds flew against a midnight-blue sky. "No title," I told them. "Did your grandmother buy this for you?" I turned the page. Although the typeface looked more antique than any of the other children's books I remembered reading in recent days, it was still handsomely set. A pen-and-ink illustration of more birds, their paths so close that they seemed nearly identical, graced the right-hand page. I lifted it up to show them. "Birdies?" I said, hopeful to trigger some kind of recognition. "Nice birds?" Nothing.

Clearing my throat, I began to read. "*Old legends speak of a time when the earth was young and the winds were alive with flocks of birds,*" I said, tracing the words with my finger. Was it my imagination, or had the boys perked up a little at my recitation? No, they were actually paying attention, their eyes wide and alert. Encouraged to get a reaction, I kept going. "*And most favored of all the birds was the Order of the Storm Ravens, whose very wings bring comfort to the persecuted and terror to the unjust.* Wow, these are big words for a kid's . . ."

The head-splitting noise that followed made me drop the book and clap my hands to the sides of my head. I'd gotten a reaction from the twins, all right—an unending keening so high and shrill that it felt as if my eardrums might burst and bleed. It sounded like some kind of terrible alarm, or an air-raid siren in cramped quarters. The twins' mouths were round, bottomless Os, and the sound they made was so perpetual that I wondered how, or even whether, they were breathing.

Marshall appeared in the doorway, his robe discarded and his dark hair in a mess. His mouth moved, creating words that I couldn't discern. "Make it stop!" I yelled at him.

Roughly, he grabbed me by the wrist and pulled me out into the hallway. My teeth ached as the sounds assailed my unprotected ears once more. "What did you do?" he repeated, yelling nearly as loudly as the boys.

"Nothing!" I assured him. "I was just reading them a story!"

"A story couldn't do that! What story?" At his demand, I pointed to the book that lay open on the floor facedown. He marched over and picked it up, examining first the cover and then the inside. He flipped through the pages roughly, nearly ripping them from the binding, before stalking toward me again. I'd never seen him so angry in my life. "Corydonais!" he shouted.

I cringed. "Coriwhat?"

"Where did you get this? *Where in the hell did you get this?*"

"I don't know!" I said, shaking. His fingers dug into my arm, sending strands of fire up my shoulder and neck. What had I done wrong? Reading a book aloud shouldn't have caused this kind of havoc. "Marshall, I don't know! I just picked up the book! It's just a fairy tale! I don't know where it came from! What's Cori . . . Corydonais?"

"Who visited the house today? Did you let anyone in?" His questions battered my already-worn nerves. "Did you let some stranger into *my house*?"

"No!"

"*Cease that noise*," he thundered. The house seemed to shake to its very foundations from the deep noise coming from his chest. Yet the twins stopped their screeching, their expressions returning to lifeless, placid normality.

My ears still rang from all the yelling, and tears stung my eyes. "This," said Marshall, brow knitted as he fumed at me and waved the book in the air, "I'm burning. And not a word about it to Mother, tomorrow." He stomped from the boy's room, a quivering bundle of rage. At the last moment, he whirled and pointed at me. I feared his voice would be raised again, but this time it was softer, though no less steely. "Go to sleep, Samantha," he ordered.

Underlit by the pale gleam of the two clown night-lights, Marshall's features seemed strange and alien—almost inhuman, in a way. Right then, standing there with my ears still ringing and my brain frazzled from the noise, I realized something I'd known all along. All the memories in the world didn't make Marshall my husband. This was not my life. Not at all. I closed my eyes and listened to him walk away.

I didn't dare disobey his order, though I had questions. Oh, did I ever have questions. I crept to the bedroom and pulled the sheets over my head while I listened to the patio doors open, followed by the sounds of Marshall starting a fire in the brick barbecue. Somehow I knew its flames couldn't compete with the heat from my burning face.

Chapter Three

The moment my daisy-colored high heeled shoes hit the brick of my front stoop that next morning, two enormous black crows from the phone lines above swooped down and attempted a Tippi Hedren on me. They might have been hawks, or orioles, for all I knew. Whatever the species, they were as big and black as my mood. I squinted as they flew off into the too-bright sun, cawing at the tops of their considerable avian lungs.

I hadn't come outdoors for a spot of bird-watching, anyway. I'd come to meet the damned milkman, whose cheerful van had stopped outside mere moments before. Ever since I'd risen after a sleepless night, I'd been listening for the sound of that van. All during my awkward, silent breakfast with Marshall I'd dreaded that it might come too early, and once he'd given his tie one last straightening and walked down the street to the bus stop, I'd rushed to the window seat in the living room and sat there, waiting. "Good morning, Mrs. Jones!" said the milkman, touching the brim of his cap with his hand. "Another beautiful day!"

My milkman looked as if he'd stepped out of an advertisement straight from Madison Avenue: *Drink milk three times a day, boys and girls!* He was impossibly tall and lean, his chin square. The guy's frame was a testament to the height-building qualities of the stuff he hawked. And now that he was here, I didn't know what in the world to say. But you know, I had a feeling I could make my wordlessness work for me. I simply folded my arms and waited for the question I knew would follow.

"Two quarts?" he asked.

That wasn't it. "Okay. Fine," I said automatically, taken a little aback by the humdrum nature of the exchange. I watched him ease two glass bottles into the cage sitting at my feet. As he hoisted himself up, I noticed with a little surprise that he looked me over closely . . . starting with my legs. When he stood at his full height and I was once more craning my neck to look at him with my five-foot-five self, we stared at each other for a moment more until I couldn't stand it. I blurted out, "Isn't there something else you want to say?"

His left eyebrow had a scar running through it, I noticed, thick as a cardboard matchstick and just as long, bisecting the jet-black curve where it peaked. "Eggs?"

"No!"

"Yogurt?"

My patience had already been worn thin by the hours of waiting that morning. "Forget the dairy. How many mornings now have you asked the other question? You know which one," I snapped, before he could offer me half-and-half.

"You do remember, then," he said slowly, his voice quiet. We'd come to the topic at last; I could tell how serious he was by the way his eyes bore into mine. To my relief, they weren't cold, like the twins', or angry, like Marshall's. Instead, they seemed concerned. Even a lit-

tle kind. With wonder coloring his voice, he asked,
"Who *are* you?"

"I don't know!" My voice was too loud. "I don't know,"
I repeated at a much more intimate level. "You tell me!
Am I insane? Was I in a hospital? Mental clinic?" Speaking my worst doubts aloud wasn't the good therapy I'd
hoped it might be. Every word made me tremble in fear,
not because I felt silly saying them, but because I worried they might turn out to be true. And wouldn't that
be a damned shame? But no, he was shaking his head.
"Did I fall? Did I hit my head? Am I crazy?"

"No. It's not like that at all."

"But you don't think I'm crazy, right?"

"No."

The relief I felt was even greater than the night before, when I'd remembered the Niagara Falls trip. All it
had taken had been one word. "So what, I have to play
twenty questions to get some answers from you? Am I
bigger than a breadbox?" He smiled a bit at that quip.
So the milkman wasn't impervious to a little banter.
Good. That made me feel more at ease somehow. "Is my
name even Samantha Jones?"

"I don't know," was all he said.

"But I'm not her?" I asked, feeling as if I was on to
something. As luck would have it, right at that moment
I heard the percussive rap of the McCuddy's front
screen door. My hand flew up to my mouth, preventing
it from saying anything more. My milkman's eyebrows
furrowed together at the noise, erasing the scar from
view for a moment. The confirmation in his eyes said
everything I needed to know. "I'm not Mrs. Goody-
goody Jones," I repeated, certain of the fact as I was
of . . . well, I hadn't been certain of much lately, but of
this, I was. I dredged a memory from some dark corner
of my mind. "Am I in the Witness Protection Program?

No, that doesn't make sense, if I don't have an identity to protect."

"It's difficult to explain." I understood he was trying to be discreet, but I needed an answer. I *deserved* some kind of answer, and I couldn't wait another twenty-four hours to get it. He rubbed a hand over his face, scraping a layer of bristles that had already grown in over the day's shave. "You'd call this place a construct. It's made to look like it's real, but it's a self-contained bubble. For the Kin who made it, it's like a toy."

"I'm in a *toy?*" I whispered, appalled. And, to be honest, a little offended. The last thing anyone wanted to be told was that they'd been stuffed into some kind of overblown version of Timothy and Patrick's Fisher-Price school bus made by someone's crazy family. Common sense told me I shouldn't be paying a bit of attention to the nonsense spewing from his mouth, but I'd abandoned common sense days ago. "Like a snow globe?" He didn't seem to understand. I shook my hands up and down around an imaginary glass sphere. "A snow globe. Niagara Falls." The nerve of Marshall, putting that little souvenir in plain sight, so it could taunt me with my own plight. "Damn him! And these are your relatives?"

"My relatives?" He seemed taken aback by the question. "No."

"You said they were your kin."

"I said they were Kin. My race, yes, but no more my family or clan than you're related to every human. Their goal is to keep you content. Unthinking. Asleep, almost, while they pump you for information."

So we weren't even dealing with something human, here. Interesting. And, quite frankly, since I was in a situation that made no logical sense, I was a little bit relieved there might be an explanation that I couldn't have thought of through normal means. "So what, you're from outer space? Is it Mars? You're a Martian? Am I on Mars, too?"

If it hadn't been for the tenseness of the situation, I almost would have sworn he might have cracked a smile. "You're not on Mars. Your people have always had legends of another race living among you. The Iroquois called us Jogah. The Chinese spoke of us as Mogui, and to the people of Europe we were fairies. Probably the correct description of us is the Peri, but among ourselves we call ourselves Kin, because . . . what are you doing?" he asked, when I almost toppled over from leaning forward on tiptoe.

"Nothing," I said, a little guiltily.

"Yes, you are." He narrowed his eyes. "Are you looking for wings?"

"Of course not!" I lied.

His eyes narrowed. "We're sensitive about that."

The Peri were, or him in particular? I made a noise of dismissal before changing the topic. "How long have you been trying to wake me up?"

He shook his head. "Not long. Less than a week."

"How long have I been here?"

"I don't know. The Storm Ravens found this place. In the real world, it sends out certain vibrations we can detect."

I recognized that name from the book. "The Storm Ravens are . . ."

"My clan. It's complicated. It's our job—it's *my* job to investigate offenses such as this, particularly when the innocent are involved." In my peripheral vision, I saw Mrs. McCuddy's head appear over the rose-tangled picket fence dividing our properties. Knowing she was keeping an eye on me, I kept my distance from the man in uniform, trying to make it appear as if we were having an ordinary conversation. Apparently the milkman had the same idea. In a slightly louder than normal voice, he hung his head and said, "I'm real sorry the milk was off yesterday, ma'am. It must be the warm weather." More softly, he added, "We don't have much time. Tell me what you know about Lily Oliver."

"Lilliwhat?" He might as well have asked me to recite the periodic table; I didn't have a clue.

"Lily Oliver." He repeated the syllables distinctly. "It's a name."

"I don't know it." With sudden hope, I asked, "Is it me? Am I Lily Oliver?" He shook his head. "Does she know who I am?"

"Is everything all right, Mrs. Jones?" Mrs. McCuddy's voice, reedy and shrill, cut through our conversation. I started a little bit, and hoped I didn't appear too guilty. "Did I hear something was wrong with the milk?"

Mrs. McCuddy's interest in me had always gone beyond mere nosiness. And hadn't she always been reminding me of my good fortune in marrying Marshall? For the first time, I looked at my neighbor and knew that she was one of the *they* the milkman had been talking about. "It was sour," I said flatly, detecting emotions I'd not felt in what seemed like ages. Anger was foremost among them. But no, I couldn't arouse her suspicions. I still didn't know what the real dangers were, here. "I'll be with you in a moment!" She seemed placated, retreating slightly. I still caught glints of her eyes through the rosebush, however. I turned back to the conversation that mattered. "Where's the stopper?"

"The what?" He raised his eyebrows, clearly not following.

If my mind had been in some kind of sleepy stasis before, adrenaline was now kicking it into overdrive. "The stopper," I repeated, thinking aloud. "Snow globes have stoppers. That's how the water gets into them. And if the water can get in, it can come out." I pointed to my noggin, feeling confident. "I used to be smart, whoever I was. And what's *Cory . . . Corydonner?*"

If I'd caught him off guard with the snow globe analogy, hauling out the word my so-called husband had used the night before positively spooked him. In a way, I was satisfied not to be the only one getting a bolt from the blue. "Corydonais? That's my name," he said, more softly. He looked askance in our neighbor's direction. "I'm Corydonais. Why?"

"My husband is not very happy with you," I told him. If I worked on the principle that the enemy of my enemy was my friend, then I was happy to have an ally.

"He found the book?"

"Did you put it upstairs?"

"Not I," he said. "An agent of mine."

"Well, he found it. And blew a gasket."

For a split second the man's lips twitched. "Good."

"Young man, are you gloating?" I said, trying not to grin.

If he had been, it didn't last long. "I meant it as a warning. I can't come here again," he told me, bending over to take the empty bottles from the bin by the door. They clattered into the basket he carried. "It's too dangerous now."

"But . . . no!" For the first time in heaven knew how long I had some of the answers I'd craved. Okay, so nothing he'd told me about fairies and snow globes should have made any more sense than the average ramblings of the smelly homeless guy who rants at you outside your local McDonald's. Crazy as they were, though, they resonated with more sense than the notion of me ensconced in suburban bliss. So he couldn't just *leave.* I despised when people just upped and left me. "Cormorant! You can't!"

"Corydonais," the man said, slightly pained.

"Cor," I implored, abbreviating.

He touched the brim of his hat again in a polite farewell, but paused before he left. "Something is binding you to him. An object. That's your stopper. No, I don't know what it is," he added before I could ask. "But if you don't find it . . ."

"What?" I asked, demanding the answer. "What? I'll suffocate in here forever?"

"Sorry. I really am." Oh. That was it, wasn't it? I could tell by the pity in his eyes that I'd hit the nail on the head.

Fear tightened its icy grip around my heart. Somehow I thought finding out the truth would be more liberating. "So find this stopper thing and destroy it for me," I hissed, feeling desperate. "Please!"

"I can't," he whispered back, equally urgent. "That would be too easy. There're rules in here, and the rule is that only you can break the link. So find it, and destroy it."

"That's it?" I almost cried. "That's all you can tell me?"

"Heaven helps those who help themselves." I hate platitudes, but I could tell he was trying to be honest and kind. "We appreciate your business, ma'am," Cor called out from halfway down the sidewalk, using his cheerful milkman's voice. I could detect an edge to it, though, that wasn't there before. "Have a good day, now!"

He was already in his van, engine started, before I could summon words to answer him. "Wait!" I wailed, as the buttercup-colored vehicle spluttered off. "Who's going to deliver my milk?"

Honestly, it was unbelievable how much of the stuff my imaginary family went through.

Chapter Four

"For the love of God, Samantha." Marshall was still up-set. He'd come home in a foul mood, slamming the front door behind him and throwing down his briefcase while ripping at his necktie, obviously spoiling for a fight. "I don't know what's gotten into you lately. Hello, Mrs. Gilly!" he called out to a neighbor on her front porch, changing his voice from an angry growl to mock cheer.

We were walking down the street in the direction of the cul-de-sac where the fearsome Mrs. Jones lived, ar-guing all the way. It was a sight more honest, at least, than having to pretend I liked the man, whoever he was. Or wasting time commenting on the beauty of the sunset—because when you're trapped in some sort of snow globe, or construct, or jail, or whatever this place was, why bother admiring what never, ever would change? "It's not my fault the babysitter didn't show, Marshall," I said, not bothering to lower my voice. Keep-ing up with his furious pace was hard enough in my knee-length skirt and heels. "I didn't drive her out."

"Oh, was it the twins, then?" I'd never heard him so snide before. In what little memory I had of the time I'd spent in this bubble, my only recollections were of feeding him night and morning and listening to him sink putts before bedtime. Any emotion at all beyond sheer minimal brain activity was a novelty. Of course, wasn't that true of most guys? Wait, where had that come from? "They're such hellions, what with the not-talking stuff, is that it? She couldn't take it any more?"

"Maybe Nikki couldn't take the heavy-handed sarcasm," I snapped back. I didn't know why the girl hadn't shown up in the afternoon, or why her mother had told me over the phone that she didn't think Nikki would be sitting for us anymore. Almost immediately I stumbled on a crack in the sidewalk. If my heel snapped, maybe I could return home and sulk for the rest of the night. "And it doesn't matter, since Mrs. McCuddy agreed to watch after them, does it?"

"Maybe, just maybe, Nikki couldn't take the *mess*. It looks like you ripped the house apart!" For a moment, when he stopped and clenched his fists together, I thought that Marshall might tear his own hair out. But no, instead of attacking its shiny, gelled perfection, he waved his fists around his ears, puffed out his cheeks with air, and stomped his foot.

He wasn't just upset. He was livid, and I was guessing it was fueled by the incident the night before. My husband—my imitation husband, as I preferred to think of him now—was absolutely purple with rage that someone had somehow gotten into the house and left that storybook in his brats' bedroom. I didn't know who could have snuck in so blatantly without anyone suspecting. The only people who'd stepped foot in the house were my nuclear family and our babysitter, so . . . oh.

I suddenly had an idea of why Nikki might have quit so suddenly.

"Honestly, Marshall. Don't be such a baby," I said loftily, bolstered by the realization that though they might have disappeared from view, I still had at least two allies out to help me. Or at least to infuriate a mate so artificial he might as well have been Kraft processed cheese on a soy burger. "You're worse than the twins."

"All I am saying is that a man goes to work in the morning and works hard to provide for his family, and in return he expects certain things when he comes home—dinner on the table, a smiling family, and a tidy house."

"Very nice, Mr. Cleaver. Besides, I was reorganizing," I claimed for the umpteenth time since he'd come home. That is, if by *reorganizing* I meant tearing the house apart from stem to stern, searching for that elusive object that bound me to Marshall. Okay, so maybe I'd dumped all the silver onto the table, happy that I hadn't had any part in picking out the hideous pattern, and torn through all the closets in an attempt to look for the mysterious stopper. And maybe I'd ripped all the clothes from our dresser, hoping to find something ominous and supernatural, like a crude linen bag filled with mysterious herbs and gypsy mojo. Or maybe a shrunken head. Unless Marshall Jones was working his voodoo using vacuum bags and napkin rings, however, I had been out of luck.

"Everything okay there, Mr. and Mrs. Jones?" One of our neighbors, a gray-haired fellow peering through the heavy frames of his glasses, waved from where he watered his rhododendrons. "Not having an argument, are you?"

"No, of course not, Mr. Makowski." Marshall laughed lightly, grabbed my hand, and started swinging it as if we were honeymooners. Although honestly, I didn't think that even honeymooners acted so goony.

"Wouldn't do to have the Riviera Lane lovebirds fighting, now," laughed the retiree.

"Russ, you old rascal!" Marshall laughed along with him, yanking me in the direction of the street's end. I tried to reclaim my pulverized fingers, but Marshall wasn't having it. In silence he stomped toward his mother's home, refusing to say one more word to me.

Honestly, at first I was fine with that. After all, reason kept whispering to me to keep my cool and not to let my temper flare. I didn't really have much of a clue of what Marshall might be capable, beyond taking innocent women and plugging them up in constructs. Constructs that looked an awful lot like what I'd consider a real-world hell, for that matter. That thought sobered me slightly. I couldn't just mouth off at the guy and not expect any consequences.

It might have been my imagination, but the house belonging to Agnes Jones seemed to have been built using blueprints scribbled with superlatives. It was the biggest, the darkest, the broadest, and the best-kept of all the tidy abodes up and down the lane, sporting boxwoods with the most sharply trimmed edges, banks of the prettiest pink miniature roses, and the greenest lawn never to have a leaf fall on it. Come to think, of all the houses up and down the street, it was also the most fake and definitely the most foreboding. I didn't think I could go in. "I have a headache," I announced, suddenly stopping in my tracks.

I was rewarded by a self-inflicted Indian burn around my wrist. Despite the friction, Marshall didn't let go. With surprising strength, he hoisted me toward him, making me lurch forward and nearly trip once again. "Woman . . . !" The low, almost feral intensity of his growl made me catch my breath; my rib cage suddenly felt like an echo chamber for the rapidly beating heart inside it. "*Don't test me.*"

We stood at the bottom of the steps leading up to the large front porch on which my mother-in-law never sat or, as far as I knew, stepped foot. Marshall's face was mere inches from mine, his eyes boring into my own. At that moment, I knew that despite the show of devotion he must have been forced to display during our mock marriage, this man thoroughly hated me. "Let go," I said. Though my jaw was set, I sounded tentative, even to my own ears. "I'm going home."

"Samantha." Marshall's voice was pure acid, dissolving any determination I might have built up over the last twenty-four hours. "The two of us are going to go into Mother's house. We are going to be sweet and agreeable, and have a wonderful dinner." I opened my mouth to protest, but found that I couldn't utter a single word of contradiction. Something strange was happening. With every suggestion that Marshall made, I felt the same cool, calming sensation I associated with sucking on a menthol lozenge when I had a bad cough, only through my brain instead of my chest. "You are going to behave," Marshall continued, leading my numb legs up the stairs. "And you are going to answer every question Mother asks. Do you understand?"

Automatically—too automatically, I realized with apprehension—I nodded. "Yes, Marshall dear," my lips said.

"Much better. Good girl," he murmured. I realized now that this was how he'd kept me so insensate to my situation all along. I'd been anesthetized. Hypnosis or modern pharmaceuticals or whatever the hell it was, he'd managed to wallop me with such massive doses of mental Novocain that I was numb to everything save the simple daily tasks he set me. And it was oh, so tempting to give in to the sweet, comfortable glow.

This time, though, I wouldn't. "Of course I am, darling," I said, the amiable tone of my voice coming too naturally. "I love your mother. I can't wait to see her."

Detecting no insincerity in my voice, he nodded and, with his hand at my back, turned the front doorknob and ushered me in. It was only after the door closed that I remembered how spiders injected anesthesia into their prey before binding and devouring them.

Not a comforting thought.

"Marshall! Samantha!" As always, Agnes Jones stood at the top of the winding staircase at the back of the entry hall, poised and waiting. Oh yeah, this dame was definitely the black widow of the spiderweb. She wore a trim and matronly dress of jet charmeuse trimmed with white and studded with glinting buttons. And with her dark gray hair pulled back into a severe bun, Mama Jones reeked sophisticated malice. She wanted something from me and wasn't even bothering to disguise it. She seemed to want to eat me right then and there, and it was all I could do to keep myself from making sure her house hadn't been built by gingerbread contractors and that I hadn't suddenly grown pigtails and left a trail of breadcrumbs behind me.

"Aren't you looking delicious, dear?" she said, making me more than a little worried that she might be able to read minds. I let my conscious self duck a few toes into the cool waters of oblivion still coursing through the front parts of my brain.

"She's been looking forward to dinner all week, Mother." Marshall approached the grand wooden staircase and held out his hand to guide his mother down the last few steps. I meekly followed them into the living room, with its antique furniture and the abundance of photographs and the portrait of Marshall's late father that hung over the mantel. Everything looked as carefully set as a stage, and just as artificial. "You know we enjoy our time with you. Don't we, Samantha?"

"Of course we do, Mother Jones," I intoned, settling down on the edge of a divan, knees together, ankles delicately crossed. "We're so grateful for everything you do for us."

"Such a dear." When Marshall's mother walked, there was none of the erratic, careful motion one might expect from a woman of a certain age. She glided smoothly and surely, swooping down into the armchair across from me, her fingers interlocked. She gave her son a sideways glance as she leaned in and, scary-woman-to-addled-daughter-in-law style, asked, "How are we feeling this week?"

"Quite well, thank you for asking," I said, smoothly. To my side, I noticed Marshall pressing his lips together and shaking his head slightly. "Hasn't the weather been pleasant?" Apparently, under pressure, I could make bland small talk with the best of them.

"Oh yes, certainly." As if trying to decipher whatever Marshall was trying to tell her, Agnes Jones turned to him while asking me, "Should we expect another visit from your lovely parents this year, Samantha?"

I opened my mouth to answer, but instead found myself stammering. "My parents?" Why wasn't the correct answer coming smoothly? "Maybe my mother . . . I don't have a father, I think . . ."

"Of course you do." Marshall sounded sure of it.

"I think my father left," I said doubtfully. "When I was young."

"Nonsense, darling," said my husband. He was using that voice again—I recognized it now. "They came to visit us last summer, remember? We had a barbecue on July Fourth. You enjoyed the sparklers, and then we watched the fireworks from the backyard afterward." As he spoke, filigrees of remembrance began to curl through my head. I could hear bratwursts sizzling on the grill and smell the scent of fresh-cut grass, and see my mother talking to Mrs. Jones at the picnic table on our patio while a chubby, white-haired man joked with an apron-wearing Marshall at the barbecue. But that white-haired man was not my father. I knew it.

Marshall's little Peri parlor trick of implanting false memories in my head was definitely the kind of thing that a girl definitely might find handy for convincing nice police officers she hadn't been speeding. "Oh, that was a wonderful time." I sighed happily, pretending to enjoy the recollection.

"Mother?" Marshall nodded in the direction of the closed double doors that separated the living and dining rooms.

"That's right, dear," said Mrs. Jones. "You get a drink while Samantha and I have a little talk. Just us girls." Her eyebrows rose in perfect, elegant arches while she pulled her mouth sideways into something approaching, but not quite a smile. "Sit back, dear. Relax." Her low alto seemed to soothe me, to make me want to obey and trust her.

The insurgent in me hated being manipulated. Was I even slightly in control of my actions? To make certain, I told myself to scratch the side of my nose with my index finger. My hand rose readily with no resistance. "It's so good to be here," I murmured, glad that my relief didn't reflect in my tone. It might have felt as if I was a marionette dangling from my mother-in-law's fingertips, but I could cut the strings if I wanted.

"Now, Samantha, I'm going to ask you some questions," she said leaning forward with her hands clasped. "And you'd like to answer them, wouldn't you?" It wasn't so much a question as a command. I nodded, still smiling.

"It's going to be useless." From the back of the room,

next to a small bar area, Marshall had poured himself a whiskey. He sprayed a small amount of seltzer into the amber liquid and swirled it around. "I don't know why you keep trying." Strange, but his accent seemed to have changed slightly.

"Marshall." The single word carried more warning in it than all the klaxons of a fire station. Then, just as suddenly, it was sugary-sweet once more. "Samantha. Dear. Tell me about your friend."

"You're my friend." That was my own response, I noticed. The real me, that is, since I intended it to be slightly sarcastic. Marshall snorted in the background.

"Of course I am, dear. Your good friend. I mean your other friend. Lily. Lily Oliver."

"Lily Oliver," I repeated. I'd heard that name before. My milkman had asked me about her. "I don't know . . ."

"Yes, you do, dear. Marshall heard you asking about her. Before you came here to be happy. Think hard."

I shook my head. I honestly didn't. And quite frankly, the rebellious part of me didn't want to. "I don't know anyone named Lily Oliver," I said, as though we'd been talking about the fine weather recently.

"She doesn't *know,* Mother." Marshall chugged his drink and let the glass fall onto the wooden table. "How long have we been at this now?" It was a question I was interested in myself, but I kept my eyes focused on the shuttered back windows and the chintz curtains surrounding them, pretending I couldn't hear. "Long enough to know that these weekly get-togethers aren't doing anything."

"Child," warned Mrs. Jones. She still studied me as she spoke to her son. "Use a coaster."

"I'm tired of this." I did notice that before Marshall strode back to the living room's center, he slipped a cork square beneath his discarded tumbler. "Tonight it ends. Let's pull up stakes. Leave the stupid bitch here with the drones. She'll never know the difference." I shivered slightly, not liking the sound of that.

"I decide when this game ends," Mrs. Jones said. For a moment I wanted to cheer her on, because I had the distinct impression if they left, the Borgias here weren't the type to give a girl the key out of her own prison. They both spoke with the same strange accent now. My brain had to work a little extra to convert the strange syllables into words I could easily comprehend. When Mother Jones's son laughed, she finally turned to face him. "What?"

"If you don't decide soon," Marshall told her, "Corydonais and his fine little clan will decide for you. Oh yes, Mother dearest," he added, seeming to enjoy Mrs. Jones's sudden stiff posture as she jolted to her feet. "Your spies didn't tell you he'd infiltrated your blind alley, did they? Well, he has, and it's a wonder that he and the rest of his ravens haven't swooped down to collect us. If they haven't gotten to *her* already." I could tell the thought had occurred to him for the very first time. The sudden suspicion caused them both to jerk their heads in my direction.

How I managed to stay placid and unmoving throughout their scrutiny is a wonder. My armpits prickled with heat, and I worried that my fair complexion might redden and give away the entire game. *Stay calm,* I warned myself, as the seconds dragged out to what seemed like weeks, months, eons. I could scarcely hear from the pounding of my heart and the heavy, sludgy motion of blood through my veins. I don't know how much time passed before my serene demeanor and charm-school posture convinced them I was unaware of the real topic at hand. "When did this happen?"

So terrible and queenly was the woman's voice that it flattened all of Marshall's arrogant cockiness. "I don't know," he said with a volume only a quarter of what it had been. His eyes refused to meet her challenging stare. "Yesterday. At least. I don't know. But neither do your drones." He sounded defensive.

Without another glance at me, Mrs. Jones stalked to the closed massive double doors that led into the dining room. "That changes things," she announced, flinging open the doors. She marched through, followed by Marshall. He turned and pulled them shut, while I remained motionless and in the same position I'd held since I'd settled onto the sofa.

That didn't last for long, though. How could it, with the adrenaline pumping through my system like fire? At least its raging heat eradicated every trace of the tranquil inertia the pair of them had willed upon me—because, believe me, there was no way I intended to sit obediently on that tacky sofa and wait for the two of them to brew up my doom. "Okee-dokee then, Samantha," I murmured. "What first?"

I crept across the Oriental rug to the double doors. Trying to listen in was a risky business, I knew, but you know what? No one else was there to stand up for me. I mean, I didn't see that Cordovan guy leaping out of a phone booth to come to my aid, damsel in distress I might have been.

This was real life. Okay, it wasn't my *real* real life, but it was the reality I'd been stuck in for a little while, and I was going to have to cope with it. "White knights only show up in fairy tales and Renaissance fairs," I growled to myself. I remembered hating those fairs in my previous life, I realized. The thought I might be reclaiming my own self, little by little, gave me hope.

With my back to the right-hand door, I put my hand on the knob and gave it a twist. At lightning speed my mind ran through all the things that could go wrong—it could have been locked, or squeaked, or been loose enough to let out a warning rattle—but thankfully, noth-

ing did. As if I'd willed it, the latch slid smoothly free,
and I was able to draw back the door without the hinge
creaking. The pair of them were still talking with the
same unusual articulation, somewhere far within. Far
enough, anyway, that I could lean forward and listen
without risk of being seen. ". . . bet he's not as tough as
they say," Marshall was saying. I heard a clink of something metallic being set on the dining room table. How
many endless, dull dinners had I endured at that table?
Too many to count, but from the sound of things they
were laying out the silver for another. "Why not just
show him what we're made of?"

"Never. To take a stand is premature at this point.
Hand me the cloth. This one has a spot on it." I'd heard
Mrs. Jones sound lovey-dovey many a time, and icy and
stern, but listening to her try to summon a bravado that
I knew was entirely false fell into the novelty category. I
mean, she'd obviously been given the worst news, and
there she was, worrying about water spots on the silver.
"That's better," she said with obvious satisfaction, setting
the utensil on the table.

"At least I won't have to pretend to be that one's mate
any longer," Marshall said, arousing my instant ire. How
many Meatloaf Mondays had I made possible for that
bastard? And hello, how bad a wife could I have been?
"She has the stench of humankind on her."

Oh, that was getting entirely *too* personal. "They all
have that stench," said his mother, adding another utensil to the place settings. Like she was fresh as a daisy?
Let's just say I'd hate to have been that old bat's gyne-
cologist. "One learns to ignore it." I had to resist a sudden temptation to sniff my armpit. "Are we nearly ready
for her?"

"Not quite." Marshall laid something down with a
clatter. "One more to go."

Exactly how many places were they setting out? Was

the rest of the neighborhood coming? Careful not to attract any notice by creating sudden shadows, I leaned around the crack in the doorway and gently tilted down my head, letting my eye scan the slender shaft of visible space. I saw first the grandfather clock that sat in the corner, and then the head of the old oak table, barren of any forks or spoons. I had to lean out a little more until I found them, standing side by side near the window.

Over a padded length of fabric they stood, huddled together like the conspirators they were. "This is my favorite," said Marshall, holding up a gleaming metallic object that glinted from the light of the chandelier bulbs.

"It has a lot of history," hissed his mother, regarding the object fondly. "It was your father's."

Once again I froze, barely able to breathe. The object in Marshall's hand wasn't an ice cream spoon. No, it was a massive sickle, its blade sinuous and lethally sharp, its metal seeming to have been formed and flattened by hand. "That's why I like it," Marshall said, running something in his left hand over its length—something like a handful of a dried flower or weed. He laid it onto the table next to all the other, smaller, similar implements the pair had been cleaning. There wasn't a single piece of Mother Jones's silver in sight.

A blue-white bead of coldness ran down my spine. Judging by that sickle, Marshall's late father must have moonlighted as the Grim Reaper. I backed away from the door, tiptoed into the hallway, and crept out the front door. I didn't care that it latched behind me. I didn't think I'd be going back voluntarily.

Chapter Five

I couldn't escape. Where was there to run? Ever since Cor had jolted me back to full consciousness, I hadn't ventured any farther than the tiny cluster of stores at the street's end. I was willing to lay the entire fifteen dollars and thirty-five cents in my little pink purse that this snow globe of a suburbia didn't extend beyond the cat food aisle at the back of Miller's Groceries. Riviera Lane was my little world, and every one of those apple-pie houses contained an enemy or two. True, not all the enemies had a weapon that could gut a hefty water buffalo with a single stroke, but I couldn't turn to any of them for help.

I had to find the stopper, I knew. And I had to find it quickly. If something were binding me here, something I could hold, it wasn't going to be lurking in the china cupboards of the neighbors. No, it was going to be at home. And that's why, when I burst through the front door and startled Mrs. McCuddy in the living room with her knitting, I didn't even pause before snatching the evening paper from the hall table. "You can go home," I told the neighbor. "Dinner was canceled."

"Why, Mrs. Jones!" Mrs. McCuddy was so startled that her ball of fluffy white wool bounced to the floor. "I've just settled your lambs down to sleep!"

"Go home, Mrs. McCuddy!" I yelled, throwing open the French doors to the patio. I'd managed to wad up sections of the paper into makeshift balls by then, which I tossed onto the ashes of the picture book Marshall had torched the night before. Haphazardly, I grabbed the metal tin of lighter fluid that still sat next to the clumsy stone barbecue, and squirted it over the newsprint. All it took was for a single red-headed matchstick to ignite everything with a massive *whoof* of heat and air.

"But dear! You seem distraught!"

Distraught, hell. I hadn't been so lucid in my entire life here. It was good that Marshall and his mother hadn't stuffed our house with anything beyond the bare basics of what a newly married couple might have accumulated in only a couple of years. I went straight to the wedding album that sat on the built-in bookshelves, dragged it out, and had wrenched from its pages the photographs within by the time I got back to the patio. Up in flames went the black-and-white shot of a nervous-looking me in my white gown against a hedge, clutching what looked like a bunch of lilies in my arms. Lilies—hah! They had a sense of humor, those two. Or at least a particularly sadistic streak. Onto the pyre I added the laughing snapshots from the rehearsal dinner, the grouped photos around the altar. The last portrait in the book was the eight-by-ten of Marshall and myself, exchanging adoring glances as we held hands, the lilies on prominent display. I tossed it onto the briskly burning flames. "That wasn't it," I muttered.

"Samantha Jones! What has gotten *into* you?" Mrs. Mc-

Cuddy had watched the ceremonial burning of my wedding album with a dropped jaw. I ignored her as I went to grab the baby albums from the shelf. She was just a . . . what did they call them? A drone. "Are you insane? Well, I . . . ! I'm going to get Henry. Henry! Henry!" she screeched, as if that deaf old fart could hear her from so far away. "Come see what Mrs. Jones is doing now!"

There was no time for niceties. I ripped the scrapbook pages from their spine in handfuls and tossed them onto the fire, indiscriminately squirting in more lighter fluid to keep everything ablaze. When I'd run out of scrapbooks and photos, I retrieved the correspondence Marshall and I were supposed to have written each other the summer he'd been in Germany, after college. I grabbed the forged letters from the lacquered box in my bedroom, burned them and the red ribbon with which they were tied, and tossed on the lacquered box as well. From the desk in the spare bedroom I set afire our official certificate of marriage and the results of our venereal disease tests (clean as a whistle, I'd been), as well as all the copies of our electrical bills, tax returns, canceled checks, and a copy of *Playboy* that lurked in the back of a drawer. I threw on some stuffed toys from the boys' bedroom, my copy of Dr. Spock, and a paperback edition of *The Da Vinci Code* in which apparently I'd never gotten past page twenty, and the only copy of the *TV Guide* we had.

In short, if it could burn, I tossed it on the fire. I built a fire so high that it seemed to warm the black night sky above, alarming the birds so that they circled above, cawing loudly. Their black undersides glowed orange with the flames. Still nothing happened.

I was halfway through cutting my old wedding dress into sections with the garden shears, tossing them onto the inferno, and enjoying the sight of the blaze consuming the gauzy material (what, was I really going to wear it again?) when Marshall appeared. The McCuddys were behind him, each with one of the boys in their arms. They all stared at me, aghast. I gave Marshall a challenging look and tossed another chunk of silk and taffeta onto the fire. He stared at me, utterly dumbfounded.

"Honey, I'm home!" I suggested.

"Samantha," he said, obviously trying to suppress every emotion.

"Samantha," I mocked, not caring any longer. I'd been caught. I knew I would. I made a show of looking around. "Where's your muscle, Marshall? Back at her house with a Bloody Mary and a Geritol chaser?"

"Samantha, something's upset you, that's obvious." Oh, so he was taking that route, was he? Fine, let him try his funky mind meld until his little sickle-clutching fingers fell off. I crossed my arms and let him have a go, just for old times' sake. "You're not upset. You had a delicious dinner at Mother's."

"You're a very lucky young woman, Samantha Jones!" said Mrs. McCuddy, on the same loop as always.

"Mrs. McCuddy, if you could get the boys away from this," Marshall said, before turning back to me. "We're the perfect couple, Samantha," he reminded me. "We're in love."

"Oh, Marshall," I said, in the voice of a simp. "I do love you, darling."

"You do?" he said, almost leering at how easy it had been.

"Yes, I do. Do you love me?"

"Yes, darling. Of course!"

"Even despite my human *stench?*" I said in my real voice. "Gotcha!" Savagely I ripped through the skirt of my wedding dress and tossed the last two sections on the fire. Nothing. "Let's cut the crap, Marshall," I said, feeling reckless and backed against a wall. "I know you're not my husband. I know this isn't my life. Where's the stopper? For the snow globe?"

While the McCuddys looked at each other in astonishment, Marshall tightened his jaw and motioned for them to step back. "Snow globe?" he asked.

"Yes!" In exasperation I pushed him aside, stepped into the living room, and from the armchair retrieved the little object I'd tossed in the "to burn" pile a little while ago. "Snow globe. A globe. With snow. Snow globe." I took the little reproduction of Niagara Falls and viciously agitated the sphere in a similar manner to how I wanted to wring their necks. "I know this place is a snow globe and there's a stopper that will let out all the water. And me." Inspired, I turned and threw the glass ball at the barbecue. Mrs. McCuddy shrieked. It exploded against the hot stones with a crash and a sizzle of water against the fire that instantly turned to steam and smoke. Still nothing.

"Fine." Marshall's voice had changed. No longer was it careful and devoted and guarded. I was now hearing the actual man behind the mask, and he sounded both sullen and angry. "Set the house on fire for all I care. I won't be living here after tonight."

"Fine!" I yelled. "After seeing your Boy Scout knife collection, I was making you sleep on the couch, anyway!"

"Hah-hah-hah." His lips curved into a sneer. "Joke all you want, but once I'm gone, that's it, Samantha." He tried to step closer, but at that moment the fire roared up higher than the barbecue's chimney, setting the birds squawking from the electrical line they'd chosen for their safety. He backed away from the noise and heat, one hand reflexively in front of his face. "Your 'stopper' won't work then. You'll be stuck here. Stuck in this tiny little box all by yourself until you go mad."

"I'm already *mad*," I yelled at his back. He was leav-

ing. This was it. Oooo, but I wanted to bean him good.
I followed him into the house. "I'm already stark raving
bonkers, thanks to you, you stupid . . ." From the mantel I grabbed one of the china figurines and let loose. It
shattered against the television cabinet, leaving a
crack across the screen. He kept walking toward the
front door.

"Samantha Jones!" Mrs. McCuddy sounded cross.
"How could you be such a wicked, wicked girl? What
has gotten into you?"

"Oh, shut up," I growled, chasing after Marshall.

"Hasn't your husband given you everything? A lovely
home, fine, sweet children, a handsome car, a beautiful
ring, everything that most girls would sell their souls to
have? And here you are, simply wrecking . . ."

"What," I asked slowly, "did you say?" Marshall had
frozen as well, his hand suspended in midair, barely
touching the front doorknob. The stupid drone had
given me the clue I'd needed, bless her. Now it was my
turn to smile. "Well, well, well," I said, suddenly feeling
sure of myself.

"Samantha." Marshall was using his Svengali voice
again, but I wasn't falling for it. I shook my head and
backed toward the patio. "Don't," he warned.

"Oh, I'm gonna," I told him, stepping over the thresh-
old. My right hand tugged at my left ring finger, which
was slightly swollen from the heat. I yanked off the diamond ring that bound me to my ersatz husband, and
shaking my head at him, tossed it into the center of the
flames.

Nothing happened, and for a second I was certain
my confidence had been ungrounded. When I looked
up, though, I saw the absolute loathing in my former
husband's eyes, and knew, with a stab of savage satisfaction, that I'd done the right thing.

And then everything happened.

* * *

Sometimes in the seconds after I've fallen asleep, I have the sensation that I'm falling. In the split second I'm dreaming, I'll trip on a stair or trod somewhere I shouldn't, and find myself plummeting into the softness of my mattress, startling myself awake. What followed after I destroyed my ring was like that, but infinitely longer. Grays and blacks rushed around me, and during the long seconds that followed I kept wondering when I'd jerk to consciousness and find myself sleepily clutching my pillow.

That wakening never came.

I did sense a scurry of motion around me, though— tiny breezes that seemed to come from dozens upon dozens of fluttering objects. The flapping and fluttering of their wings seemed to slow the velocity of my travel, though I couldn't even have told anyone in what direction I was moving, or how fast. There came a moment, however, when everything around me went very quiet. The stillness receded, replaced by sounds I recognized. Honking horns. People talking in close proximity. Laughter. Normal life.

"Jeez, lady!" I stumbled backwards when someone knocked into me. "Don't drink so much."

I opened my eyes to see two youths glaring at me as they walked by in the direction of a metal structure pointing to the night sky. Hundreds of other people milled to and fro, avoiding where I tottered in the middle of the sidewalk. I recognized those familiar arches— the Eiffel Tower. An elaborate, golden hot-air balloon had landed beside it. I was in the City of Lights, Paris. Only . . . wait. The lights in Paris weren't primarily neon, were they? Nor did they advertise Céline Dion.

It was Paris, the theme resort hotel. I was in Las Vegas. I *lived* in Las Vegas, I realized happily.

"Lily?" I heard behind me.

I turned. Cor the milkman stood there, his height and lankiness accentuated by the black slacks and a black sweater he wore instead of a uniform. His shoulder-length hair hung in a decidedly modern fashion behind his ears. Peri he might have been, but he looked like the leader of some indie-rock ensemble. "Samantha," I told him, shaking my head. "Sam. Dorringer," I added. My real surname sounded strange on my tongue. "Not Oliver. Definitely not Jones."

"That's nice, but . . ." Cor grabbed me by the ragged jean jacket I seemed to be wearing and turned me around.

The crowd of partying tourists had parted some distance ahead, shrieking and drawing away from a pair of four-legged animals that seemed to be surveying the scene. "Pigs?" I said wonderingly, looking at the line of rough, short bristles running from their heads down their spines, and the sharp, glistening tusks that curved from their mouths. The identical animals were larger than they should have been, somehow, and infinitely more menacing.

"Boars," Cor corrected. While one of them sniffed the air, searching for something, the other tossed its head, obviously impatient. "And not just any boars. Hunting boars." When I looked to him for explanation, he said, "Those, my dear, are your precious twins."

At that moment, the animals spotted us. "That doesn't sound good," I said.

"It's not."

We hesitated only a second as the vicious porkers began charging across the pavement. Tourists scattered in their wake, attempting to avoid the animals' razor-edged tusks. "I'm going to suggest we get the hell out of here," I said, turning and grabbing the milkman by his arm.

"Concurred," he yelled as we both began to run.

Chapter Six

"In Las Vegas," I yelled out over the sound of seven drivers punching seven fists into seven horns all at once, "if there's an accident involving a car and a pedestrian, it's the pedestrian who's liable, even if he's the casualty. Hold *on* there, cowboy!" I banged the heel of my hand down hard on the hood of a taxi that tried to nudge me, and instantly regretted it. Against the traffic light, Milkman-boy had managed to make it to the island in the middle of the road; my left foot was still smarting from having to vault over the barricade that kept tourists from wandering out into the intersection of the Strip and Flamingo Road, so I wasn't as lucky. "Sheesh!" I yelled, once I was clear and standing on the thin strip of concrete. "Why couldn't we take the overpass?"

"This is faster. And if there's an accident between a pedestrian and a ravening hell boar, who's liable then?" he asked. Without warning, Cor grabbed my hand and began pulling me out into the southbound traffic. Bad idea, because a Volkswagen nearly ran the both of us down.

"Hey, assholes!" Another of Sin City's squadrons of taxis slowed down once we'd leapt back to safety. Its driver, a rotund dark-haired fellow, leaned out the window. His bushy black mustache had obviously been styled from the *Gene Shalit Handbook of How to Get Away with Never Trimming Your Facial Hair*; it quivered with outrage. "There's a crosswalk!" he bawled, hanging on to the steering wheel while he leaned out the window. "You people are supposed to use the freakin' crosswalk! That's what it's there for! Freakin' drunks!"

"I'm so sorry." Cor bent over and addressed the man politely, which was more than he deserved.

"Sorry! What's the matter with you, you little fairy!"

"Peri," Cor replied in the mildest of manners, though I could tell he was bristling.

"Hey, Super Mario!" I said sharply, resenting the driver's slur. "Get your behind back to Luigi and the Mushroom Kingdom already. Yeah, you heard me!" I called out to his retreating license plate when he sped far away from the crazy woman.

"Is this what you're really like, Sam Dorringer?" asked Cor.

I couldn't tell whether he was surprised, or disappointed, or what. "When I'm being chased by—wait," I told him, seeing a break coming in the stream of traffic. At the right moment, I grabbed his arm and stepped off the curb, dashing with him toward the barricade on the Strip's west side. His large, strong hands encircled my waist as he helped boost me up, before he began climbing over the waist-high metal. "When I'm being chased by crazed animals, yes! Those were Timothy and Patrick?" Already the unreality of that construct I'd been trapped in was beginning to recede. The fact that we were going to meet our deaths either by crazy Vegas taxi drivers or by menacing pigs was a little galling, true, but at least I knew this fear and the running and heat and sweat and adrenaline were *real*.

Cor was tall enough that he hadn't had much of a problem sliding back down to the sidewalk; he helped me get my leg over and hoisted me down with ease. "I know it has to seem outlandish to you, but in Peri constructs, real-world creatures assume forms different from their normal . . ."

"Oh, I'm not questioning the plausibility of it," I said absently, looking around for an escape route. In front of the Bellagio, the dancing fountains swayed back and forth to one of those bombastic pop tunes sung by an Italian tenor. Families and excited groups of Japanese sightseers clustered around to observe with their video cameras. They didn't attract my notice as much as the couples who watched with their arms around each other's shoulders, the women's heads sometimes leaning against the men's shoulders. I bet none of *them* ever got kidnapped and forced to starch their husband's collars. "There's very little I wouldn't put beyond you Peris at this point, trust me. What gets me is the fact that Marshall and Mommie Dearest thought it would be hil-*ar*-ious to give me Desperate Housewife pigs as children."

"They're not pigs. They're Boars of the Hunt."

"Yeah, well, you can give me the Peri-tastic history later," I said, taking a few tentative steps in the direction of the Jockey Club, further south. "We need to get as far away from those rabid . . ."

As if on cue, from behind me I heard the sounds of screams and chaos, accompanied by a metallic noise that sounded like the entire cast of *Stomp* falling down a flight of stairs. Cor and I both wheeled around in our tracks to see that in the caged walkway over the streets, people were fleeing down the stairs. Two shadowy shapes barreled through the enclosure, one of them swinging its head from side to side so brutally that it caused the whole structure to shake and shudder. An entire section of the metal now dented outward, from the inside. I glared at Cor. "*They* took the overpass."

I didn't have to be Nancy Drew to get the clue that we needed to get our butts on the run again; the bacony versions of Timothy and Patrick were having a little difficulty navigating the stairway down from the overpass, which would buy us a little bit of time, but not very much.

"Come on," I called out, grabbing at him and running back toward the Strip again.

"I thought you were afraid of putting the speeding cars in danger with your hundred and thirty pounds of soft self," he remarked, though he didn't hesitate in hoisting me back over the barricade for a third time.

"Hundred and twenty-five, thank you," I said, though, thanks to the situation, it wasn't with the greatest of confidence. And of course, there was the fact I'd been packing on the meatloaf.

I doubted the management of the Bellagio was going to be happy with the way the boars were disrupting their fountain show; from what I could see over the barricade, the creatures were circling around the crowds, herding them into small clumps. Their dangerous snouts sniffed the air, trying to find us but not succeeding. I couldn't even begin to count the number of people who were trying to flee the scene, but the only spectators who weren't running away to safety were a few oddballs who seemed to think it was part of the show. After all, when you can walk up and down the Strip and see a pirate spectacle, gondoliers, roller coasters, and a volcano, what's a crazed porker or two?

One of the twins—honestly, I was beyond telling which was which at this point—lowered its head and dashed toward a bristly browed man trying to capture everything on his camcorder. I winced when, a moment later, I saw the poor guy fly through the air over the fence and landscaping, only to land in the Bellagio lake with a splash. At the same time, the other of my darling former sons battered his head into the barricade when he discovered it was too tall for him to climb over.

"Do Boars of the Hunt have concrete skulls?" I asked as we dashed to the east curb where we'd begun.

"I need to get high," was all Cor said.

Despite the fact I was straddling the rail like a pony, I stopped my climb over the barricade. "Are you serious?" I asked. "That's all you can think about right now?"

He didn't seem to understand. Then again, he hadn't had the succession of loser boyfriends I'd historically attracted, including the stoner who'd been arrested for possession in the Marina Pacific Best Western's banquet hall men's room on senior prom night. "Someplace far off the ground," he explained to me in a loud and deliberate voice, as if I were dim-witted or foreign.

"How about the Eiffel Tower?" I pointed to the highest spot around. Down the street, a light blinked slowly atop the casino's landmark. Another loud barrage of the steel separating street and sidewalk brought any further conversation to a halt. From what I'd seen, the typical male Peri didn't run any faster than I did. Against those bloodthirsty monsters, we needed every advantage we had. Together we helped each other off the barricade for what I hoped was the last time, and began booking our way once more past Bally's in the direction of the mega-resort directly south. "What are Boars of the Hunt trained to track down, anyway?" I wheezed out, trying to ignore the squashed-lung feeling in my chest.

"The worst of escaped prisoners," said Cor from beside me. "Oh, and lesser demons on the Blighted Plains of Nefarion."

Oh. Well, I *had* asked, I guess.

Over the sounds of squealing tires we heard the sounds of two cars colliding, followed quickly by the impact of another, and then another. I didn't know what was loudest—the shattering glass, the yelling, or the outraged oinking. I only hoped no one was getting hurt. Including us. "Do you have currency?" Cor asked, seeming as unwilling as I to look back over our shoulders at the carnage behind us. "Money," he added.

"I know what money is," I whuffed out.

"Do you have any?"

"I don't know!" I didn't have a purse on me, that much I knew. I appeared to be wearing a long-sleeved baseball shirt I dimly remembered buying at Eddie Bauer, and a pair of khaki-green cargo pants. Knowing me, I probably had something stuffed into one of my pockets.

"Don't you humans usually ask cash of each other to visit these places?"

There hadn't been any judgment in his voice, but merely being reminded that we were different made me put my guard up a little. "Oh, it's totally free to get into all the fabulous attractions on the Blighted Plains of Nefarion, is it?" I snapped. Running was difficult when I was busy leaning over to examine the contents of my pockets. Apparently when I'd been kidnapped by the Kin, all I'd had on me was a fossilized pack of Trident, a scratched-off losing lottery ticket, and a twenty-dollar bill.

I brandished the latter in front of Cor's face as we plowed through the ambling crowds. Poor people. They didn't know I was bringing mayhem in my wake. "Is that enough?" he asked.

"I don't see you adding to the Samantha Dorringer Defense Fund," I pointed out.

"I'm just trying to save us . . ."

"You save you, and I'll save me." For a split second I jerked to a stop, and then thought the better of it. I could still hear the tourists yelling not so far behind us. My knees regretted being summoned into activity once more. "I don't need a knight in shining armor." He didn't say anything. "I did a fine job of getting out of that Peri construct all by myself, you know. *After* you walked away," I pointed out.

"I didn't walk away."

I wasn't going to have this argument right now. He had left me, and at the time I'd resented him for it. Once again, I'd managed to pull myself out of a sticky situation when no one else had given a damn, thank you very much. "Okay, whatever." I was out of breath and tired of the bickering. Thank goodness we had just reached the closest of the Eiffel Tower's legs. "It's still twenty more dollars than you have. Oooh, wait." I'd remembered my back pockets. My fingers went exploring and came up with a plastic card. "Visa!" I exulted.

He'd sprinted the last few dozen yards to the elevator entrance, where a bored-looking youth in a black vest, fussy white shirt, and a jaunty beret guarded the empty line. "Les tickets, please," I heard the kid say to Cor, holding out a pale hand.

"I don't have any tickets," Cor explained as I caught up. I rested my hands on my knees and panted heavily. "We need to . . ."

It had obviously been a long day for the boy in the beret, who was probably a UNLV student working his way through school. Barely looking at us, he droned, "Vous can't go into Le Eiffel Tower without les tickets."

I pointed at Pigageddon behind me. "We really have to . . ."

"Vous can't go into Le Eiffel Tower without . . ."

"Credit card," I huffed out, shoving the Visa into his grasp. "I have a credit card."

"Les tickets to Le Eiffel Tower are sold in Le Gift Shop in Le Lobby," the little snot informed us. He took a look at my Visa. "And your credit card expired two years ago, ma'am."

"Miss, *s'il vous plait!*" I corrected. There would be no ma'am-ing while I was still under the age of thirty. "And that's ridiculous," I said, looking at the four-digit date on the front. "I just used this card . . ." Well, on the day I'd been abducted. I'd used it at Starbucks, if I remembered rightly. "Recently."

He handed it back with a shrug. "I hope you don't end up in Le Jail for it. *Ma'am.*"

"Listen, you little punk," I growled.

Cor held me off with one of his broad hands. "We really need to get off the street," he said, managing to sound more sane than I ever could. With a gentle ding, the lift's doors opened. "The elevator's here. No one's using it. Couldn't we take it to the top?"

"S'yeah, right," snorted the kid. "Les tickets to Le Eiffel Tower are sold in . . . *holy merde!*"

We'd been so intent on trying to make our way past the sentinel that we hadn't noticed the bedlam that had caught up with us. Not three dozen feet away stood the twin boars. Foam dripped from their mouths onto the still-hot pavement, puddling in sudsy pools. Those unblinking, intent eyes were the same as when they had been toddlers, only now they were charged with rage and the need for revenge. "Cor?" I asked, my voice sounding more trembly than I intended.

He whirled; the elevator doors were shutting. We both lunged and, with all our might, wrenched them apart. "No! No!" squealed Beret Boy, jabbing at the door-close button with both of his hands. "Don't let those things in!"

Neither of us said anything as we waited for what seemed like an eternity for the doors slowly to seal.

Through the diminishing crack, we watched as the boars charged. There was a terrible thud when they struck the elevator door right as it shut. Our companion squeaked and clutched his hat for comfort.

And then we were off and up. I admit to heaving a massive sigh of relief before asking in a terribly small voice, "They can't push buttons, can they?"

"I think we'll be all right," Cor said. His hand was on my shoulder, I noticed. I let it stay there, not really minding it so much for the moment.

Neither of us really knew what to say to Le Ticket Taker. By the time we'd ascended 460 feet into the air over the darkening Las Vegas skyline, he'd curled up into a ball on the elevator floor and was busy working his way through his third Hail Mary. Somehow we both seemed to think it was best to leave him there, once the doors slid open again. Cor flipped the button that halted the elevator as we left.

"Now what?" I asked as we walked out onto the platform, where only a few visitors stood. Most of them were busy craning their necks in the southwesterly direction, where police cars were just beginning to arrive at the scenes of the multiple accidents in the Strip, and where screaming crowds were running in every direction away from the Eiffel Tower. From our vantage point it looked as if they were all specks of dirt that some vast, invisible entity was blowing away. "We don't stay here all night, do we?"

"Le Eiffel Tower Experience closes at 12:30 A.M. daily," whimpered the ticket taker from inside the car, before he let out a sob.

"You need to stay here," Cor said. He looked into my eyes to make sure I understood. "Do you hear me?"

"I'm not deaf." Nor was I stupid, nor had I done anything wrong to deserve such a paternal tone. "Why, where are you going?"

He pointed a finger upward. Everyone else was so busy peering down that it had never occurred to me to look above us. Despite the light pollution streaming from every building in the Las Vegas skyline, from this high it was possible to see bright clusters of stars in the velvet blue sky. Birds circled the tower in long, lazy swoops. One of them let out a raucous caw.

"Up?" I pointed as well, so that we both looked as if we were testing the wind direction.

"Just wait for me," he said. He wore an expression I'd never seen on him before; it was the smile of a man happy to be doing what he did best, and I couldn't account for it at all.

"All right," I said, simply.

And then he was off. At first I confused the rush of light and fog and black feathers around me for the birds that had been wheeling around the tower in increasing numbers. It was only when I saw Cor leap into the air, transformed, that I realized the feathers were part of him. Through a transmutation I'd witnessed but hadn't comprehended, he'd become one of the birds. Aloft, his wingspan was broad, his flight swift and strong.

The world lit up for a half-second with a brilliant flash of lightning; thunder quickly followed. The black birds that had been flying randomly around the tower were now soaring in formation, up, up into the heavens. Then, in a massive circle they dove back down again until they zoomed by with a rush of air. In their wake came rain—a deluge of pelting, cold rain that fell from the heavens in angry torrents, filling the world with noise and confusion. The people sharing the tower observation deck with me ran for the safety of the elevator car, but I stood there in the storm, watching through the flashes of lightning for signs of Corydonais.

It was too dark and rainy to see him, of course. What I could see, however, was how quickly the streets cleared in every direction as pedestrians sought the shelter of the nearby casinos. The hubbub from below vanished. I don't know how long I stood there in that gale with my hands resting on the railing. My clothes were soaked, and runnels of water dripped down my hair and neck and face, but I didn't care.

When at last the inundation subsided, leaving nothing but a few droplets and the sound of flash-flood waters rushing through the streets, he appeared beside me again in a flutter of feathers and soft noise. "You're wet," he announced. He was wetter than I; his long hair hung limply in strands, and he appeared to have lost his shoes. No, there they were, on the grating; apparently he'd kicked them off earlier and left them to soak. "We sent your boys home," he added, when I didn't say anything. "Hope you don't mind."

I didn't know what to say. I was too busy trying to piece things together. "You really are one of those things. The clan of the cave bear things. I thought it was just a title. Or a club," I babbled. "Like the Elks. Only they don't turn into real elks."

"The Order of the Storm Raven." He nodded. "Are you okay with that?"

"Hey," I said, shrugging. "You do what you gotta do."

"You have a home?" he asked. I nodded. "Maybe we could dry off in it?"

We walked to the still-open elevator, where the inhabitants within were listening to the ticket taker tell some incredible story about a dozen killer pigs from Borneo trying to kill him. "So you *do* have wings, huh, fa . . . ?"

"Don't say it," he begged.

I smirked. "Fairy boy?"

He winced. "Yes. I do have wings." Then, viciously, he added, "*Ma'am.*"

Chapter Seven

"This is where you live?" Cor stood with his hands on his hips as he surveyed the site. I can't say I blamed him for the dubiousness. After all, we were staring directly at a rack of orange plastic shopping carts near the edge of a vast asphalt parking lot, where an hourly laborer-for-hire had fallen asleep with his back against the poles.

"This is it," I said, trying to figure out where I'd gone wrong. "I mean, no, this isn't it. I don't live in Home Depot. But this is where my apartment is. Should be."

"Are you sure you're not tired?"

I looked around, blinking. I'd had a very long day, it was true, and the time had to be close to midnight. Some things shouldn't change overnight, though, and a giant hardware superstore appearing on the block where you used to live qualified. "No, I mean, there's the 7-Eleven where I grab my coffee in the morning, and the dry cleaner's where I get my court clothes done when I have to testify, and there's the garage where I got my car fixed when it broke down . . ."

Not until my voice had trailed off did Cor speak. "Court?" he asked. "Are you wanted?"

"Hah!" I snorted. "Not on any level. No, I'm an insurance investigator." Why was I standing there staring at the Home Depot as if I expected it suddenly to disappear and reveal my old adobe-style, un-air-conditioned apartment building? "Cor, exactly how long was I in that construct?"

Was it my imagination, or did he look decidedly uncomfortable? "The subjective experience of time is different inside a Peri construct, as it exists outside both the worlds of the humans and the Kin," he began.

Oh, no. An academic approach. That didn't bode well. I tilted my head. "I'm a big girl. I can take it." Actually, I wasn't sure I could, but it appeared as if I was going to have to.

"How long did it feel like you were in there?" I considered his question for a moment, but with all the false memories I'd experienced inside that poor man's recreation of *Bewitched,* it was really tough for me to guess. "From what we can guess, you were in that construct for perhaps seven of its days before we found it."

"And you spoke to me first, what, a week ago? And it took me several days to hear you?" He nodded. "So that's two weeks." I turned back to the massive Home Depot, which had obviously been there a while. "Two weeks."

"Again, your subjective two weeks . . ."

I turned away from the parking lot and confronted him. "Do fairies not have any balls?" I snapped, unhappy with him and with the world in general. "How hard is it to come right out and just say what you have to say?" I let out a frustrated growl and began stomping over to the corner, where I stabbed at the pedestrian crosswalk button I'd pushed so many other mornings before.

He followed, sounding not too happy with me. "A lot of my kind find that word pretty derogatory, you know."

I didn't look at him. "Balls?"

"*Fairy*," he told me. "It gives the wrong image. You say *fairy* and people think of miniature winged creatures at the bottom of the garden. You picture those girls from Cottingley in their post-Victorian finery, surrounded by flapping little . . . insect people. It's demeaning." The light turned green and I set out over the crosswalk on the still-wet streets. "Humans have given us so many names over the centuries. How hard is it to use one of the others? And for the record, anatomically, there's very little difference between the males of your species and mine." When I didn't reply, he asked, "Are you angry about something?"

"Yes!" I exclaimed from the far curb, turning around. "I asked for an answer, and you pussyfooted around it."

"Samantha. All of this has to be disorienting for you," he said, dragging his fingers through his long hair. I realized he must have been as frustrated with me as I was with him. "My only motive was to keep you from being overwhelmed . . ." He stopped at the sight of my eyebrows, both so high that they might have been hoisted by zeppelins. "Well, it was."

"So basically," I summarized, using the crisp diction I'd occasionally summoned in the past for my court appearances, "you've forgotten the fact that so far I've coped quite well with discovering I'd been abducted from my own world and tucked away playing mommy in Barbie's Malibu Scream House. And considering everything, I *thought* I'd done fairly well at not turning into a gibbering idiot while I was being chased by killer pigs."

I turned and marched in the direction of the 7-Eleven, my goal, while I continued talking. "And lastly, I managed to stay *just* on this side of sanity when I watched you turn into a bird and chase after said pigs with what I can only assume are your Peri cronies. Oh, accompanied by a storm right out of the Frankenstein movies."

Inside the bright oasis of the 7-Eleven, cold air washed over me as I pushed my way through the doors. I ignored the siren call of the snack foods and marched over to the magazine rack, where on the top shelf dozens of nudie rags lurked behind cardboard dividers. "But I can take it," I continued, leaning over and picking up a copy of the *Sun*. "I can cope with the fact that it's—" My eyes scanned the date on the front page, while my head did some quick math. "Three years and two months later than I thought it was." I tossed the paper down. "See? Fine. Because at this point, I don't have a choice. No taksie-backsies." I crossed my arms and stared at him.

"Are you all right?" he asked.

"Of course," I said, bluntly. "I have to be." Then reality hit me, square between the eyes. The sensations came like a sharp pain—starting like brain freeze from one of the Slurpee machines grinding away at the back of the store, and then multiplying in intensity. I clutched the skin right above the bridge of my nose and exclaimed, "Oooooooh, crap!" as I tried to cope. I felt as if I'd just whacked my head on a low basement ceiling trying to come up the stairs, and all I could think of wanting was to clutch my head and be alone with my pain for a little while. "Oooohhhh, God!" I moaned, both arms wrapped around my skull, now.

The clerk behind the register stared at me over the tops of his spectacles. He was a tiny little scrap of a fellow who looked like a more grizzled and whiter version of Sammy Davis Jr. "Is she okay?" he called out.

I couldn't help it. I had to crouch down and curl myself up into a squatting fetal position. "She will be," Cor called out.

"Is she a junkie? I don't want no junkies in here." The clerk jabbed his finger at me. "If she's a junkie, get her out."

"I wish I were a junkie," I wailed. "Then it wouldn't feel so awful."

"That's it!" With surprisingly swift steps, the clerk came at us with a broom. He made sweeping motions in our direction. "Get out, you junkies!" The threat of being O-Cedared to within an inch of my life was laughable, but I realized how I must have seemed to the poor old guy. Obediently I rose to my feet, still shaking, and let Cor guide me to the door. "And don't come back. Junkies!"

When we were back out in the hot, muggy parking lot, I tried to smile in apology to the clerk who guarded the door, but he only replied by shaking his broom angrily. "I'm sorry," I told Cor. I felt miserable and guilty, and the realization that I hadn't done anything wrong didn't help. Three years! When I felt his arms around me, I didn't object. A good hug was exactly what I needed. I rested my head on his chest and relaxed there. I felt miserable and guilty, but I had to shake it off. I was shaking it off. There. It was shook, or as shaken as it was going to get. What choice did I have, right?

It was funny, how a Peri's arms felt very much like those of the guys who'd held me, over the years . . . shortly before they'd all moved on to the next chick who batted her pretty little lashes at them. He smelled like a man, too. A slightly sweaty man whose clothes still bore the moldy scent of dried rainwater. I moved my ear to his left pectoral, and then his right, concentrating intently. "Sam," he rumbled in his baritone, startling me with the sudden noise. "You're not trying to listen if I have two hearts, are you?"

"No!" I exclaimed, separating myself from him. "Where did you get that idea?" Strange, but I got the impression he didn't quite believe me. And how had he figured out that had been exactly what I was doing? "Let's see if we can find a hotel. I'm exhausted." We'd begun walking back to the street when I realized something. "Oh, no!"

"What?" he asked, probably afraid I was going to have another panic attack.

This was the worst cut of all. "I just realized I'm *thirty-two,* now." I'd lost three of the best years of my life! "That stinks!"

He cleared his throat. "Well, technically . . . you've only aged the two weeks you were in the construct."

"So I'm still twenty-nine?" I don't know why that little detail meant so much to me, but I was grateful to have something—anything—left that was really mine. "All right," I sighed. "I feel better, then."

We walked on in silence for a while. "I'm four hundred and thirty-two," he remarked after a while. It sounded as if he was trying to console me, and I felt a wave of affection toward him for it.

I grinned. "Trust me. You have no idea how young that makes me feel."

The Palm Frond Motel (or, as its neon-impaired sign stated, the PA F OND EL), which I remembered as being a haven for transients a mere two blocks from where I once lived, had three things going for it. First, it had a vacancy. Secondly, the manager didn't seem to care that we were dirty and without luggage. And third, said manager didn't look too closely at the expiration date on my credit card before running it through their mechanical carbon-copy machine.

However, upon opening the door to room 207 and listening for the telltale sound of vermin scurrying away from the sudden light, I could tell we had a problem. "There's only one bed," I pointed out. Cor stepped into the room and turned on the wheezing window air-conditioner. He looked at the dark faux-wood paneling and the rickety chairs, the tiny television bolted to the desk, and then inspected the ubiquitous instructions on how to operate the porn channels. "And there are two of us," I added, when he gave the mattress an experimental prod.

"What? Oh!" His furrowed expression cleared so that once more I could see the thin scar that bisected his eyebrow. "Puritanism?"

"No!" I objected immediately. "I'm not a . . . don't be silly." I didn't push the point, especially with someone who might have actually known a real Puritan. I let the door swing shut behind us, and locked it.

"You slept in the same bed with a stranger every night for the last two weeks," Cor pointed out. He eased himself onto the mattress, back stiff, and regarded the bedcover dubiously. Yes, but that had been entirely different, I wanted to say. "I don't have to stay in the room with you," he said. "I'd prefer to, though, simply so I can make sure your ex-husband and his dame don't send their boars to sniff you out again. For my peace of mind, it would be," he interrupted, before I could protest. "I know you're perfectly capable of looking after yourself. You've said so a hundred times." He sighed at my lack of response. "I will sleep on the floor."

Was I really that abrasive about the issue? I squelched the objections of independence that had been brewing. Besides, the fact that he was being chivalrous kind of touched me, loath as I was to admit it, even to myself. "Lord above, you're not sleeping on the floor," I said, shuddering to think of what kinds of filth and contagion the linoleum harbored. "We'll share the bed. And I won't make you build walls of Jericho with the pillows. Oh, that's from *It Happened One Night*. It's a movie," I explained.

From his steady regard, I could tell he thought I was

babbling. "First dibs on the shower," I said, trying to lighten the uncomfortable mood. Really, all I wanted to do at that point was climb into a moderately clean bed, pull the covers over my head, and let the sleepy-time brownies do their work. No. I banished that idea. With my luck, tonight would be when I discovered that there actually were sleepy-time brownies, only I'd mistake them for oversized roaches and squash a few with my flats before discovering they were Cor's best buddies.

At least I felt better after the shower. In addition to the complimentary shampoo/conditioner and a quarter-sized bar of sandpapery soap, the Pa Fond El management had also thoughtfully provided a miniature bottle of mouthwash. I was guessing the courtesy had been intended for businessmen returning to work after their two-martini-and-a-hooker lunches, but who was I to question an opportunity for fresh breath? I took a swig, spat, and looked at myself in the mirror. Now that I was free of the burden of my Marcia Cross flip, at least I had my own short blond hair back. And I didn't *look* three years older, so that was something.

I could have used a flossing and a change of clothes, but for tonight, my baseball shirt was going to have to double as a nightie. At least it covered up enough so I didn't feel entirely exposed. Still a little steamy from my quick rinse, I shyly rubbed my head with the towel and set my folded cargo pants on the dresser. "It's all yours," I said, trying not to stare. Though Cor still sat on the bed's edge, while I'd occupied the bathroom, he'd removed his shirt and shoes and sat in nothing but his tight black slacks. His left arm reached over his right shoulder, as if he were trying to scratch a hard-to-reach itch in the middle of his back. "I guess it's sanitary, if you're worried about that kind of thing," I said, my eyes darting to and fro.

He wasn't wrong about how much a Peri and a human were alike—or at least a Peri and a swimmer who put in a lot of gym time. Though he was lean and possessed an enviably flat stomach, his chest sported layers of hard muscle that were impossible to ignore. It was difficult not to notice how developed his arms and shoulders were in particular, especially when they both were adorned with large tattoos in dark ink that crawled from just above the elbow to his shoulder blades. Like the twined serpents of a caduceus, they were, but with the complexity of a more modern tribal tattoo. These sinuous twinings, though, I felt sure were tribal in a way that rock stars and bikers could only dream of. In a way, that's what made them difficult to look at. The tattoos were private enough that staring at them felt a little too much like gawping at someone deep in prayer.

I cleared my throat again. "Sorry," he said, jolted out of his abstraction. Different species or not, he clearly was as tired as I. Not too tired, I noticed, to let his eyes travel the length of my legs. He smiled guiltily when he realized he'd been caught. Wincing, he reached to the middle of his back once more, using his right arm to force his left down further.

I couldn't help it. I took another look at his chest. Most girls would have envied me right then, being locked in a hotel room with a specimen like that. "Oh, hey," I exclaimed, suddenly concerned. "You're hurt!"

He grimaced slightly when I plopped down on the bed next to him. "It's not bad."

A cut ran several inches below Cor's right shoulder blade. Since it wasn't bleeding, I suppose that technically it was merely a bad scratch. Still, it was raised and red enough to make me alarmed. "Let me get a washcloth."

"Sam, it's okay," he called out, but I was already doing the Florence Nightingale thing by retrieving a cheap washcloth, what was left of the sandpaper soap, and a plastic tumbler full of warm water.

"Did one of the Boars of the Hunt do this?" I asked, dabbing at the wound with the washcloth. Up close, the tattoos adorning his shoulders were even more intricate than I'd realized. They almost seemed like a labyrinthine collection of letters and illustrations woven into a sheath for the ropes of muscles his arms boasted. He shrugged, taking a sharp intake of breath when I scrubbed too hard. "Cor," I asked, "who are these people? These Kin, I mean. Marshall and his mother."

He let out a long sigh. "I honestly don't know."

I suppose I wanted an answer that might explain why they'd done something so inexplicably vile to me. Like, they were the Bonnie and Clyde of his kind, or had at least appeared on *Peri's Most Wanted*.

"One of the things my clan investigates are reports of rogue Kin interfering too much in the affairs of man. Following up on a lead was what helped us find their construct." He stretched, arching his back.

I'd at least wiped away the dirt and flecks of blood from the laceration. I used the washcloth's dry end across its length. "Why'd you help me?" I asked, more softly.

"Because," he said, so slowly that for a moment I thought it was his entire answer. "That's my job." Now that I was done, he pulled himself up. "I think I'll take that shower now. Why don't you get some sleep?"

I nodded, feeling a little bit sad inside. At heart, I knew it was because I was so very tired. Part of me was disappointed, though, that helping Sleeping Beauty to waken had been just a by-product of Cor's job. After the day's craziness, maybe part of me was hoping to hear someone say that they'd helped me out because they thought I was worth saving. Craziness. I shook my wet head and tried to grin. I'd had enough attention for twenty-four hours . . . or three years, even.

Martha Stewart would not have approved of the thread count of the Palm Frond's linen or the fluffiness of their pillows, but the former were reasonably clean and the latter serviceable, once I doubled it over. I closed my eyes and listened to the trickle of water from the bathroom—and must have fallen asleep immediately, because when I opened my eyes in what seemed mere moments later, the room was completely dark and quiet, save for the sound of breathing beside me. After a brief hesitation, I turned over. Cor faced away. His shoulder, barely visible in the blue-gray shadows, rose in rhythm with his breathing.

I watched for a while, trying to get my head comfortable on the pillow again. Wings had sprung from those shoulders, not long ago. What did it feel like to fly? To have the ability simply to leap into the air and zoom away from everything, without thinking of what you left behind? I'd never know.

Sleep overtook me again, but in my dreams I was weightless and floating. That would have to do.

Chapter Eight

Somewhere in my dreams I thought I heard the sound of a thunderstorm—the confusion of a rush of wings ushering in the bang and reverberation of the clouds, followed by the sounds of a deluge. I startled awake, panicked and not recognizing my surroundings. Yet I knew that someone was supposed to be in the bed next to me. The fact the covers there had been pulled back, to leave only a hollow where a body had been sleeping, made my pulse quicken. My throat began to constrict. The man with the tattoos. Where was he?

"I'm sorry," said a familiar male voice, right before I'd graduated from a mere sleepy anxiety to a full freak-out. Cor rushed out of the bathroom in his black slacks, his fingers hurriedly buttoning the cuffs of his open shirt. His hair was messy and his feet were bare, as if he'd tumbled from bed only a few moments before I'd awoken. "I don't know why . . ." Someone banged on the door right then, nearly making me jump right out of my skin. Someone using the side of a fist to make the maximum amount of noise, it sounded like. No wonder

I'd dreamed a thunderstorm. Instinctively, I clutched the bedclothes around me, not really knowing what to expect when my Peri friend peered through the door's peephole and swore. "Don't worry. I'll get rid of her," he said to me, before releasing the chain, unfastening the latch bolt, flipping the deadbolt, and wrestling with the knob lock. Yes, it was that kind of hotel. "Listen," he said to whoever was out there in the too-brilliant desert morning light. My eyes began to water from the stuff. "It's still early. She's asleep."

"It's ten o'clock in the morning!" I heard a girl's voice say. I recognized that voice, I realized; I sat up and cocked my head to identify it.

Cor tried to hush her. "We both had a very long day, as you well know. . . ."

"But it's *ten o'clock*, and I brought doughnuts, and that's what they eat for *breakfast* here." I heard the girl say. A head appeared over Cor's obstructing shoulder, as if she were trying to leap up to catch a glimpse of me. "Is she awake?"

"No." Though soft, Cor's voice was firm.

"Nikki?" I called out, raising myself up to a kneeling position. "Is that you?"

The door opened wide as the girl burst through. "Mrs. Jones!"

"Jones isn't her real name," Cor said with a scowl.

"Hi! Whatever. I told you she was awake," she said to Cor, shoving him aside. "Okay, I found this most *amazing* food that you've got to try," said my former babysitter, depositing no fewer than four green-and-white boxes onto the foot of the bed, the topmost of which she popped open. "You won't believe how *amazing* these are," she said, pinching out one for herself and another for me. "I watched them being made, and they pour a river of hot sugar syrup over them, and they come right off an incredible machine and they put them in the box *while they're hot*. Eat it!" she encouraged. "Eat!"

"I've had Krispy Kremes before. And you know, they make them every day. You didn't need to buy out the store," I assured her while I obediently bit into the still-warm pastry. Since I hadn't eaten for nearly a day, the sugar hit my stomach like a brick. I didn't care. I was simply happy to know that the only person I'd actually liked in that vicious construct had been a secret ally of mine. "I can't believe it's you!" Admittedly, Nikki had changed a bit since the last time I'd seen her. Gone were the pigtails, replaced by a shaggy black bob that covered her ears and most of her eyes. The softer side of Sears had been discarded in favor of the harder edges of Hot Topic; she sported Doc Martens and baggy black flares with tattered hems, a black T-shirt with the name of a band of which I'd never heard, and a lot of jewelry she seemed to have picked up at the nearest S&M boutique. "You've gone Goth!"

"And maybe she should just be gone," Cor said, leaning heavily on the doorknob. "Sam needs to dress."

"Nooooo!" She licked her sticky fingers and flung back the lid of the top box. Only four doughnuts remained.

"Yeeeeees," he said.

They repeated the exchange a few times more, with him growing more impatient and she more wheedling with each rehash. I, in the meantime, had risen from the bed, opened the curtains to admit a modest amount of light, and shuffled to the restroom in search of that mouthwash by the time the argument wound down. "You two sound more like brother and sister than . . ." Light dawned. It was so obvious, with their dark good looks and their similar faces. Even their penchant for black clothing was the same. "Oh my God. You are!" Nikki didn't deny it. Cor stiffened and looked displeased, as though he didn't want to discuss it. "How old are you?" I asked the girl, who in her Goth getup didn't look any more than sixteen or seventeen.

"Two hundred and sixty-one," she promptly replied.

"A very *young* two hundred and sixty-one," Cor said. His arms were crossed. Uh-oh. There was something going on here.

"Don't let me get in the way of your sibling disagreement," I said, taking a swig of the mouthwash directly from the bottle and returning to the bathroom to spit. "Pretend I'm not here."

"He's still mad at me for being your babysitter," Nikki called out. I heard someone—probably her—switch on the television, and then someone—probably Cor—just as swiftly turn it off. "Because he likes being the hero all the time."

Cor barked out a word of roughly eight syllables, the first few of which sounded like *Nicolina*. I assumed it was her unadulterated Peri name. "I explicitly told you that some things are far too dangerous for a young . . ."

"And I specifically told *you* that I could be helpful. And I was."

"That doesn't justify the risk you took," Cor said, just before a muffled series of thuds assaulted the room door again. "Who . . . ?"

"Oh, I was supposed to tell you they were waiting outside," I heard Nikki say as I sponged off my face with a wet cloth and tried to tame my hair.

"Who?"

"Landemann. And your gurrrrlfriend."

Nikki's tease made me shut off the water and cock my head, alert. Cor had a girlfriend? Even not knowing much about the courtship of his race, the word made any relationship he might have had sound kind of plebeian. Fairies were supposed to be regal and tragic creatures, wafting around like the Lady of Shalott. Who actually wasn't a fairy, come to think. But anyway. They weren't supposed to have "girlfriends." Then again, they probably weren't supposed to be eating a five-pound sack of sugar in the guise of Krispy Kremes, either.

I heard the door being unlatched again, followed by the sounds of someone walking into the already-crowded hotel room. "Nikki didn't tell you I was outside, did she?" said a woman's voice. I envied that voice, husky and confident where my own was a nondescript alto.

"I told him!"

"After I knocked?" Nikki didn't answer the woman's question. "As I thought. Corydonais, this place is a slum." All the Peri I had heard speak so far had possessed a bland, slightly Midwestern accent, but the gurrrrlfriend was different. Her words were difficult to understand in a way I couldn't exactly pinpoint. My brain seemed to be doing the thing it had done with Marshall and his mother my last night on Riviera Lane—the same kind of busywork it was accustomed to doing while watching a movie or TV program populated with British actors. It took the slightly alien pronunciations and re-formed them into words I could understand. "We could have arranged better quarters."

"I don't care much where I sleep," Cor replied, adding another of those complex, multisyllabic words to the sentence's end that I assumed was her name. Ginger, it sounded like to my crude ears. "You and I both know I've spent the night in worse places."

"Not by much."

I swear, I could hear the Ginger creature sniff. I imagined her looking around the room and sneering, and maybe even drawing one of those long Peri fingers across the bureau to check for dust. Different species she might have been, but I knew this wench. Snooty, elegant, and probably a supermodel by any standards. The next thing out of her mouth was going to be another rude remark, I just knew.

But boy, was I wrong. "Someone's hiding," she whispered. She meant me, I realized, eavesdropping as I was in the bathroom with the light off. "It could be one of them. I'll handle this."

Oh, God. There was nothing I needed less than some vigilante Peri grappling me to the floor of that Lysol-forsaken establishment. As much as I hated the idea of stepping out and confronting Pixieland's Next Top Model, I knew it was either that or a wrestling match. So I stepped out with the wet washcloth in my hand and a bright smile on my face, as if I hadn't heard anyone new come in. "Bathroom's all yours," I chirped. Then, "Oh."

I'd been completely wrong about Ginger. She wasn't tall. She wasn't elegant. Snooty remained to be proven. Don't get me wrong—she wasn't a dump truck. But the woman I'd imagined was nothing like the tiny little bundle of energy coiled in a defensive posture before me. In her black tank top, fatigues, and army boots, she looked like either a kickboxing instructor or the red-headed bouncer at a fashionable lesbian bar. For a very long moment, we stared at each other. Her eyes took in my bare legs, my makeshift nightshirt, my face, and my messy hair, and then almost imperceptibly, her muscles relaxed. I wasn't a threat at all.

"This is Samantha Dorringer," Cor said. I'd almost forgotten about him. He stood with his arms crossed next to the door, as if he expected even more visitors. Next to him, in a mirror stance, was a barrel-chested bald fellow wearing an impossibly thick mustache, a black T-shirt, and a leather jacket, who appeared to be trying out for the role of bodyguard to the Village People. Landemann, I was guessing. He looked about fifty, which probably meant he'd been born when dinosaurs roamed the earth. "The human from the construct."

Without even so much as a nod of greeting, Ginger turned her back on me. "*Eirethin.* You were right about one thing," she said with her strange accent. "You really don't care much where you sleep, do you?" The remark hurt; I felt as if I'd been physically slapped across the face. Nikki's mouth compressed into a tight little pucker of disapproval, but Cor was emotionless. "Oh, Corydonais, don't you find it cliché, how very much like your father you're turning out to be?"

He said her name again, this time using it as a warning. I'd been wrong a moment before. He wasn't emotionless; he was struggling to keep his feelings under control. Selfishly, I hoped a few of them might involve a little outrage on my behalf. "I'm not my father."

"Then why are you wasting time?" she asked, pacing around him. "And why are you bringing your family into matters that are best left ignored by the Kin?"

"I am definitely not—"

"You are. You allowed Nicolina to enter the very same construct that you forbade me and all the Kin of your own clan to enter. She has no calling and no allegiances, and worse, no discipline."

"Hey!" said Nikki. To my ears, she sounded a little bit guilty.

Landemann had said nothing during any of this, and for a moment, Cor looked as if he might follow suit. "Your wild years were not so very long ago," he said quietly. "If you cared to remember them, you'd know that what Nikki does is beyond my control."

"But we were wild together, Corydonais." The girl sounded as if she was imploring him. "You kept me in check. I followed you then, just as I follow you now. You are my commander."

"And you know that the pair responsible for the construct are exactly the type of rogue Kin our Queen has ordered your commander to bring to justice." I'd never seen Cor sound so firm, or despite his disheveled appearance, look so regal. "Their offense may have involved this *Eirethin*," he added, gesturing in my direction, "but it affects both her kind and ours."

"Fine. I've sworn to obey," shrugged the girl, refusing to follow the sweep of his hand. "It's the vow I took. But you make it hard. And this—" She jabbed a thumb back at me. "I don't know what to say."

"Then say nothing more," Cor advised. I added a mental *yeah!* to the sentiment. He reached for the knob and pulled open the door, admitting a blast of desert heat and light to the room. "Thank you for bringing Landemann to me."

Ginger took the cue and stepped underneath the doorjamb. "It's the least I could do." She turned. "Nikki, I'm sorry. I . . ."

"Nah, I know I'm a pain." Nikki looked for a moment as though she were going to inhale another doughnut, but instead she closed the lid of the Krispy Kreme box and let her arms hang down over the mattress's edge.

I'd been silent long enough. "Nice meeting you!" I called out, waving a hand.

Had Ginger actually turned her head in my direction to give me a look, it would have been of disgust. Instead, the electrical outlet nearest the door bore the brunt of her displeasure. "I'll be outside if you need me," she said to Cor before leaving.

"Well, well, well," I said, once the door was closed and the air conditioner had begun to grind away to cool us down. "I have to say I applaud your choice of girlfriends, mister. Very classy. Classy like constipation, actually."

Nikki let out a guffaw. From the grimace that crossed Cor's lips, I knew I'd struck a nerve. Frankly, after having stood there in my skivvies and put up with Ginger's insults, I was feeling a desire to get a little of my own back.

"Samantha, this is Landemann," said Cor, obviously wanting to change the subject. "He's long been in my service." Ah, he was a bodyguard type, then. My guess had been right. Landemann nodded at me from his at-ease position, but his face remained blank. "And that." Cor gestured at the closed door, then sighed. "That was my second-in-command. She's . . ." In the pause that followed, I supplied many words that completed his sentence, most of them having their roots in rich old Anglo-Saxon cursing. "Difficult," he finally finished.

"She's not much of a second," Nikki said, sitting up. "She doesn't even want to find the ones who kidnapped Samantha."

"Most of these rogues aren't threats to the Crown." Cor crossed over to the bed and sat down by his sister. "How many false alarms have we seen over the decades?"

"Whatever." Nikki's mouth twitched. "She should just join the dropouts. She and they think the same. Nothing matters, right?"

"You, mouse, are just like me." Cor smiled, then reached out and nipped Nikki on the nose. "You'll never be a dropout, will you?"

"Hardly." The girl rolled her eyes. "Not a chance."

I barely knew these people—these Peri, anyway. Peris? Perii? I had no idea. Yet the exchange touched me. I didn't care if they were different from me in more ways than I could probably imagine, or that their entire race had shared our world without us knowing or believing. They were here, and they were real, and they cared about each other in the same ways we did. Watching the affection that Cor and Nikki shared made me, alone on my dark side of the room, feel a little bit friendless and a little bit isolated. It also made me come to a decision. "I want in," I announced.

Cor raised his head and swept back his hair with a hand. "In?"

"I'm in," I repeated. "You're after Marshall and Mother Jones. I want to help. No, shut up," I told him, knowing that his open mouth meant he was going to try to talk me out of it. "Don't say no to me. I'm not the sister you can pick on just because she's littler."

"Yeah!"

Nikki's encouragement spurred me on. "Besides, I'm not a kid," I said. "I'm mature and know what I'm saying. No offense."

"No offense?" Nikki's support vanished as she made an appeal to her brother. "I'm two hundred and thirty years older than she is!"

"And you've spent most of that in a Peri enclosure, away from this world," Cor said. I felt unexpectedly pleased by his support. "I'm sorry, but it's true," he added, when the girl began to object.

"Sorry, kiddo," I told her. "I honestly didn't mean anything. You didn't have three years of your life stolen from you. I did. And three years for me means a lot more than it does for you. A hell of a lot more." She nodded, conceding the point. "I mean, at this point, what have I got? I can't waltz back into my job after a three-year absence. I've got no apartment. God knows where my stuff is. I broke up with my ex six months ago—three years and six months ago, now—so there's nothing on that front. What's left for me besides going home to live with my mom and becoming one of those bitter old ladies who keeps a hundred cats? Nuh-uh," I said, leaning against the bureau. "That's not my style. I want to help you catch these guys."

Cor nodded. "I understand why you'd feel that way. But you've no idea how dangerous my line of work can be."

"After the last couple of days, trust me, I have an inkling. Besides. I was there on the inside, remember? I know more about them than you."

We stared at each other, gazes unwavering. This was a face-off I was determined to win, however, and I forced my eyes to bore into his until at long last, he turned his head. "Fine," he said. He held his jaw clenched sideways while his nostrils flared. No matter the race, stubborn men were all alike. Any exultation I might have indulged in, though, was thwarted by a terse, "We'll see what happens. That's all I'm promising."

"Is it because I'm *Eirethin?*" Cor cocked his head at my question. "Is that it? What does it mean?"

"It means *outsider,*" said Nikki. "Human, really. Outsider to us." I wasn't surprised by the answer—I'd kind of guessed at it through the context, though I thought that maybe it meant something more like *untouchable.*

"It's an old word," Cor said. His right hand was stroking the stubble of his cheek as he watched me. "Where did you hear it?"

"From her," I said, pointing at the doorway Ginger had just exited. "Then you said it, too."

"You heard what she said?"

"Of course I heard," I said, grabbing my grungy cargo pants and beginning to stuff my legs in them. "She stood right there and insulted me."

Cor didn't seem to be getting it. "You *understood* what she said?"

"She basically acted like I was the Yoko Ono to your John Lennon." Oh, he wasn't going to get that. "Like I was your hoochie mama. I mean, tart," I said, searching around for some kind of concept a Peri might understand. "Mistress. Only, on the cheap side."

"I think I can figure out what a 'hoochie mama' is," Cor assured me, amused. I grimaced slightly when I saw Nikki mouthing the words to herself, probably to pull out at the least opportune moment. I should have remembered what Ginger had said about their father, before dragging that one out. From the sounds of things, he'd been something of a dog. "What I meant was, you understood the words she said? Every single one of them?"

"Well yeah. I'm not deaf." The brother and sister looked at each other, then. Nikki had her eyebrows raised. "She was speaking plain English."

"No," said Cor. His sister shook her head. The way they studied me made me feel suddenly self-conscious. "She wasn't speaking English at all."

Chapter Nine

Hats off to you, Thomas Wolfe, no matter how wrong you were. Apparently you *can* go home again. It's just that when you do, all you'll think about is how lucky your parents were to get their property cheap, back in the days before the area you grew up in was fashionable. Because now that you're grown and the old neighborhood's been redeveloped to within an inch of its life, the best you can afford there is part-time rental of someone's garden shed. And even then, you'd probably need roommates.

"I can't believe you grew up in Venice." At a rest stop along our trip from Vegas to Los Angeles, Nikki had swapped her riot grrrl duds for a more subdued, feminine look involving jeans and a flowing lilac top. With her iPod strapped to her waist, she looked more at home skipping among the expensively groomed banks of flowers growing along the canals than I ever had.

"Yeah, I know. Muscle Beach, the boardwalk, Santa Monica Pier, it's kind of a big California cliché," I said, agreeing. I'd spent the afternoon in a van packed with

Storm Ravens camouflaged to the nines in outfits purchased from the army surplus store (yes, I asked), who had done very little other than stare at me throughout the entire road trip across California. Being out in the fresh air and on my feet again had made me a little giddy. My stomach was already in knots. "Just don't start singing the Beach Boys, please."

"I think what Nikki means is that Venice is basically the biggest hub in this country for Kin," Cor said, looking around alertly. Landemann straggled behind us; in his Cuban guayabera shirt, dark sunglasses, and Bluetooth earpiece, he looked like a typical portly middle-aged Venice dweller out for an afternoon walk.

"You're kidding," I said, stopping and turning by a garden planted heavily with Birds of Paradise. "Seriously?"

"It's like, the epicenter of Peridom," Nikki supplied helpfully. "You didn't know?"

"Well, I always got two dollars from the tooth fairy, which was pretty generous." My poor attempt at humor flopped miserably. These two probably didn't even know what a tooth fairy was. "No, I had no idea. Are they around us now?" I asked, whipping in a circle.

"Are you talking about Kin, or ghosts?" When I ignored the sarcasm, Cor asked, "Which house is your mom's?" I shrugged, suddenly vague, not really wanting to tell him. "You don't know?"

"Of course I know." I sighed, tried to think of some comical excuse that would explain my reluctance. There weren't any, though. "I can't do this. I mean . . . no. I just can't."

Nikki held up her hand to shield her eyes from the California sun while she looked at me with pity; Cor reached out and put a hand on my shoulder. "She's your mother," he said, his voice kind. "You have to."

"I don't. She probably thinks I'm dead, anyway. She's probably made her peace with it and when I show up it'll just open all the old wounds. There'll be tears. Rivers of tears. She'll probably faint." Cor's squeeze was sympathetic as the words poured out of me. "I mean, I can't face it. I just can't."

"Nikki? Give us a moment?"

The girl looked up, then let out the faintest of exasperated sighs when she realized she was being dismissed. "Fine. But the chances of me becoming a dropout increase exponentially with every passing minute you leave me alone in Venice," she warned him. "C'mon, Landemann," she said, beckoning the pit bull standing five paces behind us. "Let's take a walk."

Cor confirmed the bodyguard's silent inquiry with a nod. We watched the two of them stroll off the way we'd come. "Now," he said in a quiet voice, once they were out of earshot. "Which one is it?" Sullenly, I pointed to the home next to the one where we'd stopped—a familiar, ivy-covered stucco cottage whose unassuming, adobe-colored exterior seemed out of place, surrounded by homes that had been tarted up and expanded beyond their humble beginnings. The house was a proud little lady surrounded by Paris Hiltons, and I both loved and dreaded meeting her again. "You're scared."

"No," I said into my palm. Pressing my hand over my mouth seemed safer for a moment; it could keep the gulps safely suppressed and any stray tears within inches of my fingertips. Then, because he was being so kind, I admitted, "Yes."

For a moment he said nothing. I wondered if he might let me walk away. "What are you frightened of?" he finally asked.

I shrugged, feeling helpless. "What if she doesn't remember me? Okay, I know that sounds silly, but what do I say when she starts asking questions? What if she has a heart attack when she answers the door? I mean, she's only fifty-four, but I don't know, if I were seeing the daughter I thought was dead for three years, I'd probably have a little sit-down on the pavement, too." Once I started speaking, the words simply tumbled out. "What if she hits me? What if she's so mad that she hauls off and socks me one for putting her through hell? Don't get me wrong, she's a very nice woman, a lot nicer than me, but I haven't been the best daughter, Cor. I missed her birthday two years ago. Five years ago, I mean. I promise to call every two weeks, but then stuff happens and I'm tired at night and suddenly I realize it's been six weeks, instead. I was a terrible teen, too. What if she decides I'm not worth it and shuts the door in my face?"

"Do you honestly think she will?" Cor hugged his own broad chest as he listened, one long leg pointed, his head cocked; his hands had vanished into the sleeves of his dark gray cotton sweater so that it looked as if he wore a particularly comfortable straitjacket.

Out in the canals, a duck kicked up a solitary ruckus as it paddled by. "No," I admitted. "And that's just going to make me feel guiltier."

"You can't feel guilty about something not under your control."

"Oh-ho-ho, can't I!" I retorted to his chiding. Then, curious, I asked, "Hasn't your mom ever made you feel guilty? I know you fair . . . Peris have them. Marshall certainly had a hell of a mother."

Cor's lips spread across his face in a wry smile. "No, despite what some of us would have you believe, mothers are much the same across both worlds. I know mine certainly expects more from me than I tend to give her."

"You?" I asked, incredulous. "Saver of damsels in distress, champion boar fighter, all-around do-gooder, and leader of a bunch of crazy crows in charge of thunderstorms? That's not enough?"

"I'm not in charge of thunderstorms. Storm Ravens

presage thunderstorms, but the storms themselves are only a side effect of the work we're sent to do. Besides," he said, uncrossing his arms and putting his hands on my shoulders. "You're changing the subject. March."

"You are not the boss of me, mister!" I growled when he began propelling me in the direction of the ivy-covered arbor that admitted people into my mother's yard. "I haven't made up my mind yet! I need a fairy re-straining order!"

"You need to see your mother, and I do, too." Somehow, although my body was at something of a forty-five degree angle, he managed to get me onto the little wooden porch.

"Why do you need to see her?"

"Because you, Samantha Dorringer, have an unusual capacity for understanding the speech of the Kin." His head bobbed down while he spoke to me. I suspected he was trying to keep his voice low so he wouldn't draw my mom's attention prematurely. "From what you tell me, your father has passed away, so . . ."

"I didn't say he was dead." My mouth twitched at a subject that had long been a sore spot for me. "I said he was gone. He ditched my mom and me to run off with some other woman when I was twelve."

"I'm sorry." Maybe I'd been a little vehement. "But there are only two ways that you could understand us when we speak. The first and more probable is to live among us for a length of time and absorb it. Which very well could have happened when you were in the Riviera Lane construct for so long. The other is to have been born to it, as children of the Kin are. And considering the lovely-I'm-sure Mrs. Dorringer . . ."

"Mrs. Neale," I grumbled. "I changed to my mother's maiden name when I was eighteen."

"Considering the lovely Mrs. Neale lives and has always lived in Venice, which is . . ."

"The epicenter of Peridom." I remembered what Nikki had said earlier. Suddenly I got what he meant. "She's not! She can't be." The last two weeks of my life had been like the White Queen's philosophy in *Alice in Wonderland*—I'd had to believe not only in six impossible things before every breakfast, but another hundred between lunch and dinner. The notion that my mom could be one of them, though, was simply ridiculous.

"That's why I want to see her." Arms crossed again, he took a few steps back toward the weed-covered arbor until he almost disappeared into the evening shadows. I stared at him, not at all believing what he was suggesting. "Well? Go on."

"Fine," I said, knowing I was at last facing the horribly inevitable and unavoidable, like tax day, or yet another bad Will Ferrell movie. "But I'm just doing this to prove a point."

"So long as you do it," was his smug reply.

I sighed. I hated him. No, I didn't. Cor was a nice guy who just happened to have the misfortune of making me do what I ought. But I sure didn't like being here. I raised my hand. After a very long hesitation, I knocked three times.

Scarcely before I had an opportunity to hope she might not even be home, the door flew open. My mother stood before me, peering at me over the top of her reading glasses. Her hair had been black the last time I'd seen her, thanks to an almost religious devotion to Clairol products. Now it was a dark silver cloud that surrounded her head in a stylish wave. Her face had more wrinkles than I remembered. I couldn't help the tears that had begun to spring to my eyes—seeing her was simply the best thing that had happened to me in a long time. "Mom?" I said, my hand leaping to cover my quivering lips.

"Samantha!" Her arms flew open immediately. I

found myself enveloped in a brisk, vigorous hug before she thrust me back and took a quick look at me. "You're looking thin. But isn't your timing perfect, dear? Come in, come in. Did you bring a friend? You did? Wonderful" I hadn't noticed before that Mom was carrying a clipboard, but she waved it at where Cor stood by the rosebushes. "Hello! I'm Barbara Neale. Samantha's mother. Come in, won't you? We need bodies."

And that, I'm afraid, was my long-dreaded reconciliation with my mother after three years in a supernatural holding cell. Both Cor and I found ourselves being hustled into the low-ceilinged cottage, with its familiar clutter of books and forgotten coffee mugs and cats dozing on the Mission-style furniture. "Barbara? Who's with you?" I heard someone call. A wide-berthed woman with vaguely pink hair, roughly my mother's age or a little older, sat deep in the leather recliner that had once been my dad's. She stared at me, a Burmese on her lap, a biscotti in one hand, and a jar of Nutella in the other. "Is it one of your students?"

"Don't be silly, Doreen. It's Samantha. I know you remember my daughter, Samantha."

"You have a *daughter?*" Doreen was so incredulous, and her implication of my neglect so plain, that for a moment I wanted to dip her head in the chocolate-hazelnut mix.

"Yes, of course I do. I've always had a daughter. Now, you stand like this, dear," she said, handing me a spear, then positioning me in the broad division between the living and dining rooms so that my back was to the archway, and my throwing arm in the air.

Yes, a spear. Cor's eyes popped out at the sight of it. "She's a professor at Occidental," I explained in a murmur, while Mom took a few steps back and studied me. "Classical studies. She uses a lot of different props in her classes. Making history come alive, you know. She could pull out a Hydra's head from the fridge and I wouldn't be surprised." When I saw Cor scrutinizing my mother even more closely after that statement, I hissed, "A fake Hydra's head, doofus! Not the real thing!"

At last satisfied with my placement, Mom leaped forward and began manhandling the Peri. "Stand up straight. Shoulders back. Look down your nose at this lowly mortal."

"Excuse me?" both Cor and I said in unison. I was so shocked that I brought the tip of the spear down onto my sneakers, and then immediately regretted it.

"Don't lose your pose!" For fifty-odd years, Mom was still mighty spry. Her hands wrestled me back into position, and then went to work on Cor. "You are a follower of Eurytion at the wedding feast of Pirithous," she told him, and then to me, as if it explained everything, "We're doing the Centauromachy."

"Is that your son?" Through a mouthful of biscotti, the woman in the recliner appeared dubious. "He's too lean to be a centaur."

"I don't have a son. Only a daughter. Samantha. She's right in front of you!"

"You're right," Cor the Eurywhatever murmured, seemingly afraid to move out of the position in which my mother had arranged him. "She's not Peri."

"Too human?" I whispered back.

"Too crazy," he grinned.

Hah! Told him so. If I had any ability to understand the Kin, it was from three years in the construct, not any genes I'd gotten from her.

I cleared my throat when my mother stepped back to give us the eagle eye again. "Mom, I'm really sorry I haven't called in . . . a real long time." I'd decided I might as well give my speech while we were standing around in a tableau. Maybe with that Doreen person present, she might not yell so loudly. "I had an opportunity to go to, um, Morocco, and ended up living there for a while." Cor scrunched together his eyebrows and mouthed the word *Morocco?* at me, prompting me to mouth back the words *Shut up!* "I know I should've called, or something, since you were probably worried, but . . ."

"Oh, Morocco!" she exclaimed, drawing out a dusty long sword from the umbrella stand. "I remember some particularly lovely sunsets over the city of Oujda."

"Well, I wasn't in Oujda," I said hastily. "I was in . . . Marrakech."

"Tangier," Cor said at the same time, accepting the sword that my mother folded between his hands. While she raised both his arms up above his head, it was my turn to goggle at him.

"I was in Marrakech, and met Cor and his little sister in Tangier." Improvisation can be fun! Except, of course, when it isn't, and I was getting deeper and deeper into the muck.

Mom's head cocked. "Sister?" she asked. "Is she with you?"

"She's outside . . ." Cor began to say, but Mom was already out the door.

It wasn't too very long after that all four of us had been pressed into service. Cor and I were posed in the archway's center, weapons at each other's throats. He represented, as my mother explained, a wine-maddened centaur guest intent upon despoiling one of the human bridesmaids, portrayed by a cowering Nikki. Who needed very little coaching, by the way, and who was so pleased by my mother's encouragements that her postures of terror and woe had grown increasingly melodramatic and silent-filmy. Landemann, on the other hand, had resisted all direction. He now merely stood, helmeted, behind Cor with his hands on his hips, sunglasses still covering his eyes. Apparently he was portraying some kind of passive centaur Teamster intent on making sure that his men weren't being asked to rape and pillage past the ratified end-of-workday time.

"Perfect!" my mom exclaimed, happy at last. She retreated and sat on the recliner's arm with Doreen, crossed her legs, then collected a biscotti from the plastic package and dipped it into the Nutella. "Now that, as I was telling you, is what I speculate that missing metope on the Parthenon's south side would look like. It's the only logical sequence of events."

"But that's all speculation," said Doreen, squinting at us. "Why does anyone care about centaurs, anyway? They're mythical."

"No, they aren't!" Nikki looked as startled as everyone else when she realized the gaffe she'd made. Clearing her throat, she said, "I mean, aren't . . . those . . . chocolate cookies?"

Mom handed the girl the unchewed biscotti and took another. "Doreen, the entire story of the Centauromachy is an expression of the Hellenistic cultural war against the Persians, which occupied a great deal of the energy and philosophy of Greek culture. You can't ignore . . ."

I couldn't take it anymore. Cor might have strong shoulder muscles, what with all that wing-flapping and all, but I wasn't about to stand there indefinitely, defending Nikki's honor with a six-foot-long polearm. Whatever the Centauromachy was, it sounded interminable. "Mom," I said. "I don't know if you've noticed, but I'm kind of grungy. I was hoping I could wash up a little, I guess. Or something." Something. This was the part where I was supposed to be throwing myself on my mother's mercy, begging for succor. Actually, I wasn't really certain what *succor* was. It sounded vaguely vulgar. But I was pretty sure I wanted some.

Crunch. My mom took a bite of biscotti and looked at me as if she'd just noticed how disheveled I was in the clothes I'd been wearing for days. Or years, depending on your perspective. "Well Samantha, why don't you just pop your things in the washing machine and change into something fresher?"

She wasn't making this easy, I realized with an internal groan.

"My boy, Charles? Whenever he came home from college, he *always* brought a duffel bag full of dirty clothes," Doreen said from her chair. "And he *always* expected me to do it. As if I wanted to launder soiled Fruit of the Looms just because he was the fruit of my loins. Fruit of the Looms! Hah!" She bit so savagely into her biscotti that it exploded into crumbs.

"Samantha's not in college, Doreen. She's thirty-two years old."

"Twenty-nine!" I protested.

My mother gave me a pitying look. "Oh, Sam. You're too young to start lying about your age already."

"The point is," I said, trying to reel the conversation back from the edge of insanity toward which it had tiptoed. "That I really don't have anything to change into, I'm afraid. My bags—our bags . . ." I looked at Cor for a little help, but apparently in the Blighted Lands of Nefarion and other haunts popular with the Peri crowd, they're not required to lie extemporaneously. "The airline lost them."

"When we left from Las Vegas," Nikki said, trying to be helpful and failing miserably.

"I thought you all arrived from Marrakech?" That Doreen. Always stirring the crap.

"Marrakech," said Nikki, forming her mouth into a little O. "Sorry. I didn't know about Marrakech," she said to me in a stage whisper.

"I think Samantha's point is that she wouldn't mind a little time in the powder room," said Cor, gathering the spear from me, a loaned veil from his sister, and plucking off the centurion's helmet that sat on Landemann's head. The spear and his sword he put back into the umbrella stand, after which he set the remainder of the props on the living room coffee table, then paused to pet one of the two cats on the sofa. "We certainly don't want to impose . . ."

"Oh, Mr. Donais, aren't you sweet to help put things away." Guessing from the way she pronounced it, Mom had heard the last part of Cor's name and wrongly assumed he was of French extraction. She scuttled over to help Nikki out of her supine position. "But Samantha, why not get a change of clothing from your room? There should be plenty there."

"My room?" I asked. "When I left for college, you changed my old bedroom overlooking the canals into an office." She nodded, trying to explain. "You called it your scriptorium."

"I meant the garage. Now that I've gone green, I remodeled it into an apartment. And when your things arrived from Las Vegas . . ."

"Gone green, my ass." Doreen snorted. "Cadging rides from me and all your other SUV–owning friends does *not* make you green, Barbara."

I was too busy staying upright to listen. "My things?" I asked, stunned. "You have my things?"

"That's what I was saying," my mother explained patiently. To Cor, she shook her head. "She was always impatient."

Damned right I was. Impatient enough to sprint through the dining room and kitchen and out the back door to the two-story garage that overlooked the street in back of the canal. In my day it had been the repository for all my old toys and bicycles before they eventually made their way to the Salvation Army, and later on for all my father's clothing and books once the bastard had deserted us. Its dark depths had been the spot where I'd had my first make-out session, in the backseat of my mother's Tercel with a boy named Myron Leblatski; it had also been the spot where, for two short weeks when I was fifteen, I'd secretly attempted to cultivate a smoking habit and only ended up with a burn on my forearm, a bad cough, and a guilty conviction I'd given myself cancer.

The garage was dark no longer. Sometime in the last three years, Mom had redone the entire thing with drywall and new flooring, recessed lights, and an honest-to-God bathroom with shower stall where my dad's golf clubs had once lurked. Glass block windows let in light from the street, and skylights made the open first floor room even sunnier. A set of carpeted stairs led up to a second half-floor and a closed loft space that I assumed had been finished in a similar style.

But most marvelous of all, my worldly possessions were there. Everything, from what I could tell—which wasn't much, but it was still my stuff! My very own, wonderful stuff! My IKEA sofas lined the far wall, surrounded by the other cheap furniture I'd picked up when my income allowed. The velvet Elvis I'd gotten from a garage sale (on the reasoning that every Las Vegas apartment deserved to feature a velvet portrait of the King) hung on the clean white wall. My rugs were rolled up and stacked in a corner next to boxes and boxes of who knew what, bulging at their taped-down seams. Some of my clothes were still on hangers and lay on the sofa, while a few of my old familiar suitcases lay on the floor nearby, presumably filled with the smaller items. Never mind that I'd been a poverty case when I'd lived in Las Vegas. This was like the best Christmas-Day spread ever. My insides practically squirmed with an urge to run over and tear everything open.

"I had planned to rent it out to a student or two, but when Hugh brought your things, it didn't seem to make sense any more." Hugh? My ex? I didn't get it. Mom stood in the garage door, leaning against the wall. One of her hands rested on her chin; a faraway look was in her eyes. "Besides, you know how snooty the neighbors are. *If you cleaned up your garden your house might be as neat as ours, Mrs. Neale. Your bungalow could really use a coat of paint, Mrs. Neale, I could give you a recommendation if you need one.* They'd never let me rent to a student. It would offend the gods of gentrification that they worship. One with greedy, meddling hands. A Hecatonchires, really."

Though at the moment my mood was so elevated that I would've granted anyone anything in the wish department, I wasn't really in the mood for one of my mother's explications of Greek mythology. "What did Hugh have to do with anything?" I asked.

"Well." Mom didn't look directly at me, which gave the impression she was trying to choose her words carefully. "You . . . left for Morocco . . . after breaking up with him. So naturally he felt guilty about how distraught you must have been to go without a word to anyone."

I put down the small box of CDs I'd been toying with. "Distraught? Why would I be distraught? He'd gotten engaged. Oh." Duh. Of course, I realized, putting it all together. Poor emotional Sam, unable to cope with the engagement of a former boyfriend she had dumped—repeat, that she had dumped—six months earlier, became unhinged and jumped off the Hoover Dam. Or ran away. Any dramatic scenario would do for the aggrandized ego of Hugh, that chuckleheaded chump. And of course he got to be the good guy who cleaned up the mess everyone thought I'd left behind. Goddamn him. "That's interesting."

"Your Cory seems like a nice young man." My mother

smiled and crossed her arms as she came in and settled on a footstool.

Cor wasn't there. It occurred to me that it might be a good time to take advantage of my mother's expertise. "Mom, what do you know about something called the Peri?" I asked, abruptly. "I don't know if you've run across the term before."

"Oh, the Peri! Did you hear about them in Morocco? Well, it's Persian folklore, actually. A mythical race of fallen angels." I raised my eyebrows at that, though perhaps I shouldn't have been surprised. Did anyone look more like a fallen angel than Cor? "I believe that legend has it they were denied Paradise and put on the earth to do penance."

"Penance?"

"For their sins."

"Interesting," I said, without betraying any emotion. I could see that being true for Cor, if there was any accuracy to it.

"And then there's Gilbert and Sullivan, of course. *Iolanthe*. Subtitled, *The Peer and the Peri*. But I think your sudden interest in folklore is a cover-up, dear." I began to flush a little at being caught out. How did she know? "How long have you and Cory been lovers?"

I've heard the word *spit-take* used in situations like this, but until the moment my mother asked that particular question and I responded by gagging on the saliva in my mouth and hacking for thirty seconds like one of her cats with a hairball during shedding season, I'd never really known what it meant. I'd really thought she'd figured out the true nature of Cor and Nikki, not that she was taking a stab at my sex life. "Mom!" I protested.

"You're quite old enough to have a frank discussion with your mother, Samantha."

"It's not the content, it's the assumption. We're not lovers. I mean, we're friends. We've been through some things together. He's helped me out of a couple of tight spots. But we're not—I mean, he's good-looking and all," I rambled. When I'd brought home heavily tattooed, long-haired boyfriends in high school—and I had—it was solely for the purpose of shocking my mother. Now, a dozen or so years later, here I was feeling a vague sense of relief she actually liked Cor, and a little bit of guilt that I wasn't able to provide her with the son-in-law she'd be sure to hint about any minute now. "But we're not lovers."

"Well, the way he looks at you!" she said with meaning. I didn't know quite how to reply to that. Privately I'd decided that trying to pump her for more information would seem disingenuous. "And that funny, good-looking man of his. Landemann? What is he?"

"He's kind of a butler," I suggested, rejecting the concept of bodyguard as likely to raise questions about whether Cor was a rock star or a drug dealer.

"Well, they're all welcome to stay for as long as necessary. I've already shown Nikki the spare bedroom. You can stay out here, upstairs, of course, and Cory and his manservant—doesn't that sound grand!—can stay down here on the sofa bed. If you want."

Those last three words, soft enough to sound like a mere afterthought, were so wistful that I couldn't help myself. On my knees I crept over until I was next to my mother. I gave her an impulsive hug. She smelled the same as I remembered, a mixture of fabric softener, herbal tea, and cat fur. "Of course I want."

Our hug, long overdue, seemed to last forever. The good kind of forever. The forever you don't want to end. While still in our clinch, she said to me, "You'll tell me next time, won't you? If you go away for so long?"

She had been worried, after all, I realized. Here I'd assumed our casual reception was a symptom of her not even noticing I'd been gone. But in that quiet moment, surrounded by all the stuff of mine she hadn't dared throw away for three long years, I had an inkling how she really felt. "Mom!" I said, separating from her and brushing the fine gray hair from her face. "Were you really worried?"

She smiled at me. "You're a big girl. You know how to take care of yourself!" I nodded, not denying it. "So of course I wasn't worried about you!" Mom bit her lip and rose to her feet, sniffing slightly and then trying to pass it off as dust, or an allergy. She crossed the room toward the exit, turning only when she reached the door. "Samantha? Was that why you went to Morocco? Because you were upset about Hugh's engagement?"

After a moment, I nodded. That nod took a lot of gritting my teeth and biting a foul-tasting bullet, I might add. "Sure," I agreed. "That was why."

We were a lot alike, my mom and me. Neither of us was very practiced at lying to each other.

Chapter Ten

For a second night in a row, I dreamt of storms roiling in the distance, at first formally announcing themselves with a rumble. After an appropriate pause, the thunder repeated itself like an echo in reverse, intensifying where it should have faded. Although I was still half-asleep, I could see a white flash of light through my eyelids. Automatically I began counting the seconds. *One-Mississippi. Two-Mississippi.* I'd counted to ten by the time the third percussive clap sounded; it was enough to wake me.

In how many unfamiliar places had I awoken over the past weeks? At least this mattress was my own, though it and the box spring lay on the floor in the bedroom while the frame parts still leaned unassembled against the wall. I was alone tonight, I remembered after a moment's groggy confusion. When another flash of light and lingering roll of thunder sat me upright, I thought of Cor. Had he left? Mild panic prickled at my skin, to think that he might have vanished from downstairs without telling me.

After I stood up, feeling the newly laid carpet between my toes, I remembered in time not to walk too far in the direction of the street, where the second-story roof sloped down to a point well below my height. I pulled on a pair of jeans and a short T-shirt lying on the suitcase nearby and stole across the room. The doorknob twisted almost silently when I turned it. When I stepped out onto the landing above the living area below, none of the floorboards squeaked. It was as if the genie of the lamp had granted me an unspoken wish I'd made not to make any noise as I crept barefoot down the stairs.

Not that I could have been heard over Landemann's raucous snores. From the light seeping through the skylights, I could tell he lay on the loveseat in a pair of surprisingly formal pajamas. Part of me wanted to stop and take a look at his face bereft of the sunglasses he always wore, but I didn't dare venture too close. On the other side of the mound of boxes and debris from my former life, my sofa lay covered with sheets and a spare pillow Mom had produced from her linen closet. They'd obviously been slept upon, but no one was there now. Cor was gone.

Fine, I told myself in classic pep-talk style as I slipped out the door and into my mom's handkerchief-sized backyard. So what if the guy had left me alone and gone off on one of his little frat-boy, paramilitary missions to bring thunder to the masses. Big freakin' deal. So what if he hadn't included me on whatever mission had to be carried out at four in the morning? What could I have contributed, anyway? I was just a powerless nothing compared to the Peri. They didn't need a cheerleader.

It had been a while since I'd gone without shoes, so the paving stones were chilly and hard underfoot as I took the path beside my mom's house out to the canals.

Although I stubbed my toe on a garden hose reel blocking the path there, I didn't make enough noise to wake anyone. I let myself out the gate and onto the hedge-lined walkway, where the concrete was warmer and still dry, despite the crackles of lightning to the north.

Across the canal, in one of the more extravagant houses to have been remodeled over the years, mood lighting revealed the details of an expensive kitchen for anyone who happened to be passing; its luminous glow revealed the low arch of the footbridge connecting our two sides of the canal. For a moment I leaned on the metal pipe at the bank's edge, peering into the distance—for what reason, I didn't really know, since the only times my eyes came into focus against that vast black-blue sky was when the lightning streaked from above to split it in half. On an impulse, I tiptoed a few feet down to a small wooden dock Mom shared with the next-door neighbor, and smiled when I reached its narrow end. Tied to a dowel was mom's little skiff, a tiny flat-bottomed boat she'd acquired years and years before after we'd moved into the Venice house. As long as I'd known her, she'd been fond of donning a big, floppy sun hat, her bathing suit, and a pair of her biggest sunglasses so that she could float in solitude by the dock with a book. It was me who would be floating for a little while tonight, without the book or the floppy hat, but just as alone.

L.A.'s warm weather is different from the furnace blast of Las Vegas; it's gentler and capable of more variations than mere *hot* and *freakin' hot*. Tonight was one of those perfect warm nights, not so sticky that it threatened to drive me back into air-conditioned depths, nor so cool that I felt I needed a sweater. Even the breezes from the approaching storm didn't bother me. I enjoyed the way they felt, playing over my skin.

There's something wild about watching a storm on

your own, isn't there? It makes your stomach feel queasy as you sit and wonder when the next bolt of lightning might strike, or where, all the while knowing that the light and the sound are inevitable. From Mom's little skiff I had an enviable view of it all, too—the dark skyline, the violent flashes reflected in the gentle water, the sleeping houses that would leap into silhouette with every fresh strike. I'd always privately mocked her little afternoon excursions as sitting in a leaky rowboat on the smelly water surrounded by even smellier ducks, but this particular spectacle suited my mood.

"Is there room for two?"

"Holy—!" Not only did I nearly tip the skiff over when I startled from my reclining position into a near-squat, but there was a moment when I thought I'd lose control of my bladder, or bowels, or worse, both. "You scared me!"

"Sorry." Cor knelt down on the dock, leaned out, and helped to steady the little boat. He seemed to be wearing an untucked striped dress shirt and a pair of dress slacks, inevitably black. Like me, he was barefoot. "I should've warned you."

"Yeah, you think?" I growled, trying to calm my still-thudding heart. Then I realized something. "Hey. Why aren't you with your buddies out there?" I pointed in the direction of the storm.

I could have sworn I heard him sigh as he pulled the skiff closer to the little dock and began to lower himself down into its bow, carefully balancing himself so that we didn't spill. "I wasn't apprised of this particular exercise," he said, curiously unemotional. "Which means that either an emergency arose, or I wasn't needed." Cor settled down onto the plank at the boat's front, hiking up his pants legs so that his calves were half-exposed. "Or wanted."

"Who would do that?" I asked, outraged on his behalf. "No, it's that Ginger creature, isn't it?" It was the first time he'd heard my abbreviation of her name. I heard him chuckle a little at it. "Well, don't just sit here. Go out and join them."

"If I'm not wanted, I'm not going."

"Why not? I would. I'd just show up and be all, *Hey, peeps. 'Sup? Where's the party and why wasn't I invited?* You're the one who's supposed to be heading up that motley crew, aren't you? Show them who's boss."

"That's a decidedly human approach," said Cor. "We handle it differently."

"How?"

Cor toyed with the boat's rope. "Confrontation is not a favored trait of the Kin. To show up and challenge Ginger would be weakness on my part. It would let her know that her snub stung. If it was a snub. I'm not needed on every run—I'll let this pass. Then, at some appropriate time, I'll find a way to let it be known that it was not appreciated."

"Oh, my God. Confrontation might not be favored among your people, but passive-aggression apparently is. Like that book you had Nikki slip in the twins' room."

"That was a warning."

"You say po-tay-to, I say po-tah-to. You say warning, I say pointless game of cat and mouse. You and your crew could have come in and cleaned house without resorting to playing those pranks. All you ended up doing was making Mommy-and-Me haul out the big knives."

"No," said Cor, firm. "A construct's very much like a soap bubble blown around the people who create it, and the prisoner, if there is one. Slipping in is possible, but dangerous to the construct itself. Too many people attempting to invade it could have been catastrophic for everyone, including you. Why do you think I was so angry with Nikki for following?" He let that sink in for a minute. "You might call it passive-aggressive, but my kind respond to subtler tactics than your . . . your . . ." He grasped for the word. "Your Rambo bullying."

"Rambo!" A flash of lightning punctuated my exclamation, unfortunately revealing the fact that I was laughing. I counted to five before the thunder followed, insistent and urgent. "You, sir, have just dated yourself. When's the last time you saw a good old-fashioned human movie?"

"I've seen plenty." Cor's pride seemed slightly perforated. "We live in your world quite a bit of the time, Samantha. We know what you do, how you think, what movies and television you watch, how you dress. We know how to pass as you."

"Ooooo, they move among us!" I said in my scary movie voice. The wind whipped up, rocking the boat a little. When he didn't say anything in response, I waited a moment and said, "Sorry. I'm still wrapping my head around the whole concept of there being an entirely different species of human on this planet, and anyway, what do you mean, you're here quite a bit of the time? Where do you go when you're not here? What planet is that Bloody Plains of Nefarion on, anyway?"

"Blighted," he corrected. "And it's not on a planet. It's in a different . . . dimension, you might say. Or plane. Elsewhere. Not here. Our worlds are much smaller than yours. Some are large and deserted, like the Plains. Most are only the size of a very small city. Though they all occupy the same plane, each is disconnected from every other."

"Like Juneau," I said, unexpectedly. I hastened to explain. "Juneau's the capital of Alaska. You can get there by boat or plane, but there aren't any roads connecting it to the outside world." I don't know where I got that.

I caught a quick glimpse of his face, almost stark white, from another flash of lightning behind me. "Like Juneau," he agreed.

The thunderclap that followed was so loud and so seemingly close that once again I startled. "You know, maybe sitting on the water in the middle of an electrical storm isn't the best of ideas."

When I began pulling us closer to the dock from which we'd drifted, he tried to assist by giving me a boost up on to the ladder. "What, you've never been hit by lightning before?"

"No! And I'm not starting now!" I hadn't quite gotten my sea legs, yet. Trying to maintain my balance on a wobbly dinghy in the dark was too much of a feat to accomplish when I wasn't exactly sure what he was trying to help me do. "You go first," I suggested.

I envied the easy way he exited the craft without even making it teeter. On the dock, he knelt down and held out his arms for me. "Come on."

"All right." I didn't sound quite as confident as he. His hand, large and strong, took mine as I grabbed the ladder with the other. Once I had one bare foot on a rung, he hauled me up. Naturally, I overbalanced; he toppled gently backward onto his butt, laughing a little as he hit a sitting position. The boat gently eased away from underneath me into the water, jerking to a halt when it reached the length of its tether. "Sorry."

"I'm okay," he said, scooching forward. He took my other hand as well, so that he was my sole support. "Are you?"

"I'm fine," I breathed. In the lightning flash that followed, I could see exactly how close our faces were to each other. Another quickly followed, and it seemed as if in less than a second the distance between us had narrowed even farther. "If you let go, I might fall," I warned him, voice low.

His reply was just as soft. "I won't let go, then."

"Okay," I whispered. When I took a step up, bringing my head up to his level, I felt the warmth of his legs, spread on the ladder's either side. He didn't pull me up any farther. "Is something wrong?"

"No." He let go of my right hand. I reached for one of the dock's support posts. Right as I anchored myself, I felt the gentle touch of his hand against the back of my head. "Is something wrong with you?"

His mouth was so close to mine that every word tickled my lower lip. "No," I said. "Not at all."

My eyes closed the moment we kissed, though I saw a blinding flash of lightning through the lids and heard the thunder that followed. My left hand dropped his and swept beneath his hair, twining into the thick thatch. My toes scrabbled for the next rung of the ladder; he rolled backward, carrying me up and over and atop him. I'd never imagined his lips and tongue being so soft, so pliant as they pried mine apart. To be honest, I hadn't permitted myself to imagine his lips at all, but now they were all I could think about. His lips and his hands, that is, as they slid beneath the loose fabric of my T-shirt. The tips of his fingers traveled up my spine, while his thumbs grazed the sides of my rib cage. I was a little surprised how rough his hands were—he was no pampered office boy with skin of velvet. I shivered as he traced the scoop of my shoulder blade, his fingers discovering that I'd come out with nothing beneath the thin layer of cotton.

I didn't protest when one of his hands left my back, leaving it exposed to the wind that was whipping around us with increasing wildness. My shivers made him draw me closer. I couldn't kiss him fast enough, or hard enough; my lips prickled from the pressure as he drew them in his mouth. The sides of his hand traced my breasts where they pressed against his torso. When his fingertips streaked down my sides to my waist, I tore away and gasped.

My back still was tingling from his touch as I began to

remove my shirt. He was too impatient, though; before
my extended arms had begun to struggle from their
sleeves, he yanked the shirt up over my head, pulled it
off my arms, and dropped it behind me. I thought I
might feel his hands all over me immediately, but he
paused. In the glow of the house across the water, in the
shadows from the arched overpass, I saw him attempt
to unbutton his shirt. Apparently his fingers weren't as
nimble or speedy as he needed, though, because after
a moment he simply skimmed it over his head and
shoulders, and tossed it onto the wooden dock. Lightning flashed again, followed almost immediately by the
sound of thunder. He panted opposite me on one knee,
his lean stomach nearly concave. "Come here," he suggested in a rasp.

He didn't have to ask twice. I crawled forward and
pressed my naked torso against his, enjoying the sensation of our doubly warm skin contrasted with the exposed parts of me that the wind brushed into a crazy
quilt of goose pimples. Every wind chime in Venice
seemed to come alive in that gale, sending out sounds
of tinkling bells, or lower, sonorous gongs, or percussive
rattles of bamboo into the whirlwind wrapping itself
around us. So insistent was the weather by this point
that save for where our bodies connected, I couldn't tell
where the wind's touch ended and his hands and fingers began.

His mouth left mine and began working its way to my
ear, nipping the lobe before it moved down my jawline
and onto my neck. Simultaneously, he pushed me back
so that he could draw his fingertips beneath my arms,
then under and around my breasts again, teasing the
nipples before moving in unison down my ribs to my
waist.

"Cor!" My whispered exclamation was lost in the
storm. I felt a cold pinch on my shoulder, so sharp and

surprising that it took a moment before I realized it was a raindrop. Another followed, then more, until finally we were being assaulted by the hard, heavy pellets of water falling in a rush from the sky.

I let my own hands explore him now. I'd dated a couple of well-built men before, but never someone whose musculature was so efficient, so lean; his shoulders felt more like hard machinery than flesh. In this light, I couldn't see his elaborate tattoos, but I remembered where they were and let my palms run over them. He shivered and stole individual kisses as I traced the outlines of his chest, then let my hands run lower. I unbuttoned his pants. I could already feel the firmness in his trousers that pulsed through the denim of my jeans and against me.

And then I made another discovery. "You don't have a belly button!" He cocked his head to hear me, over the sound of the rain drumming against the dock and the canal water. "A navel. You don't have one."

"None of us do." Hair had fallen over his face, ending just below his nose. Droplets of water fell onto his lips. "Navels are a human thing."

While he'd spoken, my hand had slipped beneath the waistband of his black pants and pulled back the elastic waistband of his underwear. "I thought this was a human thing," I told him, letting my fingers wrap around a hardness that grew more rigid at my touch.

My own hair had gotten soaked in a matter of mere seconds, it seemed. He pushed it away from my cheeks. "I believe," he said, holding my stare, "it's a universal thing."

Our bodies glistened and shone when lightning struck twice in rapid succession. Water ran down my face, stinging my eyes, invading my nose, and dripping down onto the few square inches of my body that weren't already drenched. When he lowered me down to the wooden planks again, my leg was bent back at an uncomfortable angle. I didn't care. I didn't care about the discomfort or the wet or the chill of the wind against my water-slick skin—I thought only about my need to have him close, and closer still. Once I was on my back, I felt the rough stubble of his chin scrape beneath my rib cage. His lips encircled my belly button, and sucked at it. When I laughed, bouncing my stomach against his face, he responded by undoing the top button of my jeans and tugging at the zipper.

Though the fury of the rain and wind was chaotic, above the commotion I thought I could hear the sound of birds, and an angry, animal wail. Lightning struck again, nearby this time accompanied by a clap of thunder from what sounded like immediately overhead. During the flash I saw Cor looking up to the sky, an expression of longing on that handsome face. I'd seen that expression once before, when he'd leaped from the Eiffel Tower in Las Vegas to take wing. I took his hands in mine. "You want to be with them, don't you?" I said, my ears still ringing from the thunderclap.

"More than almost anything. I love being in flight. You would, too." He moved his hands to each side of me as he balanced himself. His head drooped; it nuzzled against mine. "But not more than this," he murmured into my ear. "Not more than now."

The next bolt of lightning struck equally as close as the last. The thunder chaperoning it, angry as the Old Testament God, seemed to last forever. Not too far from us, I heard the sound of an electrical transformer popping; several cars began to bray their shrill alarms. We cowered before the phenomenon, not moving for a moment, until we were certain that it hadn't been meant for us. "We should get indoors," I said, my fire temporarily dampened, but not snuffed. "You might have survived a lightning strike, but I'm far more delicate."

He sprang to his feet, eager. "Indoors is fine," he murmured in my ear, after he'd helped me up and turned me around. "In your bed. Warm and dry."

My T-shirt was around, somewhere. He helped me find it on the dock, and held my waist while I slipped it on. Though the material was cold and soggy, it wasn't any worse than the rest of me. I took his hand and led him back toward land and the sidewalk. "What about Landemann?" I asked, suddenly remembering the sleeping log on the sofa. "Won't he, you know, hear?"

"I'll ask him to step out," Cor said, helping me spring onto the concrete.

"Step out? Into this? That's inhumane." I supposed the word could apply to the Peri, too.

"What do you suggest, then?"

"I don't know. Doesn't he have some kind of Peri cloaking device he can use to block everything out?"

We hadn't heard any thunder since the last, immense clap; a more distant rumble sounded now. "Landemann isn't Peri," said Cor, as I opened the side gate that led beside my mother's house. "He's human."

"He is?" For some reason, that made me stop and look at him. I don't know why, but I liked him a little better for having a human in his entourage. Beneath the overhang beside Mom's house, we were out of the brunt of the rain. "Well, that's even worse," I said, sticking up for my race. "You can't tell the man to stand out in the rain just because he's human. Like a dog."

I was teasing, of course, but he didn't seem to take it that way. "What do you mean?" The grip he had on my hand intensified. "I have never, *never* mistreated that man," he said, making sure I could see his face.

"Fine!" I hadn't intended to create a scene, especially one I didn't understand.

"I've done more for him than anyone else. Anyone."

"Okay!" I reached down and fastened my jeans. "I get

it. You don't want to get him wet. We'll figure it out when we get inside." He didn't say anything, but at the same time, his grip only lessened slightly. "Come on," I urged. "Or have I ruined everything?"

"No," he finally said, after a wait that seemed interminable. "You haven't ruined everything." That was better. Still weird, but better. I offered him a smile, which he repaid with another of his sweet kisses. "There's history between Landemann and me," he said.

"Tell me sometime," I whispered.

"I will."

"But not now."

"No, not now."

We were in such a hurry to rush back to the garage that it wasn't until we were halfway across the yard that we noticed its door was open, and that lights were on within. Silhouetted in the door stood Ginger. She was soaked; her khaki-colored tank top clung to her form as if it had been molded to her. "Oh. There you are." By the way my brain seemed to process her words a little more slowly than normal, I could tell she was speaking in the tongue of the Kin. Despite that, it was impossible to miss that her tone was confrontational. One of those passive-aggressive Peri things, I supposed, trying to make Cor feel as if he should have been aloft with them, even though he hadn't known they were taking flight. She looked over our drenched forms, her eyes lingering especially long on Cor's shirtless torso. "I'm glad you've been out enjoying yourself," she snapped.

"She can understand you," Cor said calmly, in his own language. Then in English, he repeated, "Samantha understands our tongue." He seemed to be warning her not to rant about me again, as she had last time.

But Ginger didn't seem to care. "Things happened while you were out playing," she said, with a nasty emphasis on the last word. For the first time, I noticed that inside the garage apartment, a number of the Storm Ravens milled about, still in their silly paramilitary fatigues.

"What?" asked Cor. Then, with sudden panic, "Landemann?"

"Yes, Landemann." I didn't know whether it was a grudge against me, or whether Cor's second was an actual nasty piece of work, but she seemed to sound smug. "We found him unconscious in the alley. He was probably out looking for you when *they . . .*"

She didn't get a chance to finish her sentence. Cor had already dropped my hand and run into the living area, where the bulldog-like bodyguard had been laid out on the carpet. "Landemann," he said, kneeling beside him.

I followed, my hand over my mouth. Horrified, I saw that the bodyguard had a wound in his side, where blood had soaked his shirt. More blood daubed his face, and one of his hands appeared to have a gash across it. Ginger stood beside me, ignoring my presence. "This is what I tell you again and again," she said to Cor. "You can't keep them as pets. Over and over you tell me that he protects you, but it's the other way around. It always will be, Corydonais. You know it. I know it. We *all . . .*"

"That's enough." The command made Ginger shut her mouth immediately. Finally she turned her attention my way, her eyes ablaze. I could tell she was judging me. To her, I was little more than another of Cor's playthings. His lapdog of the moment.

Then again, I realized, maybe I was.

"Call an ambulance," Cor ordered.

"We already have, sir," murmured one of the Storm Ravens watching the scene.

"Is there anything I can do?" I whispered. Cor shook his head and sat back onto the floor, Landemann's hand in his. He didn't have to say anything; I knew from the expression on his face that he was blaming himself. Hadn't I just accused him of neglecting the guy only moments before?

When finally he looked up at me, stony and poker-faced, all I could wonder was whether he blamed me, as well.

Chapter Eleven

"Well, I just don't understand how Mr. Landemann could have stepped outside and gotten gored by a wild beast." My mother, for perhaps the 175th time in the last day and a half, shook her head and asked the same question aloud. "They think it's a boar of some kind. What other kind of animal gores? A dog I can understand. Even a coyote. But they bite. They don't gore."

"Unicorns," said Nikki with such confident authority that I narrowed my eyes at her, suspiciously. With a smile at the girl, Mom set down a plate of chocolate-covered graham crackers on the coffee table, then quickly stepped back so she didn't get accidentally struck by the girl's flying fists of famine.

"It's a damned ugly world out there, Barbara." Doreen was back. From what little I'd been able to glean, the woman had taught physical education and coached women's soccer at Oxy before she'd retired. Her visits appeared to coincide roughly with my mother's late afternoon snack, which accounted for the decidedly unathletic figure. "I wouldn't be surprised if it were a gang."

"A gang? In Venice?" Mom helped herself to one of the graham crackers and chewed it thoughtfully. "But the paramedics said very distinctly that the type of wound Mr. Landemann received corresponded to the entry profile of a pointed tusk, not a knife or gunshot."

"So?" Doreen had hauled out the Nutella again. My teeth ached a little at the sight of her dipping one of the chocolate cookies into the stuff, especially since I knew it would give Nikki ideas. All I could say was that I certainly hoped Storm Ravens got dental coverage.

"So, apparently you're suggesting that there's a gang of youthful thugs running about armed with tusks." Mom finished off the last of her cookie. "Let's notify the local news crews about that one, shall we?"

"Spanish explorers introduced wild swine to California as early as the late eighteen-hundreds as both a source of food and in order to clear the land," Nikki suddenly said from her seat on a cushion on the floor. One of Mom's Ragdolls lay in her lap, while from the coffee table, the Burmese nudged her shoulder for attention. "In the early nineteen-hundreds, the European wild boar was imported and let loose for the purpose of sport hunting, and over the past century the two species have interbred and become feral. They have a high reproductive rate. Twice a year they have litters of four to fourteen piglets apiece." She noticed the strange looks I was shooting her from across the room. "What? Your mom's computer gets the Internet."

Mom looked pleased. "See, Doreen? Boars are not outside the realm of imagination. Gangs. Honestly."

"Well, it could have been." Doreen shrugged.

"I suppose we should be grateful it was only a shallow wound. Poor man!" With one more sigh my mother took yet another cookie. "But what I really don't understand is *how* Mr. Landemann . . ."

"Can we not talk about this anymore?" I requested, suddenly. I'd been curled up in my mom's desk chair at the room's other end for what seemed like forever, fending off the interested advances of cats while trying to ignore the semi-obscene satyrs on the amphora occupying the desk's center. Those satyrs were getting a heck of a lot more action than I was, even considering the night before last. "You've been round and round and round it so many times that it's driving me absolutely stark, raving crazy."

"Well, excuse us," Doreen muttered to herself.

My mother lifted her eyebrows. "I'm sorry, dear."

"Thank you." With my chin resting against my knees, I looked at my feet. They were dirty. Had I showered since yesterday morning? Oh yes, very late last night, after Cor's cortege of Storm Ravens had come back from the hospital with a stitched-up Landemann in tow. That seemed like a very long time ago. "Talk about anything else, but not that."

"Of course," Mom said brightly. She opened her mouth to speak, thought the better of it, and closed it again. Doreen sighed and hefted herself forward to grab another cookie. Nikki tried to keep her frantic crunching to a minimum, but its sound filled the room, easily beating in volume the ticking of the mantel clock and the moist sounds of another Ragdoll licking its most private parts on the sofa. I waited. And waited. Nikki was clearly unused to human domestic squabbles, and Doreen didn't appear to want to help out any; Mom sat there helpless. At last, her conversational nature abhorred the silent vacuum, and she blurted out, "Twenty-three stitches is quite a lot, isn't it?"

"That's it!" With a single raised eyebrow, I stood up,

straightened my shoulders, and drew myself up to my not-too-impressive height.

"But Samantha."

"No," I told Mom. "You could have talked about your work or your cats or your sisters or anything else, but you had to bring up the one thing, the *one* thing . . ."

"She needs to get out, I think," Mom said to Doreen, who stared at me with hostility.

"Let's go down to the boardwalk," Nikki said, catapulting up from her cushion. "It's a really pretty day out."

"It's always a pretty day out, here," I grumbled, but I let the Peri grab my hand and tug me in the direction of the back door.

My mother smiled approvingly. "That's right. You girls go out and get some fresh air. All this moping around isn't going to make Mr. Landemann heal any faster."

I thought of reprimanding her for bringing up That Topic again, but I knew inside it wouldn't do any good. There simply wasn't any escaping it. Just like, I realized when I walked into the tiny backyard, there wasn't any escaping the Storm Ravens. Big black birds surrounded the property. Some sat on the fences between the yards, their wings fluttering as they preened; others had plumped down on the utility wires up above. Dozens sat on the roofs not only of my mom's garage and house, but on those of the neighbors as well. Not all of these numbers had been in the cramped van the other day; reinforcements must have flow in, since.

"Venice looks like a freakin' Hitchcock set," I muttered.

Right as I spoke, two of the birds swooped down from the sky to the garage doorway, the black of their wide wings reflecting all the colors of the rainbow. Before they landed, in a crazy trick of the light, they seemed to extend and lengthen; their dark, glossy feathers disappeared, and two proud Peri, male and female, stood upright on the pavement.

"Hey!" I called out to them. I knew it was irrational, but I was angry, they were in front of me, and therefore I started to lash out. "Could you guys please not do that here, in broad daylight? You're in full view of my mother's kitchen window." I swept my hands at all the overlooking houses nearby. "Not to mention everyone else in the city. Your little metamorphosis thingie might be nothing to write home about among your own kind, but among us mere mortals, it gets a little attention. All right?"

The male stared at me with that impassive mien that so many of Cor's followers seemed to cultivate so effortlessly; his companion looked me up and down and said, "Sorry," though it was evident she wasn't.

I was about to lay into the little chickadee when, with surprising strength, Nikki hauled me alongside the garage and out the back gate. "You are way out of control."

"I am not!" Among yesterday's confusion, I'd discovered that Hugh had not only packed up my former life in Las Vegas and given it back to my mother, but that he'd also somehow gotten my old Mini Cooper out of impoundment and driven it back as well; it sat parked on one of the side streets near the house. Although my mother had allegedly gone green and forsworn driving, from the nearly full tank of gas and the cat hairs I'd found all over the black seats I had more than a vague suspicion that she'd been using it when she thought nobody was watching. I unlocked the doors with a push of my remote and waited until we were both inside before saying anything else. "Okay, I am, but I've got grounds."

"Uh-huh." Nikki strapped herself in. "You know, we could walk. It's only like, four blocks."

She was absolutely right, of course, but I'd already committed to the car and didn't want to look like a damned fool for changing my mind. "Your brother hates me, for one thing."

"Oh, he does not."

I pulled out into the narrow little side street and gingerly backed up, hoping I wouldn't get hit by a bigger, tougher car. "He hasn't spoken to me." Not since the morning before, at least. Nothing important, anyway. Things like, *The waiting room's too crowded, why don't you let Ginger take you and Nikki and your mother home?* didn't really count. He hadn't even looked at me as he'd sent us home. And what had I done, really? Had touching me made Cor violate some fairy code of ethics? Was being with me really so repulsive an act? Once he'd come to his senses and I wasn't there to sully his fine, Peri hands, was getting rid of me the only thing he could think of to do? I mean, if that were the case, then I really didn't have to defile the guy with my human touch. Honestly. I could do without it, I told myself as I maneuvered the car out onto Ocean Boulevard in the direction of the beach. Oh yeah. I could do without it, easily.

We didn't talk to each other for the next three blocks until we'd parked on the street in front of one of the few remaining independent drugstores in town, and stepped out into the brilliant midday sun. I slammed the door shut and, as if we'd actually been speaking aloud, continued the conversation. "The doctors said Landemann's wound was only superficial," I sniped. "Why does he have to spend every moment by the guy's bed?" *My* bed, I might add, which I'd ceded to the bodyguard when he'd been brought home all stitched up. "I know he's a bird and everything, but he doesn't have to be the real Florence Nightingale."

"My brother's relationship with Landemann is complicated." Nikki seemed to know where she was going; I tagged along behind her as she navigated the downtown area and strode in the boardwalk's direction.

My attention pricked up at that. "Cor said something

like that when we were . . ." I bit off that particular thought when Nikki turned her head to look at me. "Nothing."

"You know," she replied thoughtfully, stepping out to cross Pacific Avenue. I followed obediently, like a little girl behind her mother. "If you really want to keep your sex life with my brother a secret? You might not want to do it outdoors with a bunch of gossipy Storm Ravens overhead." I must have flushed, because she rolled her eyes. "Oh please, Sam. I am not unacquainted with the pleasures of the flesh." If she hadn't been wearing a pink Hello Kitty T-shirt and speaking with all the sophistication of a teenage girl who stayed up late every Wednesday night to vote repeatedly for the dreamiest *American Idol* contestant, I might not have let out a sharp laugh. "Fine," she said loftily. "In a few minutes, I'll prove it to you."

"What, you have a Paris Hilton sex tape out there?" She didn't answer, pretending to ignore me. "All right, fine. I'm sorry. You're an experienced woman of the world. Now, tell me what the deal is with Landemann and your brother."

"He honestly didn't tell you?" she asked. We were passing an enclosed cloister not far from the beach that, with its high exterior walls and spiky gates, looked more like a military compound than a private residence. Nikki's tone grew excited as she turned around and said, "Did you know Angelica Huston lives here? She's a famous movie star!"

"Yes, I know," I said, wondering if there was a Peri Ritalin equivalent I might give the girl to cure her ADHD. "Landemann?"

"Oh. He's from our sire," she said. Then, seeing I didn't understand, she added, "Our sire fathered him. With a human."

The news hit me like a sack of wet sand. "He's your

brother? Your little brother?" Impossible as it seemed, with Cor and Nikki's relatively youthful looks and the bodyguard's middle-aged spread, he was still hundreds of years younger than either. Nikki shook her head on that one. "But you have the same father. He's your half-brother, isn't he?"

She shrugged. "No. It's just not like that with us. If our sire had fathered a child with another of the Kin, we would call him *brother* without reservation, even if our dames were different."

"You make it sound like dog breeding," I marveled, slipping on my sunglasses.

"But when one of the Kin mates with one of your kind," Nikki continued, leading me onward, "there's no relationship between the offspring. And it kind of is like dog breeding. I mean, if your father arranged for your golden retriever to get pregnant, you'd feel about as much of a blood relationship with the puppies as we would with someone like Landemann. Oh my gosh, no offense!"

"None taken," I assured her, even though at heart, I was slightly vexed at the comparison. "Especially considering my father left my mother for some bitch." Some surfer dude hauling a board back to Pacific Avenue overheard the comment as we approached; he raised his eyebrows. Then he grinned at Nikki and exchanged a nod with her. "Do you know him?" I asked, curious at how they seemed to recognize each other.

"No." She gave him a final glance and shrugged. "I mean, he's one of the Kin, but I don't know him."

"How can you tell?" I looked over my shoulder at the kid, with his crazy, shaggy hair, board shorts, and enviable skinniness.

"You just can. I told you, when Kin leave Resht for this world, Venice is usually where they stay. The portal's here. That's why it's the epicenter of Peridom."

She smiled brightly at a middle-aged man passing by who wore a raincoat despite the good weather. He was a balding fellow with a red face and tiny eyes who appeared to be talking to himself. "I don't care," he said aloud, to some invisible companion. "No, I told you, I don't care. Stop telling me that! I told you, stop!"

I turned to watch him walk in the direction of town as he continued talking to himself as if it were the most natural thing in the world. "Is the crazy guy one of yours, too?"

"The crazy guy is a human talking on one of those thingies you have. Bluetooth."

When she tapped her ear, I instantly felt foolish. A trio of high-school-aged girls trotted by, laughing and giggling and nearly knocking into us. "Okay, they're mine," I said. I could tell because their shirts exposed ample quantities of midriff. "I can tell by the belly buttons. Unless they're painted on. Do you do that? Oh, good Lord, listen to me, I'm becoming paranoid. I'm going to end up barricaded in some garden shed in Encino babbling about pod people."

"I'll tell you who's who," promised Nikki. Before us lay the sand and the ocean, while Venice Beach's acres of tourist shops stretched to either side along Ocean Front Walk. When I squinted against the sun, I could see boys playing basketball in the concrete courts beneath the palm trees, and surfers and wading couples beyond. Growing up here had made this sight so commonplace that I'd taken it for granted. I'd been away long enough, though, to realize how lucky I'd been. How many thousands upon thousands of people had stood at this very same intersection and been awestruck enough to want to grab a piece of the California dream? Not Nikki, apparently. "Okay, I'm going to take you someplace, but you can't tell anyone," she said, suddenly coy. Once I'd promised, she beetled off to the north, waving at the proprietor of a cheesy T-shirt shop on the corner. "That's one," she confided.

I still couldn't figure out how she could tell, so I decided to return to our original topic. "So tell me. If you don't regard Landemann as a blood relation, then what's with your brother and the hovering nursemaid act?"

"Guilt, I guess." Nikki tossed back her brief answer like a hot potato she didn't want to be caught holding. Knowing that I wanted more of an answer, though, she sighed. "Sheesh, okay. Cor's going to k-i-l-l me for talking about this, but I'm going to say it and drop it. Okay?" She stopped in front of a circular rack of bikinis, fingered a couple, and then faced me, plainly uncomfortable. "Landemann is not the only child our sire fathered by a human."

A crowd had gathered around a quartet of young women putting on a jump-rope show on a cleared, flat stretch of the boardwalk. *Double Dutchess,* read the card they'd placed in front of a canister half-full with bills and coins. Two of the girls had short blond hair; the other two had long, curly tresses that bounced and shone in the sun as they all performed some impossibly complex choreography with their ropes. It was more like dancing than schoolyard jumping. "Nicolina! Hi!" called one of them, winking and waving as she did a quick handspring through the waving ropes.

"Kate Rock!" Nikki hailed her Peri friend with a wave before returning to our conversation. "There've been like, dozens, even before Cor and me. He's the only one I've known, though. And he's probably the last."

My curiosity couldn't help itself. "Probably?"

Nikki looked from side to side and lowered her voice. "Probably, because our sire's not in a position to do that anymore. It's because of Cor, and ever since, he's got this weird *thing* about Landemann. Okay?" She turned away. "I don't want to talk about it anymore," she added, as we passed the piano guy who sat on the boardwalk's grassier side.

Everybody knows the weird piano guy on Venice Beach. He's a dirty old coot with an enormously frizzy, long beard in braids who hunkers down in front of an old, out-of-tune upright, playing songs and abusing the masses. "Oh Christmas tree, oh Christmas tree," he sang. "Give me some damn money please. Thank you!" He nodded at two married tourists boasting University of Wisconsin shirts who tossed some coins into his jar, before launching into another charming ditty. "Chestnuts roasting on an open fire . . . Jack Frost nipping my damned nose. If you don't want me to cut the cheese, give me some money, you skanky hos. Thank you!" The last was to Nikki, who dropped a dollar bill into the jar and gave him a sunny smile.

I recognized that smile. "Don't tell me—!" I gasped, looking back at the (for lack of a better word) musician. He'd been crazy and profane since I'd been a kid.

Without warning, the piano guy broke into a lyrical tickling of the ivories that was totally at odds with his usual stubby-fingered banging. "I believe, if you do, that fairy tales can come true . . ." he crooned, Sinatra-style, before pounding out the inevitable conclusion: "So give me some damned money."

In awe, I followed Nikki down the sidewalk, dodging Rollerbladers and bicyclists and joggers with glistening muscles. "So where is this Resht place? Wait," I amended, so I wouldn't get the whole other-plane lecture. "*What* is this Resht place? I though Resht was a human city in the Middle East somewhere."

"There's a Resht in what you call Iran. It's where the Kin first stepped foot in your world. The portal's moved since, though. The real Resht is the largest of our remaining cities," Nikki explained. She seemed happier to be on a topic other than her brother. "And oh, my gosh, is it ever boooooooring. It's probably the most boring place I've ever been in. Which admittedly isn't many. That's why so many drop out and come here instead." She waved at a pair of bored-looking, teenaged oddities wearing layers of tights, kilts, ripped shirts, and sporting blue braids, piercings in their lips, and kohl around their eyes. I couldn't even tell what gender they were, though I was guessing the one with homemade pink fairy wings decorated with Christmas garland was a girl. "Like that," she whispered.

She and her brother had talked about dropouts before. "They drop out of what?"

"Out of the Kinlands," Nikki said. "I mean, for good." To emphasize how serious it was, she jerked her head back in the direction we'd come. "They stay here. For the rest of their lives. And after a while they get old and crazy, and die. I mean, everybody dies eventually, but, you know." She stopped and grabbed my arm. "Oh my gosh, there he is. Look. No, don't look."

I didn't know which direction I was supposed to be avoiding—down the walk where a few diehards were exercising in the blue-caged Muscle Beach enclosure, or at the curly-haired jogger who turned to smile at us, or at the little puppet theater playing to a group of delighted children on the sandy stretch nearby. Finally I followed the laser beams of Nikki's burning excitement into the storefront nearby, a dirty-looking sliver of retail space purporting to specialize in reggae and island music. Behind the counter, hair clumped into reddish white-boy dreads, was a gangly youth boasting so many tattoos that both his arms were covered in sleeves of ink; the skinny legs sticking out of his shorts and into his ratty Converses were gradually getting filled in as well. "Oh, Nikki," I groaned. "You don't have a crush on *that* guy, do you?"

"No!" She seemed offended that I'd ask such a ridiculous question. "But isn't he the cutest? His human-style name's Adam."

"Cor wouldn't want you getting involved with a dropout." I knew that boy's type. Hell, I dated that boy's type from the time I was old enough to don a training bra.

"He's not a dropout!" We both regarded the boy through the shop's window as he bopped around to the loud music. "He's just taking some time off before he finds his calling. A lot of us do that."

It sounded vaguely religious, the way she talked, but at the same time I couldn't shake the image of Eurail passes, backpacks, and smelly youth hostels. "Calling?"

"A calling's like a talent. It depends on the form you're able to shift into. Everyone has one. Well, Kin do, anyway," she added, with a quick look of apology. "I don't, not yet. They don't manifest until you're nearly grown up. So hopefully soon." I detected a note of wistfulness in the sigh that followed.

"So do all the Kin shift into birds?" I wanted to know.

"Oh, no! It's always animals, though. Mammals and fowl, and usually not the really big ones. I mean, I don't know of any Kin who can shift into like, giraffes. Or elephants." Nikki chewed her lip thoughtfully. "It does seem like there are a lot of birds, though. I think it runs in the family. Cor's talent is flying, of course. All the Storm Ravens have that calling, because it helps them get to trouble faster. But there are lots of others. Like, this girl I knew turned out to have a calling for assassination, and she could shift into a panther."

"Assassination. Fantastic," I said, remembering that the most my own high school friends turned out to have a talent for was emptying baskets of fries at the golden arches.

"Well, I mean, that's unusual. I had two friends who had a talent for filing."

I blinked. "Filing?"

"Filing really efficiently." She nodded. "They're hummingbirds, I hope I don't get that one. If I do, it'll mean I have to spend the rest of my life in the libraries of Resht, and of all the booooring places in Resht, that's the worst. Oh gosh." She flinched, then giggled into her hand. "He saw us."

"Listen," I told her, trying despite myself not to smile. "Why don't you go talk to your Adam friend? I'll just have a seat and wait. Okay?"

She looked over her shoulder at the Rasta-styled Peri and bit her lip. "You don't mind? I won't take too long." I shooed her away. "Thanks!" Within moments of flying into the shop, she was engaged in a lip-lock with the kid. I discreetly averted my eyes. Maybe she did know the pleasures of the flesh, after all.

I settled down on a bench partly in the shade of a palm tree. Despite the eclectic information I'd siphoned from Nikki, I was less confused now than I was before. Small wonder Cor didn't want to talk to me, when I'd basically accused him of treating his brother no better than a dog. And they were brothers, in my eyes, whether the Peri saw it that way or not; I was touched that Cor would be so protective of both his siblings, no matter how close the blood relation. It was sweet, really. I didn't know what Cor could have done to his father to stop his womanizing, but—oh, wait. Ginger had accused him of being like his father when she'd found us together in that hotel room, hadn't she? Worse, since we'd actually come within inches of doing the deed, did that make her right?

Somehow I thought I'd rather endure a hundred root canals than see Ginger proved right.

From the little marionette stage nearby, the puppeteers started making a commotion. "Do you believe in fairies?" said a voice from behind the stage, while below a wooden figure danced on the strings. "Say quick that you believe! If you believe, clap your hands!"

Several mothers and fathers who were watching the performance with their kiddies began applauding, hoping to get the kids clapping along with them. Harder and harder they pounded their hands together, trying to bring Tinker Bell back to life. One little girl looked especially teary at the thought the little fairy might die. When the puppet rose back to life, though, slowly, weakly, and then finally flying around the stage with vigor, she burst into smiles.

I rolled my eyes and looked to the heavens. "You have got to be kidding me," I told them. "It's a freakin' Peri propaganda factory out here." No wonder the real estate prices were skyrocketing in Venice, with all the fairies moving in and gentrifying the place.

Chapter Twelve

The one lamp I'd managed to find and plug in cast a spooky glow across the garage's living quarters. Shadows from the piles of boxes fell ominously across my lap, where I sat on the sofa; if I wanted to see anything, I had to hold it up and peer at it from below. That was fine. At least I was alone, for a change. I'd shooed away the Storm Ravens an hour before. Storm Vultures, it felt like. More and more had invaded my living space throughout the afternoon and evening—from what I could tell, for lack of anywhere better to go. Cor wasn't moving from Landemann's side, and Ginger surely hadn't been giving Cor much breathing room since the attack. All night, a score of the Ravens had huddled in the living room and talked among themselves in small clumps while I vainly looked through boxes and tried to figure out my ex's packing system.

Oh, a couple had been helpful, jumping up to help when I needed to get down one of the higher, heavier cartons, or giving me a hand with cleanup when I popped open a sealed box that exploded in a shower of foam popcorn. I can't say they were unfriendly, but the atmosphere hadn't been chummy enough to compel us to hold hands and sing "Kumbaya," either. And that had probably been because of Ginger, who stood outside the bedroom for most of the evening with a scowl on her face, setting the tone for the rest of the flock. But even she hadn't put up a fuss when I'd asked everyone to leave so I could get some rest. My garage, after all. I hadn't intended to turn it into some kind of Motel 6 for the wee folk. No, wait. Those were leprechauns, weren't they? No matter. The Kin could roost outside on the telephone wires if they wanted, but I had to have a bed to sleep in.

Not that I'd intended to fall asleep right away. As soon as they'd gone, I'd attacked the boxes with vigor. It was good to find more of my old clothes, and nice to unearth things like old DVDs I'd forgotten, as well as the kitchenware I'd accumulated when I hadn't been eating my dinners in fast food restaurants or ordering Thai takeaway. Yet what I'd really been looking for lay, quite naturally, in the bottom box at the very back of the pile, labeled MISC. STUFF, just like most of the boxes I'd been through that evening. My papers.

I'd just flipped through my passport with relief, checking to see if the expiration date had passed, when I heard the door open above me. Though I heard footsteps on the carpeted stairs, I didn't look up. I knew who it was. I simply didn't know if I could look at him, right then. Not yet.

He padded forward and stood a few feet away. I continued to look through the box, tossing aside a rubber-banded packet of newspaper articles my mother had thought I might find interesting, and discovering underneath a whole parcel of unopened mail that must have arrived after my disappearance. Some of them looked like bills, too. Ooops. He continued to loom there, silent, while I continued to pretend to ignore him. Finally I couldn't take it any longer. "I think I'm probably on Nevada Power's shit list," I said, brandishing a few of the mails I'd received. "I've heard a rumor they bring out the big goons for punks like me who don't pay their bills, too."

Still he didn't say anything. I looked up, and found him wearing nothing but a pair of dark plaid flannel pajama bottoms. It was damned *unfair* of him to stand there in that careless posture, shirtless and lean and so pleasing to the eyes, when I was trying so very hard to steel myself against him.

"How's Landemann?"

"His fever's broken."

"Oh, good! Of course, some of these overdue notices were probably from even before I got abducted," I told him, waving around another handful of unopened bills. "I've never been the kind of person who really remembered to pay things on time. Shocking, huh?"

"Is that really what you want to say to me?" Cor asked, his voice quiet.

"No." There was a lot I wanted to express, but I didn't know where to begin. My heart ached from the heaviness of it all, but everything I'd learned that afternoon and the day before seemed so tightly wound that I didn't even know how to unspool the first thought. "I'm just making noise." Noise that ceased the moment I stopped moving my lips, since he still didn't contribute. What did he want from me? An apology? Fine. I'd apologize. I was a big girl. It wouldn't kill me. "You know, it was kind of stupid of me to say the things I said about Landemann. Especially because . . . well, Nikki told me about him."

"Did she?" Cor's arms crossed over his chest, deepening the cleft between the muscles there.

From the expression on his face, I knew he was wondering exactly what. I picked my words carefully, so I wouldn't offend. "She told me that Landemann's the offspring of your sire, so you feel some, um, personal responsibility for him. Which is cool. I get it." Still he looked at me. How far was I going to have to grovel? Again, I didn't care. Everything I had in the world was right there in that room, packed into boxes I couldn't comprehend. An apology was no extra burden. "So if I upset you by the things I said . . ."

"Samantha Dorringer, you are an idiot," was his unexpected response. I blinked and looked up, a little bit stung, yet there was no malice on his face. "No, seriously. Why in the world are you wasting your breath trying to make amends to me when I'm the one who acted like a damn fool? Can I . . . ?" He gestured to the sofa, which I was hogging.

I moved over and waved to the cleared area. Instead of sitting on it, though, he swung his feet onto the cushion I'd warmed while he perched on the sofa's arm, facing me. "This is what amazes me about your kind. You feel guilty about anything that's not your fault. Bad things fall from the sky and kill people, and you beat your breasts and wonder what you could have done to prevent it. People die and get hurt when you're not there, and you lament to the heavens your faults. People desert you, and you spend the rest of your lives not pointing the finger at them for leaving, but blaming yourselves."

I stiffened, wondering where this could possibly be going.

"You didn't do anything wrong," he concluded. "Stop the self-condemnation."

"Oh, like you're one to talk," I retorted, still stinging. I'd never, ever blamed myself for my father abandoning us. That was his own shame to bear every night for the rest of his life. "Aren't you doing . . . what's the word?

Aren't you expiating for what you did to your sire? Crap. I'm sorry."

I hadn't meant to say those words, exactly, but in my vexation they'd come popping out. His face was a study, right then. I honestly didn't know whether he was going to curl up and mourn, or stand up and walk away. He did neither. After a moment of holding his head between his hands, he nodded. "Nikki has an awfully big mouth."

"She didn't tell me details," I assured him, wanting to apologize more, but wary of it after his big speech of a moment before. "And I wasn't supposed to say anything, so don't take it out on her." I'd be blabbing about her secret boyfriend next, like some kind of gossipy eighth-grader.

For a very long time, Cor looked at me, his elbows resting on his upright knees. In the dim light, his eyes were black and shiny as obsidian; the edges of his tattoos seemed to be creeping up and over his shoulders as he tugged at his fingers. "I never really understood our sire's desire for women of your kind," he said at last. His words came slowly at first, like the creaking of a trunk lid pried open from its rust. "It's not dishonorable among Kin, but it's not . . . hmmm. If you had two families of your kind joined together while the children were young—a woman with several children of her own marrying a man with . . ."

"Three boys of his own?"

He nodded without recognition. Apparently *The Brady Bunch* didn't play in Resht. "Yes, like that. And say all the children grow up side by side for many years with the same affection as brothers and sisters of the blood. Only two of them decide they want more." I nodded, being slightly revolted by the notion of the Bradys locking the closet door for a quick game of Seven Minutes of Heaven. "That's how we regard it, after those of my kind have grown up in the same household as those of yours." His hands spread wide, indicating that he wasn't talking about my mother's house on the Venice canals, but something much grander. "Not wrong, but . . ."

"Squicky."

He shrugged, not recognizing the word. "It's simply not encouraged, given our differences. We've watched you evolve over the millennia. Many of my race wouldn't admit it, but we've evolved alongside you. So most Kin wouldn't even think of mating with humans—the option wouldn't occur to them. That's the point I wanted to make."

"But it happens? I mean, obviously it happens, if children are being born. I doubt Landemann's the first and only." When he nodded, reluctantly agreeing with me, I suddenly felt defensive. Vulnerable, almost, especially when I remembered what had passed between the two of us on the dock, during the storm. I hadn't liked that word he'd used a moment before. Mating. It sounded so clinical. "So, this urge some of you have to be with us, what is it?" I wanted to know. "Just a physical hunger? Some kind of kinky Peri sexual release?"

"For my father, yes, it was," he said, his words blunt. I think he could tell I was beginning to sound accusatory, a tone I was already regretting. "Maybe for others like him, who are careless and hurtful enough to take their pleasure where they will and damn the consequences." His harsh tone softened as he looked away. I barely heard the conclusion to his thoughts. "But it's not mere biology for all. Some Kin have fallen in love with humans, over the centuries. Deeply in love. It has happened."

I was glad to hear him say so, though I knew the words that followed didn't sound it. "And you?" I hated the veiled hostility in my voice. I hadn't intended to go to this place, I honestly hadn't. I sounded like a child on the verge of a tantrum, needing reassurance.

"I am not my father, Samantha." He sighed. "Over the years when my father would leave his station and spend years in the world, dallying with one of the human women who had caught his fancy, my family and I would turn our heads and pretend not to notice, knowing that sooner or later, her spark would burn out and he'd return. Until the next time, anyway."

I swallowed, not knowing what to say. It wasn't the first time I'd had the longevity of the Peri thrown in my face. What wouldn't half of Hollywood give to learn the secret of their eternal youth? I could see it now—vast spas and Scientology Centers in the city of Resht, where the studios would store their stars between shoots, then trot them out again looking scarcely a day older, years later. L.A. might be deserted, in fact, if the secret got out.

Suddenly feeling very frail, I directed my attention back to Cor. "The primary purpose of the Storm Ravens is to keep the courts of the Kin free of corruption. We investigate irregularities and purge our lands of those who would abuse the trust given them. A few decades ago, one of the investigations I'd undertaken showed that my sire had not only been siphoning royal money to provide for the human woman he was seeing but also that when he thought he might be found out, he created a construct for her." My eyebrows raised at that. "Yes, he had told her too much, and she was not discreet. He intended to put her in there indefinitely, along with the child she'd had by him, to cover his misdeeds. By the Queen's order, I escorted him to the construct instead." His voice grew low. "He stays there to this day, unaware of who or what he is. And when the woman would have abandoned their child, I took him."

"You mean Landemann," I whispered. "I'm sorry."

Then, just to make things crystal clear, I said, "That's not an apologetic *I'm sorry*. That's kind of a *Wow, it's a shame you had to do that to your own sire,* kind of *I'm sorry*. Mixed in with some *Thank you for telling me that story, I'm sorry it wasn't under better circumstances*."

He smiled a little at my pathetic attempt at humor. "As I said, I never understood what my father saw in human women. Until now. It feels like . . ." Again, he grappled for the words, rubbing his fingers together until he caught them. "It's like throwing the thinnest piece of paper imaginable into flames. It quickly turns to ash, but while it leaps in the draft, how beautifully it dances and how brightly it burns! I see that in you, Samantha. There's fire in you. You blaze. It's impossible to ignore. You want to *do* things, to make things happen." Cor shook his head. "So few of our kind are like that. We don't change. We stagnate. That's why so many of us leave the Kinlands and live among you."

"I can't make things happen like you," I said, a lump in my throat. He seemed so sincere. "I'm only human. I can't change into a bird and fly, or make thunderstorms with my wings. I can't change into whatever shape it is that becomes a deadly Peri assassin. Or even makes me good at filing. I'm just one of a hundred bazillion humans, powerless. A grain of sand."

"You underestimate what grains of sand can do," he told me. "Under pressure, they can shore up and become solid stone. The foundation for great buildings." Without warning, he knelt down on the sofa and laid one of his hands across my cheek. It was so warm. Warm as the flames he'd been describing. His lips drew closer to mine. "Thank you for burning so brightly," he murmured, as he leaned in for a kiss.

"I . . . I . . . I can't." Like the blazing Kleenex I apparently was, I squirmed out of Cor's much-too-comfortable embrace and danced my way over to the sofa's far corner.

"I really can't. We can't." I'd surprised him. He honestly had thought we'd simply pick up where we'd left off the night before. "It's just not right."

"Why not?" I could tell through the fabric of his pajama bottoms that he'd become half-aroused by our near-kiss, and that the excitement was dwindling rapidly. I averted my eyes, feeling self-conscious about looking. "Yesterday morning . . ."

"You said it yourself, Corydonais," I said, grabbing the box of papers and putting it firmly in my lap, where it would be squarely in the way of any more temptation on either of our parts. "I'm ash. Or I will be soon enough, while you'll go on and on and on long after I'm gone, until the day comes that you'll remember the other night and smile and then think to yourself, What was her name again?" The hurt I felt saying these things was physical; it made my lungs and heart ache. Here I'd just received the highest compliment I'd ever received from anyone, Peri or human, and I was having to spurn it, though every impulse told me not to. Typical me, though, to think of falling for someone utterly unattainable.

"I wouldn't," he said.

"Maybe you wouldn't. But Cor, I couldn't face it," I said, feeling both beaten down and deflated. "What if you did like me enough to stay with me for a few years? Every morning I'd be staring at myself in the mirror. I'd be looking for the wrinkles on my face I knew would never arrive on yours, looking at the gray hairs and the spots and the pull of time and gravity. Every morning I'd be wondering if that would be the day you'd decide that my spark had burned out, and that I'd come home to find you gone. I don't want to be abandoned."

He reared back, astonished. "Abandoned! Samantha!"

I recognized the rebuke for what it was. "I know, I'm not being fair. You're a nice guy. A great guy." I'd splayed a hand across my face while I'd talked, and now I peered at him between my fingers. He was a hell of a handsome guy, too, and I was an utter fool to say the things I was saying. But what else could I do? I had to protect myself. "I don't want to be my mother, Cor."

He reached up and ran his hand through his hair, brushing the long strands from his face. "What in the world does your mother have to do with us?"

"You don't know what she went through after my dad abandoned her. What *we* went through. You don't know how it is, to come home from school one day and just see vacancies everywhere. Empty hangers in the closet where he kept his clothes. Quiet in the evenings, instead of the sound of his music or his TV programs. Nothing on top of his dresser. Mom had to invent an entirely new life for herself after that to fill in the gaps, just so neither of us would be bothered by what was missing. But we were bothered, Cor. The thought of you leaving me . . ."

He looked pained at my portrait of the future. "I wouldn't do that."

"You'd have to," I said, jutting out my jaw to keep the tears from coming. I couldn't even look at him, mere inches away from me. When he tried to protest, I cut him off. "Don't be naive. You're not Nikki. You know that one day, you'd have to. We both know it. Your life span is so much longer than mine. You're going to be young-looking for centuries more! It's just a bitch that men age so damned well, even when they're Kin," I said, trying to make a joke so that I wouldn't erupt into tears.

He didn't find it particularly funny, either. In fact, Cor stared at me, stunned, as if it really was the first time he'd thought about these things. For all I knew, maybe it was. "We could figure out something," he assured me. "Listen, Sam. I could take you to Resht. Then your life span . . ."

I laughed helplessly. "Take me to a place where I

could stagnate? You said it yourself, Cor. You're attracted to me because I burn so brightly, and going there would snuff out my flame. Don't ask me to content myself with a life that never, ever changes. You might as well embalm me and put me back in Riviera Lane."

Cor still was looking for solutions. "Or I could make a permanent life out here . . ."

"And become a dropout?" I shook my head. "No. You're intended for more important things. Neither one of us should have to give up what makes us special. Don't you understand?" He shook his head, slowly, as if it were too heavy to move. "If we were to start something, all I could be assured of was little moments between us, here and there. They'd feel good, but they'd still be nothing more than hundreds of tiny moments. And Cor, I want a lifetime together. A real lifetime. So. Let's just not travel down that road, okay? I'm happy to be your friend. I'm happy to work with you to find Marshall and his mother. Or dame, if you prefer. You'll get your justice, I'll have my revenge. After that, though, we cut it clean, and go our separate ways. Okay?" It wasn't okay. I certainly didn't feel okay, anyway. The lump growing in my throat had reached the general proportions of Rhode Island, from the feel of it, and every breath I drew felt like poison in my chest. From the quick look I made in Cor's direction, he didn't seem all that happy, either. "That's just the way it has to be," I concluded.

"I thought—" He clenched his mouth shut, and turned his head. "I'm not—" Finally, after much effort, he sighed and sat back in the opposite corner. "Is that really what you want?"

No, it wasn't. Not at all. I kept my words clipped and precise so that I wouldn't let emotion overwhelm me. "That's what I think is best for the both of us. And yes, it is what I . . . ah-ha!" Down at the box's bottom, under a crapload of random pens and take-out menus, I found what I'd been looking for. My brown leather notebook. I pulled it out, discarded the box, and immediately began thumbing through the pages.

"A diary?" Superior race or whatnot, those Peri sure knew how to put on a good sulky face.

"My case notebook," I explained, tapping on the cover. "I thought it was in the car, but Hugh must have cleaned out my glove compartment."

"Oh, Hugh did, did he?"

Was Cor jealous? Of a guy he hadn't even met and that I hadn't seen for months and years, even? If so, he was being ridiculous, and I didn't have time for it. "Anyway," I said with meaning, "it has all my field notes from my job."

"I don't understand." Though he was still slightly piqued, I could tell he was focusing more on what I was saying, than on what I'd said a few moments before. "What did you do?"

"Insurance investigator. I told you. It wasn't all that interesting for the most part." I stopped at some of the earlier pages on which I'd scribbled small memoranda that would eventually make it into my final reports. "People would claim more injuries for themselves on an accident filing than they'd really had, so I'd go out and talk to the neighbors, keep an eye on them for a week or so, to see if they really did have whiplash or whether they were just wearing a brace and wincing a lot. Sometimes it was fun. Once, I had one of the Las Vegas robber barons claim some stolen artwork—Rembrandt etchings." I pointed to the relevant page. Talking about work made me feel more grounded, which is exactly what I needed after having Cor pull the world out from under my feet. "One expense-account trip to Switzerland, and I found it hanging on the wall of an apartment that only he and his mistress knew about."

"Fascinating. So you'd rather go back into the business than be with me?"

"Listen, Mr. Snotty Pants," I retorted. "Get over the blue balls and work with me here. This is relevant. Because I'm certain . . ." The last quarter of the replaceable notebook inside the folder was empty, but I stopped flipping on the last page. "Oliver. Harland Oliver." That got his attention. "That's the name of the man I was investigating the day I was abducted. Life insurance claim."

"Oliver, as in Lily Oliver?" Cor leaned over to look at the notebook, scribbled in my incomprehensible notation. "Is that Chinese?"

"Shut up." I snatched the book away. "I had an address in Summerlin. I don't think I checked it out. Does that jibe with your information?"

He shrugged. "I don't have any information. Just a name." Obviously I didn't understand, because he explained. "Much of the energy required for a construct involves weaving the names of the people involved into its fabric. The pair that abducted you obviously didn't know much about you, because the construct was woven around the name of Lily Oliver. Riviera Lane was intended for her, not you."

"For her!" I gargled the words.

"It was probably meant to be comforting for her. A happy place. Obviously she's someone important to them."

"Obviously," I echoed. A happy place for her, maybe. Hell for me. Part of me was slightly miffed that they hadn't even bothered to find out to make my own construct for me. Sheesh.

"Fine. We head for Summerlin tomorrow," said Cor, rising from the sofa. That was more like it, I thought to myself. Action, instead of moping. "I'll notify Ginger."

Wait, that wasn't more like it at all! "Wha'?" I mumbled. "Why her?"

"She and I are spearheading this inquiry," he said, as if it were obvious. "Of course she'll be coming. Don't worry. You'll still be involved." Was it my imagination, or did he sound slightly condescending? It was a tough call, honestly. He seemed genuine, but why did I keep having a mental picture of the two of them consulting only each other and leading the questioning while I ended up sitting in the back of the Storm Ravens' van, just me and a Sudoku puzzle? "I know you want to see what happens."

Darned right I did. I allowed him to squeeze my shoulder when he left, quietly exiting out the door into my mother's backyard. Oh, I was sure that Ginger would be glad to hear the news that someone else had done all the spadework for them to get their little Raveny investigation started again. The someone else being me, specifically. I was soooo glad that I, with my mayfly-like lifespan, could have spent so much of it doing *her* some good.

Well, screw that. No, wait, I couldn't just go haring off on my own. This whole Oliver thing was deeply mired somehow in the Kinlands, and I needed Cor to explain the parts of their culture or customs that I didn't understand. If Harland Oliver had been faking his illness to get workman's comp, I could probably go it on my own. But this was much more complex. Without Cor, I was hopeless.

Or was I? I smiled to myself as I thought up an alternate plan. Cor would be livid, but I didn't mind a little righteous fury on his part so long as I could make the point that I was sufficient without him. It hadn't been him from whom those bastards had stolen. It had been three precious years of *my* short existence.

Cor came back into the room from outside. "Leave at ten tomorrow?" he asked, closing the door.

"Oh, sure," I said, yawning. I made a show of it, as I tucked the notebook beneath the pillow on the sofa. "I guess I'd better get to bed, then."

Cor nodded, hands in his pockets, drawing the flannel fabric around his waist low onto his hips. He didn't look as if he knew whether to kiss me goodnight, or simply retire without pushing it. At long last, he chose the latter. "I guess that's that, then," he said, shuffling to the stairs. "Unless you've changed your mind about . . ."

"Mmmmmm." I stretched and pretended to smile. " 'Night."

He sighed. " 'Night." Halfway up, he turned. "Hey, Sam," he said. "Good work. So you know."

I flipped out the light as he closed the upper bedroom door behind him. Yes, I knew. My work. My time. My life.

Chapter Thirteen

All during our little secret jaunt back to Las Vegas, Nikki kept up a running travelogue sites. By eight in the morning, I was made cognizant of the fact that the city of San Bernardino was established by the Latter-Day Saints, that it was host to the National Orange Festival every September, and that the first McDonald's restaurant had been opened by the McDonald brothers there in 1948. An hour or so later, we learned that Barstow's original name was Camp Sugarloaf and that it had been mentioned in a famous song called "Route 666." (Me: "I think it's 'Route 66,' Nik." Her: "Are you sure? Because I'm pretty sure it's about the devil.")

I was already regretting sneaking out of my mom's house so early in the morning. By three hours into the journey I was craving talk—any kind of chatter, even the most boring—to keep my eyelids from closing along some of the most boring stretches of road the United States Department of Transportation had ever committed to concrete. Luckily, Nikki came through. "The Mojave Nature Preserve's amazing natural features include the Kelso eolian sand dunes, the Joshua Tree forests, and fascinating volcanic features like the Cinder Cone lava beds and the Hole-in-the-Wall," she announced from the backseat.

Beside her, his head dozing on her shoulder, Adam snickered. "Hole in the wall." Nikki hit him. Good thing, because I would have if she hadn't. "Sorry, babe," he mumbled. "It's just funny, that's all. Hole in the wall. Hole? In the wall?" In my rearview mirror, I saw him pinch her somewhere in the midsection. Though she swatted him again, she giggled and let him move his head down to her chest, where he made soft little yipping noises, like a Chihuahua.

Fantastic. I'd managed to go on a Magical Mystery Tour with two teenagers, one of whom appeared to be straight out of the cast of *Dazed and Confused,* and the other a contemporary of Marie Antoinette and just as ditzy. They'd come as a package deal, however; even a promise of Egg McMuffins and as many boxes of Krispy Kremes as she cared to take with us couldn't entice Nikki when she'd planned to sneak away from the Landemann watch and spend the day with her secret boyfriend. Recasting the excursion as a 100 percent Genuine Classic American Spontaneous Road Trip Complete with Unlimited Snacks from Quaint Roadside Stands that would simultaneously let her spend quality time with the tattooed wonder and get her out from under the scrutiny of her brother for most of the day, though? Worked like a charm. Part of me felt a twinge of guilt at involving the girl in the very same affair that had gotten me abducted the first time around, but my instincts told me having one of the Kin around might be necessary. Plus, she'd proven she could take care of herself. She was a bit like me, that way. I suspected the trait was one of the reasons I liked her so much.

"Dummy," she murmured happily into those white-boy dreads that hadn't been washed in God only knew how long. Involuntarily, I wiped my mouth.

"You're the dummy," he said, pinching her nipple through her shirt.

She slapped his hand. "You're the dummy!"

Like I said. I was sleepy enough that I was desperate for noise.

The address in my notebook that I'd scrawled down several years ago was for an apartment building in the Hills North division of Summerlin—and a very nice apartment building, at that, next to a park with a spectacular view of the mountains. I mean, I'd dreamed about apartment buildings like this, with their tennis courts and swimming pools and landscaping that didn't consist of a solitary cactus in a pot outside the manager's office, when not so very long ago I'd been living in Vegas' rank armpit. When I'd arranged Nikki and myself decorously outside the designated apartment number, however, I discovered that Harland Oliver not only no longer lived at the address, but apparently hadn't lived there three years ago when I'd been conducting the investigation.

The pretty apartment manager verified the information after she took a thankfully quick look at my no-longer-valid investigator's license; she'd been employed by the leasing company for less than a year, had never heard of an Oliver living in the complex, and didn't seem all that inclined to help me find the guy. "I'm sorry," she said, adjusting the lapels of her company-issued blazer, and looking at her gold watch. "We're awfully busy today."

"I'm checking out a suspicious insurance claim," I explained. "So I was thinking that maybe, just maybe, you could see your way to giving me the name of the person who occupied the apartment three years ago? And a forwarding address if you have one." When the woman furrowed her pretty little brow and looked like she might object, I smoothly added, "I know you'd hate to get the police involved."

"Oh, no," she agreed, big brown eyes wide open. "Not the police."

Five minutes later, Nikki and I stepped out into the high-temperature kiln that is the typical Las Vegas morning, me bearing a slip of paper scribbled with a new address. "Do you have a persuasive calling or something?" she asked. "Because that woman did everything you said."

I laughed. "No. Persuasive it might be, but it's not one of your callings. It's psychological," I told her, tapping a finger to my temple as we walked across the parking lot. "Every average law-abiding person has a secret fear of the police. Law enforcement's the grown-up equivalent of the old bogeymen. Mention them casually, and most people will do anything to keep them away."

"Oh," she said. I could tell she was storing away this nugget in her head for future reference, somewhere among the data about the Californian wild boar and the greater imports and exports of Barstow. "So what now?"

Adam was asleep when we returned. His jaw hung slackly on his Marley T-shirt, and the gaping cavern of his mouth emitted a distinct snoring noise. I leaned in and picked up my notebook from the passenger seat where I'd left it. Uncapping my pen, I consulted the slip the agent had given me, and copied down the name and address. "We are going to visit a Ms. Chassidy Smart in southeast Las Vegas," I announced. "Maybe she'll know something about our mysterious Mr. Oliver."

I really could have done with less mystery, personally. I wasn't working with a full toolbox, here. In my old job, I would have gone out on an investigation with a fairly thick claim file that contained as much background on the claimant as we knew, a laptop, a cell phone, and my digital camera. I'd even had a pair of night-vision goggles for a couple of cases. I might not have been James Bond, but at least I'd sometimes felt like a geeked-up Nancy Drew. Now all I had were my instincts and my personal notebook, which didn't have much at all in the way of clues about what the case had been. *Possible fraudulent life insurance claim, C.O.*, was all it said after Oliver's name. I just wish I'd had more of a recollection on how far I'd gotten with this particular case before Marshall and his mother or dame or whatever had put the smack-down on my memory. I didn't know who had died, or who had attempted to make an illegal claim. The case was not only cold by this point, but developing icicles.

I'd work with what I could, however. What choice did I have? Not much, that was for certain.

Nikki and Adam both snored in the backseat while I navigated through the vicious midday traffic. They slept through our drive from Summerlin into the area east of McCarran International, and the rapid decline in economic status between the two. The neighborhood off Paradise Road was anything but utopian; the commercial strip was a land of by-the-hour hotels, dive bars, discount cigarette shops, and nail salons. Pornographic litter spilled onto the streets from newspaper boxes stuffed full of the full-color escort ads; they had been trampled over and over again nearly into pulp. The residential street that was my destination wasn't much better, being little more than a slab of concrete onto which had been plopped down a number of old cinder-block motels converted into furnished monthly rental units. This was the kind of place I'd used to come with my pepper spray tucked in one hand, half-wishing I had a gun.

The kids were still snoozing when I parked the car in front of the La Bel Age Residence Court between a vintage rusted Duster with a FOR SALE sign on the sheet of plastic sheeting where the back window used to be, on one side, and a pickup truck covered with stickers of both Calvin and Hobbes urinating, on the other. Given that the neighborhood looked like a *CSI* crack den set, I thought it wise not to roll the windows down more than a couple of inches, and hope that the Society for Prevention of Cruelty to the Peri didn't catch up with me when I left them alone in the heat. Not that I really understood how they could sleep, anyway; the roar of planes swooping overhead every three or four minutes was so deafening that it would have woken the dead.

"Yeah?" The woman who answered my knock in the half-basement apartment peered around the door with suspicion in her eyes. Though I guessed she was only in her late thirties or early forties, she easily looked twenty years older. I was surprised, frankly, that she could get her hair through the opening. It was enormous. Blond and frizzy, curled in springy strands that resembled the filler in stuffed animals more than anything that naturally occurred in nature, it had been dyed to the color of Dijon mustard and tied up into something that resembled a sheaf of wheat. Or a bundle of asparagus, take your pick.

I already had my expired insurance credentials out and in the air. "Hi there," I said. "Chassidy Smart? I'd like to ask a couple of questions."

"Aw, shit," she replied, once she'd scanned the card in my hand. "I don't have time for this."

"Ma'am. Please."

The woman heaved her shoulders and threw back the door. "Look. I just got back from work and it was a bitch of a day and I don't *need* to spend my damned *time* talking to you people again. I thought this was over with." Work, I was guessing from her outfit of flesh-colored tights and tuxedo-styled bodysuit, had to be as a cocktail waitress in one of the sleazier casino bars aimed at the locals. Or perhaps the hard-of-seeing.

She didn't close the door on me, though. That meant something, and I didn't mind using it to my advantage. "Only a few more questions, Ms. Smart, and we'll be out of your, um, hair. Our records show that you are a former resident of Summerlin, at . . ."

"I don't give a good hard crap in a bucket about your records." From behind the door, she produced a lit cigarette, from which she took a long, slow drag. From the tobacco habit I'd attempted to cultivate in my teens, I recognized it as a Virginia Slims. "Why should I? If you'da given me the money I was supposed to get when I asked for it, *then* I might be interested in talking. I don't have to give you jack shit." She could have slammed the door on my face at this point, but she kept talking. "Yeah I used to live in Summerlin and if you scumbags had given me that damn check I'd still be there instead of this dump."

Her insurers had turned the case down after my disappearance, then. That was more than I knew before. She'd told me the reason for her downward mobility—but what I didn't quite get was her motive for sharing. "We periodically review our investigation files when we run across cases in which we still have unresolved issues," I said, trying to sound only marginally interested. When she stared at me, I dumbed it down a little. "Sometimes we still have questions."

"Are these questions gonna give me the money you shoulda given me in the first place?"

I shrugged and smiled. I wasn't dumb enough to make promises. All I wanted to do was give her enough hope to spill. "Maybe you could invite me in and we could talk about it."

She sucked long and hard on the cigarette and stared at me through mascara-caked eyes. "I don't think so."

"Tell me about Lily Oliver," I suggested quickly, before she closed the door.

"Lily!" she sounded surprised. "What's she got to do with it?"

Bluffing in poker is one thing. At least in poker you know what you don't have. I was betting blindfolded, here. "Could you tell me your relationship to Lily Oliver, Ms. Smart?"

"Relationship!" Her mouth puckered in distaste. "I don't like kids. She's Harland's get. I guess I would've been her mama, if . . ." Suddenly she grew guarded. "I don't like kids," she repeated.

I tried to make a sympathetic expression. I liked children, myself. I wanted to have some, someday, if I could ever get another male of my own species to look my way. Whenever I ran up against one of these unapologetic kid-haters, I started to grind my teeth a little. "How old is the girl now?"

"Now?" She shrugged. "I ain't seen her in two, three years, since Harland bit it. I don't know. Seven, probably." Chassidy dropped the cigarette onto the stoop, mere inches from my feet, and stubbed it out with her bedroom slipper. Then, just in case I hadn't picked up on what she really thought of me, she blew the last lungful of smoke into my face. "What's in this shit for me?" When I raised my eyebrows, she elaborated. "What am I gonna get out of these 'questions' of yours? Because I know my rights. I don't got to say nothing."

"Maybe your answers will keep you out of jail," I heard someone say behind me. Nikki had left the Mini; she stood behind me with her arms crossed, trying to look stern in the pastel yellow tank top and running shorts she'd borrowed from my wardrobe. Adam, I noticed, stood a dozen yards away, puffing a cigarette of his own. At least Nikki hadn't tried to pass him off as the cops. The private look she shot at me when I gaped at her was knowing. She was trying to pull the same stunt I'd used on the rental agent in Summerlin.

Damn it! There was a reason I'd always worked by myself in the past! I held my breath. To me, Chassidy looked like a cornered wild animal trying to decide whether to run, or fight. Finally, she snarled, "I know my rights. You don't get to accuse me of stuff I ain't got no part of. What Harland done is Harland's own business. I told that to you and the police back when I was in Summerlin. I told you I didn't know nothing about how he faked his accident."

Her voice was so high-pitched and shrill that I knew she was going to try to shut us out of her apartment. And what could we do then other than pound on the door and beg? We had no authority. One call to the police about my out-of-date investigator's license and I'd find myself sharing a small cell with a mullet-wearing bulldog named Butch. "About that accident," I said, trying to invade the door so that she couldn't slam it easily.

"You ain't even from that insurance company at all, are you?" With unexpected energy, she snatched my identification from my hand, looked at it, and threw it on the ground. When I dropped down to retrieve it, she took the opportunity to bark out, "You get out of here before I call the police! Go on, get!"

"I wouldn't do that, Ms. Smart." Before Chassidy had a chance to maneuver her considerable hair back into the apartment and completely slam the door, Nikki stepped forward and spoke. Despite the fact that she looked like a high school girl heading out for track and field practice, she spoke with a gravity and authority I'd never heard from her before. "We are in a position to make your life considerably more comfortable." The door stopped swinging just as the edge hit the frame; it bounced back enough that we could see Chassidy's eyes, black and glittering, in the darkness beyond. "In fact." Nikki dug into her pocket and pulled out, much to my surprise, a small wad of bills. Carefully and deliberately, she counted out five of them, all hundreds. "I believe this may change your mind, hoochie mama." I wanted to groan. Of all the times to pull out that phrase!

Chassidy didn't seem to notice, though. "That's nothing." She opened the door a little more and looked through, sideways. "I can get five grand in one night's tips if I wanted." Nikki shrugged, began to stuff the bills back in her pocket, and nodded at me to go. "Wait."

Frankly, I was dumbfounded. It was as if Nikki had deliberately been hiding from me, all the time I'd known her, two-hundred-odd years of experience in dealing with difficult people. For all I knew, maybe she had. These Peri seemed to be capable of anything. "So we can come in?" asked the girl, the money still in her hand.

After a moment, the door opened. Chassidy backed away, and we stepped in. Because it was more than half belowground, the apartment was cooler than the parking lot by far, even without air conditioning; its inside, however, reeked of tobacco, Wind Song perfume, and armpit sweat. I left the door partly open so that I wouldn't pass out from the smell. A pile of ratty shoes covered the floor near the door where Chassidy kicked them off after every work shift and let them lay. The grungy furniture was littered with candy wrappers and copies of the *National Enquirer* and *Star Magazine*. Well, at least I knew who was buying those things, now. I stuck my hands in my pockets, lest I accidentally touch any of the countless unsanitary surfaces. Across the room, by a cordless telephone sitting on a portable garden chair, Chassidy was nervously grabbing another cigarette and lighting it. "I don't got to tell you nothing," she mumbled. "They told me a long time ago they wouldn't press charges, seeing as it was all Harland's doing."

I decided to take charge of the questioning again. "What was Harland's doing?"

"His insurance scam." It took her a minute to get the cigarette going. She sucked so hard I thought the entire thing would shrivel to ash in mere seconds. "He was gonna marry me, after. That's the only reason I went along. He thought up the whole thing. Drove to L.A. when he knew there was going to be a bad storm and rented a wave rider. Then he drove it off into the ocean. It came back by itself, with some of his clothing ripped and tangled in the motor or whatever." Her voice was soft, almost reflective. At the same time, though, she kept an almost hungry eye on the money that Nikki held in her left hand. "Said that someone would wash up eventually and I could say it was him. And it did. Drove all the way to Venice a month later just so I could look at some chewed-up mass of nothing and say it was Harland. Then the insurance people got involved and the police and they found out it was some asswipe from Encino, and I had to be all like, how was I supposed to know one bloated fugly body from another? Shit." She tapped out a long ash into a whiskey glass sitting on the TV.

"Why did he do all that?" I asked. I was pretty certain she was telling us the truth; I'd become fairly good at weeding out the liars from the rest, when I'd been working, and there was a certain resignation in her voice that led me to believe she didn't have much to hide anymore.

Chassidy shrugged. "Scared." I needed more than that. After a moment, she complied. "He'd been getting a lot of money from this freaky guy for like, three years. I only saw him once, didn't look right to me. I don't know what he was dealing, though. Drugs, something, I don't know. He wasn't a user, though. He just had all this money. We moved to Summerlin on it, nice place.

Whole lot nicer than this. Even had a white BMW." She sagged against the archway leading to the kitchenette. "Then he got scared, and since he wouldn't be getting no more cash from his buddy, he thought of the insurance thing. He said he and the brat had to disappear." My poker face must have fallen for a split second, because she wrinkled her nose at my reaction. Defensively, she said, "She was a pain in the ass! Couldn't eat McDonald's like other kids, oh, no, had to have special food. Little princess, she was. He thought she was a brat, too. He called her a taint. That's what I heard him say once—Lily was a taint."

I felt Nikki's fingers on the back of my arm, squeezing. She must not have liked the way the woman talked about the girl, either. "Why was she tainted?"

"Hell if I know. She wasn't like, a flipper baby or nothing." Nikki squeezed my arm harder, to the point that it stung. I moved slightly away while Chassidy kept talking. "All I know is that I was supposed to tell people that her mama from Georgia came to get her after he died. Don't think she had a mama in Georgia. Not one that was living, anyway."

"So they're both still alive?" I looked at Nikki when Chassidy seemed to admit that they were. "Where are they?"

She'd reached the limit of Nikki's generosity, apparently. Catlike, the cocktail waitress lurched forward and snatched away the money, folding it into a wad and tucking it into her fairly ample bosom. "I don't know." She chewed on her thumb.

She was lying. Her eyes slid away from mine, like mercury down a slope. I was about to call her on it when Nikki said, "Five thousand dollars for his location. No negotiations," she added, when the woman looked as if she might try to argue for more. "That's all it's worth to me."

"We aren't going to hurt him," I assured Chassidy. "All we want to do is talk."

"I don't give a damn if you *do* hurt that son of a bitch." Chassidy went from sly to feral in a heartbeat. "Fuck him up for all I care." She glared at us with some strange sort of defiance, enjoying our shocked reactions. "Whatever. I don't care."

"So do we have a deal?" I wanted to know, pushing back in reaction to her shove.

She nodded. "Yeah. But I can't give it to you right away." She looked out the window. "Come back tomorrow."

"Tomorrow!" I didn't want to come back the next day. I hadn't intended to spend the night, much less spend it with Cor's sister and her puppy-crush in tow. "That won't do."

"Yes ma'am!" Chassidy's tone made it clear she thought I'd been high and mighty with her. "It'll have to do. I gotta make a call, make sure he's where he was the last time we talked. Make it nine o'clock." Her black-lined eyes narrowed until they were slits. "And I'll take that five grand now."

"Think again." Nikki wasn't having any of it. "Not until you deliver the goods."

Deliver the goods? My little Nikki? She wouldn't look at me when I cocked my head and stared. "Fine." Chassidy caved. "Tomorrow morning. Five thousand. And I don't want nothing over hundreds. Got it?"

"Got it. See you tomorrow, then." Nikki turned and strode out of the room with her shoulders back, as if she'd negotiated high-stakes bribes every day of her life. I nodded at the woman, not really trusting the way she'd retreated into the corner again, or the way she studied us through those slits. Once the apartment door was closed and the smell was behind us, I realized that the girl was muttering something under her breath as she walked down the sidewalk in front of the so-called residences. I caught up so I could hear. "Ohmygosh ohmygosh ohmygosh," she muttered in rapid syllables. She waited until we were a good distance away before she turned and looked at me with wide eyes. "Oh my *gosh*. I can't believe I *did that*. It was just like *television*."

"Nikki!" I snapped. We weren't that far from where Adam stood with his back against the wall, gazing at a billboard across the street advertising a strip club. I grabbed her by the arm and marched her to the building's end and around the corner. "What in the hell did you think you were doing?"

"You should be glad I was there," she said. "She's—"

"You could have screwed up everything!"

"I didn't!"

"No, you didn't, but you might have! Oh," I said, squeezing a hand to my forehead. "I sound like your brother, don't I?" I closed my eyes and tried to calm myself down. "My heart's beating so fast. Faster than the time a guy in Sparks drew a rifle on me."

"Sam, you have to know—"

"And that money!" My lids flew open again. "All that money! Where did you get so much money? Oh my God, five thousand dollars!"

At that, she winced. "Yeah, about that. It's an old trick of the Kin. In twenty-four hours, it'll turn back into twigs." I gasped. "Oh, don't. Corydonais would k-i-l-l me for doing it. It's not 'honorable' in our family, especially with what our sire . . . anyway." Her face flushed slightly before she opened her blue eyes wide and changed the subject. "That's not the important thing, though. You've got to listen."

"So tomorrow she's going to open up her bag to spend that money on crack or booze and it's going to be gone," I muttered. "Or she'll spend it *today* on her crack and her dealers will find twigs in their pocket tomorrow and come back to rough her up. Fan-freakin'-tastic."

"Will you listen to me!" We'd been speaking in low voices, but to get my attention, Nikki spoke up. In the dank tunnel of cinder blocks, the echo was like a slap in the face. "Lily. I know what she is!"

"Meaning?" I knew what Lily was, too. The daughter of some drug-dealing fraudster, that's what.

"That creepy human said the father said she was a . . ."

"He said she was tainted, yes. Which is a cruel, inhuman . . ." Nikki was glaring at me, so I shut up. "Go on."

"That Chassidy woman overheard wrong. Harland Oliver didn't say Lily was a *taint*. He said she was a—" The last word in Nikki's sentence, I recognized now, was in whatever native language the Kin spoke. "Your people used to call it *teind*. It's like a tithe. Something you give up. Oh, there was a famous song about it in your history, but your kind move so quickly. Tam Lin? Thomas the Rhymer?" I shook my head. "It's about a woman named Janet who rescues Tam Lin from the Faerie Queen. He's a teind to Hell, and she drags him from a white horse and holds on to him while he changes into all kinds of animals, and if she holds on to the end, she gets to keep him, but if she lets go . . ."

"To *Hell*?" I asked, my voice raised.

Nikki looked decidedly uncomfortable. "That's what teinds are. It explains a lot, Sam. The special food? Food from the Kinlands. To purify her." Just to intensify the hackles that rose on my neck, a dark shadow crossed the sunlit entry where we stood. I jumped at the sight of a large black bird swooping down to the parking lot nearby. Nikki laid a hand on my arm to calm me down. "It's a crow. Not a raven."

"I can't tell the difference!" I looked at the bird and shuddered. I'd been worried about Cor or his spies finding me all morning.

"Ravens have a bigger beak, and their tail feathers are kind of wedge-shaped and . . ." Nikki let her words trail off when she saw I wasn't in the mood for an encyclopedia entry. "Sorry."

"So that's where all the money was coming from? These people were accepting money in exchange for a little girl?" I spat, a foul taste rising in my mouth. "A helpless little girl! Marshall and his mother were *buying* a human to purify and use as what, a *sacrifice?* I can't believe this." Apparently Nikki felt she had, for once, said enough. She backed against the opposite wall and regarded me with compassion. "I'm sorry, Nikki. This just absolutely disgusts me. I am so ashamed of my people right now."

"It kind of sounds like he had a change of heart, though. She said Harland got scared. Maybe he realized what he was doing."

"Yeah, he realized he was going to hand his daughter over to some strangers as a sacrifice for cash, then turned to insurance fraud so he could keep his damned white BMW," I snarled. "What a keeper. Where do I sign up for some of that?"

"I told you it was serious. They probably still want her. That's why I offered Chassidy a lot of money for the information." She grinned. "I was good, huh?"

I ignored all fishing for compliments. "You offered Chassidy a lot of twigs, Nikki."

"Yeah. Well." At least she had the decency to look shamefaced.

"What do they want her for?" I had to know.

"Ask Cor." My mouth twitched. "You can't avoid him forever. He's not dumb, Sam. He's going to figure out where you went this morning. Hey, don't get like that.

I'm on your side. Anything that shows my big brother he's not the only capable one out there is fine by me. But you know you're going to have to see him again sometime."

"What are you, my conscience?" I sighed, and looked at my watch. "We're going to need to find someplace to stay."

"Cool!" Nikki looked delighted at the thought of a night in Sin City. "My treat? I don't mind. But I need to find a bush or something," she said, sticking out her head and looking around.

The Peri. The only creatures in the world for whom money does, apparently, grow on trees.

Chapter Fourteen

"You haven't changed a bit!"

"You've said that, what? About seven times now?" I put my elbow on the bar and immediately jerked it back when I felt the ice covering its surface bite against my skin. That twenty-five-foot expanse of ice and cold metal was one of the key features of Mandalay Bay's Red Square restaurant. While it might have been good for keeping shot glasses of vodka chilled, it wasn't built for comfort.

Hugh Bleeker sat on the stool next to mine, handsome as he'd been during the months we'd dated, and dressed to kill in a camel Armani blazer and chocolate-brown slacks. Wisely, he kept his elbows to himself. "I mean it, though. Honestly, Sam, you don't look like you've changed a bit since the last time I saw you, what, four years ago?" His eyes traveled up and down my form, while I tried to look cool and elegant. No small feat, considering I'd left the house that morning wearing the blandest of outfits and not realizing I'd have to wear it for twenty-four hours straight. Still, my V-necked top was simple and plain enough, and I'd managed to keep from spilling anything on my slacks, and my flats, if not exactly pretty, at least weren't in bad condition. In fact, I was probably in better condition than Hugh was used to.

"Something like that," I said, giving him the eye as well. Hugh had always been one of those good-looking men who knew how to make the best of their irregular features. His almost too-narrow face he'd topped off with a short, expensive haircut that de-emphasized how small and close together his eyes were. His mouth, on the other hand, was by most standards too big for his face; he compensated by always smiling and exposing his bright, white teeth. No, it was still Hugh, all right. The only thing different was the band of gold glinting on his left ring finger. "You look good too," I told him. "Marriage must agree with you."

"It does when I agree with Ellie," he joked, flashing those pearly whites again. Back in the days when Hugh and I had seen each other, I'd fallen for him pretty much on the merits of the smile alone. "You never met Ellie, did you? Nice girl. Nice girl," he added, when I shook my head. "We don't always see eye to eye, but who does, right?"

Hugh and I certainly hadn't, most of the time. We'd broken up because he'd eyed a UNLV Hotel Administration major, and I'd eyed her phone number in his pants pocket. Of course, I don't know what I really should have expected from a guy I'd originally met while tailing a whiplash victim at Caesar's Shadow Bar, who'd come up to say hello to me with his arms around two very different and very drunk girls; the concept of fidelity had always been the last thing on his mind. "Whatever she's doing agrees with you," I told him.

"I was surprised you called," he admitted, slugging down the rest of his vodka. He motioned for the bartender to refill our glasses. "Delighted, but surprised. I think most of the world had given you up for dead. I know that sometimes things get crazy after a breakup." He wrinkled his nose then, to let me know he understood, and reached out to give me an unexpected chuck on the chin.

"Yeah." A single word, prelude to a sentence like, *Yeah, listen, thanks for telling everyone my disappearance was because I was distraught about your cheating ass, dillweed.* I smiled, though, trying to keep it civil. After all, he had gone to the trouble of packing up my things. "How about that? Crazy." With a dramatic flourish I assumed was supposed to resemble some kind of Russian ceremony, the bartender placed two more vodkas down onto the ice-covered bar. The faintest traces of vapor, visible from the lights underneath the bar's frosty surface, wisped from the glasses.

Why had I experienced an unidentifiable urge to call Hugh after all this time? Okay, for him it had been four long years since I'd broken it off with him, though to me it had been a mere six months. Partly it was because, for the first time in a week, I wasn't being held hostage or running in crazy circles from supernatural threats. Apparently I'd become a little bit of an adrenaline junkie, from all that. The prospect of spending an entire evening in my hotel room alone seemed dismal, while Nikki and Adam were out watching the pirate show at Treasure Island and taking in the sights of a city that very probably was the exact opposite of their beloved Resht.

Mostly, though, all I'd wanted was a little closure. Surely this whole caper would be coming to an end tomorrow, when we found the Olivers and I again let the Storm Ravens take over their own business.

He slugged down half the fiery liquid, staring at me over the top of his glass the entire time. Waiting, I guess, for me to make the next move. "Basically I just wanted to take a few minutes to thank you for, you know. Cleaning up after me, when I left for Morocco." I gritted my teeth both at the lie and the vodka, which was stronger than any of the domestic brands I was used to. "I left a mess, and you went above and beyond and all that." This wasn't coming out the way I intended. "If I'd returned . . . from Morocco . . . to find nothing to my name, I wouldn't have known where to begin." Picking up my life would be tough enough, after Cor and his Storm Ravens left. After they left. My head didn't want to travel down that particular road, yet. "So you're the tops, yadda-yadda-yadda, and I know my mom thanks you, too."

"Aw, your mom's a sweet lady. Shame you don't take after her." My eyebrow shot up, and he exploded with laughter. "I kid! Jeez, don't get so wound up." He finished the rest of his drink in a single, fluid motion, rearing back slightly as the liquid fire trickled down. "If you're buying, I'm getting another."

I was getting down to my last few bills before I'd have to resort to Nikki's twig money, but I threw a twenty onto the ice and nodded at the youth behind the bar. And that's when I saw him. Cor, sitting at a table near Red Square's entrance, hunched over and turned in our direction. His long hair hung on either side of eyes that bored holes through me. God only knew how long he'd been there. In his usual dark, dressy clothing, he'd blended in so well with the early evening crowd that I simply hadn't noticed him.

But oh, I surely couldn't escape noticing him, now. I felt certain that he'd meant for me to see him, too—in his black pants and shoes and a dark striped shirt with the top three buttons undone, watching me. At first, I panicked; I felt like a schoolgirl about to be sent to the principal's office, red-handed and scarlet-faced. After a moment, though, the Russian fire coursing through my veins made me bold. I gulped down what was left in my glass and slammed it onto the ice before the next round could come, then tossed back my head so the air vent above me could cool my face. That's when I realized Hugh had been talking to me again. "Sorry?" I said.

"I was just saying that there's something about you, these days." Hugh leaned forward so that he could speak a little more softly over the bar's babble. "I don't know. You seem energized, or something. You're a little spitfire, now. It's really attractive."

Though the comment really hadn't merited it, I let loose with a long peal of laughter, carefree and bubbly, and patted Hugh on the wrist. Midway through my little show of mania, a gawking tourist family entered and threatened to stand squarely in the sightline between Cor and myself, so I had to prolong the gesture until they'd finally moved their Iowa corn-fed butts out of the way. I finished off with a fluttering of my eyelashes and a hearty, "Oh, you!" Obviously I'd surprised him. I never had been a flirty girl, and apparently spitfires weren't the type to bat their lashes and go all gushy at the drop of a hat. "I bet your wife loves your sense of humor."

"How about we don't talk about Ellie?" Hugh moved in close and smiled. "Let's talk about us."

Oh, crap. I'd stuck sex-scented bait on the hook and reeled in a stinkfish. Laughing lightly, I swatted away Hugh's hand from my leg. "Don't."

"Come on, Sam." I recognized that tone in his voice. It was the *Come on, let's do it in the back of the Hummer. Nobody'll see* tone, the *Come on, the tablecloth practically touches the floor and we can both keep poker faces here in this fancy restaurant, can't we?* attitude, the particular timbre he took on when one of his buttons had been pushed and he was feeling particularly randy.

"Didn't you say you had a hotel room? The sex between us was always fantastic."

"Sex? Was that the thing we used to do where you'd roll off me after and then run to check your hair in the mirror?" I said with a grimace. Sometime between when I'd made the fatal mistake of playing the femme fatale and that moment, Cor had left his table. I'd been looking around, desperately trying to find his tall and lanky frame among the young lovelies who kept coming into Red Square in pairs. And there he was, in the middle of the bar, only about a dozen feet away. "Kidding! Don't," I laughed, dabbing at Hugh's hand and hoping he'd remove it again from my knee. While still trying to maintain a lighthearted mien, I pried his fingers from their death grip on my patella. "Seriously, don't."

"Baby," he said, still confident that I'd fall for his dubious charms. "It's okay. Ellie and I have an understanding. Nobody's going to get hurt, here. We're all adults."

"Hugh." I'd had enough. I didn't care if Cor saw me looking miserable. I couldn't lead my ex on any longer. "That's not happening." Without warning, the hand that had already been prying open the lock tried to shoot through the gates. I stopped him from making a clumsy, drunken grab at my upper thigh and glared him down. "Stop it, seriously."

He grinned and grabbed my other hand. "You've always been crazy about me. Why else would you call me?"

"Closure," I growled. Each of us had one of our fists wrapped around the other's wrists.

"Keeping your legs closed isn't going to accomplish that," he slurred. "One more bang for old time's sake, and we'll call it quits. Okay?" He leered at me. "I was hoping you wouldn't turn out to be a bitch, like you used to be."

I've heard of people seeing red before, but in that moment of rage I saw white. It felt like one of those cinematic editing tricks, where everything on the screen loses all color and form and then slowly fades back to normality from a bright nothingness. When I came to and was thinking normally again a second later, I had an empty glass in my hand. And on the front of Hugh's chocolate-brown trousers, a dark, wet stain was spreading. The sight made me want to laugh, though not as much as the expression on Hugh's face. With his arms extended, his eyes wide open, and his mouth in a perfect O shape, he looked as if he'd been frozen in marble in mid-goose.

"Bro," I heard someone say beside me. "Did you wet your pants?"

At the sound of Cor's perfect imitation of a louche lounge lizard, several people in the vicinity turned to gaze at Hugh's 'accident.' Titters began to reverberate across the wood-and-concrete lounge, particularly from the women; most of the guys guffawed and looked away from the sight out of sympathy or embarrassment. After what seemed a very long time, Hugh stood all the way upright; the remnants of my drink that hadn't been completely absorbed by his pants dripped onto the floor in a small puddle, causing the crowd around us to wince. Very soon, they were all groaning aloud—a chorus led, I realized, by Cor, now no more than a foot away. Then slowly, very slowly, as if he loathed the feeling of the wet material against his privates, Hugh began to walk away, still wearing the same horrified expression.

I watched him go without any regret or much in the way of pity. Once the hubbub around us had died down, I lolled my head at my Peri friend and shook my head at him. Then I collected my bag, smiled apologetically at the bartender leaning over the icy bar and gaping with dismay at the puddle on the floor beneath Hugh's chair, and began walking for the exit.

Cor loped behind me. "Have a good date?"

"My little meeting with Hugh was not a date," I snapped.

"Oh, that was . . . ?" He feigned surprise. "That was Hugh? The ex? Really? Because somehow I thought any ex of yours would be a little more . . . continent."

From Red Square's more rarified interior I couldn't hear any of the ordinary sounds of the casino, but once we'd stepped outside, the clanging of slot machines and the chatter of gamblers and tourists were back in full force. "That wasn't very funny."

"No? You were about to laugh," Cor pointed out. "I'm not the one who threw my drink on him."

"Maybe not." I stopped in the passageway and confronted him face-to-face for the first time since I'd snuck off that morning. "How did you find me, anyway?"

"It wasn't easy," he said, grim but pleasant. The answer wasn't good enough for me. I jutted my neck forward, waiting. "Fine. We combed the city. Ginger and two Ravens spotted two Kin in front of the Mirage volcano that turned out to be Nikki and Adam. She squealed."

"The little quisling." My mouth twitched, and then my legs took over. I don't know why, but my instinct was to flee from the very sight of Cor, and therefore they began to carry me back in the direction of my tower elevator. I didn't argue with them.

"You must have known we'd come when we'd found out the two of you had snuck out," he said, catching up easily. My short little steps were no match for his long strides. "Whose idea was it, Nikki's?" I didn't say anything. "You shouldn't have listened to her."

We were on the escalator leading down to the casino level. I turned and remarked, "Yes, that's right, she's

Lucy, I'm Ethel, and I'm so weak-minded that I can be talked into just about any harebrained scheme. We're going to steal John Wayne's footprints from Grauman's Chinese Theater next. Want to join?" I stomped down the remaining few moving steps and into the slightly smoky casino interior. "It was my idea, Cor. You pissed me off, and this is how I paid you back." I threw my hands up in the air. Not a great move, when it turned out that I struck a woman in the head who'd been playing Ms. Little Green Men. "Sorry," I told her. Then to Cor, I added, "Not much of a dancing flame now, am I?"

"Why didn't you say anything last night?"

"Because you had it all planned out and wrapped up, didn't you? You and Ginger, swooping in to the rescue, while poor old dopey wingless Sam sat in a car somewhere, waiting for all the pretty birds to come back. There wasn't a place for a little grain of sand in your strategy, was there? Admit it."

I'd touched a sore point somewhere, I could tell. Good. Though honestly, I couldn't tell you why in the world I was so angry with the guy; half of what I said felt simply like bluster over being caught. "I'm not used to working with your people. I'm used to being among you, because when members of my race go rogue, your world is where they hide. It's a bigger place. But I've never had one of you as a spunky sidekick, and I've never—"

"Landemann," I pointed out.

"Landemann's a special . . . fine." All at once, he capitulated. "You got me."

I felt a savage stab of triumph over that one. But good lord, did they have to build these casinos so *large* these days? I turned at the cashier's cage and headed in the direction of my elevator. "And in case you haven't noticed, I'm not anyone's spunky sidekick."

"If you'd have let me finish," he said, plainly annoyed,

"you would have heard me say that I've never had to work with a human who demanded to be an equal partner. When it comes to you, I shouldn't treat you as anything less. You'd kick my ass if I did. So yes, it's difficult to figure out exactly where you fit in." My pace slowed, a little at first. Then I turned to face him. He stood before me with his arms at his side—not helpless, exactly, but disarmed. "But I intend to fit you in. I always have."

"Good," I told him, expressionless. What he couldn't see, however, was the little smile on my face when I turned. I didn't speak again until I'd jabbed the elevator button. "I suppose Nikki told you all about what we'd discovered."

His mouth twitched. "It did sound as if you had a productive morning." He cleared his throat. "I think Ginger was more surprised about how much you two found out than I was."

I couldn't really savor that little bit of information as much as I wanted to. "Cor?" I asked, stepping into the shiny metallic elevator once the doors opened. I pushed the button to the fourteenth floor. "What's a teind for?"

He considered for a moment before replying. "Millennia ago, in the distant days of the Peri," he finally said, once the doors had closed and we'd begun ascending with the faintest of rumbles, "when our race first set foot on this world, we found we were not the only sentient creatures walking its surface. The proudest among us found their new brothers and sisters crude to their eyes—little more than apes who were barely able to stand upright enough to lift their knuckles from the dirt. All they saw were the defects, the flaws, without seeing that those very same flaws were the reason we had been sent into exile." My mind went back to what my mother had told me about the supposed origins of the

Peri. From her mouth it had sounded like fable. From his, it sounded like a history richer than human imagining. "Our queen then was among those who wanted to retreat from this new world to a land where only Kin could walk. And so she made arrangements to do so, in a world we once would have scorned."

"In Hell," I concluded for him. "Like in that poem Nikki mentioned. Tam Lin. You made a pact with Hell."

"Yes and no. The lands were not directly governed by him whom your people might call the ruler of Hell. But he gave my people access to those lands in return for a sacrifice. A pure soul, or one purified to be close enough." I almost jumped when the bell rang for my floor. My arms were covered in goose pimples when I stepped out into the hallway and onto the spongy carpet. "Every seven years, she offered this teind. Occasionally they were Kin—the misguided among us who volunteered to be teind, out of conviction for the cause. More usually, they were culled from among your children."

"That's barbaric!" I protested, angry, stomping in the direction of my room. "That's no better than the worst of us."

My voice sounded unusually harsh in the cloister-like sanctity of the hallway. "I know, Samantha," he said, trying to calm me down. "That's why we stopped the practice over two thousand years ago, when the old queen was dethroned and her followers expunged. And that's why the Kinlands are so fragmented and disconnected from each other today, and the gateways to Resht are so few. Without teinds, the Kinlands are slowly disintegrating."

I'd extracted my key card by the time we reached my room, but I turned and leaned against the doorway instead of opening it. The indignation fluttering within my breast a moment before had calmed some—after all, it was kind of tough to hold an entire race to task for crimes committed thousands of years before when my own often wasn't doing too hot, itself. "What's this have to do with Lily Oliver?"

"It sounds as if your friend Chastity . . ."

"Chassidy," I corrected. "It's the kind of name that unfortunate kids get when their parents can't spell."

"She heard Harland Oliver say his child was a teind. Nikki said something about a special diet she'd been on."

"Probably food from the Kinlands?" He nodded. "It purifies?"

"Your men of science would say it changes the body's composition so that it can better withstand the transition from this plane to that of Hell. Its ruler likes the teinds to survive once they're there. For a little while." I closed my eyes, pained, not wanting to hear any more. He leaned against the other side of the door, hunching slightly so that we were more at face level. "There are other rituals, some discarded, some still observed. A designated teind used to ride only on snow-white horses, back in the days when folk rode them. They originally were given fresh flowers to wear in their hair, though I think . . ."

"The BMW," I said softly. Then, at Cor's puzzled look, I explained. "Chassidy said they had a white import car. Kind of an expensive one, too."

"That's part of it, then. After the purification, the teind is taken from this world and put into a construct for seven days. At the end of that time, there's a ceremony in which what they treasure most about themselves is taken, to humble them. Then they are turned over."

"But why were they doing this to Lily, if your people don't offer teinds to Hell anymore?"

"Our queen does not." His blue eyes flashed with some expression I didn't recognize. "The people of

Resht do not. But there are two who apparently wish to. They made an investment in the girl, and I'm willing to bet they'd rather claim her as she is than start over."

"But why?"

"With the sacrifice of Lily Oliver, they hope to claim a kingdom of their own, where they can reign supreme and unchallenged. By our laws, that is treason, the crime my order is sworn to avenge." A shiver trickled down my spine. I would not have wanted to be a Peri deserving of Cor's brand of justice. "We're on the same side, Samantha. You and I both want the same thing."

It was at that moment I knew he didn't quite trust me yet. He wanted to, I could tell. After my runaway act that morning, I wasn't certain I would've trusted me, either. "I don't want to be the spunky sidekick," I warned him. "I'm not a sit-in-the-car kind of girl, and I never will be. I'm not the damsel in distress who you have to worry about rescuing, and I'm not the chick in the horror movies who runs from the monsters screaming and then conveniently trips and falls on her face so they can catch up with her. Got it?"

"I think you've made the points more than abundantly clear." He grinned, which at least let me know I wasn't annoying him. "Are we good, again? Fresh start tomorrow, the two of us?"

I held out my hand so we could shake on it. "We could use a fresh start. Done." I nodded, pleased to be agreeing with him again. I liked Cor. I liked someone who could actually keep up with me. If only I'd realized earlier in my life that it would take a man with wings to do it.

I must have been standing there for a while, goony-eyed and wistful, because he finally broke the silence between us with a legitimate question. "Are you actually going in your room? Or were you waiting for your boyfriend with the urinary problems?"

"Classy," I commented, jolted out of my reverie. "Classy remarks from a jealous fairy."

"Do you have to use that word?" he asked, pained. "I most certainly am not jealous of that vapid, smug . . . and anyway, I'm not sure I'd talk about jealousy, prone as you are to it whenever Ginger is around."

I made an astonished face. Or, I should say, mock-astonished. I wasn't so much surprised at the accusation itself, as at the fact he'd noticed. "Lies," I snorted, fanning myself with my keycard. "I have no feelings of any sort about Ginger. I'm sure she'd love me out of the way, though, so she could jump your bones without any interference. I've seen the look in her eye."

He sighed. "If you want the truth, she jumped my bones, as you put it, a long time ago. Once only. Roughly around the time your people were inventing the steam engine. There, are you happy?"

I can't say the news really thrilled me, but I wasn't surprised. Besides, with that kind of time having elapsed, it really was like ancient history. "Thanks for the honesty," I conceded, trying to be gracious. Then, because I had to know, "Did you like it?"

"What?"

"It. Her. Bone-jumping." Either he wasn't getting it, or he was playing dumb. "Did you like having her bony carcass all over you!"

"Hmmm, oh yeah." He nodded gravely, then pretended to wipe his chin. "Mmmm, so good. So good that it's kept me satisfied for two hundred and forty-three years." I felt a little bit abashed. Maybe I had let my jealousy show a little bit too much. "Actually," he said in a way that promised juicy details to follow, "we weren't that compatible. She was kind of . . ."

"Mean?" I suggested, after waiting an appropriate length of time for him to finish. "She pinched you, didn't she? I bet she's a biter. She looks like a biter. Did she pierce your nipple with her canines? I bet that hurt."

"Are you done?" he asked.

"Maybe." My upper lip curled as I thought about it. "All right. I'm done."

Cor smiled at me, his arms crossed. "Bossy, is what I was going to say. I felt the entire time as if I was being given a final exam for a lecture I hadn't attended, and that she was grading me even before I'd turned in my essay." I smirked. Figured. Somehow, knowing that little tidbit made me feel a little better. Cheerful even. "So. Are you going in?" He nodded at the door.

Oh. I'd forgotten we were standing out in the hall. "Excuse me," I said, prompting him to step aside as I faced the doorway. I slid the glossy card into the slot and watched the lights flash from red to green. The maid must have come in while I was out to turn down the sheets and leave the bedside lamps on; the room was suffused with a warm, low glow. Once the door was open, I turned. "By the way, I never said that you could come . . ."

When I turned to issue my decree, I found myself facing the door opposite mine; Cor wasn't there. I did feel a rush of air above my head, though, and heard the flutter of feathers. By the time I turned around, I caught the confusion of air and light and smoke as he transformed over the king-sized bed, plopping down on the mattress from midair into a cross-legged posture. "I'm sorry. What did you say?"

I sighed and let the door slam beside me, flipping the switch that turned on the lights. "So unfair," I commented, deciding to give in rather than argue. The cheesy grin on Cor's face made me glow from the inside; it was a refreshing change to see him boyish and playful instead of set on rescue and vengeance. How many times had he referred to our respective species as brothers and sisters? It was small moments like these, when I knew we both shared the same emotions and impulses, that I really felt it could be true.

The problem was, the feelings I had when we were alone together were never anything approaching sisterly. Simply looking at him made me desire another taste of his skin against mine. I wanted to bathe in the feelings aroused by his angular good looks. I wanted his arms around me once more, but I was too damn proud to admit it.

Awkwardly, I put my hands on my hips, and then in my pockets. I didn't know what to do, or what to say. "You know, it's getting late," I finally ventured.

"It's eight-thirty."

Damn these hotels for leaving clock-radios out in the open where anyone can see them and use them against me! "Yes, but."

Cor wouldn't take that as an answer. He uncrossed his legs and slid up toward one end of the bed, flipping off the light on the little table next to it. Then while I shifted uncomfortably from one leg to the next, he turned off the other. In the darkness, I heard him rise from the bed, kick off his shoes, and shuffle across the carpet. Then, with a scrape of rings against metal, he swept back the heavy curtains covering my window, so that the lights from the Las Vegas skyline filled the room with a blue glow. Against the pinpoints of light and the neon radiance, Cor's silhouette occupied the window's center. I watched while he unbuttoned his shirt.

"Cor," I whispered, when he walked slowly toward me.

His baritone was lower than usual when he spoke. "Would you rather Hugh was here?" He reached for my hands and held them, rubbing my palms with his thumbs.

"No. It's not that."

"Then shush."

I couldn't. Not as simply as that. I still had all the same doubts and objections from the night before. Every time I attempted to contemplate the enormity of them, I felt lost and helpless. It was like trying to imagine infinity all over again. "You scare me," I told him. His hands moved up to my wrists, and then my elbows, drawing me closer. "You really do."

"Am I really a monster to you?" I felt his chin graze my cheek as his lips moved to my ear, pausing to whisper there. "Tell me the truth."

I shivered. He rubbed his hands up and down the gooseflesh that formed on my arms. "No," I replied. My eyes closed while he breathed warm air onto my right ear. "You're an angel, aren't you?"

His chest rumbled in amusement. "I am no angel, Samantha." I felt a twinge of disappointment when he moved away from me. "No angel at all."

Cor wasn't leaving, though; he knelt down before me in the darkness, only visible when the feeble light glinted in his eyes. I wasn't certain what he was doing until I felt his large hands around my feet, helping me off with first one shoe, then the next. Up my legs they traveled. I felt a tugging at my waistband, and then a sense of freedom as he released the pressure around my hips. He shucked down my pants like he might the skin of a banana, smoothly and without effort. I braced one hand against the wall as Cor pulled each pant leg around my feet. The cool air played around the skin of my naked legs; with my eyes shut, I could feel him standing and blocking the breeze from the blower beneath the window. His fingers skimmed beneath my blouse, pulling it up and over my head. "I'm worried I'll like this too much," I murmured. With my arms in the air, it felt as if all my resistance was draining from my fingertips down to the floor.

"Are you seriously worried?" he said. I felt his lips on

my neck, gently suckling at the skin there before moving on to the underside of my jaw. "Why would you agonize over something we both want?"

"I'm human. I'm built for worry," I mumbled.

His arms surrounded me, supporting me. In the blackness I could barely tell which way was up. Somewhere in the confusion I found myself being laid on the bed, its silky sheets chilly against my skin. I couldn't protest, nor did I want to. I felt as if I was trapped in that deliciously dozy moment between sleeping and waking, when only the most elemental of sensations mattered—the warmth of his skin against mine, the softness of his hands, and the trembling he seemed to awaken with every touch.

Oh yes, I wanted this to happen. Wasn't I the one reaching up to unbutton his shirt, unable to divest him of his clothing fast enough? I wanted to run my hands over the curves and hardness of his arms, to feel the planes of his chest and stomach beneath my palms. Once the shirt landed with a soft whoosh on the floor, my fingers danced over his flat stomach, rubbing in wonder the smooth area where there should have been a hollow, but wasn't.

"You are so smooth," he marveled. I gasped when he pushed me roughly toward the headboard so that he could rake the light stubble on his face across my stomach. His tongue flicked in and out of my shallow navel. He was as fascinated with it as I was with what he lacked, I realized with an echo of laughter.

I pushed my pelvis up into the air when I felt his knuckles run along the outside of my hips, pulling down my panties until they tangled around my knees. He and I both wrestled them off, eager to get rid of them. Finally I kicked them from my foot and heard them knock over the plastic cups on the table at the bed's bottom. "Oh, God!" He buried his face into the sensitive area where my leg connected to my hip. His tongue passed over the skin there, seeming to burn wherever it touched. "Don't!" I cried.

He lifted his head. "No?"

"No, I mean yes! Don't . . ." He returned to his ministrations before I could gasp out the last word of my command. ". . . stop!"

"Are you sure?" he asked, taking me literally. "All right then, but it's a pity to halt the boat midstream."

"God damn it," I growled, exasperated beyond belief. I just wanted the good sensations to go on and on.

The faint laughter I heard relieved any frustrations I might have had; he was toying with me. Soon he was back at the job, his tongue alternating between long, sensual lapping and tickling and dipping into more sensitive areas with its tip. His hands brushed over my stomach, my legs, the backs of my calves; he pushed my knees into the air and held them there as he seemed to dive into parts of me that didn't seem able to take—or deserve—such attention.

I don't know how long the sensations went on, but I felt pressure growing. I felt like a boiler in an old-fashioned building, groaning and protesting at the load as it pumped out heat. Then, without warning, the sensations stopped and the heat began slowly to ebb. "What's wrong?" I asked.

"Take off your bra," he ordered. In the dark, I heard the sound of his belt buckle clanging as he ripped it from its loops. It was quickly followed by the sound of his zipper, and by the dance he performed as he tried to remove the rest of his clothing. "I haven't removed a woman's brassiere in more years than I can recall, and I don't know how they're fashioned these days."

"It's not *that* tough," I commented, hastily reaching around to unhook myself. "I'm sure you could figure it out."

"Fine, teach me later." With a lunge, he was on top of me. My breasts pressed against him, enjoying their first introduction to his chest. His lips pressed against mine while his tongue forced its way into my surrendering mouth. One of his hands moved up my neck through my hair, sending my scalp into tremors that felt like a schoolgirl blush. "I don't care, right now."

I could feel his flesh pulsing against my thigh, hotter than skin should be. His hips ground against mine in a circular motion, prompting me to respond in kind. It felt as if we were locked into a private tango, the music for which only he and I could hear. "You have to tell me," I said, before I abandoned all common sense for the pleasures of the moment. "Are you likely to give me anything nasty I'll regret if we do this?"

"There's no chance," he assured me.

I trusted him, but I still had more questions. "And what about, you know? Protection?"

"You won't become pregnant tonight," he said, panting through the interruption. "It's not my . . . how do you say it? Time of the month." I couldn't help but laugh, which didn't make his oral conquest of my breasts right then all that smooth an expedition. "What?"

"Oh. You're serious," I said at last, surprised. I honestly had thought he was trying to make a funny.

"Among the Peri, it's the male of the species who has a limited window of fertility on a regular, predictable basis," he began to explain. "Our philosophers think that because we've traditionally had a matriarchal society, over the millennia it developed as a response to . . ."

"Cor," I interrupted, before the pressure building between my thighs subsided any more, "teach me later. I honestly don't care right now."

His teeth shone blue-white in the glow from the skyline. "Right," he agreed.

Our pelvises continued pressing against each other as our lips joined once more. His hand cupped the back of my head as he pulled away; I felt the tip of his penis, warm and wet, nudge against me, tentatively at first, as if questioning me. My own hips answered the query by rising up to meet him, my legs parting not only to grant him entry but also to seize that which they desired. And then, effortlessly, he was inside me, warm and firm, my softness yielding to a hardness I couldn't, and wouldn't, deny. His head turned so that my cheek pressed against his long, thick hair. Into the pillows he uttered a wild, wordless exclamation of pleasure that gladdened my heart. I placed one hand on his shoulder and another against his round buttocks, pulling him all the way in, hoping that I'd hear him cry out again.

He did. And in a few minutes, my own shouts of astonishment and joy joined his, until our breathing came too wild and fast and heavy for the cries to continue.

Chapter Fifteen

Apparently the same principle of making friends I'd used many years ago when I'd gotten my first insurance investigation job applied to the Peri. A couple of bags of bagels and a tub of flavored cream cheese was all it took to be promoted from the suspicious outsider to everyone's best pal. "Here you go!" I said cheerfully to one of the Storm Ravens, handing her a napkin that cradled one of the bagels I'd picked up on the way. "Cinnamon-raisin with pumpkin pie cream cheese. I hope that's okay. There's hazelnut coffee and something else, French vanilla decaf, in those boxes over there," I said, pointing to the open hatch at the rear of my Mini.

The Peri, whose name (as far as I was able to gather), was something like Lanallaioni, smiled broadly, then gave me an impulsive hug. "Thank you so much!" she gushed. Then, with a quick and guilty look over her shoulder, she skipped away to the coffee. I watched with a grin as she opened her jaws wide to bite into the massive hunk of bread before anyone could stop her.

The someone in question, of course, being Ginger.

Here in the parking lot of the little strip mall where we'd rendezvoused with the Ravens, she'd been sitting in the van's front seat with Cor, going over all the intelligence they'd gathered over the last twenty-four hours. It made no sense for the rest of us to stand around and yawn while we looked in the windows of the closed Takee Outee Chinese restaurant or the empty former travel agency, so on impulse I'd crossed the street and come back overloaded with breakfast-y goodness. Once the second-in-command's boots hit the asphalt when she jumped out of the driver's seat, however, they all scattered and tried to stand with their backs to the woman so that she didn't see them with their contraband. It was all very boot camp.

The redheaded Raven couldn't really ignore the munching or the steam rising from the cardboard cups, however. She gave the deserted parking lot a quick look-around, pulled her mouth into a grim line, then strolled in my direction. "Good morning!" I said, once she was close enough that I couldn't pretend not to see her.

Her tiny head bobbed ever so slightly. "Looks like you're quite the domestic goddess this morning." Ginger didn't sneer exactly when she said the words, but I could imagine how judgmental a comment it could become with only the slightest of inflections.

"They're bagels," I said, picking up the cardboard box and holding it in front of her. "Would you like one? They're fresh."

She regarded the open container as if I were offering her a nice hot Petri dish of botulism accompanied by a ptomaine chaser. "We're accustomed to carrying our own rations."

There was affront and reproach intended in that simple remark. After the night before, though, I was in a good mood. No, I was in a fan-freakin'-tastic *great* mood—the kind of disposition that I'd experienced only one or two times before in my entire life. I felt like Snow White whirling around in her flowy dress while my wildlife companions danced and sang around me in Disney colors. It was the kind of mood in which I didn't so much walk around, as waltz on my tippy-toes, and in which I could overlook the litter in the gutters and the used syringe lying in front of the nail salon and see only the pretty colors of the early morning sky over the mountains, and the hazy mist as the sun rose.

In that kind of mood, all I had to do was remember what a bossy nipple-chomper she was, poor dried-up little thing, and everything felt all right again. "Oh, a little bagel never hurt anyone, Ginger."

At that moment, one of the Ravens came back for another round of the cinnamon-raisin and pumpkin combo. The bagel he fished out of the box wasn't really so little, since it was roughly the size of a baby's head. Ginger raised her eyebrows, and said something unintelligible. "Beg pardon?"

"Jin-jur-na-turn-i-a," she said very slowly, enunciating each syllable at a high volume, as if I were Thicky Mc-Thickerson. "That's my name. Not Ginger. And maybe in the future, you'll let me keep the responsibility of giving my people morning rations."

You know, after two hundred and forty-three years of not gettin' me some, I'd probably be a wee bit cranky, too. Remembering that fact made it all the more easy to ask the question that was foremost on my mind. "What's with the paramilitary jargon, Ginge? And the gear?" I pointed at her outfit of camouflage pants and tank top. I didn't get the boots, the little cap that matched the pants, and the whole look that made them look like Operation Desert Fairy Storm. "Doesn't it strike as kind of strange, borrowing your whole regimen from *Eirethin* military culture?" Ooh, I'd struck a nerve there. Her face, already pink from too much sun, grew even redder. "You must be more democratic than I thought."

I rather enjoyed the tortured silence that followed, in which Jinjurnaturnia wrestled with herself rather than betray the slightest emotion that might have let me know I'd scored. At long last, without frothing at the mouth, she finally managed, "Any system in which discipline is the bedrock has much to admire."

"Fascinating," I said, taking a bite of bagel. It really was delicious, though I admit I regarded the bread as a mere delivery system for the mass of pumpkin pie cream cheese I'd spread across it. "So you like humans, after all? I'd kind of gotten the impression you wouldn't be sorry if we were all wiped out in some kind of planet-wide mishap. Or is it just me you despise?"

Mean, I knew. I couldn't help myself, though. I had Cor and she didn't. Simple as that. Nyah. I listened to her bluster, but my eyes rested only on the object of my passion as he stepped from the passenger side of the Raven's van, studying the clipboard in his hand. He smiled at me and loped forward, looking as out of place among all the camouflage as I did. From the side door, Landemann straggled out, sporting his usual dark glasses and shiny goombah-wear. If it weren't for the fact that he was stiff when he tried to straighten up, and that one of his hands was still covered with mummy-like bandages, it would have been hard to tell that he'd been in the hospital only two days before.

"How's it going? Oh hey, bagels," Cor said, reaching into the box I proffered. He turned and motioned for Landemann not to exert himself; the bodyguard eased down onto the van's floor with his legs on the ground. "Excellent. I'll take two. Are we behaving?"

The last question seemed more directed to Ginger than me. She pursed her lips, looked at the ground, and stabbed the toe of a boot at a parking line. "We were just talking about discipline," I cut in, trying to save her some embarrassment. "Not of the spanking variety," I murmured with meaning, loud enough to be heard.

Cor had to clear his throat to regain his composure after that remark; Ginger had the grace to look away and pretend she hadn't heard, though I was glad she had. "So, let's talk about this morning," he suggested, trying to keep things professional. "We were discussing what you and Nikki found out yesterday."

"Is Nikki upset about not coming?" I asked, interrupting. Her brother had basically forbidden her to be within a mile of the second meeting with Chassidy, on pain of being sent back to Resht.

"I might not be able to convince you to keep from sticking your nose into danger, but the offer of a fancy breakfast buffet took the edge off Nikki's annoyance," Cor admitted. "We'll pick up her and that boy after the exchange. Ginger?"

"I've taken the liberty of posting two of our Ravens at Chassidy Smart's address." Ginger had given Cor a stricken look at his use of my nickname for her, but she kept plugging along. I began to suspect that Cor might have been lecturing her in the van about good manners in front of the helpful human. "The latest timeline is that she left home last night to report to her job at the Lucky Leprechaun Casino, and returned at approximately seven-forty-five this morning. As of fifteen minutes ago, no one else has been seen approaching the door."

Cor nodded, then drew up the clipboard. "Now, the plan is for the team to follow us to the complex. We'll park. I'll stand cover for you outside, while the Ravens cover the perimeter."

"Cover the perimeter?" I asked, shaking my head. "Who are you, Jack Bauer in *24*?"

"It's standard procedure," Ginger informed me. Or

rather, informed my kneecaps, since she couldn't bring herself to look at Cor and me standing together.

"You'll make contact with Chassidy, obtain the information from her on the whereabouts of the Olivers, and you'll give her this."

He unfastened a manila envelope from the board, and handed it to me. I undid its metal clasp and looked inside to find a stack of crisp hundred-dollar bills secured with a slip of paper around their middle. Fifty of them, I was presuming. "Twig money?" I guessed.

"No, it's not *twig money*," he growled. "And if Nikki uses that old trick again, I give you full permission to take a willow switch to her behind. I don't care how old she is." I nodded, not sure whether to mention that I'd been tempted, much more than I cared to admit, to allow the girl to pay for our hotel rooms the night before with twig money. "We have what you'd call discretionary funds. This strains them a little, but it's worth it."

"All right." I folded the envelope over on itself until it was of a size to stick into the back pocket of my cream-colored jeans. "Anything else?"

"The exchange should be pretty straightforward," Ginger said. With a straight face, she added, "A monkey could handle it."

I was considering asking Cor if I could hit his second-in-command, but the stern look he gave her, followed by a not-so-subtle clearing of his throat, was punishment enough. She turned her head away from me yet again, and reddened once more. "Are you ready?" he asked me, when done.

"Aye-aye, Cap'n!" I clicked my heels together and saluted. Lana, the Peri I'd given a bagel to earlier and who had returned to my trunk for more coffee, snickered slightly, earning a glare from her superior female officer. My watch said fifteen before the hour. "We should go now," I told Cor.

He nodded. I noticed that at the first up-and-down motion of his head, the watchful Storm Ravens all sprang to attention and began moving to the van. When he said, "Wait," they literally halted in their tracks.

"What is it?" Ginger asked.

Cor sprinted around to the back of my Mini and bent over. "Cream cheese," he said, licking a little of it from his thumb. "What? Landemann really likes cream cheese on his bagels." When Ginger shook her head in barely suppressed disgust and stomped off to the van, he threw me a quick wink and whispered, "Someone hasn't gotten any in a while!"

"That's what I was thinking!" I giggled.

Despite the playfulness, though, once we'd finally gotten underway, Cor was all business again. His eyes darted every which way as I navigated the Mini through Las Vegas's morning traffic, nudging my way through the mass of yellow taxis heading to the airport to pick up incoming tourists. At some point his hand drifted over to my side of the car, where it lay companionably upon my leg as I drove. It was such a commonplace and comfortable gesture that I luxuriated in the simplicity of it, though I didn't call attention to my enjoyment of his touch with anything other than a smile. Part of me was afraid that if I did, it might vanish like a frightened butterfly.

The rusted-out Duster still occupied the same space in the lot of the La Bel Age Residence Court. It had probably been there for years, I realized; the owner could have moved away or died in one of these makeshift apartments, mummify in the desert heat, and no one would have been the wiser. It was with that cheerful thought that Cor squeezed my knee and said, "I know you don't want to hear what I'm about to say."

"If it's the lecture about how I should be letting you do this, then you're right," I admitted. "Honestly, Cor, it's a simple cash exchange for information. Nothing could be simpler. When you start talking about how I shouldn't be doing things, it just makes me feel shoved to the side."

"That wasn't my intention. I care about you," he said. "I just worry."

I was touched again by the straightforwardness of the statement. So much so that I instantly regretted letting my prickly defenses come into play again. "I'm sorry I'm so defensive," I told him, leaning in to give him a kiss. Our eyes studied each other at close range. "But it'll be a breeze." Then, because I could see the Ravens' van as it pulled into the parking lot of the convenience store down the street, I sighed and sat back, in case the sight of me smooching their commander demoralized any of the troops. "Okay, let's do this thing."

"Wait." Cor put his hand on my wrist, letting it rest there while he strained his neck to see out the passenger-side window. Did he see something I didn't? No, he was obviously waiting for a signal. A raven swooped down onto the hood of my car, its widespread claws scrabbling for a hold on the shiny surface. At least, I was assuming it was a raven—its tail feathers, black and iridescent and shining with every color of the rainbow in the sun, looked wedge-shaped enough. Its beak opened, letting out a low, guttural rattle that didn't even sound avian. "All right," he said. "The Ravens are getting into position. You can head out."

As I undid my seatbelt and slid from the Mini, Cor gave my hand a quick squeeze. Through my sunglasses, I watched as one of the Ravens exited the side door of the van and walked around to its front. Where she disappeared from view, a dark-winged bird soared over the parking lot and into the sky. Fine, I didn't mind. They could send as many Storm Ravens as they wanted;

all of them couldn't make me feel as secure as my solitary milkman.

Businesslike, I walked briskly in the direction of the stairs leading down to Chassidy's apartment level. Like the last time, I didn't hear any signs of life from the other apartments—but then again, anyone who was living in that low-rent a district was probably still sleeping at nine in the morning, after hooking or pushing drugs all night. Cynical of me, but I'd lived in Vegas long enough to know that the people living in transient hotels were most likely not ministers, doctors, and members of the creative community. I turned once I'd reached my destination to let Cor know I was ready. He was already exiting my car and making his way across the lot to the stairwell I'd just taken, where he stood at a good distance away. He nodded.

I rapped at Chassidy's door after making sure I still had the packet of money in my back pocket. My intention was to bring it out early in the conversation and show it off a little, letting her know that it was hers for the taking if she came through with the Olivers' address. *This is what you want, right?* I planned to ask. *Then give me what I want.* Chassidy wasn't the kind of woman who'd care much about my motives, I knew; she just wanted the dough. I knocked at the door again, thinking that perhaps she hadn't heard me the first time.

That's when I noticed that her door was cracked. My knocks had dislodged it, but it had definitely already been off the latch. Even through a chink that small, the aroma of the tobacco within was overpowering enough to make me gag a little. I pressed my ear to the opening to listen—though for what, I didn't know. All I could really hear was a repetitive clacking noise in the distance. "Ms. Smart?" I called out, knocking at the door again. Then, "Chassidy?"

There was no reply. My first reaction was annoyance; I'd encountered enough subjects in my old job who'd skipped town the minute they knew they were under investigation. Why should Chassidy be any different? She could have taken the twig money Nikki had slipped her yesterday and hauled ass to Reno. Yet that's when I remembered that she couldn't have. The surveillance the Ravens had from their eye in the sky, so to speak, said that Chassidy had arrived home a little over an hour before and hadn't left. She had to be in there. Perhaps she'd merely fallen asleep.

"Ms. Smart?" I yelled out through the crack. I tried pushing the door open, but something was keeping it from opening easily. It only gave another inch, letting out more of the reek of cigarettes and sweat. "It's Samantha Dorringer. My associate and I were here yesterday morning, Ms. Smart. Won't you come talk to me?"

Maybe she'd fallen asleep, because I still didn't hear anything other than the persistent rattle from somewhere inside the apartment. I didn't know what was hampering the door. Had she barricaded it? That didn't make sense. I leaned all my weight against it and was satisfied to feel whatever was behind the cheap wood give, and then heard a little metallic rattle as the door's chain prevented me from opening it any further. She had to be inside, then, if the door was fastened that way, right? I took a deep breath so I wouldn't have to inhale any more of the stink, and turned my head so I could look with both eyes inside.

"What is it?" Cor asked in nearly a whisper, when a moment later I had galloped hell-for-leather down the concrete in his direction, my hand over my mouth. I pointed back at the apartment. "Is something wrong?" All I could do was run back to Chassidy's door, stabbing my finger at what I'd seen beyond. He knew something was amiss, but beyond seeing the chained entry he couldn't tell what. "Is she gone?"

"Foot," I told him, gasping in the air my depleted lungs so badly needed. I thrust my finger down toward the floor. "Foot!" I repeated. "There's a foot on the floor!"

He shook his head and, when I pushed him forward to look, peered through the crack I'd created. He uttered a curse in his native tongue that I didn't understand, though I got the gist of it. "Maybe she's passed out. Can you hear me in there?" he called. "Are you okay?"

I didn't know. I was having a very, very bad feeling about all of this. "Break it down," I suggested. He looked at me with mild surprise. "Fine, I'll do it," I growled, trying to shoo him out of my way so I could take a running launch.

To my amazement, once he'd regained his balance from my off-kilter attack, he pivoted on one leg, lifted the other, and kicked the door squarely by the doorknob. It shuddered and bounced almost shut, but not before the Peri let loose with another forceful kick that caused the chain to pop out with a splintering of wood and a metallic clatter. The door bounced with a thud against whatever was behind it, then closed. We both leaped for the knob.

Chapter Sixteen

"Oh, God," I said, once we'd slid inside Chassidy Smart's dim apartment. The atmosphere within was thick as Los Angeles smog, and immensely more toxic; the only fresh air was coming from an open window in the bathroom, where the crooked blinds flapped in the breeze. I could only take quick looks at Chassidy, where she lay on the floor. Every look was successively more horrifying. "She's dead, isn't she?"

"Very dead," Cor agreed, kneeling down to look. I didn't know whether he was stoic about violence after three hundred years of human wars and turmoil, or if he was actually jaded by bloody corpses in his particular line of work, but he didn't seem as disturbed as I by the sight of a woman lying on a carpet soaked with her blood. "This isn't good."

Some understatement. "You think?" I asked, a little hysterically, before I tried to get a grip on myself. "Oh, Christ," I said, suddenly clenching myself around the middle. "Fingerprints." Cor raised his eyebrows. "My fingerprints are on file with the state. It was something I had to do for my investigator's license. If they find them here . . ."

"Did you touch anything?"

I thought about it, and shook my head.

"Are you sure?"

"I'm pretty sure," I said, looking toward the bathroom. That was safest. There wasn't anything other than a mere mess there. "I remember thinking how disgusting everything was."

"What about Nikki?" There was no mistaking the urgency in his voice.

"I don't think she did, either. Most of the time we were outside. She would have touched the cash."

He relaxed. "That should be disappearing in a few hours."

"Do you have fingerprints?"

"Of course we have fingerprints," he replied.

Listen to me, I thought. A woman was dead mere feet away, and here I was asking about Peri fingerprints. The brain copes in funny, funny ways sometimes. I forced myself to look at the poor woman again. Chassidy's face was turned away from me; her crazy head of hair was matted with blood. Her body was crumpled up, seemingly because of the force with which Cor had kicked in the door. She seemed to be wearing a bathrobe. There was blood on the walls, too, I noticed for the first time—a thick splattering of it on the back of the door and the wall next to it, that had dripped down to the floor. She must have been trying to get out the door when he'd gotten to her. No wonder it had been unlocked.

Cor saw me following the almost horizontal spray of the stuff with my eyes. "Her throat was cut," he explained. "Deeply. She would have died almost immediately."

I'd had enough for the moment. "But your guys said no one came in."

"The bathroom window." He stood, careful not to let his hands grab on to anything.

"I'd already thought of that," I told him. "It's too small for someone to break into." Because the apartment was mostly belowground, the window was up near the bathroom's ceiling. It was maybe two feet wide and a foot tall. Maybe a determined child could have squeezed through it, but not a cold-blooded killer.

"We can't stay here," Cor decided. "Someone might have heard."

"The police would have been here by now if someone had heard her being killed and called," I suggested.

"What about when I broke open the door?"

He had a point. Hands thrust deep into my pockets, I pushed past him.

"What are you doing? We need to go," he urged. "I don't want you anywhere near this place."

"I'm not leaving without what we came for." Though how we were going to get it, I didn't know. "This is our only lead!"

I saw him hesitate. For a moment he looked as if he intended physically to pick me up and carry me out, but then he relented. "I don't like this. Make it quick," he ordered. "And don't touch anything."

"Where are you going?" I asked. He'd pried open the door again with his foot and was trying to squeeze out without touching anything. I felt a little panicked at the thought of being left alone with what was left of Chassidy. "Don't."

"I need to get a Raven," he said. "I'll be just on the other side of the door."

I felt a little better at his reassurance, but not by much. Once the door had slipped closed again, I made my way to the kitchen. What was I supposed to be looking for, exactly? A road map to the Olivers' hideaway? A diary? I doubted that Chassidy could have written a coherent sentence. An electronic organizer with all her addresses and secret notes? Unlikely. The only thing that Chassidy Smart had collected in her miserable apartment were ashtrays, empty cigarette cartons, and old copies of the *TV Guide*. Which made searching pretty easy, actually. Even in the kitchen, the apartment had very few drawers; the ones that I opened with my shirt as a buffer between the knobs and my fingers were filled with matchbooks and salt and salsa packets from fast food restaurants. The refrigerator was empty of everything save Budweiser, and precious little of that. There weren't many knickknacks or photographs or anything beyond the clothes in the closet and the pile of shoes that Chassidy's corpse lay upon to tell much about her at all.

"Find anything?" Cor asked, creeping back into the room. He used his shirt to open and close the door as well, I noticed.

"No," I sighed. "No address books. Nothing. Wait." Like a sudden injection of adrenaline, energy coursed through my veins. I had an idea. I ran over to the aluminum garden chair where the cordless phone sat. It was an ancient model—modern sleek cordless handsets would have run, frightened at the sheer imposing bulk of it. I picked it up with my shirt-cradled hand, and pushed a button. "Hah!" I crowed. "Write this down."

"I don't have a pen."

Neither did I, though I did have my notebook in the Mini. "Fine, memorize what I'm about to say." I read out a phone number. "310 is an L.A. area code. West side. Whoever this is, Chassidy called them about fifteen minutes after Nikki and I left yesterday."

Cor looked relieved. I didn't know whether it was because I'd found some possible something out of all this mess, or whether he simply was happy to have had a human who would have thought to check the recently dialed numbers stored in a phone. I flipped back to make sure there were no more calls, and then placed the handset back into its base. "Can we go now?" he asked, obviously wanting to leave as quickly as possible.

"Yes. We'll phone the police, right?"

"One of the Ravens will. *After* we're far away. Come on."

I took one final look around the place, though. My eyes still skipped over the corpse near the door. I couldn't quite take in the reality of that, yet. "Wait," I told him again. This time I got an exasperated groan in reply. "I want to see the bathroom."

"You can go in a McDonald's!" he growled.

Funny. I ignored him. The bathroom was a serious mess. A blue boa lay over the mirror, and near-empty perfume bottles littered the back of the toilet. The tub hadn't been washed in eons, apparently; the sight of the fuzz around the drain made my stomach roil. How did someone get in through that window? It didn't seem possible, given that the window itself tilted in only at a sixty- or seventy-five-degree angle. There was no screen to the alley outside, true, but it seemed as if only a small animal could have possibly come in through what was obviously intended as the most meager of ventilation.

"I notified Ginger and the Ravens. Let's go," Cor called out. "I mean it this time."

"Fine!" Yet I didn't move, because I'd noticed something out of place, lying on the bathroom floor. Cor had the door open, so that light was streaming inside onto the crime scene. I only had a split second to dip down and scoop up what I'd seen, tucking it under my blouse as I tiptoed out as quickly as I could. My stomach was in knots, now. More so even than when we'd discovered Chassidy Smart dead.

"Put on your sunglasses. Give me your keys. I'm driving." Cor held out his hand as we walked at a high speed back to the staircase. "Yes, I know how," he added, before I could ask.

I handed them over. He unlocked the doors with the remote, looking around to make sure nobody was spying on us as I folded myself into the small car. He shot the driver's seat to its furthest position back, jumped in, and shifted into reverse as soon as the engine ignited. I didn't speak until he'd navigated us out of the La Bel Age's parking lot and down the street. "Cor," I whispered. He looked at me, then back at the road. "I think I know who killed Chassidy. Or what," I amended.

I thought he'd nearly run us off the road, he swerved so suddenly. A station wagon next to us honked loudly; the driver gave him the finger for veering into his lane. "What?"

I pulled out the objects I'd found from underneath my blouse, where my left hand had been clutching them. Two feathers, one broken. Both black as jet. Cor swore again at the sight of them. "I thought they were part of one of her costumes. She had a blue boa in there. But these aren't blue, and they're not the same kind of feather." He seemed to be having a hard time keeping the car on the road. Nervously I kept silent for a minute while he looked over his shoulder and then at the mirrors so he could maneuver over a lane. Not until we were pulling into the lot of a twenty-four-hour Kinko's did I feel safe enough to keep talking. "Think about it, Cor. Who else could it be? The door was locked from the outside. Only something smaller than a person could have fit through that window. Like a squirrel. Or a bird." He yanked the car to a stop, lurching us both forward. Then he grabbed the intact feather and began to examine it. "It makes *sense*. If Marshall had known about Chassidy, he could have come here on his own years ago. Only the Storm Ravens knew about her."

"No," he said, shaking his head.

"You haven't been out of my sight since last night," I continued. "But one of your order . . ."

I nearly startled out of my skin when I heard a rapping on my window. I wouldn't have been surprised if it had been the Ghost of Chassidy Past, but it was only Ginger, who'd appeared from nowhere. I didn't see the van nearby, so I guessed that she'd followed us in the air. "What's the problem?" she asked Cor.

"Was the guard watching the back alley last night?"

"No need, without any way for anyone to get into the apartment." He handed her the feather in his hand, and I displayed the other. "Damn," she said, her mouth working into a grimace. "We screwed up."

Personally, I wasn't wild about him sharing my evidence. He might have trusted her, but as far as I was concerned, the chick was a suspect. Heck, I wouldn't have put it past her to attack Chassidy out of spite because I'd produced her as a lead. *Nice. Way to be harsh, Dorringer.* I winced at myself.

"Do you have any ideas about which of the Ravens might have done this?" I asked her.

Whoa. I don't know what I could have said to make her react so strongly, but I could see Ginger's anger flare and spread out like the sparks from a Tesla coil. Her nostrils flared. Her eyebrows crunched, and her jaw jutted out. For a moment I thought she was going to haul off and sock me. "Calm yourself," Cor barked at her. From the strange timbre in his voice, I knew he was addressing her in their own tongue. She responded immediately, stepping back from the vehicle and shaking her head.

"What?" I wanted to know.

"These aren't from a raven." Cor reached over and accepted the whole feather back from Ginger. "What do you think, crow?" he asked her.

She nodded, reached over me, and pointed to the

feather's shaft. Apparently she was pointing out a detail that only ornithologists or actual birds might notice. "Definitely crow."

Cor shook his head. "This is not good, Jinjurnaturnia."

"No, sir."

"So it wasn't a Storm Raven." I made more of a statement than asked a question. In a softer voice, I added to Ginger, "I'm sorry. It's not false guilt," I said, for Cor's benefit, though I still spoke to her. "I didn't know any better."

"Obviously." The redhead glared in my direction.

"Ginger . . ."

My hand flew to Cor's wrist. I didn't need him reprimanding his second-in-command every time she was short with me. For one thing, that would end up being an awful lot of reprimands. "Listen, I'm really sorry I insulted your order. I know you're proud of what you do. Maligning you or any of your men or women was never my intention." All I got for what I thought was a pretty handsome apology was a brusque nod of the head and a twitch of Ginger's jaw, but that was understandable. I'd be prickly, too, if she'd badmouthed the Greater Las Vegas Professional Society of Insurance Investigators. "But here's the thing. Who else knew that Chassidy existed?" They looked at each other with dawning understanding. "It was just us three, and the Storm Ravens. I don't think that either of you blabbed about her to someone else, but if one of your other people knows someone who can turn into a crow, now's the time to find out."

There was a long moment of silence in which the two Peri studied each other's stony faces. "In our history is a sect we don't often speak about," Cor finally said, his words slow and deliberate. "They caused unspeakable harm."

He tilted his head at Ginger. I couldn't tell whether he was indicating she continue, or what. She nodded, though. Apparently he'd just been checking his theory with her. "I would hate to think you were right."

"They took the forms of crows, and were among those who not only wished to separate themselves from the human race, but also advocated its elimination." Cor's face looked grim.

I can't say mine was any more cheerful, after hearing that news. "Who are they?"

"They were known as—" Cor paused portentously before continuing. "The Order of the Crow."

I am ashamed to admit that I giggled slightly. Part of it was sheer lightheadedness from the heat. Most of it was a certain sick unsteadiness from the memory of Chassidy's remains, sickeningly curled up on her apartment floor. A lot of it, however, came from the name's sheer anticlimactic lack of oomph. I was expecting something juicy. Even "The Legion of Doom" would've done. "I can't wait to see your Order of the Spotted Titmouse," I muttered.

"What?" I waved away Cor's inquiry and put my hand to my mouth. He continued conferring with Ginger. "But the Order of the Crow was purged, centuries ago."

"Or it was thought to be," Ginger corrected. "It could have gone underground. I don't know."

"Deep underground. Even their old rituals were expunged from the codices. Only a few of us know of the details," Cor said. Then to me, he explained. "They used ritual implements—certain weapons—unique to their order that have been forbidden since. They were one of the three cults against which the original Storm Ravens were formed to fight."

"Even I don't know anything about them," Ginger admitted.

I cleared my throat. "Ritual implements?" They both stopped their conversation and looked at me. "Wrapped in cloth, maybe? With, like, the Colonel's secret recipe of eleven herbs and spices?" Ginger wasn't getting me, I could tell. "When I was stuck on Riviera Lane, the night I got out, Marshall and his mother were unwrapping these . . . things . . . that had been wrapped in cloth. Tall sickle things. On sticks. They'd been wrapped up with dried herbs or flowers."

Cor's eyebrows had shot up during my description. "Sickles on sticks?"

"Is that bad?" I asked.

He nodded. "Very, very bad. There's a reason that many of your race have long associated the image of death with a scythe. It began with the Order of the Crow."

They still weren't getting it. I had to lay it out plainly for them, which I did with no little degree of impatience. "Fine. Fantastic. They've been hiding out in plain sight for eons. But don't you get it? One of your Ravens has to be a Crow."

"Impossible." Ginger seemed sure.

Cor nodded. "It can't be one of the Ravens."

"Well, someone they know, then, or associate with . . ."

Ginger once again didn't like me impugning the honor of her followers. "Maybe it was someone who followed you," she snapped. "You're so inconspicuous in this vehicle, after all." Her hand slapped the top of the Mini.

"Hey!" I felt outraged on its behalf.

"Nikki has an unusual talent for knowing when other Peri are around," Cor said. "Better than either of us, even. I think she would have spotted one of the Kin."

"That's true," I said, remembering how easily she'd picked out her own kind during our afternoon on Venice Beach, on the trek to the CD shop. The memory of Nikki and Adam locking lips that day triggered a crazy thought in my head, and as I ran it through all the various outcomes, I started to feel sick to my stomach. When finally I looked at Cor again, my face was white with certainty. "Unless we brought him with us," I whispered. When he didn't understand, I said, "Adam. The tattooed boy."

He startled up, immediately unbuckling his seatbelt. "How much did he know?"

"Not much," I said, feeling miserable. After all, I'd kept the enemy supplied with Funyuns and Mountain Dew for most of the previous day. "We didn't say a lot in front of him. But, oh, crap. He was alone in the car with my notebook. And he was standing outside the apartment when Nikki and I were in . . . and we left her at the hotel alone with him this morning." With every word, I was more and more convinced I'd left Nikki with the enemy. "I thought he was just some kid!"

"Our kids are not the same as yours."

"I know. Shit." On my right I felt the slightest of breezes, and heard a flap of powerful wings. Without waiting to hear anything more, Ginger was already aloft, zooming southward as swiftly as she could fly.

Cor was out of the driver's seat in a flash. I nearly broke the amateur speed record for unfolding myself from a subcompact car and vaulting over the hood, before he could join her in flight. "Do you still remember that telephone number?" he asked. "The one Chassidy called?" I nodded. "Then do what you have to, on your end. Take Landemann."

"I will," I promised. His legs bent as he sprang into the air; with a chaos of cloud and beams of light and sound, he shifted his shape and propelled himself upward. "I'm sorry!" I called after him. I yelled my regret to the small spiral of sand whirling in the empty parking lot, however, for he was already little more than a vanishing black speck in the southern sky.

Chapter Seventeen

I'd thought my trip to Las Vegas had been endless, the day before. It was nothing, compared to my drive back to Los Angeles. Every mile I placed between myself and Sin City, stretched my patience further and further; I wondered when that thin, invisible cord linking me to Cor might snap. I didn't know where he was, or Nikki, or anyone; the only thing I could keep in mind was my mission.

I'd promised to uphold my end of all this, while Cor tracked down his younger sibling. That meant that the first thing I did, after I'd watched him and his second-in-command wing off without a word of farewell, was to find a way to call that phone number. Apparently while I'd been away, cell phones had completed the last phase of their plan of utter world domination; what seemed like the last remaining public pay phone on the streets of Las Vegas, outside a liquor store, was battered and covered with graffiti. It was also grimy enough that I resisted lifting it to my mouth, for fear of the plague. But I did, and grimly performed the task before me.

It hadn't been easy. When Harland Oliver answered the phone, I'd had a devil of a time keeping him from hanging up. "Who is this?" he'd kept asking, with a distinctive Southern twang to his voice.

In the meantime, I'd kept repeating one question to myself, over and over again. "Is this Harland Oliver?" I'm sure it hadn't helped that I was near hysteria, myself. "My name is Samantha Dorringer," I kept telling him. "I'm a friend."

"Who is this? How did you get this number?" he'd asked, over and over again. Plainly he was alarmed.

"Chassidy Smart gave it to me," I'd said, slowly and distinctly. "Mr. Oliver, listen to me. This is a life-or-death situation, here. Did anyone else call you after you talked to Chassidy yesterday morning?"

"How do you know Chassidy called me yesterday?"

Although I'd been in a parking lot of a strip mall, barely able to hear over the traffic and the sound of the airplanes passing overhead, it hadn't taken a keen sense of hearing to pick out the mania in the guy's voice. "Mr. Oliver," I'd said, more and more certain that I was speaking to the man in question. "This is a serious matter. Chassidy is dead."

There's been an awful pause after that, when for more than a few seconds I'd been sure our connection had been cut off. I'd been just about to bang the receiver on the exterior wall of the liquor store when finally he'd said, "What did you do to her?"

At that point, I'd exploded with agitation. "I didn't do anything do her! They did. They murdered her, Mr. Oliver, in cold blood. I was there. I found the body. And if you don't listen to me, they're going to do the same to you and take Lily as their teind, no matter how well you've hidden her. Is that what you want?" He didn't reply to that, but at least he hadn't hung up, either. "Are you listening?"

"I'm listening," he said, in a very small voice. I could tell he was shaken.

"Good. Now, did anyone else call you between yesterday and this morning?"

"Lily's school," he said, thinking it over.

"Anyone else?"

After a long pause, he said, "There was a man, early this morning. Maybe two hours ago. It woke me up." Pressed for details, he'd squeezed out a few more. "He asked if I had a daughter, then hung up."

That was exactly what I hadn't wanted to hear. "That was your old friend," I'd explained to him. "The one who wanted to take Lily away from you. The one you ran from. I'm not one of those people, Mr. Oliver. I'm like you. I'm human. I don't want your daughter taken any more than you do." It had been a lie; part of me was still so angry with a man who'd knowingly sell his daughter to strangers that I wanted to snatch the girl away and make sure the likes of him never saw her again. The whole thing sickened me—but as I kept telling myself over and over again, I couldn't be both judge and savior. "I'm coming to help, but your friend is going to be able to get to you a hell of a lot faster than I ever will. Are you listening?"

"I'm listening," he'd said in the same small, scared voice.

"Good. Then I need you to do exactly what I tell you. Where in L.A. are you? What?" I asked, as another jet roared overhead. "*Where?*"

And that's why it had been with a sense of impotence that I'd gotten in my car and driven around the southeastern streets of the most glamorous and gritty city in the world until I'd finally spotted the Ravens' van still parked outside the Takee Outee. I'd parked and left the engine running as I knocked on the van's windshield, smiling at Landemann, who was slowly baking within.

"Come on," I'd told him, sighing. "We're going to Catalina Island."

"Freakin' Santa Catalina Island," I muttered now, to myself, over the roar of the car's air conditioning. We were about halfway there, I was guessing—and could the miles go any more slowly? I didn't think so. The speedometer's needle hovered a little above the seventy mark, but the entire trip so far had been so interminably slow that it seemed like it was taking place underwater. In an ocean of maple syrup. With police department wheel locks on my rear tires. "It figures that Harland Oliver would hide himself on the island of expensive condos and day spas."

Landemann said nothing. Par for the course. I'm afraid that my Mini Cooper hadn't been made for big guys like him, but Cor had insisted he go with me. Even with the seat slid to its furthest position, and even at a steep recline, Landemann looked like a giant Macy's Thanksgiving Day Parade balloon strapped into a child's amusement park ride. He stared at the road ahead impassively, through the shield of his sunglasses, hands perched on his thighs.

"Have you ever been to Catalina?" I asked him. Not expecting an answer, I talked on. "My dad took me there once. It was just him and me, one Saturday, when I was twelve. We took the ferry over. I don't remember much about it. I do remember worrying about being sick on the ferry, but he sat next to me at the very front and held my hand and told me to breathe deep, and everything would be okay. I didn't get sick. Which I guess is a good thing." Something black and feathered swooped across the highway in front of me. When I craned my neck to see, I could tell it was only a carrion bird in search of lunch. "I kind of remember going on bicycles. And swans? I think there were swans somewhere. Mostly I remember the ice cream. It was a good day."

People could say what they might about Landemann, but I had to admit he was a good listener. He hadn't interrupted me once, during all that.

"That would have been right before he left, actually. He left us, my dad," I explained. "Walked out and never came back. Didn't even take his clothes. Catalina was probably his way of saying good-bye, come to think."

Had it been? I'd not connected the two, before. Had he taken me out there that day, just the two of us, knowing that within a matter of weeks or days he'd be walking out without a backward glance? I bit my lip, trying not to think about it. Thanks to years of refusing to think about him, I didn't have that many memories of my father left. Now I'd tainted one of the last remaining ones.

I changed the subject, talking to keep my mind off the monotony and the dread. "Do you enjoy working for Cor? Corydonais, I mean." Still not expecting an answer, I sighed. "I can't imagine it's easy working for the Kin. I mean, they probably don't even offer comp time."

The relentless sun blazed at an angle on the driver's side that began to burn my cheek; I adjusted the visor to block it out, sighed once more, and gripped the steering wheel tightly in preparation for another long leg of tense silence.

"Mr. Corydonais is the kindest person I know."

I almost startled from my skin. I hadn't ever expected Landemann to give me an actual answer. I'd actually come to think of him as some sort of elaborate prop, like the corpse those two bums wheeled around in the movie *Weekend at Bernie's*. But no, he was actually speaking, and his voice was softer and gentler than I'd expected.

He didn't look at me when I turned my head, but he said something more. "There isn't anyone else I'd rather work for."

I nodded. I'd had my sunglasses sitting on top of my

head for a while, but at that point I pulled them down over my eyes. I didn't want Landemann seeing how that testimonial had made tears sting the corners of my eyes, so I made believe it was the sun.

For another fifteen minutes we sat there in a silence that, while not exactly companionable, at least wasn't tense. Then Landemann spoke again. "Where am I?" I was so sure that whatever painkillers the guy was on had him addled beyond belief, that I was about to explain to him what we'd been doing for the last three hours. But then, when he added, "In the girl's car. Yes. Catalina."

He was talking on a cell phone, I realized. "Is that Cor?" I yipped, shooting my hand out to grab it from him, good manners be damned. "Can I talk to him?"

We swerved, of course. That's usually what happens when one removes one's hands from the wheel and one's eyes from the road. The Mini's tires groaned in protest as we ran over some kind of rumble strip designed to frighten sleeping drivers back into their lane; the wheels up dust and gravel when I swerved back onto the asphalt. Landemann snapped shut the clam-style phone and turned his head in my direction, staring at me long and hard through his sunglasses as though I were crazy.

" 'The Girl' just wanted to know what was going on!" I protested, feeling thoroughly rebuked. "Was that Cor?" The bodyguard shook his head. "Was it someone who's going to tell Cor where we're going? Is it someone who can tell him to call you?" Maybe I was crazy. I certainly sounded it. Holding on to the steering wheel tightly with my left hand, I held out my right. "Fine. Can I see that phone?" When Landemann didn't reply, I sighed. "I'm not going to pull anything tricky. I'd like to call my mother. Would that be all right?" He still didn't so much as move a muscle. "My mother? The woman who, though she didn't know you from Adam, waited over five hours in the hospital emergency room to make sure you were okay? The one who laundered your sheets after you arrived home? Can I call her, please? Or will that be cutting too much into your rollover minutes?"

There was really only one way this battle of wills would end. Just as I could have predicted, Landemann reached into his pocket, withdrew the mobile phone, and handed it over.

"Thank you!" I said, trying not to smirk. Of course, my basest impulse was to check the call log and dial the last number in it, just to see if I could find out what in the hell was happening with Cor and Nikki. I refrained, though. I had my end of this mission to uphold. Besides, I didn't think I could figure out the phone's advanced functions one-handed. "Mom?" I said, after I'd punched out ten digits and then the little dialing icon. "I need to ask you a big, big favor. What're you doing this afternoon? Do you want to go on a little trip?" I looked over at Landemann, who was watching me through his Blues Brothers shades. "What do you mean, who's going?"

I found out exactly what she meant when I pulled up in the tiny street behind her house a little over an hour and a half later, only to see my mother's round, smiling face looking for me over the gate. At least she was ready to go, it looked like; we wouldn't have to make much of a pit stop at all. "I'm so glad you can come," I said, breathless as I stepped from the car that I hadn't even bothered to turn off. I opened the gate so I could grab her by the arm and escort her to the car. "You see, it's like this." I'd spent the last hour of the trip perfecting the story I'd be telling her that might explain the things I needed her to do. It was my mother we were talking about, here—the woman who, instead of reading me fairy stories when I was growing up, had let me cut my baby teeth on *The Iliad*. She couldn't handle the truth. "There's a man on Catalina Island I have to see who . . . what the hell is all this?"

Parked on the mossy brick pavers was an entire assortment of paraphernalia. A wicker basket lined with red gingham. A small cooler. A beach umbrella, and a canvas bag printed with a purple kitten, that held towels. Another canvas bag filled with shoes, sunblock, and a prominent copy of *Bulfinch's Mythology*. "Just a few things for a nice day on the island!" said my mother, surprised that I'd asked. "Should I put them in the trunk? Hello, Mr. Landemann!" Her hand fluttered in his direction.

There seemed to be something particularly unstrung about the way she tiptoed to look over the top of the pickets in order to see him. It was then that I noticed what she was wearing. Barbara Neale, from whose loins I sprung, had traded in her baggy-jeans-and-sweatshirts schlubwear and her invisible-academic jumpers and turtlenecks for a look I'd never seen before. Now, true it may be that I'd been out of the picture for the last three years of her life and during that time she may have fallen under the influence of fashion makeover shows on cable, but I was fairly certain that it had been a long, long time since I'd seen my mom wearing a sleeveless, strapless sundress in a bold and eye-catching red floral print. And when it came to headgear, I was pretty sure I'd never seen her wear anything more than a Dodgers baseball cap—certainly not a wide-brimmed white hat with an ivory scarf tied around its dome, suitable for Hepburn to wear to a royal garden party. Audrey, not Katharine. "Why are you so dressed up?" I asked. "When I told you we were going on a manhunt, I didn't mean . . ." That's when I gasped. "*No!*"

With great dignity, my mother turned from her scrutiny of my Mini and minced over on her low heels—heels!—to pick up her bag and the cooler. "Are we ready?" she asked, primly pretending not to notice my surprise.

"You little *minx!*" I might not have been any taller than my mother, but I was a heck of a lot faster. I firmly blocked her path, arms crossed. "You're interested in *Landemann?* Don't try to pretend. You're a terrible liar."

She turned her head to the side. I could tell she was biting her lower lip. "And what if I was? Interested, that is? He's of a certain age. I'm of a certain age."

"Mmm-hmmm," I agreed, with my eyebrows raised.

"We're both unattached, if I'm not mistaken. I'm sure he has many interesting stories about his job as a butler. So why don't you . . ." Her cheeks puffed out in frustration. "Why don't you just mind your own beeswax, young lady?"

"Oh, Mom," I laughed. The rush of love I felt for her at that moment was so overwhelming that for a moment, I nearly forgot about the utterly craptastic day I was having and the stress I felt. Nearly, but not quite. "Fine," I said, hurrying her along. "Use all your siren skills to lure Mr. Landemann into your sticky web of lust."

"I think you're mixing your metaphors, Samantha," she said, her face grave.

"Whatever. Just haul ass. And we're not taking any of this stuff. Except maybe the picnic basket," I amended, grabbing it. I hadn't eaten anything since the bagels that morning. "And the cooler. And that hoodie, for me. Honestly. A beach umbrella? It would never fit in the Mini. You might as well try to bring an elephant."

"Barbara?" As if my spine had suddenly been yanked from its socket, my head lolled back at the sound of Doreen's querulous voice. She stepped out of the back door, pulling it shut behind her. She wore an enormous pair of pink shorts, a Provincetown T-shirt, sunglasses, and flip-flops. "Barbara! I can't find the Purell."

Instantly I turned to Mom. "No."

"But, Samantha," she explained in a whisper, trying to sound quite reasonable. "On Saturdays Doreen and I usually visit the flea market together. I can't just leave her."

I couldn't scream outright, not with Doreen waddling closer. But did Mom really not notice me doing my best imitation of my teenage days, with the rolled eyes and the tapping foot and the general look of surly curtness? Apparently not. I was going to have to vocalize. "No," I growled.

"I can't," she repeated, even more softly.

"No!"

"There's plenty of room. Look. We'll leave the cooler behind."

"Barbara?" said Doreen, affixing a green plastic visor to her head. "I hope you told her I have to ride shotgun, else I get carsick."

"Please?" asked my mom.

I put my foot down. My car. My journey. For once in my lifetime with my mother, I got to have the last word. "Absolutely, one hundred percent not!"

Chapter Eighteen

"And that is how the doctors finally managed to get rid of them," Doreen was saying by the time we climbed off the gently rocking Catalina Express. "It's like I told your mother. Plantar warts are just one of those things you always think happen to other people, and not yourself." She'd been talking to me the whole damned trip. Which, as any weekend Catalina tourist would know, is not that short. There was the interminable drive in Los Angeles pre-rush-hour traffic, during which Mom and Landemann sat wedged in my tiny backseat, shoulders and knees pressed together. I'd had to listen helplessly to Doreen's chord-by-goddamned-acoustic-guitar-chord recap of the NorCal women's music festival while mere inches behind me, my mother urged Landemann to sample some of the picnic-basket treats from the gourmet market. We were scarcely out of Venice before she had him opening a jar of garlic-stuffed olives and plucking one out for himself. Soon after, she was extending a package of Japanese rice crackers for him to taste; by the time we reached San Pedro, the old hussy was lean-

ing over and actually inserting dark chocolate biscotti
into his mouth with her own fingers, ignoring the disap-
proving glares I kept trying to shoot her in the rearview
mirror.

After the drive, there was the wait on the pier for the
Catalina Express to board and leave, and finally the
hour-long trip across the water. All that time, I couldn't
take my eyes off the sky. Relieved as I was not to be driving any longer, the cramped quarters of my little vehicle
had at least seemed to contain my anxieties, squashing
them down to human size. Beneath the blandly blue
California skies, though, they seemed to balloon in size
until they seemed unmanageable and endless. I
couldn't stop looking upward, though, hoping for some
glimpse of the jet-black birds who'd become so en-
meshed in my life over the last week. It was up there
that I longed to be, flying with Cor, instead of remaining
earthbound, listening to Doreen rattle off a complete
list of all the foods she could no longer eat after having
turned fifty-five. God, anything but that.

"Oh, Mr. Landemann," my mother giggled, her left
hand resting on his crooked right arm. Somehow she'd
managed to accomplish the impossible, in the confusion
of exiting the ferry; on her nose rested the bodyguard's
never-removed sunglasses. Without them, Landemann's
portly face looked naked and pinker than normal; his
eyes were tiny and a shade of blue similar to the eyes of
the Peri side of the family. "You really are one of the most
interesting men I've known."

"You give those back!" I hissed. Since my mother was
too busy flirting like Scarlett O'Hara after too many
mint juleps—I practically expected her to pull out a fan
and flutter her eyelashes at the man—I was left with the
responsibility of hauling all the crap she'd brought with
us. God only knows that Doreen, still talking to no one
in particular about the difference between plantar

warts and bunions, wasn't going to hook her arms around the basket and the cooler and the overnight bags they'd both packed. So it was up to me, hampered by the weight of my mother's entire pantry and cosmetics cabinet, to compete with all the city people disembarking with us for transportation.

Mom ignored me. "Have you ever been to Catalina before, Mr. Landemann?" she asked, taking a moment to survey the broad sweep of white and blue that was the little city of Avalon, huddled at the mass of greenery leading to the steep hills. Hundreds of boats were docked in the bay, the lines of them sweeping out to the ocean in a semicircle that ran parallel to the beach. Something flying above caught my eye, but when I shaded my brow and looked up, it was only a small plane gliding toward the mountaintop airport. "It's a sweet little place to visit. I worked here one summer when I was in college, at one of the ice cream parlors. Can you imagine me, scooping ice cream?"

The look that Landemann gave her, with his eyes squinched up with smile lines, seemed to indicate that not only could he imagine it, but that in his vision of her summer job she was doing unspeakable things with the Tin Roof Sundae. And now that we were at our destination, I'd had just about enough of that.

"Taxi!" I yelled, shoving the cooler in Landemann's hands. Hey, I knew he was still recuperating from his gore wounds. The cooler was the lightest of the bags I'd been struggling with.

"I'll find one," he said.

"Oh, it speaks," I commented, as he walked by. I'd been sure his remark had been more for my mother's benefit than mine. "We're kind of in a hurry here, if you don't remember!"

At least then he broke into a trot. Why didn't these people understand how serious this all was? Admit-

tedly, I hadn't told my mother any of the whys and
whats of our outing, and I intended to keep it that way.
But of all people, Landemann should have known better! Maybe he'd been stuffed with too many of my
mother's imported figs.

I wasn't complaining when, mere moments later, an
elderly driver wearing the Catalina Transportation Services uniform came jogging over from the main thor-
oughfare to relieve me of my basket and bags. He
began to hustle them to his van, shooing away people
to make a clear path for us. Landemann must have
strong-armed him severely, or else given him a pretty
hefty bribe. Several of the wandering crowd who had
made it to the few waiting cabs well ahead of us and
should have been taken first stared at us with no little
hostility as our little group shambled by; on an island
where precious few motor vehicles were allowed and
most people got around by bicycle or golf cart, the
competition for shuttle service was sometimes fierce.
"Elderly mother," I explained to one, who huffed dra-
matically and crossed her arms when we passed. "She's
feeble."

"Feeble like a goddamned ox during tilling season,"
Doreen snorted in her loudest voice, as the cab driver
tried to help her into the front seat of the van. "She
teaches tai chi at the senior center."

"Thank you, Doreen," I said, loudly.

"She can beat me at arm wrestling any day."

"I said *thank you*, Doreen." The driver shut the door.
My mother was already in the rear seat; Landemann
held out a hand so that I could climb in through the
van's side door and into the middle. When it came to
picking between the two generations of Dorringer girls,
however, I noticed that he went with the older variation.
Finally, with a united chorus of dirty looks from the peo-

ple we'd ferried over with, we were off, navigating through Avalon's quaint streets.

The Sycamore Plaza Hotel was one of those elaborate century-old monstrosities near the beach at the far end of the harbor boardwalk, erected when the nation was apparently under the impression that if there was space for a window, no matter how tiny or oddly shaped, it could and should be crammed in there. Throw in a massive tower over the corner entrance and a half-dozen decorative turrets, trim with gingerbread, and you had one of the typical architectural aberrations that dotted the Avalon skyline. I wasn't there to criticize building design, though; I'd chosen the Sycamore off the top of my head because it was one of the few spots around town that had stuck in my head enough to pick as a meeting point. So anxious was I as we approached the building that part of me considered simply leaping from the car and racing it there on foot, but I resisted. I couldn't ignore the thudding of my heart, though. Hours and hours I'd come for this meeting, and the fact that my destination was only yards away was making me itch all over. I wanted it all to end.

But there we finally were, pulling up to a stop on the street in front of the hotel's entrance. Without so much as a look over my shoulder, I grabbed the door's inside handle and slung it back behind me, jumping out into the cool and slightly briny seaside air. Up the red-carpeted steps my feet tripped, carrying me into the decidedly modernized interior of the Victorian folly. Although the designers had furnished the lobby with formal-looking chairs, they were as plush and comfy as you'd find in any upscale hotel, without any of the hard edges. From the bright and decidedly modern check-in desk, a pair of clerks smiled at me blandly, but I ignored them. Instead, I looked wildly around the empty room.

I'd *told* Harland Oliver to meet me here. He'd promised he would! Was I late? Had he given up and gone away?

Refusing to think of other, more disturbing, alternatives, I marched up to the desk and attempted to plaster a simulacrum of goodwill on my face. "Hi," I said to the clerks, barely able to hear my own voice over the pounding in my chest and my impending high blood pressure. "I was supposed to meet a couple of friends here. You wouldn't have happened to see them, would you? A man and a little girl?"

Although they'd been friendly enough before, in that professional public demeanor kind of way, when I qualified my question with that one basic description, their faces fell. "Oh," said the guy on the left, suddenly more interested in whatever scraps of paper were on the desk in front of him than in me. "They're in the Internet lounge."

I said a quick thank-you to his blond tips and ran in the direction he pointed, to a little room near the rack of tourist brochures and an old-fashioned, closed shoeshine booth. Although the room was dark, the PC inside was on, giving the two faces within an eerie glow. "Harland Oliver?" I said to the man from the doorway. The screen's blue radiance made his eyes seem larger than they really were. Or maybe I'd startled him; certainly at the sound of his name, he shrank back into a defensive position, one hand on the computer's mouse, and the other on the back of the chair where his daughter sat. "Lily? Lily Oliver?"

The girl swiveled at my voice. "Huh?"

And she really was just a kid, I realized. I'd known it all along, of course, but somehow in my head over the last two weeks, the name *Lily Oliver* had become inflated to almost mythic proportions. I wouldn't have been surprised by an otherworldly cherub with flowing hair and an unearthly voice, or an oracular tyke in ghostly robes. But she was just a little second-grader in overalls and a striped shirt, with blond, slightly wavy hair, as cute and no more unusual than Drew Barrymore had been at her age. And I mean the Drew Barrymore of *E.T.*, not the Drew Barrymore of *Firestarter.* "I'm Samantha," I explained. "We talked on the phone. Are you guys all right?"

The father stood up when I walked into the room and switched on the lights. When he moved, I could instantly tell why the clerks hadn't been too wild about his presence. He stunk. They both did, of what I instantly assumed wasn't so much body odor or filth, as fish. The scent was so pervasive that it seemed to unfold from their clothing as Harland picked up Lily from her seat and took her into his arms. My nose twitched and stung at the intensity of it, though I tried not to let it register. "You tell me," said Harland. His southern twang sounded more like a rattle. "You tell me if we're goddamned all right."

"Ssssh." I looked over my shoulder to see my three traveling companions setting down their bags in the lobby's center. I waved in their direction to let them know where I was.

"I mean, I haven't even been able to look outside for the last three hours," he complained, bouncing Lily up and down in his arms. She lay her head on his shoulder and stared at me. "All I know is that you're the one calling me up, scaring me half to death . . ." In the distance, long and low, came a rumble of thunder. All three of us looked up at the unexpected sound—Harland's face apprehensive, Lily's placid, and my own hopeful. "That doesn't sound good," he whispered.

"No, it's good. It's very good," I assured him, feeling suddenly confident again. The Storm Ravens were nearby, I knew. "I need you both to come with me. Come on," I said, holding out my arms toward Lily. I didn't think I was strong enough to carry such a big girl for long, so I helped her down to the floor, took her by the hand, and started to lead her from the room. "Everything will be all right. What did you tell her?" I asked him, privately, as close to his ear as I could, despite the protective barrier of fish odor keeping me away.

"Nothing," he said. "I didn't tell her about Chassidy, if that's what you mean. Or anything about . . . those other people."

The Kin, he meant. The Order of the Crow, whom he'd so willingly aided and abetted as long as the checks had kept pouring in. Harland Oliver might have looked no more extraordinary than any other guy—in fact, with his receding hairline, his sun-damaged complexion, his too-big checkered shirt, and his mucky jeans, he seemed more like the polite homeless people I used to see panhandling in Las Vegas and quickly ignore. But I couldn't forget that the one exceptional act he'd taken in his life had been vile and unforgivable. I couldn't think about it without feeling the anger grow inside my chest. He'd tried to sell his daughter to strangers, and this is where the consequences had landed him. Not only him. Me, as well. I couldn't forget that Harland's greed had shaved away three years of my life, too.

"Mom," I said loudly, unable to address him. "This is the little girl I told you about. Her name's Lily." I stroked her hair as I introduced her; Lily looked up at my mother with wide eyes that were unafraid, though not exactly friendly. "Lily, sweetie, this is my mother. She'll be watching after you while your daddy and I go out to meet some people."

"What?" I heard from behind me, as Harland gulped audibly. "Wait a minute."

"Hello, Lily!" With Doreen settling herself down in the largest of the armchairs, my mother bent over and placed her large hat on the girl's considerably smaller head. Almost immediately, Lily's hands reached up to adjust it, a grin on her face. "Oh, you like hats, do you? We'll get along just fine, then. Don't you have remarkably blue eyes?"

"Get a room," I told Mom. "Don't worry about the money. Get something comfortable, and shut yourself in there until I come back."

"My daughter makes it sound so grim," said Mom, her eyes crinkling as she beamed at Lily. Her enthusiasm was infectious; the girl was shyly smiling back. "We'll watch The Cartoon Network and order room service, won't we? And maybe have a bath," she added, nose wrinkled. Hand in hand, the two of them went to the desk to check in.

"Don't talk to any strangers, unless Mr. Landemann knows them," I called out to my mother. Landemann still stood next to me, sunglasses back in place, I noticed. He stood with the same attentive air as when I'd first met him, guarding Cor. Easy target for gourmet-market goodies he might have been, but at least he knew when it was time for business. "Stay with them. Don't let anything happen to her. I'm relying on you," I told him, trying to keep my voice low and private. "I know I'm not Cor, but I'm the best you've got until he comes back. You and my mother are the only things standing between them and that little girl."

He didn't have to obey me. Why should he? He'd only known me for mere days. But he slowly nodded, agreeing. "Barbara!" brayed Doreen, from the armchair. "I don't understand. We came all this way to babysit a rugrat?"

"It will be fun, I promise!" said my mother, from the desk.

"And where are *you* going?" Doreen gave me a look of utter aversion.

"Out to see a man about a bird," I declared, shoving Harland Oliver ahead of me. "Keep walking," I snapped, when he protested. I didn't let him say good-bye to his daughter; she didn't even notice when he and I disappeared through the leaded glass of the front doors.

"I get the feeling you don't like me," he said once we were outside beneath the darkening skies.

"You're right," I admitted, sounding snide. People were walking by on the streets, so I tried to modulate my volume. "Forgive me. I have a hard time warming up to men who'd sell their little girls."

His face reddened. He stopped in his tracks, forcing me to turn around. "They said—!" he huffed, grinding his jaw. "They said they were going to take *care* of her. They said she'd have a better *life*. You don't know how bad it was before they started giving us money. I didn't have a job. She didn't have a mother." He must have seen me mentally playing the teeny-tiny violin because he started stabbing a finger to emphasize his points. "I didn't *know* what they were going to do. They put these pictures in my head like she was going to be taken care of for the rest of her life. I mean, I don't know what they did, but I could *see* what they were telling me, right there in my brain, like a movie or something. She was on a throne, and had the prettiest clothes, and everyone loved her. Like she was going to be some kind of princess, or celebrity, or something. Lady, I couldn't give her that kind of life! I was this guy on unemployment. A serious loser. And Lily was this pretty . . ." His lower lip quivered slightly in what I could tell was the prelude to a breakdown. "She's my pretty little girl I wanted to give the world to. How was I supposed to turn that down?"

It had never seriously occurred to me before that Marshall could have duped the guy. I could almost see the seductive logic behind the imagery they'd painted for him. If I'd been in his situation, I immediately recognized, I might have done the same thing. "You're her father," I said at last. "You're supposed to turn down offers that are too good to be true."

"You can't judge me like that!"

"You're right." Although I knew I was being more gruff than I perhaps had right, I continued. "One hundred percent right. I can't judge you like that. I'm not qualified. Never mind that because of you, those same people kidnapped me and kept me hostage for three years, Mr. Oliver, just because I happened to make a routine insurance inquiry into your whereabouts after your feigned death. Oh yeah." He looked shocked at that news, and I was glad for it. "Three very long years of my life just *gone* because of what you were going to do. But you're right, that doesn't give me any right to judge, not at all. And it doesn't matter that right now, at this moment, they've kidnapped one of the people who was trying to help you and your daughter. Someone I'm very fond of. None of that matters, Mr. Oliver."

"I didn't know," he muttered, suddenly not able to look me in the eye. He was still dark as a cherry.

I felt another wave of exasperation for the guy. "Of course you didn't. How could you? But you know now, and what you're going to do to make up for it is take me to your home."

"But . . . but you told me to leave home." Harland's lower lip trembled. He didn't look as if he planned to move anywhere. "You told me it was dangerous there."

For someone I'd cherished thinking of as a scheming super-villain for so long, the guy certainly was kind of, well, a wet rag doll. I wanted to grab him by the scruff of the neck and give him a good wringing-out. Instead, I grabbed the collar of his shirt and hauled him along. We'd wasted enough time. "I told you it was dangerous for *Lily* there. Now come on."

"If it's dangerous for Lily there, then won't it be dangerous for me?" he asked, dragging his feet.

I didn't answer the question. I didn't really think I had to.

We had to take one of the island's inevitable golf carts to the Oliver's home. On almost any other evening, I would've enjoyed the leisurely twilight drive along the romantic streets of sleepy Avalon. Even though low rumbles of thunder still nibbled away at the peaceful evening, and though dark clouds from the east seemed to be streaking their way across the orange-pink skies faster than night itself, the atmosphere was still tranquil. None of the tourists still roaming the streets with their shopping bags and ice cream cones in hand seemed to worry about the possibility of rain; no one in the candlelit restaurants even seemed to hear the impending storm. Me, though? I chafed against the cart's achingly slow speed. I was actually considering hopping out of the open side and dragging it in whatever direction we needed to go, when finally Harland steered it off Sumner Avenue and down St. Catherine's Way, leading north from Avalon. Not that there was much to Catalina Island beyond Avalon, tons of trees, and a few herds of buffalo out in the wild, mind you. But before too long, after we'd left behind all the quaint in-city housing and the stretches of private road with more expensive and exclusive housing, we made a sharp turn onto a rocky, steep road leading down toward the water. The frame of a half-built resort home sat on a fenced-off site on a scrap of dusty land there; its timber frame was skeletal against the darkening sky. Harland pulled the cart to a stop by a gate, so that suddenly the only noises I could hear were the susurrus of the water and the flapping of plastic tarps in the increasing breeze.

"This is it?" I asked, gesturing to what had been built of the house. "This is your home?"

He laughed shortly, fiddling with the keys on the ring he kept on one of his belt loops. "Hardly," he said, twisting one into a padlock and releasing it with a snap. Unlatching the metal hasp, he pushed back the swinging barrier and invited me in with a sweep of his arm. "That is."

What he meant, apparently, was the construction trailer sitting on the site's edge. It hadn't even been leveled properly; one of its corners was at least a foot lower than the rest of it. A window had been broken out long ago and replaced with plastic sheeting and duct tape. "You live here?" I asked, astonished. It didn't take full sunlight to see what a run-down tin can of a home it was. No, make that sardine can—the odor grew stronger when we approached it. He didn't seem to notice, which didn't surprise me, considering the stench of his clothing. I pointed over to the main house under construction. "So eventually you can move in there, right?"

He shook his head, looking almost ashamed. "It's not my property. It's been in arrears for over a year now. No construction, nothing. I'm kind of squatting here." He already knew I thought the worst of him, so he didn't bother to wait before adding, with a defensive manner, "I know it looks like a shithole, but it's got electricity and water and phone. Lily goes to school and everything. They think her name's Jennifer, here. When anybody asks, I tell them the big house is mine and we'll be moving in next summer. I mean, I don't earn much, but I sell fish at the local market and do odd jobs and we do all right. Or we did all right, until you found me." Harland seemed uncomfortable with silence; he kept talking to fill it. "So what am I doing here, anyway? Am I bait? Is that it? You're just going to . . ."

"Sssh." I cut him off, instantly aware that something was wrong. He tried to talk again, but I clutched his arm, warning him not to make a sound. In one of the flickers of lightning a moment ago, I thought I'd seen something moving through the windows of the darkened trailer. This wasn't good. Not good at all. I pointed to the door at the top of the makeshift cinderblock stairs, and whispered, "Stay behind me."

"No problem!" he whispered back, sounding as frightened as I felt.

And I was indeed scared, I don't mind admitting. For a split second I wanted to blame the world for leaving me to face whatever was in that trailer all alone, but I knew how ridiculous that was. I hadn't been deserted. I'd undertaken the task willingly, and here I finally was at my destination after too long a journey. Sure, I would have felt better with Cor at my side, personally, but that was a luxury I didn't have. I'd done without him for years, and I could make do for now.

"Get ready," I whispered, taking a deep, fishy breath and trying to soothe the willies I felt. I needed energy, and I needed the element of surprise. As if I feared it might be electrified, I grabbed the trailer's knob and twisted, while simultaneously kicking the door wide open. "I've got a gun!" I yelled, my bullet-less canister of pepper spray firmly in my hand. "I know you're in there! Come out, and don't try anything funny!" I sounded surprisingly authoritative, even to myself. Nobody said anything, but I heard a shifting noise from the dark inside. "Get your ass out here, damn you!" I growled, stepping back. Behind me, Harland scampered away, afraid to be too close, but seemingly too frightened to run off on his own.

"Fine." A woman's voice came from the trailer, sharp and ironic. "Don't shoot me with your 'gun,' please, Samantha."

Chapter Nineteen

Electricity seemed to run from my spine along my shoulders and down to my fingertips. "Ginger?" I asked, as she emerged. She stood in the doorway, arms crossed, head tilted. I never thought I'd be so glad to see someone I disliked so much.

"Who's that?" gibbered Harland behind me. "Is she one of them?"

"Yes, but she's not one of *them* them," I told him. But frankly, at that moment, I didn't care about Harland. I rushed in Ginger's direction, only stopping short at the last moment from grabbing her and trying to shake information from her. "Where's Nikki? Is she okay? Did you find her? Where's Cor? How did you find this place? Is Nikki okay?"

She waited patiently while I rattled off my questions. "We don't know where Nikki is, though our trackers think she's on the island, somewhere. We had the number you found at that dead woman's apartment traced to this location. Do you have Lily?"

"She's safe. What about Cor?" I asked. "Is he okay? Where is he?"

"Samantha." She stepped down from the trailer briskly, taking me by the shoulder. "We need to have a little talk. Your friend will excuse us, won't he?" It wasn't so much a question as a command; she waved her fingers in his direction. "Wait inside for a moment, please," was all she had to say to get him to hurry indoors. He wasn't the only person she was commanding, however; several large, dark birds I hadn't noticed stealthed among the falling shadows opened their wings and took flight.

Once everyone was out of sight, Ginger put her hand around my shoulder and, as if we were old chums, began walking with me in the direction of the open gate. I didn't like it. It felt like I'd made some terrible faux pas, and every pace we took across that gravel-strewn work site added another misstep. "What did I do?" I asked, thinking that I'd blown some sting operation that neither Landemann nor I had known about.

"You did your job, dear." If there was anything more condescending than Jinjurnawhatever literally patting me on the back while calling me "dear," I didn't ever want to see its backside. "Well done, you!"

"You don't carry off that female-empowerment talk-show pep thing very well," I said, wary. I didn't see any recognition in her eyes. "In other words, what do you want?"

Although I'd called her on the palsy-walsyness, Ginger didn't let me out of her clutch. "I think you and I want the same things, Samantha. We want to see justice done. Isn't that right?" I couldn't deny it, though I wasn't about to make the mistake of agreeing with her. "We want to do well at our duties. And you've done well here."

"All right." I couldn't thank her. Not when part of me

was certain with every word of her faint praise, she meant to damn me.

"I mean, look at everything you've managed to accomplish. Don't think I'm not a fan of the human race. I am. I think it's amazing, what your people can manage to do in your brief life spans. You might think that what we can do is magical, but compared to you! We shift and become part of the world, but you change the world to suit yourselves. I don't think there's one among us who doesn't envy your energy and drive."

I stopped. Already we were a good distance away from the building site, close to a decaying old dock in the water that must have belonged to the demolished house occupying this lot before. Ginger might have been used to the storm winds that were whipping up both sand and water around us, but in my flimsy hoodie, I was getting chilly and more anxious. "Yeah, yeah, I know the whole grain-of-sand spiel. Cor gave it to me. What's this all about?"

"I just wanted to thank you," she said without hesitation. "You've done a fantastic job. You found Lily Oliver and got her somewhere safe—where is she, by the way?"

For a fraction of a second I had a vision of this scenario playing out like the climax of a cheesy action movie, in which the hapless heroine discloses to the seemingly friendly foil the location of the valuable stolen jewels she's found and secreted away, only to discover that the foil is really in cahoots with the mad scientist who needs the specially cut diamonds for his dimensional laser weapon. I discarded the notion as ridiculous, though I didn't get too specific in my answer. "She's in town with my mom, safe."

"Good. See? Amazing." Her smile refrigerated me more than the wind or the drops of rain just beginning to fall. "So your job is done."

It took me a moment to realize that she hadn't been

asking a question. We'd finally gotten to the point of this little tête-à-tête. "I'm sorry?" I said, trying to compose my thoughts.

One of her muscular arms reached out and squeezed mine. "You're done. It's over. You did really well. You can go home and enjoy the rest of your life now." I wouldn't have at all been surprised if she'd added, *what's left of it*. She was so patronizing, so superior so . . . *smug* in her sincerity that I was utterly taken aback. "Isn't that what you want? You've got a great mother, a sweet little house. You could take up your job again. Meet some-one nice."

Oh. I got it. Did I ever get it. "Good God," I said, jaw practically scraping the pebbly beach.

"The Crown has a standard helper's fee for this type of thing, of course," she went on, pretending not to see how dismayed I was with her. "It's not princely, but in a high-profile case such as this one, and considering the danger you were in and the length of time for which you were incarcerated, I think you might be looking at enough to start up your own small business, or at least buy some time to figure out what you really want to do with your life. Your life away from us."

There was no mistaking the threat in those last three words. "What exactly do you think I'm going to do to your Kin, Ginger?" I asked. Outright rudeness I could have ignored, or laughed at. The condescension, how-ever? It pushed my every button. I was ready to punch the bitch. "Steal them all away from you? Awww. Or wait. Is it just one in particular you're worried about? Could it be, hmmm. Corydonais?"

Naturally, she didn't get the humor of my best *Satur-day Night Live* Church Lady imitation. "You know what I'm worried my people might call a human like you, Samantha?"

"High-level achievers?" I ventured. "Success stories?"

"Fairy-seekers," she spat, crossing her arms. "Oh, you haven't heard the term? We see them all over, wherever we are, throughout all of history. *Eirethin* sluts in the coffee shops with flowing gowns and dreamy eyes. Shopping in our shops and flirting with our men. They even dress up for our Renaissance Faires in the hope of seeming like one of us." I should have *known* that the Kin were behind those bloody Renaissance Faires! "There's not an ounce of dignity in them. All they want is to seduce one of the Kin—any one of them—and bear a mongrel child. Why, I don't know. If they think the brat will have the birthright to enter Resht, they're sadly mistaken. Now, I know you're different." If her tone had been harsh and unforgiving before, now it was honeyed once more, tickling my ears with its sweetness. "You're not one of those women, are you? Of course not. But to our people . . ." She let out one of those sounds that most people render as *tsk*. "It just doesn't look good to see so prominent a member of the Kin consorting so closely with one of your species. His father . . ."

"What happened between Cor's father and his women seems about as much your concern as whatever happens between Cor and me," I snapped. Honestly, the woman was making me want to do the kind of irrational and outrageously dramatic things you only saw in flipping past a Mexican *telenovela* on cable TV—like throw a sangria in her smug little face. "I happen to care for Corydonais. I'm not in it because I want to have his baby, which by the way is an awfully regressive, if not to mention sexist, thing to say about a woman. I respect him. And he respects me."

"It's what all the Peri are going to think, whether it's true or not. And how long can Corydonais avoid questioning your motives when all his friends and family will be, with every word you say and breath you take? If he doesn't already." Ginger was back to being smug again. "Dear, why don't you just go before your illusions are shattered?"

I gaped at her in disbelief. She was threatening me with what, a public shunning? Like I cared? I was about to tell her to bring on her worst snubbed nose and icy shoulder when I hesitated. My involvement with her race might have lasted for less than a month, but Cor had been a part of them for centuries. What if our involvement—whatever it was—really did cause him to be isolated? I knew that sounded dramatic, and even unlikely. But honestly, if there really were consequences to being with me, how could I dare speak for him?

Ginger saw my doubts, in that brief moment of hesitation. I knew it by the curve of her lips. She'd managed to get into my head with the thin edge of her wedge, and I despised her for it. "We'll see what Cor says about it," I yelled out against the wind. It didn't seem too successful a bluff, unfortunately, because she didn't back down at all from her stance of self-satisfied superiority. And I have to admit: knowing that Ginger begrudged me any time with Cor whatsoever when she and he were likely going to be around for years and years after I'd gone to my cold and lonely grave really rankled. It also made me feel puny and insignificant in the face of the great wash of time.

But that scary small feeling didn't last, because at that moment we were both startled from our little struggle by the loud and raucous sound of birds overhead. Lightning streaked across the near horizon, crackling with energy; thunder followed, shaking the ground beneath my feet and rumbling so viciously that it seemed to empty every ounce of oxygen from my lungs. I sucked in air, barely aware that I'd crouched down in a defensive stance, while I watched the battle suddenly raging above. In the near darkness, I could see what looked like arrows darting across the sky, shooting in every direction. Yet they weren't arrows—they were birds, squawking and screeching over the sound of wind and rain. The commotion they made sounded like some strange language I could almost, but not quite, understand. It was frantic and energetic, frightening and staggering in its scope; I'd simply never seen so many birds aloft before, much less at war with each other.

A flash of brightness forced me to hold my hands up over my eyes, shielding them. I'd thought it was lightning, but when it didn't disappear, I realized that the storm-accelerated darkness had triggered the sensor on some kind of construction lamp on a post above the work site. It lit up the ground around us with a stark, white light, cold and desolate as moonlight and twice as terrifying. I could see plastic sheeting whipping from the walls and windows of the barely begun house in the near distance, the sideways slant of the rain beginning to fall with increasing fury, and the silhouette of Harland Oliver, emerging from his trailer to witness the tempest outside. My clothes hung heavy and wet on my skin. That had been happening a lot, lately.

Close to my ear came the sound of a shriek. I whipped around in place, stumbling backward until I trod on Ginger's foot. She put both hands on my back to keep me from pushing her over as some kind of dark-feathered bird hurtled by, mere feet from where I'd stood. Another bird seemed to be chasing it through the air. In a flurry of motion and rage, the two collided. One of them let out a great cry of pain and thudded to the ground, one wing wildly flapping, while the other hung, limp and impotent. I watched, horrified, as it twitched, shuddered, and within moments, stopped moving entirely.

"Get going!" I heard in my ear. Ginger grabbed my

arm and began running with me in the direction of the trailer. I didn't need a second prompt. My legs pumped wildly to escape the battle raging overhead. Another bird's corpse fell to the ground nearby, smacking the ground with more force than seemed possible. I couldn't tell if it was crow or raven. "Stop!" Ginger yanked me back at the property's perimeter, just outside the gate. "The trailer's not safe. It looks like that's what the crows are attacking."

I was glad she had some idea of what was happening, because beyond a vision of mayhem, I didn't have a clue. "Harland's there," I yelled at her, pointing. Water was streaming down my face and neck and matting down my hair. Pulling my hood over my head didn't keep it from getting any wetter, but at least it stopped the rivulets of rain that were surging into my eyes. When I cleared them, in the harsh glare of the construction lights I saw the silhouette of Lily's father teetering on the concrete steps outside the trailer. His fingers were interlocked and covering his head as he crouched down. His forehead was pale white as it tipped upward, trying to see where all the commotion began and ended. "Harland!" I yelled, jumping up and down. "Mr. Oliver!" Then, to Ginger, I shouted, "I've got to get him!"

"At your peril," she retorted, grabbing my chin, pointing it at the trailer, and pushing it up. I saw what she pointed at with her other hand—dozens of ominous-looking birds stretching their wings as they landed atop the trailer, calling out to each other with a cry of *caaah-caaah-caaaah!* I could now understand why a group of crows was called a *murder*. "I can't permit it."

"I have to!"

"Cor would never forgive me," she snarled, keeping a firm hold on my arm.

I couldn't wrestle from that grip; she was plainly stronger than I. I tried, though, using every trick of wriggling and twisting that I could in order to get away, while still calling out Harland's name. One wrong twist and a sharp counterattack from Ginger brought me to one knee. A sharp-edged stone cut through my skin, making me shout with pain. Right at that moment, I heard an electrical flurry—the noise of an overloaded transformer, straining and buzzing like a sound effect from a mad scientist's laboratory. Sparks erupted far above our heads from one of the power lines, blocked only momentarily from view when a number of crows swooped from the pole down to the top of the trailer to join their brethren. "Get up!" Ginger pulled me by one arm to my feet, nearly yanking my shoulder from its socket, then jerked me back like some kind of wet scarecrow. "Get away from the fence!"

Lightning struck nearby. The booming that accompanied was so astounding that it deafened me, pressing some invisible mute button on the action. In the seconds that followed, I seemed to be living in some insane silent movie. In the bright flash of light, I saw the power line, a wet black whip, snap in two. Half of it landed atop the trailer, creating more sparks where it landed on the metal roof; the other half fell and dangled limply across the tall metal enclosure we'd only been inches away from, moments ago. The acrid, tangy scent of electricity gone wrong filled the air. It reminded me of the smell of a model train set, only stronger and much more deadly. The construction lights extinguished with a sigh.

The last thing I saw in that quick burst of light was Harland, surrounded by enemy birds that had descended upon him en masse. They'd formed around him a whirlwind of wildly agitating wings and dangerous beaks, pecking and flapping at him in a frenzy. My ears still ringing, I tried calling out, but whether or not he could hear me, I didn't know. I couldn't hear myself.

The wind whipped the hood from my head, and I was conscious of Ginger trying to drag me back even farther. Quick successions of lightning followed, and with each one I caught glimpses of Harland running forward, hands and legs flailing as he tried to escape the maelstrom. One last flash, and I saw him running for the fence, hands outstretched, as if grabbing at the swinging gate might lead to his salvation. I turned my head, but not before I saw his face stretched into a rictus of agony and shock as he convulsed on the current-charged metal from which he couldn't let go. "Harland!" I called, though I knew it was too late for him. I wanted to collapse. At that point, I thought my legs might actually fail me. All I wanted was to lie down and let the storm wash me away.

Chapter Twenty

Sound began to spiral back into my ears, intensifying back to the howling proportions it had been before the last bout of thunder. I'd preferred the silence. "We're not safe here," yelled Ginger in what I realized was the understatement of the century. Still keeping her viselike grip above my elbow, she yanked me first toward the road, and then stopped and swore in her own tongue. "This isn't good," she finally called out, straining her voice to be heard above the turmoil.

"What?" I asked. I could barely see anything, now—not the house, not the water nor the trees, not even the distant glow from Avalon to the south. I thought of Mom and Lily at that point, and prayed that with all the crows creating havoc here, they were warm and dry and safe from harm.

"Not good," I heard her repeat, before suddenly pulling me in the opposite direction. All I could do was stumble along behind her, hoping that her Peri senses wouldn't lead us astray. More than a few times I stumbled over the uncertain and rocky ground, but somehow the two of us managed to remain upright. The terrible screeching of avians at war continued to surpass even the considerable volume of the storm. It felt as if I'd been plunged into Hell.

We stepped onto softer ground that squished underfoot, but only for a moment; I stubbed my toe against something hard and stumbled onto what felt like planks of wood. We must have left the building site for the beach and dock, I realized. The dread I already felt in my stomach intensified as I realized that Ginger was painting us into a corner. She was a better strategist than that! It was only then, when I blindly felt the touch of angry wings against my face and then a jab of something sharp and painful against the back of my head, that I realized the two of us had perhaps already run out of options.

Ginger's arms surrounded me tightly. Whether she meant to protect or comfort me, I didn't know. Lightning followed, its brilliant light seeming to turn the roiling water into a mirror. I was able to perceive we stood only a foot away from the dock's edge, being buffeted inch by inch toward the water. Maybe, I thought dimly over the confusion, Ginger was even looking for solace from me.

A beak stabbed my forehead, not far from my eye. As my hand flew to my face to press against it and stop the pain, I heard over the disorder a single loud bellow of *pruck! pruck! pruck!* I recognized that call. I'd heard the Storm Ravens using it before, the night Cor and I had been on the faux Eiffel Tower. It came again, loud and clear, a rallying cry—for soon every Storm Raven around us was responding in kind, until the air rang with sound of it. All the battering of wings I'd felt seconds before ceased; from behind us came another rush of wings and a cold wind that felt like a cleansing.

I sensed, rather than heard, another person join us

on the dock. A pair of long arms wrapped around the two of us, and a familiar, stubbled chin brushed against my ear. "Are you all right?" Cor asked, pressing a kiss against my temple. I nodded, hoping he'd understand despite the darkness. "And Lily?"

"She's with—"

"No," Ginger interrupted. "Don't say it here. Not until this is over."

"I'll send someone to get her later," Cor assured me.

"Her father—" So helpless did I feel that I couldn't even finish the sentence.

"I know." I hadn't even noticed until that moment that the chaos seemed to have died down. On the horizon's fringes, thunder still tickled at the skies; it seemed as if the rainstorm had been turned to simmer, rather than to off. "It's too late, now."

"You don't have to be so cold about it!" I protested, stung by what I'd interpreted as a lack of caring. "Lily doesn't have a father, now. You don't know how awful that is!"

"Samantha," he said, all seriousness. "I know the consequences."

"But—"

"Lily's only a little girl. I know." He held me by the shoulders now. In the dark I could tell he was looking at me, though I couldn't see his face. "She'll be fine, Samantha. The Kin will protect her."

"You're the ones who did this to her!" My face was already wet. Only by the warm tracks on either side of my nose could I tell where the tears were drifting. "Shut up, Samantha. I know. It wasn't you. But she won't know that."

"She'll be taken care of. She'll be all right, love. You lost a father, and you turned out all right." The reassurance warmed me, though I couldn't tell exactly why. Perhaps it was because I knew he was safe, and seem-

ingly uninjured; perhaps his touch simply made me feel
more at peace with myself after such a turbulent storm.
Maybe it had been that word he'd used—the L-word,
the one he'd tossed off so casually, the unexpected
grace note that had resonated to my heart like a glad-
some major chord. "But now, it's time to end this."

"Oh, you're so right about that." The voice came out
of the gloom behind us, echoing across the water. "High
time."

"Marshall," I whispered, whipping around. In the
murk I couldn't see so much as a single star above.
Damn these Peri and their sensitive eyes. Didn't they
know a girl could use a little flattering lighting?

As if in answer to my unspoken demand, a half-
dozen fireflies began to dance in a semicircle before
me. No, they weren't fireflies, and they weren't dancing
at all. Out in the water, bobbing up and down on the
ocean waves as they rolled to shore, were a number of
small boats. Little more than rowboats, most of them.
Although they seemed to have outboard motors, none
of them were running, and yet, most eerily, none of
them seemed to be moving out of the half-moon formation in which they were arranged, perfectly still. God
only knows who they belonged to; I would have
guessed they'd been stolen from the private landings
lining the water. "Don't move," Cor whispered in my ear.
Yeah, because I'm the kind of girl who, when she sees a
cold-blooded murderer before her, runs up to give him
smoochy butterfly kisses.

Shadowy figures stood upon the half-dozen boats,
two apiece to every craft. Each, in one hand, carried
the lanterns I'd mistaken for fireflies. Their beams of
light reached across the water, stretching soft orange
arms in our direction. All of the figures in the boats
wore dark robes with hoods that obscured their faces.
Even in the glow of the lanterns, they were nothing

more than black voids. Only when one of the boats eased forward, cutting through the water without anyone propelling it forward, did I notice that in their other hands, the dark forms carried long sticks. Atop each was a blade—lethal curves of silver that glinted in the dim, bobbing lights. Twelve identical Grim Reapers. A dozen visions of death incarnate.

"Samantha," said the figure in the prow of the moving boat. He reached up and pulled back his hood, revealing the curving eyebrows, the close-cropped hair, the face I'd learned to loathe. "It's like we're married all over again, when you call me Marshall." I looked over my shoulder at Cor when I felt him put a hand on my shoulder. There was that face again, lean and angular. My heart was glad that he appeared unhurt, but the look in his eyes was troubled. When I turned back, Marshall cocked his head, almost birdlike even in human form. "But we know more about you now than when we wed, don't we, dear heart?" he crooned. "It's Samantha Dorringer, not Jones, isn't it? Or should I say, more properly, Samantha DeRengier? It explains so much."

I didn't get it. DeWhat? "You've killed a man tonight," Cor called out, his voice carrying easily over the constant splash of the water beneath us. He stepped in front of me, almost cutting me off from view. As if to remind Marshall that the storm was far from over, dark thunder crackled in the distance.

"So say you, even as my dead lie around your feet." I turned once more. In the flickering lantern light, debris littered the beach and the land leading up to the fence, which still sparked and spluttered with electricity. Among the branches and driftwood I could see a handful of dark shapes where lifeless birds had come to rest.

Cor sounded angry as he said slowly, "You are not the only clan to have lost Kin in this battle." I turned away, closing my eyes, not wishing to think about the number of dead I'd seen in the past day. "But when the warfare of our race creates human casualties, we've overstepped our bounds."

"Who died?" Marshall sneered. His hand wandered up and down the shaft of his scythe, fondling it in a way that made me sure he itched to use it again. "Oh, our friend, Mr. Oliver? Why, who'd even notice?" He sounded almost jocular as he spoke. "A craven weakling who gave in so easily to his lusts for lucre and pretty women. A mortal who'd barter his daughter, without asking for what purpose. He's no great loss, is he?" He leaned his weapon forward, until the shaft pointed at me. "Ask the DeRengier. That's what she's thinking."

"I'm not . . . why do you . . . ?" I stammered, confused. "That's not what I was thinking at all!" I said, angry because I'd thought such things many times before I'd met the man. Angry also, because I worried I might still be thinking it, even after I had watched him die.

"No? Hmmm." Marshall shrugged. The other figures remained motionless.

"You're wasting our time." Ginger finally spoke up. She looked miserable; the rain and commotion had left her hair in short red runnels, and her face covered with mud and dirt. I wondered if I looked like I'd been run through the wringer forward and backward, too. "Where's Nicolina?"

"Oh, the girl?" Marshall snapped his fingers. The figure at the rear of his boat leaned forward and pulled up a bundle of rags. When the rags remained standing, I realized they'd had Nikki in the boat with them the entire time. "Why, here she is." With a circular motion, as if he was unwrapping a mummy, he spooled away the fabrics covering her. They dropped to her feet, revealing our former babysitter, her hands tied behind her and her feet tightly bound. Her eyes flashed as obviously she longed to call out to us, but a length of white cloth tied tightly around the back of her head gagged her mouth. Her hair hung in her face and her clothing had been rumpled, but she seemed to be in one piece.

"Nicolina!" Ginger cried. She looked about to dive in the water to swim out to the boat, but a single word in their native tongue from Cor stopped her.

"Safe and sound." Marshall smiled. "Now, where is my girl?"

"She's not yours," I growled. "She never was and never will be."

"Awww." I hated the tone of mock sympathy that Marshall assumed, and I despised being condescended to. "Sentimental, isn't it?" I didn't rise to the bait. All I could do was tremble impotently, somewhat secure in the knowledge that at least Lily and my mother hadn't yet been found. "You know, Corydonais, favored boy, that this war will not end until we have her?"

"It ends now," Cor said, firm as granite. "My clan will see that your sect is rooted out and exterminated."

"Hmmm," said Marshall, reaching out to stroke Nikki's chin with his index finger. The gesture made both Cor and Ginger bristle beside me, but beyond a subtle shifting in their stances, neither moved. "Yes. Much luck with that. You see, our roots burrow further than you would ever suspect. Your feathered friends could hunt for a lifetime and not begin to eliminate a fraction of our numbers."

"Blah, blah, blah," I said, tired of this nonsense. "You know, Marshall, the only thing you haven't done here is twiddle your evil villain mustachios. Get it over with and give back Nikki. You know you're not going to win, here. You're outnumbered." Above us, I could hear the Storm Ravens swooping in formation as they patrolled the area around us. There was no way they could be overwhelmed.

"But I," Marshall replied, quite reasonably, "have a

hostage." I backed down, having no reasonable answer for that. "Ask your boyfriend here if he thinks I'll give up that easily."

I didn't like the way that he placed an unnatural emphasis on the word *boyfriend*. Spoken so nakedly in front of everyone, he made it sound cheap and ordinary and, well, human. "Speak your terms," Cor said, saving me the embarrassment of repeating a bad seventh-grade nightmare of having to tell the class that he wasn't my boyfriend, had never been my boyfriend, and that boys were icky.

"Come now. You know perfectly well that we don't require a purified child for our teind, Corydonais." Marshall seemed to be enjoying this scene. If so, he was the only one. "One of the Kin will do. If, that is, he gives himself willingly."

"Corydonais. No." Ginger kept her voice soft. "Don't listen to him."

"Doesn't your great-dame's line still believe in the great atonement?" Marshall cocked his head again, curious. "Sacrifice, for the sins of the past?"

"The sins of clans such as yours!" Ginger shouted, as Cor gently shushed her.

"What?" I didn't understand. "What's he saying?"

"Cor. Your dame . . ." Ginger shook her head. I could have sworn I heard fear in her voice. "Your great-dame. I couldn't go home to them with such news."

A long silence followed, in which both she and Cor seemed to be having some kind of silent, almost psychic struggle. "Your duty as my second-in-command," he began to say at last.

"Screw that." The abrupt admonishment seemed to not only take him aback, but her as well. "Oh. I shouldn't have."

"You are more like the race of man than you know, little raven," he said, reaching out to sweep the hair and soot from her face. The gesture was so intimate that I wanted to avert my eyes. I should have been jealous, but somehow the exchange seemed more brother-and-sisterly than anything, well, romantic. "I mean that as a compliment. Do what you must. Perhaps you won't have to return to my mother at all."

"Why?" she wanted to know, agitated. "How could that happen?"

"Samantha." I looked up at Cor. He turned his back on Marshall, so that his face fell into shadow. I could barely see the expression there as he spoke. "You must know. I love you."

"Why are you telling me this?" I asked, my throat feeling suddenly strained. "Why now? Why here?"

"Because I want you to know in your heart that I am not abandoning you. I am not your father, and you are not and will never be your mother, heaven willing." He spoke with good humor, but my heart beat like a frightened butterfly within my chest. "I wouldn't have you wondering . . ."

His voice broke then. "Cor." My words came out feebly, barely traveling the space between us. I didn't want to believe where this was leading. "Just call in your Ravens. Get rid of him. Get your sister back."

He shook his head and took both of my hands in his. "Lily needs to be safe. We can end this here, tonight, and the Ravens can take her someplace away from danger."

"No," I whimpered. I'd somehow lost control of my lower lip. It quivered out of control.

"Listen to me," he said softly, not sounding any happier. "You refused to let me rescue you, before. Would you do me the good grace of not refusing to rescue me?"

"The clock is ticking, Corydonais." Marshall, still moving up and down on the waters, appeared impatient.

I looked up where the gloom obscured Cor's face—

his lovely, handsome face. I shook my head. "I don't understand any of this."

"Seven days. Remember, as I told you?" he whispered to me. "Seven days they must hold me. That's how long you'll have to find and save me."

"I can't!" I would have moved heaven and earth to rescue Cor from danger, if I could. But there was the rub. I couldn't move either. I wasn't of his Kin. I was just plain, ordinary Samantha, the woman who'd lost everything and had no idea of how to get it back. "Cor. I can't."

"Let me do it," Ginger offered, obviously despairing of me. For once, I was tempted to agree with her.

"She'll need your help to find where they hide the construct. But grant me the freedom to choose my own savior." Ginger looked as if she might protest, but at the very last moment, she caught herself. Instead, she nodded, and lifted the back of a finger to her nose, as if trying not to sneeze or sniffle. He turned back to me. "Do you care for me?" he asked.

"Oh my God, yes, a thousand times yes," I said. Forget my lower lip. I'd lost control of everything, by this point. My chest heaved. My eyelids fluttered as I helplessly tried to clear away the tears. I wanted to yell and scream and stop all of this madness, right here, right now, but I was helpless. "More than I want to admit. I love you. I love you, Corydonais."

"Then come find me," he whispered. Before I could answer, or beg him to reconsider, he cleared the huskiness from his throat, turned, and nodded at Marshall. "My sister's freedom, and the freedom of Lily Oliver, for my own," he announced, making a complicated gesture before his face. "I accept this bargain willingly."

Marshall's mouth drew back in a smile that was almost feral. "Let it be witnessed," he hissed. Behind him, several of the hooded figures of death raised their hands. The sleeves of their robes fell back as they wrote invisible glyphs in the air before them.

"Witnessed," whispered Ginger, sounding heartbroken. She, too, raised two of her fingers and inscribed something on a plane before her. Then she stepped back, but not before grabbing my elbow and pulling me away once again.

"No. Cor, no! Please!" I rasped out.

"I am ready." He turned. In the lantern light, he gave me one last smile. His palm was raised, as if hailing Marshall in greeting, but his eyes he kept on me. Beyond him, Marshall had set down his scythe and lantern to pay attention to something that was growing between his cupped hands. The object looked like a ball of silver light, frenetic with internal motion and growing larger with every passing second.

Until that moment, I'd never remembered a thing about my own abduction. I'd never expected to, either—I supposed it would be one of those white, blank areas of my life that would remain a mystery until the day I died. The sight of that pulsating globe of energy, though, brought back that hot afternoon in Las Vegas, three years before, when I'd been tramping to a parking structure in the blazing sun, on my way back from talking to someone in the Paris casino. Who had it been? Harland Oliver's former supervisor? Something like that. I'd just entered the deck and blinked the sun from my eyes when, from between cars, I'd seen a hand tossing at me a ball of that same silver light. And then, in my memory, there was blessed nothingness once again. I only knew that I'd woken up at Cor's urging, days later, zombiefied on Riviera Lane.

Once it had reached the size of an orange, Marshall lifted the sphere to his lips. "Corydonais, son of Mabelle, daughter of Titania," he called out. At the sound of the name, the ball launched forward, zooming toward Cor.

He caught it with his outstretched hand. "Find me." I read his lips, though they made no noise. Before I knew what had happened, the globe of light had completely encompassed him, flashing outwards to his size at one moment, then shrinking the next. Away it flew into the sky like a shooting star in reverse, zipping upward and then darting away in frantic, evasive movements as it disappeared. I ducked. Hundreds of wings set into motion as the Ravens took flight after the light. Ginger was the first among them, lunging up toward the sky on her legs and winging her way in pursuit as she shifted shape. They were trying to chase it, I realized. The light was moving far faster than they could, but they were doing their best to find out where it was going.

I was alone and unprotected on the dock, I realized. And the light was vanishing, for the six boats were silently moving away from me and toward the horizon. Marshall reached up and over his head, replacing the hood over his face so that it disappeared into darkness again. I saw him wave at me, mockingly.

If he'd been within arm's length, I would have killed him right then. And the fucker hadn't kept his part of the bargain! "Nikki!" I yelled at him as loudly and savagely as I could. "You didn't give back Nikki!"

Over the waves I heard him call out, "Oh, right! So sorry." Then, with a simple and economical gesture, he pushed the standing Peri from the boat so that she tripped over the side and tumbled into the water, headfirst.

Crap. I instantly realized that there was no way she'd be able to swim with her hands and feet bound. Trust Marshall to do something so cruel! I turned for help, but none of the Storm Ravens had remained. Cor, Ginger—all gone.

It was up to me, then. Apparently I wasn't only going to have to save Cor from his own nobility, but I was going to have to save his little sister from drowning, as well. Fine. I kicked off my sneakers and, with a deep breath, drove into the Pacific waters.

Despite the fact that I was not an able or willing swimmer, I might add. Like every other kid who lived near the beaches of California, I'd had enforced lessons at the local Y, where I'd learned a laborious Australian crawl and an ungainly sidestroke. I'd even gone through a three-week training session in lifesaving during high school, in which we'd tossed a dummy into the pool and repeatedly dragged it back to the diving board before practicing on each other. None of which had prepared me for the cold waters at night, where one mouthful of ocean tasted worse than a hundred bottles of olive juice boiled down into a foul extract.

I didn't even know where Nikki might be. I couldn't see from the salty water that stung my eyes, and though I shouted her name over and over again as I flailed my way to where I thought she might have gone overboard, I realized there was no way she could answer back. If, that was, she could even kick enough to keep her head above water.

I rose on one of the storm swells, while I swallowed another mouthful of the bitter brine and felt my stomach recoil. The sea was too rough for me to be swimming in it, I realized; I'd come out so far that there wasn't any footing to stabilize me, or even in the darkness a good indication of which way land lay. "Nikki!" I yelled again, receiving another taste of the ocean as a reward.

They always said that drowning was the gentlest of deaths. I'd never believed it. Who had started that rumor, anyway? Wouldn't it be ironic, I thought to myself as I slipped underwater, if I were to drown out here, when I was supposed to be saving someone? I'd read stories about that kind of thing all the time throughout my life.

Here I was, in typical Samantha fashion, about to become one of them, myself. I surfaced again and managed to get half a gasp of air before the rolling waters consumed me once more. My chest was burning, ready to explode with a fire that traveled throughout my entire body. My limbs were too weak to fight, any more. Beneath the waves, the up-and-down, back-and-forth motion was almost soothing. Natural. It felt like being rocked to sleep.

Maybe the rumor had been right.

I was above the waves again, coughing out water and sour air and breathing as deeply as my distressed lungs would allow. Something below was lifting me to the surface, making me buoyant, bringing me back to life again. Frantically my arms clawed for some kind of grasp on whatever it was, at last finding only a slick, leathery roundness that propelled me in a direction that I hoped was shoreward. After a few moments, the peril seemed to have passed. Although my chest still hurt and I was still waterlogged, at least I was able to keep my mouth closed during the worst of the waves and breathe when we were skimming higher. And we were indeed moving quickly, gliding through the water with more speed than I could ever have made swimming on my own.

The thing taking me to shore twisted slightly; I felt the pebbly shallows scrape my legs, so I let go and scrambled onto the beach. Behind me, whatever it was I'd been grasping jumped into the air, splashing me as it made clicking noises. I'd heard them before, somewhere, sometime, but I couldn't quite place what they were. At that moment, though, I wasn't going to try. I needed solid ground. I needed to sit.

I'd failed. Utterly and unmistakably, my best efforts had come to disaster. The tide washed in and out around where I sat on the sand with my head in my hands, no longer able to distinguish where the salt from the ocean ended and my tears began. "Nikki!" I called out, half wishing I had drowned so that I wouldn't ever have to lay this news at Cor's feet.

"What?" she replied, plumping down beside me. "Did you see that? Huh? Did you?"

I almost had a heart attack. I swear, I was so startled at the sudden presence beside me. My hands flew to her, to make sure she was real. She protested when in the darkness I got handfuls of breast and hair. But it was Nikki, all right. Her hands and feet seemed unhampered, but around her neck was still the knotted gag that previously had been in her mouth. "Holy shit, I thought you drowned!" I yelled, hugging her so tightly that by all rights she should have suffocated instead.

"I thought you were going to drown," she said. "You're really not a very good swimmer, are you?" I shook my head, half-laughing, but mostly still crying. "Did you see me? Did you know that was me? That saved you?"

"No," I confessed. "What was it? What were you?"

"A dolphin!" she said, barely able to keep the excitement from her voice. "I got my calling, Sam! A dolphin! Just in time, right? I won't have to do filing in Resht for the rest of my life!" She gave me another neck choking by way of celebration. "But forget that. Where's Ginger? Where's Cor?"

"You didn't see?"

It was the wrong question. I could feel her stiffen. "No. I don't remember much between when they gagged me and when I hit the water. Sam, I thought I was going to drown! But then I found myself changing, and the ropes fell away and . . . well, here I am. Where's Cor?" she repeated. "What aren't you telling me?"

It seemed a pity I was going to have to ruin the joy she felt in discovering her calling with the bad news about her brother, but there was no avoiding it. I took her hands, steeled myself, and there, in the dark, told her a fairy tale without a happy ending.

Chapter Twenty-one

"So this is it." Ginger, Nikki, and I stood somewhere in the middle of the great preserve of forests that comprise most of Catalina Island. Dozens upon dozens of ravens sat on every available perch in the immediate area, some high overhead, others on the low branches or even resting on the toppled, hollow tree to which they'd led us, near a clearing made by a brush fire the previous spring. I knelt down beside the blackened trunk and peered inside. I'd expected gloom, but instead found myself looking into a rotted-out interior glowing with a silvery light. The globe of energy rested only a foot within, snug in a nest of dead leaves and furry moss. In the far distance I could hear the normal, everyday sounds of the rustling forest—birds, wind, and the occasional falling branch or dashing animal. In the section where we had assembled, our hush felt more like some kind of church ceremony. The area around us was immediately silent, the ravens somber. It was as if this small section of the world mourned, even as we did.

"This is it," Ginger said. She kicked at the stump with

the toe of her boot, seeming more deflated than I'd ever thought I'd see her. I watched the tree nervously, but there was really no way that several hundred pounds of fallen tree was going to be shifted by a single prod from an army boot, even one attached to a woman with hands so strong she'd left bruises on my upper arm the night before.

Nikki was still dressed in the same clothing she'd been wearing for the last two and a half days. Although she'd managed to freshen up at the hotel overnight, she still looked the worse for wear. Of course, neither of us had gotten much in the way of sleep, while we waited for Ginger and the ravens to return with news. "Oh, Cor," she sighed, kneeling down beside me. She put a hand on my shoulder for comfort.

Usually hiking in the island's interior was limited to those who'd managed to obtain a day pass from the island's conservancy, but of the collection assembled here, only the two of us had come on foot. And only one would return. "How many days has it been in there?" I asked.

Ginger shook her head. "There's no way of telling. Time moves so differently in a construct than it does out here. It could be an hour, or a minute, or a year."

"But it's still here," Nikki reminded me. "It would have vanished if a week had gone by in there and they'd given him to . . . well, you know."

She didn't want to speak about Cor sacrificing himself as a teind to hell any more than I wanted to think about it. But that was the grim reality of what we were facing. I didn't know exactly what sacrifices to Hell went through, but I was willing to bet what little I still had in my life that it wasn't a skip in the park. "What if I can't do it?" I asked, uncertain, and not for the first time. "How can I get out?"

I didn't like the exchange of glances between Nikki

and Ginger at that point, or the concern in their eyes.
"You kind of have to do it if you go in," Nikki explained.

"You won't be able to come out, if you don't." Ginger
looked away from me as she said the words; she
couldn't face me with them. "The only people who can
exit are the creators."

"That's why Cor was so angry that I joined him when
you were being held." Nikki's hand slid down my forearm to my hand. "But you can do it! You can do anything! Right, Jinge?"

"Jinge" apparently didn't like the new nickname any
more than the one I'd selected for her, but she surprisingly didn't lash out at Cor's sister. Instead, she shrugged.
"Cor wanted you to follow him. To save him. I'm in a position where I could veto his decision, and no one back
in Resht would question me for a second." For a second, my anger began to rise. "But I think you might do
pretty well," she murmured. She managed to spare one
quick look for me before adding, "You have in the past."
I nodded, appreciating that. "You're closest to him, now.
It should be you."

"Ready?" Nikki whispered.

This was so hard. Even with Cor's little sister looking
at me expectantly, hope and admiration mixing in her
eyes, hell, even with Ginger's grudging support, it was
still so damned hard. Most difficult of all had been talking to my mother that morning, trying to keep her in the
dark while knowing that I was saying good-bye for who
knew how long . . . perhaps even for the last time.

"I have this work-related thing," I'd told her in the
lobby. We'd spent a lot of time there that morning, while
Ginger and two of the female Ravens had used the
room upstairs to comfort Lily.

"Does it have to do with poor Mr. Oliver?" she'd
asked, while thumbing through her book. "And the people who killed him?" That had been a bit of a surprise,

since Ginger and I had maintained that Harland's demise had been an unfortunate accident caused by a snapped line at the family's trailer. But I nodded, not wanting to pile on any more lies than I had to. Then she had another question. "Does it have to do with your Mr. Donais?"

"Mom." I'd kind of hoped that having this conversation in the hotel's lobby might keep me from too emotional a display. My hopes were in vain, I feared, but I took a deep breath and plunged on. "I don't know how long it will take." A month, another three years, or enough to make me the next Rip Van Winkle? "I don't want you worrying about me." At that point, I leaned across the coffee table and put my hand down on her book so she'd stop flipping its pages. "And I don't want you thinking I'm, you know. Abandoning you."

"You'd never do that." My mother had rested her hand atop mine then, squeezing it. "Do what you have to. And then come home. You'll be back soon, I know. All right?"

She'd given me an easy way to exit, and I'd appreciated it. Yet after I'd stood and turned to go, planning not to be a Lot's wife and look back, all my best-laid plans went awry. I just had to know. So I turned and said, "Mom? What's a DeRengier?"

In the time it had taken me to cross the Sycamore's tastefully appointed lobby, my mother had settled her reading glasses on her nose and returned to her book. She'd given me an odd look over the top of her spectacles at my question. "Wherever did you hear that, dear?"

"What is it? Is it a name?"

She'd removed her glasses and let them dangle on the chain from her neck. "Well, it's the name of our family, of course. Before they emigrated and it became Americanized. I think it used to be French, but there are still some DeRengiers in Great Britain." She'd picked up her book again and replaced her lenses. "And quite an odd lot, too my mother used to say, though she'd never tell me more than that." Fine. It didn't really answer my question, but I'd have to table my investigation of the DeRengiers until after this entire affair was over.

Not wanting a second round of farewells when I was feeling uncertain and sentimental enough already, I'd smiled and slipped away without another word.

I peered into the tree trunk again, not really certain how I wanted to proceed. "I just touch it?" I asked. My companions both nodded. "Nikki," I said in a low voice. "If I'm gone . . . for a long time. Just promise me you'll look in on my mom from time to time? She likes you." She didn't have to respond. I saw the answer in her face. "And Ginger, just make sure that something good happens to Lily? That would mean a lot to me."

From Ginger, an affirmative would have been nice, but she appeared to have something in her throat. "You should go before it's too late," she finally said, gruffly.

"Remember, you might not be what you are out here, in there," said Nikki, giving me a final hug. "But you'll be yourself. Cor will be, too, once you find him. He just won't remember."

"Find the key to the construct," Ginger said. She extended her hand for a brisk shake. The stopper to the snow globe, of course. I knew all about that one, didn't I? "Bring him back."

The pulsating silver object flickered inside the hollowed-out trunk, crazy lines of seeming electrical activity making its surface appear like a tightly wound bundle of constantly moving twine. Would it hurt? I didn't want to find out, but I braced myself. If I was ever going to do anything, this was the time. Without a second thought, and before I could stop myself, I plunged my hand into the still-soggy wood and wrapped it around the sphere.

Day One

Whiteness. It's like that moment after a hard blow to the head, when everything is white as snow, but before the pain begins. There's no pain here, though—just a prickling at my eyes as my sight slowly begins returning to normal. That's when I realize I'm falling. Plummeting, really, to a ground that's impossibly far below. I see the tops of trees, leafy and green, racing toward my feet

My heart's beating fast, a pitter-patter that rattles like a frenzied castanet. I can't die like this. I've come too far. Something kicks in, and I find myself flapping my arms furiously, trying to make it stop. Only I don't have arms, in this place. They're wings, and once I set them into motion, I find myself curving out of the freefall and into a soaring, buoyant glide.

Oh my gosh. I'm flying!

When I was much younger I used to have dreams of weightlessness, of floating above the ground as if on an invisible layer of water. This is far, far better. I can't see it exactly, but I can feel my beak slicing through the air as I propel forward, sometimes flapping my wings to accelerate, sometimes just enjoying the sensation of zooming across the sky like a bullet. I can feel the currents of the air, so very much like those of the ocean with their constant push and pull and their unexpected undertows. It's warm where I am, but occasionally I find myself nudging into a stream of chilliness, just to enjoy the sensation.

It's wonderful. I could do this forever. When I open my mouth, delighted chirps escape it.

Cor, though. I'm supposed to be finding Cor. I circle down to the trees, which grow close together and in abundance. I'm in a forest, but not like I was in only a few minutes before. Where had that been, again? Oh yes, California. Its scrabbly flora seemed continents away from this lush place. Here everything seemed as if an artist with a box full of nothing but variations of green had spilled his paints. It was spring; the leaves were young and pliant as I swept through them. On the ground I could see squirrels busily running from tree to tree, while on my trip down I passed a nest of cheeping hatchlings. There's movement everywhere here—birds of all types, animals I don't recognize, all of them basking in the country sunlight. The only thing I haven't seen are humans. Or the Peri who look like them.

I have to explore some more, so I take flight.

I've discovered the limits of this construct. There's an odd thing that happens when I fly in a straight line for a long distance. Though when I'm above the trees I can see an infinite distance in the horizon, there's a point when I can go no farther. It's not like a glass wall, though. I can't feel myself slamming against a barrier; I simply stop advancing and start to slide to one side. I might notice it more if I were on the ground, but here I might not even have noticed if I hadn't been paying attention. The construction really is like an oversized snow globe. Or perhaps I'm especially tiny. It's hard to tell.

Once I found out I was in a mile-long terrarium, I set out to find what was in it. They can't have captured Cor and kept him in a forest. What would be the purpose? Unless, of course, he's one of the trees. If that's the case, I'm lost. How could I tell a knotty Cor oak from any of the other leafy giants crowding the ground here?

But now I've found it. When I was navigating around the construct's perimeter, trying to figure out if it was as circular as I guessed, I came across a road. A simple dirt road that runs in serpentine curves over and across the gently rolling hills and through the valleys, disappearing from clear open land into the thicket of trees in the middle. I've followed it to the center, where it splits in

two and leads to two separate buildings. The larger
looks like a home of some sort. Perhaps as a bird I'm
smaller than I thought, because when I try to wing a
circuit around the house, it's exhausting. Its surface is
covered with round gray stones that give it a textured,
pebbly appearance. The chimneys at both ends are covered with moss, and the ivy that's crept up from the
ground to the second and third stories looks as if it's
been there for a century. It's a cottage from legend, the
kind of place you might expect to see Hansel and Gre-
tel approaching with a trail of bread crumbs behind, or
perhaps a little pig daring a wolf to blow it down.

Only bigger. Much, much bigger.

I can't see anyone through the windows, though I
alight on several to see what I can spy. On one of them,
the leaf-filtered sun catches the glass just right and I'm
startled to see myself reflected. I'm indeed small. And
round-headed. And yellow. I've caught glimpses of my
bright yellow wings when I've flown, but apparently I'm
the same color all over. I think I'm a canary, though I'm
no expert.

I fly low to the hard-packed road to discover where
the other branch might lead. I see something familiar
there—a car. One of those oversized vehicles built for
off-road travel. A Land Rover or some such, many years
old and covered with dried mud and grass. There's a
building as well, a long, low one-story construction
with a peaked roof, open in the front. It looks like a stable, though I don't smell any horses. Not that my sense
of smell works the way my human nose, does.

I'm going to investigate.

I've found Cor. I know what they're going to do to him.

Before I flutter into the stables, I make another pass
around the smaller, longer building, then take a quick
rest atop a plank of wood in front of it. The plank is, I re-

alize after a moment, a sign. When I fly a distance away, I find that I can read it, though it takes a little bit of concentration—my eyes and head seem to work differently in this form, making it difficult to focus. *East Anglia Regional Avian Rehabilitation Centre,* spell out the words.

Avian. That means birds. I fly in to see.

The building might have been stables, once, but they've been renovated since. There are still stalls, some as wide as eight or nine feet, but none of them are very deep. Some of them have been sequestered off with some kind of roped-down netting, to make them into cages. Inside of these sit some vicious-looking predators. I recognize a vulture by its bald head, long neck, and cape of feathers, but when I alight on the netting and hold tight with my tiny claws, it doesn't seem to notice me as its vacant stare sweeps by.

Most of the stalls are netted. Large, wild birds occupy them, pecking at the seed scraps that liberally line the floor. My tiny stomach flutters slightly at the sight of all the free food, but I can come back for that later. None of the prisoners look very happy. I don't think I've even seen many of the species here, before, but something's wrong with each of them. There's a swan behind netting strutting around with a cast of some sort on one wing, and a peacock that seems to have been denuded of its tail feathers. As it passes by, it cocks out its neck and gives me a baleful look as it tries to extend a fan that's no longer there. I notice then that it's missing an eye as well.

In the center, I recognize Cor. He's sitting on a perch in the largest of the stalls, and the only one without a net. I can't tell you how or why, when neither of us looks like we should, but I know it's him. He's an eagle—an American bald eagle, out here in the wilds of East Anglia. I think it's the look in his eyes that I recognize. While the other fowl here have the appearance of anger, or disinterest, or any of the things you might expect from long-term residents of a jail, the eagle appears frightened. He doesn't know why he's here, because he keeps looking around at any moment as if expecting to receive an explanation for all the craziness. Though his posture is regal, his feathers are matted and dirty. From time to time, he shivers, glancing upward. But at what?

When I land on the window ledge behind him, I see what he's been looking at. Directly opposite his open stall is suspended a large bird, its feet bound with a thin cord and hung upside-down from a cruel hook screwed into the ceiling planks. It is dead, its eyes lifeless and glassy.

I try flying around him to distract him from the grisly sight, but it only seems to daze him more. I can't talk to him. I can't talk at all, at least not in an avian language I understand. Instead, I fear that all my chirping and cheeping is only annoying him. After a long time in which I try to make him recognize me, he adjusts himself on his circular roost so that he faces into the corner, away from the gently swaying corpse of the falcon. There's no getting his attention now. I'd cry if I could, but I don't have the ducts for it.

Oh, Cor. I'm so tiny. Whatever in this world can I do for you?

Chapter Twenty-two

Day Two

I've spent the night on the window ledge, sleeping in short bursts that aren't any too refreshing but haven't left me especially tired. The slightest noise wakes me, so when I hear the sound of footsteps, I'm instantly alert, flying up to the cobwebby rafters so I can't be seen. A man walks in that I recognize immediately—Marshall. He's not the suburban husband here, or the hooded vision of death. Just an ordinary man of the country, mucky in his knee boots and dungarees and plaid shirt. A floppy leather hat covers his head.

He comes down the hall as if it's routine, as if he's done this for years, but I know it's all for show. None of these birds are real; they don't need the pep talks or the scraps of meat or grain that he tosses in their dishes. None of the birds, that is, except for the one in the center stall. He's the one that all this show is for. "Ye shouldn't be dead by right," says Marshall in a thick Suffolk accent to the falcon hanging from the ceiling. "A shame, that." He reached up and pulls down the bird from the hook, holding it by the bound feet and shuffling out. The dead bird's head dragged on the dirty, straw-and-seed-strewn ground. "But accidents come and go."

Though he hasn't acknowledged Cor with even so much as a glance, I know what Marshall is up to. The mental torture's working, too. Cor, alone of all the birds, seems to understand what's going on here. And he's frightened, shrinking down into himself to appear smaller. I think he wants to escape notice. What he doesn't know is that this entire world revolves around him—there's no escaping a performance put on for an audience of one.

I've found the stopper. I know it.

I decide that Cor needs to be cleaned up, whether he wants it or not. A feeder of water stands not too far from his perch, so I hit upon the idea of filling up my mouth with liquid and then letting it drip onto the dirty parts of his feathers. Beakful by beakful I transport water over to him and drop it down onto his head. I'm not making much progress, since I can only wet him with a few drops at a time, and it's hard work to drop my payload in the right spot when I have to hover while flapping my wings. After the fifth or sixth trip, however, Cor looks around at yet another drop falling on his matted head and rolling down along the dirty parts, and seems to notice what I'm doing, though he doesn't acknowledge it.

When I've more or less gotten the feathers of his white head thoroughly damp, he endures with nothing more than an injured dignity my fluttering and attempts to smooth him down with my wings and beak and feet. Exhausted, I perch on the ledge opposite to survey my handiwork. Or wingdiwork, more accurately. It's not great, but it's better than before. I don't care that my wings feel as if they might fall off; I want to attack the feathers on his proud chest, next. It's harder for him to ignore me this time around, when I'm hovering so close to his chest with every trip, but he somehow manages.

It's on one of my trips that I notice it—the reason that Cor hasn't moved from his perch since I've been there. Around one of his legs, right above his claw, rests a little gold shackle attached to a gold chain. The chain's long enough to give him access to his food and water, but it keeps him from flying off.

It's the thing tying him here to this construct. I know it is. What I don't know is how to get it off his leg.

Marshall brings in a cellmate for Cor in the evening, after the sun's gone down. It's a bird of prey of some sort that looks a little like a majorly oversized seagull. Though his wings are white and black, when he extends them, his underbelly is white as snow. He's proud as punch, this one. His wing has been injured, and has some kind of covering attached to it. "We'll see to you tomorrow, won't we?" Marshall asks the bird as he sets him down from his clutch on a leather-protected sleeve. "In the meantime, keep your friend company, here."

From the rafters, I watch and wait until Marshall's gone before flying down. The new bird doesn't notice me at all, but Cor shifts slightly on his perch when I alight beside him. He doesn't seem to mind when I stay there.

I wake several times throughout the night. He doesn't seem to mind me sleeping beside him.

Day Three

I don't know what to do about the fetters around Cor's leg, and it's driving me crazy. There isn't so much as a seam on the cuff itself, and the chain is attached to the post with a heavy metal bolt. I've made a few stabs at trying to pry out the bolt with my beak, but it doesn't work. I'm too small and weak.

Cor could do it, I'm sure, if he remembered who he was or why he was there. I don't even have the voice to tell him to wake up, to remind him that this isn't his life or his fate.

It worries me that Cor hasn't eaten anything. In the water, I soak some of the fish that Marshall has tossed into his dish, and carry a large chunk of it in my beak up to his perch. At first, Cor doesn't even appear to notice what I'm attempting to do. But then, after he watches me flit by for the hundredth time, he sees the pile of food and stabs at it, gulping down first one chunk, and then another, and then more. I keep bringing him food until he loses interest. Afterward, he allows me to keep sharing his perch with him.

He must think I'm his stalker canary. That's fine. As long as he lives.

While trying to bring more water to Cor in the afternoon, a sparrow watches me from the floor. He must think I'm crazy, that sparrow, but it doesn't stop me from collecting more water in my beak and dropping it onto the parts of Cor's form that are still dirty. Then something miraculous happens. The little bird cocks its head, seems to shrug, and then joins me. Like me, he dips his beak in the water, takes flight, and drops his mouthful onto the bigger eagle on the perch. He's not aiming, like I'm trying to do, and it's obvious that he thinks it's a game of some sort, but it's helpful. And in this situation, I need all the help I can get.

I'm disappointed when the sparrow disappears shortly after, but he returns very quickly with another of his kind. We go back to our water sports. It's not very long before the third bird joins in. The two sparrows are doing it for the fun, and end up splashing more water on each other than on Cor, but every little bit means one less trip for me. While they work, I attempt to pull out the bolt from the platform again, but I can tell it's not going anywhere. There has to be a better solution!

Throughout it all, Cor watches the antics of the tiny little birds around him, one yellow, two brown as chocolate. I can't tell if he's amused, or grateful, but he doesn't seem to be disappearing into himself as much as he was. Not until Marshall returns, that is. Even the little sparrows fly away with me, then. From the rafters above we watch, safe in the shadows.

Clouds of dust stir around his feet as he shuffles forward. There's something in his hand. A walking stick, it looks like from a distance. He rests it against the wall, where I can't see from my perch. "Special visitor for you tonight," he says to the new bird, who shakes his neck and looks very proud. "Yes, a very special visitor." His eyes are glinting with devilry. Though he still doesn't glance in the bald eagle's direction, I know that every atom in the Peri's body is focused on him. He chuckles. "You'll see."

Once he's gone, the new bird hops down from his perch, unbalanced for a moment from the splint on his left wing. The anklet and chain on his leg is dark and medieval in design, and it clanks slightly as he shuffles over to explore the straw around him. Although Cor has kept his head turned during Marshall's visit, he faces the front of his stall now, completely frozen. When I fly down with the sparrows I can see why every feather in his body is trembling in fear—the walking stick that Marshall has oh, so casually leaned against the wall is in fact a scythe, gleaming wickedly in the tranquil green light from the window.

* * *

I'm the leader of a pack of sparrows now. I don't know where they've all come from, but they've rallied around me as if I'm their skipper. Maybe it's because we're the tiniest birds in this aviary, and because I'm such a striking color that it's easy to find me in a group? I don't know. All I can tell is that save for the occasional robin or jay who comes looking for seed, we're the only birds able to fly in and out as we please.

Other sparrows have joined me when I try to bring food to Cor, piling little bits of fish and chaff from the stable floor onto his roost. He eats them, grudgingly at first, and then more hungrily after the first mouthful. I'm positive he doesn't move much because of the golden chain. It doesn't look as if it's hurting him. At least, I can't see any chafing or blood around the rings of his leg. No, I think it's the chain itself, the fact that it's there. If he's motionless, he can pretend he can't feel it. He won't be reminded of it, if he doesn't move.

But even he shifts when unfamiliar noises disrupt the soft repose of the forest at night. There's the humming sound of machinery, and a gentle screech of brakes, followed by the sound of footsteps on the gravel outside. I hear Marshall speaking as he and someone else enter the stable corridor. "It's so good of you to come, your ladyship," he's saying. Bare electrical bulbs of a low wattage suddenly switch on, casting a naked, white light that sets off deep shadows in the rafters that I and the other sparrows are occupying. "I've been hoping that you might be taking a look at our latest acquisition." The pair step into view. Marshall has his hat off, clutching it in his hand. I have to make a short flight to another beam in order to see his guest, but it's exactly who I think it is—Marshall's dame, today done up in riding gear and tweeds. Every inch of her is the archetypal provincial gentry, all stiff-upper-lip-itude and starched, crisp fabrics. It's the same face I knew as Agnes Jones, but in this garb she seems younger somehow. More energetic. Dangerous.

"An osprey," she says, leaning forward to inspect the new bird. On his own perch, Cor backs away to the very edge, to avoid being close to the woman. "Isn't he beautiful? Quite a specimen. A pity about his wing, though."

"Aye," says Marshall, grunting in character. "But that's about to come off." He draws a penknife from his pocket and leans down and fiddles with the splint. It only takes a few moments before the simple construction lies on the floor. The osprey shakes out his wings, the left one more tentatively at first, and then spreads them wide. He's pleased. I can tell by the way he lets out a cry, long and loud, as if he's calling to his family from afar to let them know he'll be winging his way home, soon.

"Not so fast, beautiful one," says her ladyship, reaching out to make a caressing motion around the bird's head, without touching it. "It's too dangerous out there for you to be flying on your own. We need to protect you. For your own good."

"For your own good," echoes Marshall. He walks over to the wall where his scythe lies and grasps it in one hand. My sparrow friends scatter in a panic, as if they know his intent. So intense is the fluttering of dozens of wings that for several moments all I can see is a brown blur.

"What's that?" I hear her ladyship say, as she looks up at us.

"Just birds," he tells her. "What'd you think it would be?"

I didn't hear a response, but for a moment, I'm terrified. It's possible she might spy me and see through my form, or at least notice how out of place I am among the other, less colorful birds. Hastily I fly back to my original perch, behind a column that obscures her view, praying that neither of them chose to look too closely. The other sparrows settle around me, their heads twitching in every direction.

By the time I feel it's safe enough to peer over the edge again, Marshall has the osprey in his arms. "Takes a sharp blade to clip the wings correctly," he opines to her ladyship. "It doesn't do to cut the feathers with a blunt instrument, y'see. There's blood in the feather shafts, and if you don't know where to cut . . . well, it's a pity, that's all I can say."

"I'm certain," says the woman. "It would be a pity if you were to miss. Especially with that sharp a blade."

The grin that he gives her is ferocious. The electric bulb reflecting against his eyes makes it seem as if he has no pupil at all. I already know he can't have a soul. "Indeed, ma'am. A great pity." He pulled at the osprey's wing, stretching it out to its full length, and reached for his scythe.

I can't stay. The terror is too much for me and the sparrows; our little hearts beating so quickly speed our wings into motion. Crying at the tops of our voices, we take flight, away from the shrieking and sharp, metallic smell that Marshall unleashes in the stall, away from the laughter of the woman and the alarmed squalling of the other captive birds. Out of the stables we fly, rocketing from the noise and foulness and out into the cool night air of the forest, where the trees still shake away their daytime haze in the breezes. In formation we zoom up into the air, cleansing ourselves on the currents. One by one, we split away from the mass exodus, fluttering to the ground like leaves in autumn. Only I return soonest, ashamed at having fled at all.

Marshall and his mother are emerging from the stables when I float down to its peaked slate roof. On the weathervane I perch, next to a metal rooster. "You won't be spending the night, then?" Marshall asks. "The house has been ready for you, your ladyship."

"You have things under control," said the woman, slipping on a pair of gloves. The long, black car in which she arrived purrs into life; a driver steps out and opens the door for her, waiting. "Good work, my son," she adds, stroking his cheek with much the same motion as she had pretended to caress the wounded osprey. "How proud you make me."

All he does is bow. Then he pronounces words I don't want to hear: "Tomorrow night's the end, then." The realization that tomorrow marks the end of Cor's seven days chills me. I don't have much time left.

"Good. Come to me when it's done." Her ladyship nods to the driver as she eases into the limousine's inky depths. "And then we can proceed."

I'm cold, though the night is balmy. Shivering, both Marshall and I watch as the car drives down the dirt road toward the perimeter. I wait until he's trudged back up to the house, his lantern bobbing at his side, until I fly back to where I belong.

On the hook across from Cor's stall, the osprey hangs, its feet bound, one bloody wing hanging lower than the other. There's a puddle of dark liquid beneath, soaking into the dirt. Cor is still on his perch, facing the opposite direction. In the dark, even with these eyes, I can't see him. How can I comfort him? How in the hell am I supposed to let him know that I'm even there? I'm as tiny and helpless as the form this construct has given me.

So I sit there beside him, huddling close and hoping that simply being there will offer him solace.

And after a while, I wake up in the dark to find his wing sheltering me.

Chapter Twenty-two

The Last Day

It's after midnight. I can see a full moon as round and white as a paper plate outside the window, bathing a corner of the stall with light. I can't give up on Cor. I didn't care about myself. I could remain a canary indefinitely if I had to—it wasn't so bad a life. But Cor has watched who knew how many birds before him face mutilation at Marshall's hands. He knows what's coming, and he knows how hopeless his chances are. They've made sure of that. That was the point of the exercise—to screw with his mind so that he'd rather give his life willingly than be without his birthright: the power of flight.

But while I've got two wings, two eyes, and a funny-looking mouth, I'm going to try to do something. Maybe I've been attacking the chain all wrong. I shouldn't be worrying about the bolt at all. Gold is soft, isn't it? Isn't it something people bite into with their teeth, to see if it's real? At least in the cartoons? It doesn't matter. Perhaps

I can break it on my own, and bring this nightmare to an end. It's something to do at least. I shift myself out from under Cor's protective embrace and, with the tip of the hard bill projecting from my face, I scrape the links onto the perch. My beak's hard; I can use it for breaking up the hard shells of seeds, so pecking at the metal stuns me a little, but it doesn't do me any harm.

Peck. Peck. Peck. It's not a fast process; the chain jumps every time I tap at it, meaning that I have to find it in the moonlight again before the next tap. Sometimes I miss entirely. *Peck. Peck.* The noise isn't loud, but apparently it's enough to stir some of the stalls' other occupants. They become restless, pacing back and forth in the straw, calling out tentative queries to no one in particular.

And after a while, I hear some scrabbling around me. Some of the sparrows are back, woken from their nocturnal rests, watching me curiously. If they could help me with this task as they helped me with washing Cor, yesterday . . . the thought's invigorating. Sore as my beak is becoming, I tap away at the gold, trying to hold it down with one of my feet to keep it still. Will they follow? Will they think it's a game?

It doesn't take too long before one of the sparrows leaps up and imitates me, pecking at the wood of the bald eagle's roost, but not at the chain. Another hops up and thinks the task is great fun; his pecking is closer to mine. The chain jumps and shivers when at last he hits it—and that's even better fun than before. It isn't long before both birds are making the chain shiver with their concentrated pecking, and more are joining in.

Despite the flurry of activity beside him, Cor doesn't move. I'm sure he's awake, and I'm right. When I fly to the sill to see how he's reacting, he's looking directly at me. I wish I could read his mind. If I had to guess, I would have thought the morose, almost hostile stare was saying, *Why? Why bother?*

My answer would have been easy. *Because for you, I have to.*

It's not breaking. I don't think there isn't a sparrow in the entire construct who hasn't had a go at the chain. We've pecked and nibbled and bitten it until our little faces are sore. It's not that it's made of some super-impervious metal. It's gold, all right, soft and somewhat pliable. We've bent some of the links and stretched some of the others, hammering them out to a thinness that should have broken through long ago. One good tug would do it—but we're tiny and weak.

I remember back to what Cor told me, when I was stuck on Riviera Lane—breaking the stopper was something I had to do for myself. Maybe the construct's rules mean we can't break through the gold for him. Cor has a big beak. He could crush the chain with a single bite, if he cared to. Yet he doesn't. What will it take to make him care?

I hate these bastards—Marshall and his mother. I swear to God, if I ever get the chance for revenge upon them, I'll have it for what they've done to my Corydonais.

My attitude's changed. I'm angry. I'm *raging*. Time's running out and there's nothing we can do, so I've decided just to create as much chaos as possible. Maybe it's irrational, but I've found other things for my army of sparrows to destroy. We've started on the ropes holding the netting over the farther cages. It's easier work than the chain, because the little strands tear so easily. We've knocked down the tools Marshall uses to distribute the straw from the bales at the stable's end, and have even strewn the straw far and wide.

None of this is helping Cor, I know. Yet I have to keep working. I have to keep moving, to keep trying. Something I do has to have an effect.

Still he keeps looking at me sadly when I fly by. At least he recognizes me. He can pick out the little canary who's causing such a ruckus in this idyllic countryside hell. I just wish he knew how hard I was working.

It's dark now. I can barely fly. I haven't eaten or had a sip to drink all day, it feels like. And Marshall's coming, step by slow step from the house above.

I can't watch this. Yet I can't flee. If Cor and his whole bloody race are concerned with doing penance for the crimes of the past, then I can do penance, too—and it'll be standing by Cor until the bitter end. It's my duty.

Marshall's a sadist of the first order. From my spot in the rafters I can hear him approach, slowly, methodically. He rattles his lantern, and shuffles his feet through the straw, and hums to himself to let us know exactly how far away he is. The sparrows chitter nervously around me in the dark rafters when he lets out a sharp curse at discovering the straw scattered everywhere, but I feel the one stab of satisfaction I've had in some time.

It's not enough. Mere wisps of straw can't stop him from his goal. "Why, hello there," he says to the bald eagle when he arrives. He's wearing not the country bumpkin drag. Instead, he's in his death regalia. His dark robe of rough-spun cloth trails on the ground behind him as he shuffles forward, obscuring his feet. I could see under his hood only because the lantern he carries shines upward, sending eerie, campfire ghost story shadows cascading over the planes of his face. We were forgoing the electric lights for this ritual, apparently. I can barely look at his other hand, in which he clutches his clan's weapon.

I hate this. I *hate* this certainty, this pokiness, this prolonged prelude to what is going to be the end of Cor and I both. Below me, the eagle raises his head, staring at his enemy. He knows the finale's coming, too, I can tell.

"Ready to have your wings clipped, precious one?"

croons Marshall, crouching down. He places the lantern
on the empty roost the osprey had occupied, so that it
provides a steady light that flickered only slightly as it lit
up the space. Against the other wall he leans his scythe,
making sure that Cor can see it plainly. Casually—too
casually—he reaches for one of the straws on the
ground and lifts it to the blade. Barely a touch slices it
in half. The sparrows and I shiver in absolute darkness
above him, thanks to the lantern's hood. "It doesn't hurt.
Just a few feathers, here and there." His finger projecting from the robe's sleeve, flicks the eagle's side. "You
won't even notice they're missing. At first." Hateful man.
"And then we can take you to your new home. Let's get
started, shall we?"

It's when he reaches for the grim scythe that I realize I
can't sit still any longer. It's only a matter of seconds before all my last chances evaporate. Puny creature
though I am, I find myself winging down in a furious
swoop, batting my wings furiously as I fling myself at
Marshall's face. My feet make contact with his cheek,
but I can only scratch him before I scramble aloft again,
to make another pass.

My strike is enough to startle Marshall out of his ritual, though. He looks up in the darkness, astonished.
"Who?" he yells.

I dive for him again, this time having a vague idea of
pecking his eyes out. It's a grandiose scheme given my
relative size, but desperate times call for desperate
birds. He tries to bat me away with his hands. On this
pass, however, it's not simply me that's out to get him. I
have other sparrows joining me. Our barrage is confus-
ing him, I can tell. He doesn't know where to look as
bird after bird swoops by. I can see that one of them has
succeeded in leaving a deeper scratch than the one I
managed. Blood seeps from the wound in a dozen tiny
ruby beads. My short little beak connects squarely with

the bridge of his nose and I rebound in a downward spiral.

"You!" he yells again. He's seen me—he's picked me out of the mass of brown objects flying around and hindering his murder. "I know you!" he yelled, grabbing for his scythe. Desperately I flutter upward to a beam, but not before I see Cor looking up at the mayhem with curiosity in his sad, black eyes. "I know it's you, woman!" Marshall yells after me.

He's furious. Good. Maybe I've made a little bit of a difference, after all. I don't care if he's seen through my form. I don't care if he chases me through all of this construct, inch by inch, if it keeps him away from Cor. I'm about to try this particular tack, trying to lure him out of the stables, when I hear a mighty *thunk!* beside me that shakes me to my little bones. It's the scythe blade buried halfway in the beam, only inches away from my perch. Marshall has grabbed it and brought it down in my vicinity, hoping to kill two birds, as the saying goes. The blade rocks back and forth in the wood as Marshall loosens and lifts it, preparing for another blow.

I'm not going to sit around waiting for it to fall. I let myself fall from the beam and down again, winging my way to where the sparrows are still battering Marshall with their tiny wings. I'm too conspicuous to miss, though, and he lashes out at me with the scythe, trying to bat me like a baseball. He clips me, knocking the breath from my little body and sending me flying. One of the sparrows gets the full force of the blow, spinning across the room as the wood staff connects with its body, hitting the wall opposite, and falling to the ground. I land next to its twitching remains, knowing that it could have been me. It almost had been. Aching all over, I'm aloft again, trying to get out of reach. It's difficult for me to fly, though; one of my wings is too stiff, too sore.

"Damn you!" Marshall yells. He's flailing wildly now,

trying to swipe me out of the air. "Damn you to hell, Samantha! I know it's you!"

I'm not surprised by what happens after that. Marshall is thrashing about so violently that the sleeve of his robe catches the lantern and sends it crashing to the floor. Its oil spills, burning with savage brightness in the corner.

I am surprised by this, though: I don't know whether it was the sound of my name, or whether it was simply the sight of his little canary friend in distress, but Cor rouses from his stupor. Something has awoken him enough to send him into action; something's made him care once again. His wings spread wide and proud as he lunges into the air with an angry cry.

And the chain snaps. It simply breaks, the links clattering to the floor. The pecking the sparrows and I had done stretched them close enough to the breaking point, so that when Cor came to himself, he is able to launch skyward. Marshall freezes, aware that something is wrong. When he sees Cor on the beam above, sitting next to me, his face contorts. Yet the howl he lets out is not of rage—it's of pain. His flowing ceremonial robe is rapidly being consumed by the fire spreading through the stable.

Cor and I look at each other. As if in agreement, we take flight, putting as much distance between us and Marshall's dying screams as quickly as we can. Beneath us, all the birds are escaping the inferno. The buzzards, the falcons, all the birds who were behind the netting the sparrows and I loosened earlier in the day.

Grains of sand. Though I hadn't known it, every minute action the tiniest and weakest of us birds had taken had been grains of sand, shoring up into a solid foundation of rock and ensuring our freedom. How right that seems, and how just.

We birds were sparks of light, flickering away into the darkness, away from the fire that spawned us, as the construct disintegrated into thousands of black particles.

Chapter Twenty-three

The last time I'd returned to Venice, it had felt like a punishment. All I'd been able to see were the tendrils of smog snaking from downtown L.A., the horrible parking, and the hippie-dippy crowd with their surfboards and diets of uncooked vegetables. Now, though, I basked in the lemon-yellow sun with its sweetly unchanging rays, the happy neo-beatniks in their flip-flops and dreads, the coffee shops on every corner. I could smell sweet remnants of the night-blooming jasmine planted all around the waterfront, a scent I'd always loved. Even the gaudy pink flamingos filling an entire canal-side yard brought a smile to my face as we walked to my mother's house. This time, Venice felt like home.

My mother's stucco-covered cottage sat before me once again, the garden beyond its worn wooden fence little more than a collection of tangled dead vines. It looked as if it had hardly changed. I hesitated, almost frightened to duck under the arbor framing the front gate. "Come on," said Cor, squeezing my fingers. I looked at him, startled; in the sudden sweep of apprehension I'd been feeling about letting my mother know I was back, I'd almost forgotten he was standing firmly beside me.

Which was silly, since we'd been joined at the hip since we tumbled to the ground together next to that hollow tree in the Santa Catalina Island forests. Hand in hand we'd walked away from that place, him barefoot with the legs of his pants rolled up, me dirty and bedraggled and without a penny in my pockets. So delighted to be ourselves and to be together were we that for a long, long time we did little else but sneak glances at each other with shy, giddy, almost sophomoric grins on our faces, saying nothing. And then, like a dam of words breaking under pressure, we'd started speaking.

"You saved me," he'd say, in awe.

"You saved *me*," I'd tell him.

"You actually *saved* me," he'd say, and then we'd go back to those shy grins again.

And so on. Actually, from the standpoint of an outsider, the whole thing would have seemed pretty icky. We were two insiders, though, and to us during that long stroll through the forests and back to human civilization, insiders were the only ones who mattered.

"Are you okay?" he asked again, bringing me back to the present.

I sighed. Glad though my heart was to be here, the second homecoming was no less difficult than the first. "Yes," I said. With him there, and safe, I was very okay. "Let's do this." I swung open the wooden gate and led us up the slates to the porch.

Before I knocked, I paused. I could see my mother in the living room, sitting on the sofa with a cat on either side, looking slantways through her reading glasses at a pile of student papers in her lap. She gnawed on a red pen while she considered how to mark. Her brow furrowed. She looked so old right then. How many more times could I do this to her?

Smiling at my dithering, Cor raised his hand and rapped his knuckles so that they sounded against the wooden door. Mom blinked, then saw me through the window. Almost immediately her face changed. The wrinkles disappeared and became smile lines; she seemed almost as young and elastic as when I'd been a kid. "Samantha!" I heard her cry as she strode toward the door. It popped open, and I found myself enveloped in a big comforting hug. "And Mr. Donais!"

"Ms. Neale," said Cor, his eyes popping wide as he found himself squeezed in my mother's python-like arms.

"Oh, call me Barbara, do. I'm so glad you're back. And so quickly, too!" she said, leading us inside, where one of the Ragdolls yawned wide from his position on the armchair and blinked at Cor sleepily.

Two days. That's how long we'd been gone. The first thing we'd done after finally reaching Avalon—after looking around for levitating cars and the robot servants that might have told us we'd skipped a few decades ahead—was to race for a newspaper box, just to find the date. "You told me it wouldn't take long," I joked, glad that I had been right.

"Oh, I'm so glad you're back! So much has happened!" My mother settled back down on the sofa and pushed a plate of Lorna Doone shortbread cookies in my direction. "The nicest people came for Lily, poor dear. Apparently she has some relations in Venice who were quite anxious to come get her after they heard the news." I looked at Cor. He nodded. So that was all right. "Lady Marga got out of the house and was missing for four hours! Weren't you, you naughty girl!" Mom addressed a cat so fat she looked as if she could hardly waddle across the room, much less get lost in the canals of Venice for that long. "Oh, and Cory. Just a word to the wise. Your sister had some kind of breakup with a boy she was seeing, apparently." Mom sighed. "But you know girls these days. They get over it so quickly. She's spent all of her time at the beach, swimming, and then comes home with a ravenous appetite."

"And you can tell a difference in her appetite how, exactly?" I joked.

"Well," said my mom, flustered a little. She stopped whatever she'd been about to say, finally noticing the way that Cor and I had stood next to each other with our hands firmly clasped the entire time. The sight perked her up. I mean, I could tell she was champing at the bit to scream with delight at the sight of her daughter finally hooked up with a guy of whom she approved. At the same time, though, she didn't want to give him her official stamp of approval so that I'd find a reason to drop him at the first opportunity. We'd been through this little dance a hundred times in my adolescence. "Oh," she finally mustered. Then, with a bright smile, she rallied. "Mr. Landemann's in the garage apartment. Maybe you two would like to be alone? I mean, visit with him. Alone. Together." Thoroughly thrown off balance, she sat back down on the sofa so precipitously that she nearly flattened Lady Marga to a pancake. "Crap."

"It's okay," I laughed. Cor seemed amused as well, but at least had the decency to hide it behind his hand. "Let's do something for dinner tonight, okay?" She seemed to like that idea. When we left, her eyes were gleaming not just with gratitude, but with the satisfaction of a hope redeemed.

Landemann was going to have to wait, apparently, because scarcely were we out the back door when we were besieged by Peri. Cries of *thuk-thuk-thuk!* filled the air from above, where more Storm Ravens than I could count roosted on the power lines and rooftops. Cor looked up in astonishment, genuinely taken by the surprise at the show of welcome by his troops. The corners of his lips crept upward in a show of staggered delight. On impulse, he lifted up my hand in the air with his, setting off another round of avian ovation that seemed to sweep us both up to the skies.

One of the Ravens was so excited that he'd forgotten to shift to bird form, and jumped up and down on the peak of the next-door neighbor's house. Other than him, the only other Peri in their natural state was Ginger. She stood in front of the garage apartment's entrance, heels apart, hands at her sides aligned perfectly with the seams of her camouflage pants, a perfect paragon of attention. She didn't make eye contact with either of us until Cor approached. "Sir," she barked, saluting.

Cor's slight roll of his eyes in my direction was meant only for me. "At ease, you silly fool," he said, sweeping up Ginger in a tight hug. Her eyes squeezed shut, but I wasn't at all jealous. I could see mostly that she was simply relieved to see him again. "So you won't have to give my mother any bad news, now."

Ginger rubbed at her nose. "No, sir," she snuffled, her voice gruff. Again she sniffed and looked at the ground, obviously trying to hold back the tears of happiness. Trying to regain her composure, she nodded at me and extended her hand. I was surprised she'd reached out, frankly, but her shake was genuine and firm when we connected. Too firm, maybe. I kind of wanted to use that hand again in the future. We were back to business, now. "Am I to assume the mission succeeded then, sir?"

Cor nodded at me to tell her. I cleared my throat. "One down. More to go, but one down. And he was one of the big ones."

"You didn't get the dame?" I shook my head. What I

saw in her eyes wasn't blame, or scorn, however. Just respect.

"It's a start," said Cor, echoing my thoughts exactly, though he was talking about something else. "This clan is like a cancer. It's going to take more than one strike to root them out."

"Sir." Ginger nodded. "Yes, sir." Although she'd been all business up until now, the façade suddenly dropped, along with her alert posture. "I was going to run away," she confessed. "Not from them. But I would rather have gone into voluntary exile for the rest of my life than have to return to your dame and great-dame with bad news."

"Some day you may have to," Cor told her. His matter-of-fact tone chilled me. I'd just gotten him back. He wasn't supposed to be talking like this, not already. Not ever.

Ginger didn't seem to be taking his reply too well, either. "You can't keep taking these risks. Sacrificing yourself like that was foolhardy! And avoidable!" Out of respect, I stepped back slightly. "You just can't, sir."

"But Jinjurnaturnia." Cor's eyebrows furrowed, covering the thin scar that ran through the left one. "That's what I do. It's what we all do, every day. So come on. Despite our losses, we had a victory! You know the drill. How do we always celebrate?"

The last question had been addressed not to Ginger, but to all the winged Peri crowding the roofs, fence tops, and power lines. From their beaks swelled a chorus of unintelligible replies. To my poor human ears, anyway, it sounded simply like a raucous avian ensemble—or a bird rave, shortly before the police bust in because of complaints about the noise. Ginger, however, mumbled along with her troops, "We fly."

"We fly," Cor said, grinning. I enjoyed seeing him so

confident again, so very much in his element. "So let's fly." As if startled by a sudden noise, the roosting birds sprang into the air as one, filling the canals with the sounds of their chesty cries and beating wings. Ginger, too, sprang into the air to join them, but only after taking a lingering study of her commander. Her face seemed odd, as if it wore gratitude mixed with anger.

I suspected it was an expression echoed on my own features, when Cor turned to me. "What?" I asked, when he raised his scarred eyebrow. "She's only saying the same things I'm thinking."

"But this is what I do," he replied, almost helplessly.

"I know."

"This is what I've always done. For decades and decades."

Nodding, I echoed myself. "I know."

"You wouldn't like me if I neutered that part of my life."

Cor sounded as if he expected more of a skirmish on my part, but I wasn't giving it to him. Above us the birds had begun to assemble into formation, splitting into two distinct halves that began to swirl counterclockwise around an invisible center point. "Sweetheart," I admonished. "I will always like you. I love you. You make me feel like I can do things—important things. I can't help it! But I can't ask you to change. I never could." It saddened me a little to have to utter these words, but if I didn't say them now, I might lose the nerve later. "We're both who we are. I can't ask you to abandon what you believe in any more than you can ask me to . . . to . . . have a saner mother!"

Did he understand that I truly meant what I said? His eyes were narrow with concentration as he stepped forward and took my hands in his. "I could leave it all behind," he whispered. "I could drop out. You wouldn't have to look in the mirror and worry, every morning."

I'm almost ashamed to admit that for a moment, I considered that offer. How many times in my head had I wondered about it, as a possibility? Wasn't it the easiest path? The road that I should want to take? We'd live out our lives together that way, the two of us, getting progressively older and crazier until one day we were that old couple sitting on the boardwalk bench, watching the puppet shows with smiles on our faces and our fingers entwined. We could have our own apartment—heck, a business I started and ran and even our own little house on the canal someday, if I accepted the money that Ginger had offered that night at Harland Oliver's trailer. If we followed that path, we could be starting new lives, side by side, feet firmly on the ground.

Only I knew I could never be the woman to clip his wings. If we started off that way, sooner or later I'd see the look of longing in his eyes I saw now, as he craned his neck upward to watch the Storm Ravens. They still continued to fly in two large clusters, one of them swooping up when the other pitched down, around and around in a yin and yang of symmetry. When he looked down again, I knew the yearning in his eyes was for me this time. The realization aroused into being a warm, giddy feeling; it spread from my middle up my spine and tickled my neck until it sent my cheeks into a furious blush.

I'd once told Cor I couldn't live a life with him of hundreds of tiny moments, happy though they might be. But hadn't he been the adventure of a lifetime, so far? What better could I honestly ask for than moments upon tiny moments with him that added up to a lifetime beyond what I'd ever imagined for myself? "No way. You are *not* dropping out, young man," I told him with a genuine grin. "We'll make this work, I swear. One way or another. Got it, buddy-boy?"

"All right then," he said, accepting my challenge with a broad, delighted smile that matched mine, tooth for tooth. "Got it."

"Besides, I've got a prime apartment in the heart of Venice, right on the canals and walking distance to the beach. You'll be the envy of all your Peri pals when you move in."

"I'm moving in, am I?"

"Oh yes," I said, closing the distance between us. "That is, when you're not commuting to Resht."

"It's a short commute," he promised. "Ten minutes. Walking distance, even."

"Even better."

"You're sure about this, then?" he asked, serious for a moment. "Because I want it to happen."

"Serious as a heart attack," I assured him. "Besides, you think I'm going to give up the chance to be the crazy old woman of Venice with the hottest young buck of a husband anyone ever saw? Forget it!"

His arms encircled my hips, pulling them to his. "You're already crazy," he reminded me, nuzzling my ear with his mouth. "I think it might be genetic."

I laughed at how he made my skin tickle. "Get out of here," I told him, swatting at his butt. "Go on! Go join your gang already!"

Cor gave me a final squeeze before we separated. Light and laughter were in his eyes when he knelt down and sprang up into the air, his dark clothes shifting into sleek, black feathers that seemed to bend daylight into the spectrum of colors. He was aloft, winging his way toward heaven until at last he was a mere speck, dancing in celebration with his comrades. That was exactly where he needed to be.

And there I was, gazing at him from below, the bright sun squeezing tears from my eyes as I squinted at ballet of the birds, a beautiful sight most of Venice's residents probably missed, too busy to notice with their morning commutes and drive-through coffees and news reports. In another place I'd flown with him once, my tiny self winging through the air as the two of us had coasted together through the currents.

After long, graceful minutes, Cor finally broke from the ravens, coasted to where I stood and landed, and shifted so he could reach out and take my hand in his. I answered the smile in his eyes with one of my own. "Breakfast?" I suggested, jerking my head in the direction of my apartment.

"Love to," he replied, pulling me along as he raced me there.

I was content. In this world, it didn't matter if sometimes he would be gliding his way across the sky while my feet had to remain firmly planted on the ground. We would still be flying side by side.

Coming in Fall 2008

Crate & Peril

A Novel of the Storm Ravens

by
J. D. WARREN

Chapter One

"Let's get down to business, bucko," I suggested, withdrawing an envelope from my bag. The rubber band surrounding it was the only thing that kept it from spilling out the stack of hundred-dollar bills within. "You've got what I asked for, right?"

"Jeez, Samantha," said the hunched-over man across from me. "You get more hard-boiled every time I see you. Was there some Sam Spade film festival on TCM last night, or what? Why not let a guy get a few bites in before you grill him?"

"Yeah, well, lunch is on me, remember?" I tossed him a couple of the wet-naps from the little bowl at my side. "Provided you've got the goods."

"I've got them, I've got them." At the sight of my expectant, raised eyebrows, Rooster sighed. How he'd gotten that nickname, I had no idea. Perhaps it was his red face or the flap of jowl hanging beneath his chin. He reached into his sports coat to pull out a packet of papers stuffed into an oversized manila envelope that had, quite frankly, seen better days. I was assuming the wrapper had started its life yellow, rather than accumulating the color along with the rips, abrasions, assorted stains, and general air of grime that made it look like an artifact from the crash site of a small craft midair collision. With dirty fingertips, Rooster pushed the container across the table, so that it slid next to my take-out container. I gently used the saltshaker to move it to a less contagious position. "All my notes. Everything I remember them saying."

"And how good is your memory these days, exactly?" He seemed offended by my question, but I pressed on. "Because you know, the last time that I used your services . . ."

"Yeah, and I gave you a refund for that, didn't I?" he said, stuffing three of the large-cut French fries into his piehole at once.

"The *last* time," I emphasized, "Cor went flying in to what he thought was going to be a cabal of border smugglers and ended up busting the Venice United Methodist Church Crafty Ladies Annual Crochet Challenge." I crossed my arms and dared him to dispute that one.

Through a mouth full of potato, he added, "Sheesh. I got the street number of that one wrong. I admitted that from the start. No trust, Samantha! No trust at all! It's not like I can carry a pen and paper with me when I'm on recon, is it? No," he said, answering his own question before I could halfheartedly agree. "I have to keep it all up here. In my noggin." The fellow rapped the knuckles of one hand on his skull—and I admit I half-expected it to make a hollow sound—while he nibbled intently on his corn with another. "In my brain."

Honestly, from the way he chowed down while he spoke, I would've guessed Rooster hadn't eaten in a week. "Yes, but it's a mouse-sized brain. No offense."

"None taken," he granted. How could he take offense? I hadn't meant it as an insult. Rooster was of the Kin, as his race informally termed it. He was Peri, member of a race of shape-shifters with whom I'd become entangled six months before. It was because of some nasty Peri that I'd lost three years of my life. Thanks to some of the Kin's nicer representatives, I'd managed to get back on track. Rooster's unique ability was to shift into the smallest of mice, giving him a unique opportunity to infiltrate spaces ordinary people couldn't, and to eavesdrop on conversations that shouldn't be taking place. "But it's not like my head fits less stuff when I'm smaller, you know."

I'd never seen my hired informant in his rodent form. I wasn't really sure if I wanted to. Mice and I just don't get along—something about those pink-ringed tails really creeps me out. Since my first encounter with the Peri, though, I'd taken up a career investigating little criminal irregularities affecting both their sphere and my own. Having a plant among the dirty underbelly of a race to which I didn't belong helped pay the bills. If Rooster's ratty self resembled in any way his humanoid form when he ate, particularly in the way his nose twitched and his oversized front teeth gnawed away at the cob of corn he held between his quivering fingers . . . well, I could do without witnessing that particular transformation.

"So what's in here?" I asked. Much as I disliked doing it, I picked up the envelope by the corners and looked inside. True to form, all of Rooster's notes had been written on torn scraps of paper, rolled into a wad and fastened with rubber bands that looked on the verge of snapping. Poring over them was going to be a bacterial blast. "This is all the information about the border crossings?"

"The ones I overhead, yeah. Bunch of my people making promises to a bunch of crazy-rich Hollywood types about smuggling them through the gate into Resht, telling them they'll live forever, that kind of crap." He put down the corn and with relish began chomping away at the meat surrounding a glistening beef rib. "Making them pay all kinds of money up front for a shot at the fountain of youth, eternal life, all that crap. Hell's bells if they don't buy it, too. Two million, one of these guys has paid. Four installments of five hundred thou each." He jabbed at the envelope with his index finger, adding a fresh, dark stain to it. "And that's just so far. When the Kin who's selling him lies disappears, which he's going to do whether it's because you and Corydonais pick him up or whether he just decides to move on to the next mark, the Hollywood guy is just going to start looking for a new contact."

"Fantastic." I grimaced, not meaning it. "And there's nothing we can do about the Hollywood guy, because there's no law against throwing away your money on trying to stay young forever. If there was, there'd be no Rodeo Drive." Persian lore had it that the Peri came to earth as fallen angels—or at least so says my mom, a professor in the classics and an ordinary (if slightly crazy) woman as far removed from this crazy business of mine as I could possibly leave her. Persian lore would also probably have it that the Kin were mythical, but here I was, neck-deep in their schemes and dirty dealings. Not that they were any worse than we humans, really. Some were better. The one I lived with, for example. He was good. He was very, very good.

As if reading my mind, Rooster raised his head from his frantic gorging to ask, "So how is Corydonais? Haven't seen him for a while. Yeah, yeah, I know," he added, before I could answer. "He's too recognizable. You're his lapdog now."

Oh, that was beyond the pale. "I am *not* his lapdog," I announced, making little air quotes around the phrase.

"Our investigations sometimes overlap. Cor and his Storm Ravens deal with the affairs of court. I clean up the little stuff." Did I sound discontent with that arrangement? In case I did, I added, "And that's fine. It's a living." I didn't mind checking into the little irregularities that popped up here and there, regularly enough to keep me busy five days a week or more. When one of the Kin fresh out of the capital city they called Resht fell in love and talked too much to a homegrown California mall rat, I was the one who appeared with a settlement and a binding nondisclosure contract for the girl to sign. When a group of adolescent Peri (and the Kin had a long adolescence that lasted roughly well into the third century of their lifespans) snuck through the hidden portal leading from Resht to Venice and went on a bender, I was the one visiting the bars the next morning to get descriptions and to settle the skipped tabs and bills for damages. Before I'd run into these people, this race that lived among us but that weren't of us, I'd been an insurance investigator. My current job wasn't much different, though the pay was better. And, I had to admit as I thought of Cor, the benefits were glorious. "I like it," I finished, lamely.

"Uh-huh." Rooster simply studied me as he picked up the cup of coleslaw at the plate's side and let some of the contents slide into the black hole he called his mouth. "You know, his last lapdog was a redhead. What happened there? He ditch her?"

"If you're talking about Ginger . . . Jinjurnaturnia," I said, hastily amending my sobriquet for Cor's second-in-command to her actual name, "she's still very much in the picture."

"Kinky," was all he said.

"You are disgusting." I couldn't take the gorging any more; it was too much like a feeding frenzy in the shark tank. One of my hands reached out for my take-out container, while the other grabbed for my bag so I could stuff the notes inside. "Enjoy your lunch."

"Hold, hold, hold on there, lady." Rooster's expression of enjoyment at my discomfort couldn't have been more obvious; he wore it as plainly as the smear of barbecue sauce across the lower half of his face. "We're not done here."

"Oh, yes we are. You've got your cash, I've got my information, and I'm not paying extra for the abuse. Later, gator."

I was halfway to my feet when Rooster's arms shot out and grabbed my wrist. I recoiled at his touch. I'm sorry to say that all I could think about was what his little unsanitary paws looked like once he'd shifted into rodent form. It didn't help that he kept his fingernails sharp and long. "You aren't going yet," he said, his nose twitching with amusement. When I wrenched my arm out of his grasp, he yanked back his own hands, seeming to know he'd gone too far. They hung, limp and twitching, in front of his chest. "I mean, there's more. I have a message for you."

"A message?" I cocked my head. "If it's about more money . . ."

Rooster rolled his eyes. That mischievous grin crept back onto his face. "Open your mind, wouldja? It's not about money. Sheesh. Give me a little credit. This is about a message someone told me to give you."

"Someone?" I asked, raising my eyebrows. Being around Rooster made me uncomfortable enough as it was. I liked keeping our meetings short and sweet, erring more on the short side. "Someone who?"

The Peri shrugged and resumed eating. "I don't know him. He said he had a message for Samantha DeRengier."

When I was a little girl, I used to have a toy marionette that I took an unholy pleasure in making crumple to the ground, by keeping the strings slack. Suddenly, I knew exactly how that marionette felt. I slid back into my just-vacated seat, letting gravity drag me down. "DeRengier?" I said, repeating the word. "You know my last name is Dorringer, right?"

The question was a test. He simply shrugged. "Can't say I ever really thought about your last name."

Now it was my turn to twitch. Shortly before he'd died, one of the Peris who had abducted me and taken away three years of my life had called me a DeRengier. I'd found out from my mother that it was her family's original name before they'd immigrated to the United States, but other than a cursory look in the white pages to see if there were any DeRengiers in the greater Los Angeles area, I hadn't investigated it any further. To hear the name coming from the mouth of yet another of the Kin left me sagging.

"Maybe it's not for you, then?"

"Just give me the message!" I snapped, impatient and, weirdly, more than a little frightened. Of all the places to feel apprehensive, too—the Baby Blues restaurant couldn't be any more everyday. But just the merest reminder of the night I'd had to confront my mortal enemy and nearly lose the man I'd begun to love gave me an unshakeable case of the creeps.

"Fine, fine." Rooster still seemed to be relishing his hold over me. In his tiny little head, it was probably some kind of revenge for all the times Cor and I had asked him to scuttle into out-of-the-way places in rat form to do a little reconnaissance. "He wants to meet you."

"Who wants to meet me?"

"This guy."

"What guy?"

"The guy who wants to meet you."

It is a pity that God gave me both sturdy, strong hands and conscience enough to prevent me from strangling the guy. My voice was gargled in my throat as I intoned, "What guy . . . wants to . . . meet me?"

Power is an ugly thing, people. Rooster shrugged again, grinning. "I told you, I don't know."

I made a quick decision. If he wanted to play some variation of a seventh-grade guessing game, bully for him. I'd had enough, though. I raised my right hand and flipped the fingers in a definite farewell.

"I know you're not gonna walk away," he called out to my back, but already I was smiling at the second of the restaurant's brawny, baldheaded owners as I handed over the tab along with a couple of bills. "You're bluffing," Rooster shouted, oblivious to the stares he was getting from the other midday diners. I continued to ignore him as I received my change. "Aw, come on," he groaned, when I made a beeline for the door. "Come back, already!"

I paused at the exit, hands on the glass, waiting a moment. The question I meant to ask was expressed in my eyebrows, arching toward the ceiling when I turned.

"Yes, fine, I'll tell you," he said. Now it was my turn to enjoy the irritation on his face as I marched back to the table. I rested my hands on its edge, leaned forward, and waited. "Fine. Whatever. You win."

"I always do," I commented. "Now, who is this guy?"

"I don't know." Before I could make another dramatic exit, he waved his hands and stopped me. "I honestly don't. All I know is that he said his name was Azimuth, and that he had a message for Samantha DeRengier. He wants to talk to you."

One of the things I'd picked up from working in the field of insurance claims investigations for a few years before my abduction was a good sense of who was lying to me. Rooster wasn't—at least, not now. His eyes weren't shifty. When he talked, he didn't stare at the saltshaker or anywhere else other than me. "So this human . . ."

"He was of the Kin," Rooster corrected.

"Ah. So this Peri just approached you and said he wanted to talk to me. And out of the goodness of your heart . . ."

"He gave me *money*." My informant looked pained that I'd suggested otherwise. "I'm not crazy. I'm just the messenger, Sam. That was it. He just wants to talk to you."

"Just wants to talk, huh?" I didn't buy it. "What'd this guy look like?"

I was expecting a description of a shadowy figure in a cowl and robe, face obscured by dark alley shadows, but instead Rooster replied, "White hair, kind of. Like, really bleached out. Surfer-type dude."

Which was about as far away from the answer I expected as I could have gotten, really. "All right, great," I replied, fishing into my bag. "Get him to give you a phone number or something and I'll call him sometime during the week."

I noticed Rooster was munching on a French fry and shaking his head at me. "He didn't seem that type of guy. I think if you agree to meet, he'll find *you*."

As used as I'd become to the otherworldly activities of the Kin over the previous few months, I didn't like the sound of that. Knowing that my hometown of Venice, California was the absolute epicenter of Peri activity on this continent didn't bother me. In fact, it more than amply explained why the boardwalk was littered with freaks. Hanging out with Corydonais and his Storm Ravens and watching them transform and fly off to fight evildoers, like a troop of feathered superheroes, might have been a little disconcerting the first few times, but I coped. I was even used to it, now.

Agreeing that some shape-shifting stalker could simply appear out of nowhere to visit me, however, sounded like the kind of thing I typically advised against in the self-defense classes my mom had roped me into teaching down at the local senior center. Yet I'd be fibbing if I didn't admit to some intrigue. What if this Azimuth guy was on the up-and-up? What if he had some kind of information I could use? "Let me talk to Cor about it."

"Nuh-uh." Rooster shook his head, definitely squelching that idea. "That was the other thing. He forbid you to tell Corydonais."

Well. If that was the condition, I'd had enough. "Forbid me? You've got to be kidding! Besides, Cor and I don't keep secrets," I informed the little rat, picking up my carry-out box again. This time, I wouldn't be persuaded to come back.

"Oh, you don't?"

I didn't like the tone of slimy insinuation Rooster used. He really was a repulsive little creature, and the fact that I had to deal with him on occasion rubbed me the wrong way. Maybe after today, though, I'd cut the ties completely. There had to be other among the Kin who could do what he did, with less back-talk and familiarity. "No, we don't," I told him. "He knows everything there is to know about me, and I know all about him." Or at least what portions of his multicentury lifespan I'd been able to learn about in six months. There were definite disadvantages to dating an older man, even if he looked to be only thirty. "That's the way we roll."

"Oh, that's the way you roll, huh?" The echoing thing was getting on my nerves, particularly since he did it so mockingly. "So that's why he told you all about his dame? And his grand-dame?"

"What about them?" I asked, shrugging. I didn't know what his mother and grandmother had to do with anything. True, I hadn't met them, nor did I necessarily think I ever would, but given how unusual a Peri/human romance was, I'd never really thought much about our worlds colliding. "I mean, there's nothing unusual about them, is there?"

Rooster's reply was a snort. He regarded me levelly while he continued to down his lunch. "Is there? I don't know. If you and Corydonais don't have any *secrets* from each other, any, you know, unspoken *confidences* that you shouldn't be keeping, it shouldn't be hard to ask. Right?" His sharp incisors loosened another hunk of meat from a rib bone. "Isn't that what Dr. Phil says about good relationships?"

I narrowed my eyes, not even pretending to have missed his low blow. "Tell your friend I'm not interested," I said, standing up straight once more. This exit would be the last.

"Oh, he'll be waiting around," Rooster said while I stomped toward the door again. "Probably where you least expect it." He raised his voice as I reached the exit. "A pleasure doing business with you, Sam!"

After a few minutes inside the dim Baby Blues BBQ with an even dimmer personality, the California sun was so dazzling that I had to pause to put on my shades. Once my vision was properly adjusted to the polarized lenses and I'd dug out my car keys, I tucked my bag beneath my arm, hefted the carry-out order I'd been clinging to for the last several minutes, and began walking to my Mini, parked down the street. Ridiculous, the notion that I would agree to meet some perfect stranger—one of the Kin, no less—simply because he commanded. I wasn't any Peri's to direct or forbid; even Cor had learned, the hard way, that I responded to suggestions better than to outright directions.

Still. As I marched along the pavement, passing some of the odd strays of Venice and trying out my Kin-dar to attempt to figure out exactly to which race they might belong, I couldn't help but wonder what this Azimuth creature might want from me. Given that no one else had ever called me by that particular name, I couldn't help but wonder if he knew something about the sect responsible for my abduction, three and a half years before. That would be helpful. Cor and his followers had been looking for leads in that direction.

But still! The high-handed attitude of this guy was already rubbing me the wrong way. He'd have to change his tune if he wanted me to agree to a meeting. He'd find me? People didn't find me. They made appointments, like civilized beings. They called. Sometimes they sent letters. They didn't just *find* . . .

It was at that moment, only a mere twenty feet from my little black Mini Cooper, that from the corner of my eye I saw an arm shoot out from the alleyway behind the restaurant. A masculine hand gripped my wrist. Before I could yell, it was yanking me off the sidewalk into the shadows.

NINA BANGS

One Bite Stand

Harpies don't get callbacks. That's why Daria's job as night manager of the Woo Woo Inn is the opportunity of several lifetimes. Where better to prove that in the snatch-and-dispatch business she has CEO potential? So what if she doesn't really fit the corporate image. So what if she has to nurture her inner bitch to compete. And triple so what if she'd rather take Declan MacKenzie to bed than on a one-way all-expense-paid trip to Tartarus. His sexy blue eyes and hard male body lure her into deep and dangerous erotic waters. With a monster eating guests for its midnight snack, cosmic troublemakers cooking up chaos and Declan making serious moves on her, this looks like a lot more than a...

AVAILABLE JANUARY 2008!

ISBN 13: 978-0-8439-5954-3

MARJORIE M. LIU

THE LAST TWILIGHT

A *Dirk & Steele* Romance

A WOMAN IN JEOPARDY

Doctor Rikki Kinn is one of the world's best virus hunters. It's for that reason she's in the Congo, working for the CDC. But when mercenaries attempt to take her life to prevent her from investigating a new and deadly plague, her boss calls in a favor from an old friend—the only one who can help.

A PRINCE IN EXILE

Against his better judgment, Amiri has been asked to return to his homeland by his colleagues in Dirk & Steele—men who are friends and brothers, who like himself are more than human. He must protect a woman who is the target of murderers, who has unwittingly involved herself in a conflict that threatens not only the lives of millions, but Amiri's own soul...and his heart.

AVAILABLE FEBRUARY 2008!

ISBN 13: 978-0-8439-5767-9

ATTENTION
BOOK LOVERS!

Can't get enough of your favorite **ROMANCE**?

Call **1-800-481-9191** to:

✳ order books,

✳ receive a **FREE** catalog,

✳ join our book clubs to **SAVE 30%!**

Open Mon.-Fri. 10 AM-9 PM EST

Visit **<u>www.dorchesterpub.com</u>**
for special offers and inside
information on the authors you love.

We accept Visa, MasterCard or Discover®.
LEISURE BOOKS ♥ LOVE SPELL